Under the s

sky...

"It was your money the thieves were after tonight, and you'd be dead if that bullet had hit you," Kain said.

"I was protecting what was mine," she said stubbornly, but her voice lacked the sharpness it held before.

"If I let go of you to light a smoke will you run away?"

"Run? Why should I? Am I your prisoner?"

"No." And then he said, as if to himself, "but I may be yours." The match flared and he held it between cupped hands until it blazed. The light outlined his face and turned it into a bronze mask.

Vanessa's eyes clung to the smooth skin and straight brows. He was too handsome, far too handsome, despite the jagged scar that slanted across his hard cheekbone and disappeared into the thick brown hair. The gold-tipped lashes lifted and the amber eyes looked into hers. Oh, my God! Why did she have this feeling of rightness when she was with this... stranger?

He blew out the match. "What were you thinking, little red bird, when you looked at me with those beautiful eyes?" His fingers gently fondled her cheek and looped a strand of hair behind her ear. Vanessa caught her breath sharply. She tried to move away, but he held her with his words. "Don't go."

Also by Dorothy Garlock

Annie Lash
Restless Wind
Wayward Wind
Wild Sweet Wilderness

Published by
POPULAR LIBRARY

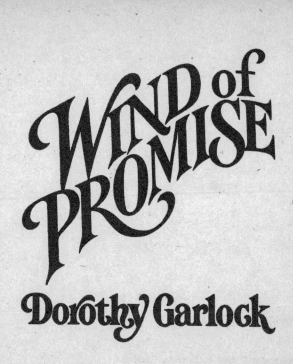

WIND of PROMISE

Dorothy Garlock

POPULAR LIBRARY

An Imprint of Warner Books, Inc.

A Warner Communications Company

POPULAR LIBRARY EDITION

Copyright © 1987 by Dorothy Garlock
All rights reserved.

Popular Library® is a registered trademark of Warner Books, Inc.

Cover art by Sharon Spiak

Popular Library books are published by
Warner Books, Inc.
666 Fifth Avenue
New York, N.Y. 10103

 A Warner Communications Company

Printed in the United States of America

First Printing: March, 1987

10 9 8 7 6 5 4 3 2 1

To a special man, with special love—
my husband, Herb

ROCKY MOUNTAIN WIND

Blowing through the towering crags
of hard rock;
across blossoming but wild blankets
of nature;
bringing seasonal and occasional
violent changes in weather;
the billowing wind of the Rockies—
the wind of promise.

Adam Mix

Chapter One

Only death would end it now.

The cheering crowd in front of the Dodge House watched the primitive game called lap jacket being played by two Negroes. It was said to be an African sport. In reality it was supposed to be a way to settle a dispute without a killing if one of the participants cried uncle while they lashed each other with a bullwhip. The fight had turned into a murderous duel; blood flowed freely, ears had been lopped off, jawbones exposed. Now each was aiming at the private parts of the other while the crowd, worked into a frenzy by the vicious fight, cheered them on.

Kain DeBolt leaned against the porch post and watched the duel. It was easy to see that the town marshal, who was overseeing the settling of the dispute, had no intention of stopping the fight. Kain turned away in disgust, stepped off the porch, and ran headlong into a woman in a dark sunbonnet with a basket on her arm. He reached out to steady her to keep her from falling. As soon as she regained her balance, furious blue eyes blazed up at him and she jerked her shoulders from his grasp.

"Get you hands off me!" she hissed.

"I beg your pardon, ma'am." Kain was surprised by the venom in her voice. The collision had been as much her fault as his, and he was tempted to tell her so. Instead, he put his fingers to the brim of his hat and moved aside so she could pass. He watched her walk away, head up, shoulders erect, indignation expressed in every line of her slender body. He couldn't suppress the grin that played at the corners of his wide mouth as her quick steps took her down the boardwalk. She swept past a drunk who had just been tossed out of a saloon, holding the skirt of her blue calico dress aside so it didn't touch him, and then turned the corner.

In 1873, Dodge City, Kansas was living up to its reputation of being a wicked little town. *The Kansas City Star,* which Kain had tucked inside his coat pocket, proclaimed it the "Gomorrah of the Plains." "Dodge City," the reporter wrote, "is the beautiful bibulous Babylon of the frontier. In truth, Dodge City is hell in a loosely tied package."

Less than a year before the Sante Fe Railroad had arrived and a station was opened in a sidetracked boxcar. At that time the infant town already had two saloons under tents and a general store. Within a month track workers, teamsters, rawhiders, whores, pimps and gamblers had flocked into town and mixed it up with the tough frontier soldiers from nearby Fort Dodge. Frame houses and false-fronted stores sprang up along Front Street. Dozens of boxcars arrived each day with grain, flour and provisions, and left again filled with buffalo bones and hides. The hides were shipped to the eastern tanneries, the bones to manufacturers for all manner of products from fertilizer to bone china. Buffalo hunting was the pillar of the town's economy, and the bull whackers who brought in the hides, the soldiers, and the railroad gangs its populace. Both the hunters and the freighters had about them a peculiar smell from their dead cargo, and remarks made about those unpleasant odors often led to gang fights and killings.

As Kain passed the Lady Gay Saloon, an overweight trollop leaned out of one of the upstairs windows and wheezed, "For five bucks I can give ya a mighty fine time."

He looked up at the bloated face and decided a man would have to be desperate, crazy, or both to relieve himself with a crib girl from the Lady Gay. He shook his head and walked on.

"Piss on ya, then," she yelled. "You probably ain't got nothin' but a little ole bitty, nohow!"

Kain grinned, reached into his pocket for a cigar, bit off the end, and paused on the street corner to light a match. People, he told himself, were the same world over. Those same words, or a cruder version thereof, had been flung at him in a hundred towns such as this. He glanced at the reflection of himself in a darkening store window. His eyes could make out no detail, but he knew what was there. A tall man, lean of body, wide of shoulder. His face was narrow and clean shaven, his cheekbones high, and his jaw strong. A bullet scar on his jaw gave his face a somewhat sinister look until he smiled. His hair was brown and wavy, and his eyes, beneath straight dark brows, were a light tawny gold. He wore a black frock coat, a fancy vest and a flat-crowned, black hat. Yet Kain DeBolt saw a great deal more than what was reflected in the window. He saw a restless man, seeking to fill an emptiness inside him.

At any time, day or night, there were about a hundred freight or light wagons in the streets of Dodge City. Now, in the late afternoon, a wagon carrying a crude wooden coffin turned off a side street, and Kain paused to let it pass. A black man playing a moaning tune on a squeeze box sat on the tailgate of the wagon and a whiskered man in black broadcloth coat and high silk hat drove the black-draped team of horses. Another resident for Boot Hill was making his last journey. The cemetery, reserved for the many characters who died with their boots on, had received its first resident only six months before and already had a population of twenty.

Kain walked past the harness shop, the dry goods store, and the Longbranch Saloon. He passed the depot where he had stepped off the train early that morning. At the edge of town he paused to take a deep breath of fresh air. Even the smoke from the locomotive that brought him from Kansas City was preferable to the stench of hides, rotten meat, unwashed bodies and privies. His dust-reddened eyes swept over the sod houses that surrounded the town. Dirty and desolate were the only words that came to his mind. The people who lived in those huts lived with despair and hardship. He would be glad to see the last of this place.

A commotion at the end of what appeared to be a peddler's or traveling troop's wagon parked in the middle of a vacant lot well back from the railroad tracks drew his attention. A dozen men had formed a circle and were laughing and throwing coins into the center. Another fight—one of the many fought each day in Dodge City, Kain thought. He started to retrace his steps back to the Dodge House when he saw the woman in the dark bonnet and blue dress running toward the wagon from the other side of the tracks. He wondered as he hurried toward the wagon if it was curiosity that had put his feet into motion or if he wanted to see her furious blue eyes again.

The woman reached the scene first.

She grabbed a shovel and forced her way through the ring of shouting, laughing men. A thin-bearded youth had a big blond man down on the ground and was pounding his face with his fists.

"That kid's a fightin' son of a bitch!" an excited male voice rang out over the jeers of the crowd.

The woman lifted the shovel and brought the metal scoop

down on the back of the man on top. She lifted it again and hit him with a resounding blow to the side of his head. The small man came up fighting and her next blow caught him on the shoulder.

"Leave him alone, you filthy, little swine!"

The short, shaggy haired, thin-bearded youth clenched his fist as if to hit the woman, then thought better of it and backed off. He spit in the dust, grinned cockily at his friends and began to pick up the coins.

"I tole ya I could do it," he crowed. "I tole ya I could beat that big ole boy into a spitball."

The woman in the bonnet stood protectively between the man on the ground and the trail hands who had fallen back a few paces when she had lifted the shovel threateningly.

"Get! Get, I say!"

"Ah, ma'am. We was just funnin'. We was waitin' on the pie."

"Funning? Why you unwashed bunch of mangy... warthogs! I don't bake pies for a bunch of lily-livered clabberheads who think it's funny to encourage a cocky little rooster to show off. Now get out of my camp! Go on, get!"

The men backed away. They were rough, but they knew that to bother a good woman in Dodge City was like putting a noose around their necks. An older, whiskered man with a bald spot on the top of his head who was holding his hat in his hand moved to the front of the crowd.

"I ain't with 'em, ma'am. I shore be sorry. I didn't have no idey 'bout the young feller there. I heared ya was sellin' pie 'n I come to get me some. We ain't had no makins fer pie since Injun Territory, 'n it's many a dusty mile pushin' that team to Dodge."

"All right, stay. The rest of you big, brave *men*," she spat the word contemptuously, "hightail it back to the dung hill you crawled out of."

"Now see here, ya ain't got no call to be so uppity." The

cocky youth was still looking around on the ground for coins.

"I've every right to be whatever I want to be. If I were *small* like you, I'd not choose to make myself appear bigger by standing on someone else."

Her words stung the youth and his head snapped up. "Goddamn! Why you . . . " He took a step toward her.

The woman in the bonnet stood her ground, holding the shovel as if it were a club. "I thought that's what you were trying to prove. I've seen your kind before—a little man who's only knee-high to an ant trying to make up for his lack of size by picking on someone bigger than himself. You're nothing but a cocky little bully!" Her clear voice was filled with contempt.

The boy muttered a few curses and his fists clenched. He was so angry he was shaking. "At least I ain't no dummy," he said spitefully, and spit toward the man on the ground.

"I'm not so sure about that! I'm surprised you've got enough brains to hold your ears apart. Run along, little *boy*. If you come around here again, I'll spank your bottom and send you home with a tail full of buckshot."

There were snickers from the men, and then a cough to disguise a laugh. The tables had turned and the men were enjoying the show. The bully was livid with anger.

"Ya . . . ya . . . bitch," he snarled. "Ya'd better watch out! That's what ya'd better do. Ya'd just better watch out!"

"And you'd better watch your mouth, kid." Kain spoke quietly, but his voice carried to each man. They turned in a body to look at him, as did the girl in the bonnet.

"Ya wantin' a little a what I give him?" The youth flashed a boastful grin at his companions before he looked fully at the man who had spoken.

"If you think you can do it, come on. I'll chew you up and spit you out in nothing flat. The best thing for you to do is to run along, like the lady said."

"I ain't runnin' along cause a duded up, spit 'n polish,

greenhorn tells me to." He put on his hat, hooked his thumbs in his gun belt and looked at Kain belligerently.

Oh, no, Kain thought. Why the hell hadn't he kept his damn mouth shut? He stifled a sudden burst of temper. The damn fool kid was probably suckled on wolf's milk and didn't have enough sense to back down.

"Don't make a move toward that gun, kid. I don't want to kill you—not that I'd aim to. That gun hand is only inches from your belly and I've been known to shoot wide."

"C'mon, George. Yore goin' to mess around 'n get yore-self killed." A youth in a flat-crowned hat and the ragged buckskins of a rawhider stepped out and took the boy's arm.

"Your friend's right." Kain stared unblinkingly at the boy.

"I ain't no greenhorn with a gun," the kid declared in a strident shout.

"I'm sure you're not."

"C'mon, George. The old man said we could collect our pay at sundown."

"I ain't forgettin' this," the boy said threateningly as he turned away.

"You'd better forget it and leave these folks alone. If the lady doesn't fill your hide with buckshot, I will."

Kain watched the men leave. They were not a bad lot and he doubted they would give the woman any more trouble. The kid and his friend were another matter. He turned to look at her and saw that the man on the ground had rolled over onto his knees and was crawling toward the wagon. Kain felt a spurt of embarrassment and glanced away before looking at the woman. She met his eyes defiantly as if daring him to comment. The big blond man reached the front of the wagon and sat with his back to the wheel, his head in his hands. An older woman hurried from around the wagon. She went to him, knelt down and placed a wet cloth on his face.

"Apple or raisin?" the young woman asked him.

For a long moment Kain stood looking at her white face. She did not move any part of her body, but her breasts strained against the soft material of her dress with her intake of air. Her brilliant eyes staring at him through the tunnel of her stiff-brimmed bonnet barred any advance on his part.

"Or did you come to buy a quirt?" Her voice came faintly to him from across the vast emptiness yawning between them.

"Quirt?"

"Quirt or pie. Which do you want?"

"Oh, uh . . . pie. Raisin."

"Get the man a raisin pie, Aunt Ellie, and collect his money. Which do you want, mister?" she asked the old man who was still waiting with his hat in his hand.

"One a each, ma'am. If'n ya got 'em to spare."

"We've got plenty. It looks like our business will be off today."

"I'll spread the word, ma'am. If ya be awantin' me to."

"We'd be obliged. You do that and we'll charge you for just one pie."

"That's mighty kind a ya." The old man placed a coin in her hand, picked up his pies and hurried away.

"A quarter, please," the older woman said as she walked up to Kain holding a platter of fried pies. He dug into his pocket and placed a coin on the platter before he selected one.

"Thank you for what you did." The woman's voice was low, but the young woman in the bonnet heard it.

"Aunt Ellie," she said sharply.

"But Vanessa—"

"We'll be selling pies again this time tomorrow." Her cool voice dismissed him.

Vanessa. A grand sounding name for a grand looking woman. Kain felt a little foolish. There was no reason to linger, but some stubborn streak in him made him want to see her remarkable eyes flashing at him again.

"I *may* be back tomorrow, it depends on the pie. Are you sure there are no flies in it?" He carefully scrutinized the open end of the pie. "They'd be hard to find among the raisins."

That brought her head around. Her brilliant blue eyes met his and held; in that breathless second her face was like the light at the end of a dim corridor. Kain took in a shallow breath and hoped to God the woman didn't know the devastating effect her magnificent eyes had on him. He shook his head as if saying no to an unasked question, shifted his weight from one foot to the other as gradually the magnetic connection between them loosened its grip. Then, as if somehow seeking revenge, he slowly ran his narrowed eyes over her face, down her slender figure in the blue cotton dress, and back up to her white face enclosed by the bonnet brim.

The woman stiffened as his eyes roamed. Her flushed face made him smile, and he knew she would like to slap him. But she controlled her temper, took a deep breath, and eyed him in exactly the same way he had eyed her. The blatant contempt in her eyes was enough to discourage even the boldest of men. This time, however, it didn't work.

"Do you like what you see?" The devilish urge to tease her couldn't be denied. His laughing eyes mocked her.

"If I was looking to buy a puffed-up jackass, I might be interested."

He let loose a shout of laughter. "Lady, you really know how to get a man where the hair's short. You did a good job of stomping that kid's pride in the mud. He's not going to forget you cutting him down to size in front of those men. That tongue of yours has the sting of a scorpion, but the rest of you looks mighty sweet. Now, I just can't help but wonder what you're hiding under that bonnet."

"Mister, my advice to you is to get the hell out of here." As she spoke she moved to the front of the wagon, climbed up on the wheel, reached under the seat and brought out a double-barreled shotgun. Handling it as if she had been born with it in her grip, she cocked it and pointed it at him.

Kain looked deeply into her angry blue eyes before he shrugged his shoulders. "You and your . . . friend have persuaded me. Ma'am," he said to the older woman, "I don't think she's got a sense of humor at all." He tipped his hat politely, shot an amused glance at the girl with the shotgun and walked away.

Vanessa lowered the gun and waited until the man crossed the tracks and started up Front Street before she leaned the weapon against the back of the wagon.

"Why didn't you get the gun, Aunt Ellie, when that bully started picking on Henry?"

"I wasn't here. I'd run over to take some pies to that poor woman who came by yesterday with that parcel of younguns—"

"Oh, Aunt Ellie! We can't feed everyone we feel sorry for," Vanessa said gently. Then with more spirit she said, "This is the worst place we've ever been in, bar none! I'll be glad to see the last of it."

"So will I, dear. It seems the farther west we go the more the people act like animals."

Vanessa went to the other side of the wagon and looked down on the big blond man who sat with his face in his hands. She knelt down and pulled his hands from his face with gentle fingers.

"Are you all right, Henry?"

His sky blue eyes between thick, spiked lashes were filled with tears. One eye was swollen almost shut and his beautifully sculptured face was cut and bruised. Light blond hair hugged his well-shaped head and Vanessa pushed it back from his forehead, then stroked his cheeks with her fingertips.

"Ah, Henry . . . I'm sorry I wasn't here," she whispered.

"I'm just not a fighter, Van."

"Of course not—"

"I didn't know what to do. I didn't want to hurt him."

Vanessa had known her cousin Henry all her life, and all her life she had been fighting his battles for him. They had been born to sisters within six months of each other, and since she was old enough to understand that Henry was of a simple nature and never raised his hand in anger, Vanessa had shielded and protected him the best she could.

"They sold some of your quirts at the store," she said eagerly with a bright smile. "Look at all this money I've got in my pocket." She opened her pocket so he could peer inside. His swollen lips quivered.

"That's about all I'm good for, making quirts."

"Don't say that, Henry Hill! I don't know what Aunt Ellie and I would do without you. It's because of you we have all this money. We should have enough to leave this place by the day after tomorrow. Here, put this in your pocket." She placed a silver dollar in his hand. "Wash your face now, and go water the mules."

"Do you think they'll come back?"

"If they do I'll fill their butts with buckshot," she said staunchly. She stood and Henry got to his feet. He towered over her even though she was considered a tall woman. Henry managed a smile of sorts, but his worried eyes showed it didn't go beyond his lips. "You'd like to see me do that, wouldn't you?" she chided affectionately. "Now get, you rascal!"

Vanessa watched him walk away. He was a fine figure of a man, tall, broad shouldered, slim hipped. She had never seen a more handsome man. Not until someone talked to him did they realize that Henry was as naive as a child. Vanessa loved him as if he were her own. Because of that love she had let Aunt Ellie talk her into making this trip to Colorado to find Henry's uncle, who Ellie believed would take some responsibility for his brother's child.

They had been in Dodge City three days; as far as Vanessa was concerned, it was three days too long. Never had she imagined a place so wicked. The farm home where she was born and had lived until just three short months before now seemed to be in some other world. At times she was so homesick she thought she would die from it. But there was no going back. The small farm outside Springfield had been sold, and the money hidden in the bottom of their wagon would help them get settled into a business when they reached their destination. In the meantime, they sold their pies and the quirts Henry made and bought supplies for the next leg of their journey in each town along the way.

Vanessa wasn't sure she wanted to go back to her old home, now that she thought of it. The people there had been unkind to her father when he returned from the war. He had been a fine doctor when he left, but the memory of the bloody battlefields had caused him to turn to drink, and the only time a patient had gone to him was when there had been no one else available. And then, more often than not, they had sought help from Vanessa because she had picked up an amazing amount of medical knowledge from her father before he died.

Vanessa leaned against the wagon and watched her aunt. Men were coming to the wagon from across the tracks, and Ellie, gracious and smiling, was dispensing the pies and taking their money. The men doffed their hats, thanked her aunt repeatedly, paid their money, and went away eating their pie.

Ellie Hill was the only mother Vanessa had ever known. Her own mother had died when she was a baby, and Ellie, bringing her own small son, had moved in to take care of her. Henry's father and Aunt Ellie had been married in Springfield, and he had gone back to Chicago saying he would send for her. Nothing was heard from him until several years after Henry was born. Ellie received a letter from her husband's brother in Colorado saying he had been informed his brother had been killed saving a small child from being crushed by a runaway team. Ellie idolized her dead husband's memory. She had a small tintype of his likeness that she looked at often. When she got out the picture, the letter, and her marriage paper, Vanessa knew she was suffering from a bout of melancholy and was thinking about the one short month of happiness she had had with the man she loved.

She watched Henry walk across the field carrying two buckets of water. Animals liked Henry; children liked Henry. Grown men had no tolerance for his slowness to understand. Henry was good help if someone told him what to do. But he had to be watched like a child whose curiosity outweighed his judgment. Aunt Ellie was right to worry about what would happen to her son when she wasn't around to take care of him. She thought it would be unfair to saddle Vanessa with the responsibility. She was convinced that she and Henry had spoiled her niece's chances with wealthy, handsome Martin McCann. He had stopped courting Vanessa because, as he put it, he wanted a wife, but not one tied to an old woman and a dummy. Vanessa sighed deeply. Aunt Ellie wouldn't believe it, but Martin McCann made her want to throw up. She wouldn't have married him if he were the only thing walking on two legs. Anyway, the relationship had ended, and the idea of going to Colorado to be near Henry's uncle took root in her Aunt's mind. And, Vanessa had to admit, her own adventurous spirit welcomed the idea.

The opportunity to make the trip fell into their laps much sooner than they expected when a traveling medicine man had stopped at the farm. He was dying, he explained, and if they would take care of him until the end and give him his pain-killing medicine, he would leave them his fine caravan and two strong mules. He had had the caravan specially built of light lumber. It was compact and neat, with two sleeping shelves attached to the sides. Every inch of space was utilized. A small wood stove heated it in the winter, and an opening in the ceiling cooled it in the summer. It was a marvelous vehicle and had served as his home for four years. The old man had lived for only six weeks after he arrived at the farm, and in the spring they had sold out and begun the journey.

Vanessa allowed herself a minute to think about the tall, well-dressed man who had spoken up for her earlier. She had no doubt at all that she could have handled the situation. More than likely he was a gambler or a railroad speculater, and she wanted no obligations to such as that. He was everything she disliked in a man, bold, insolent, much too confident. She had seen him standing on the hotel porch watching the Negroes lash each other with the bullwhips. Anyone, she thought, who could get pleasure out of seeing two men mutilate each other was little more than a barbarian. She had also seen him look at Henry and then away, as if Henry were an embarrassment. That had really set her teeth on edge. How could a man like that possibly know how confused and frightened Henry was?

By evening Dodge City was in its hip-hip-hurrah stage, and by ten o'clock the hell raising had just begun. Vanessa and Henry brought their four mules and one saddle horse close to the caravan and staked them for the night. They doused the campfire, not wanting to call attention to themselves, and settled down in their chairs near the back of the wagon for an hour of rest before going to bed. The double-barreled shotgun was within Vanessa's reach.

"I liked that man who was here today," Ellie said.

"Which one?" Vanessa asked, although she was sure she knew which man her aunt meant.

"The one that faced up to that little . . . weasel."

"Oh, him." Vanessa had removed the pins from her hair and was massaging her scalp with her fingertips. What a heavenly feeling! While they were in town she never took off her bonnet until after dark, and on the trail she wore one of Henry's old hats. Her fiery, copper colored hair drew too much attention. The thick, curly and often unruly mass covered her shoulders and spilled down her back. She was resigned to its contrariness in the same way she was resigned to the fact that God had given her pale, fine skin that had no resistance whatsoever to sun and wind. She had learned to protect herself from burning by wearing a stiff-brimmed bonnet while in the hot sun. But on this trip the bonnet had served two purposes, the most important one being to cover the mass of hair that shone in the sun like a red-hot flame and brought unwanted attention.

"I liked him."

"You liked him? Oh, Aunt Ellie, I swear. You like anyone who's polite and clean. Those duded-up, smooth talking galoots are the worst kind. That's how they make their living —smooth talking people into doing what they want. I bet he has two horns under his hat."

"Who has horns under their hat?" Henry sat on the ground between the two women with his back against a wheel.

"Vanessa is just funning, son. What she meant was the man wasn't what he seemed to be."

"I wonder if those people plowed the corn." Henry's mind was always forging ahead, flushing out one notion after the other as they came to mind.

"I imagine so," Vanessa said.

"Sometimes I wish we'd stayed home." His face twisted as he tried to puzzle through an idea. "I'd be plowing the corn and old Shep wouldn't have got killed."

"Maybe we can get another dog before we leave Dodge City." Vanessa knew her cousin was still grieving over the loss of his dog, which had been kicked to death by a stallion in Wichita.

"When's that going to be? I don't like it here."

"I don't either. I'll be glad to leave. I'm thinking we can go the day after tomorrow. I'll go back to the store in the morning and pick up the quirts that haven't sold, unless the man wants to buy them. I told him we'd take some of the money in trade."

"I kind of hate striking out by ourselves," Ellie said. "I wish we could join up with some other folk going west."

"I've not found anyone ready to leave just yet. They say a group left two or three days ago, and another one before that. Maybe we'll meet up with someone, but if we don't we'll do just fine by ourselves."

"I know, but this country seems so wild—"

"I figure we'll take the Sante Fe Trail west, and when we get to the point where it turns south, we'll go north to Denver and from there up to Greeley then over to Junction City. The roads are supposed to be passable, if not good. We've got four strong mules, a solid wagon, and Henry to take care of us."

"It'll be all right, Ma. Me and Van'll take care of you."

After a while Ellie's voice came softly out of the darkness. "I thank God every day for you, Vanessa."

Chapter Two

Kain opened the first of the two telegrams the operator handed him and read it several times. It took a moment or two for the message to take root in his mind. He had expected the news to be bad, but not as bad as this. The fortune his father had left him had been wiped out when the New York Stock Market took a sudden plunge down. He was broke—flat broke. All he owned was in his pocket, in the suitcase at the Dodge House, and in the stable at the hotel.

One thought stood out above all the others: Why wasn't he feeling something? Why wasn't he feeling as if the world had dropped out from under him? All his life he had had only to wire his friend and broker, Alexander Fairfield, and money would be waiting at the next town. He couldn't remember a time when it had been necessary for him to earn his living. Without that incentive he had drifted from one challenge to another, trying his hand at whatever relieved the boredom at the time: mining, riding shotgun on a stage, rounding up wild horses or gambling when the notion struck. He had hired on to make a cattle drive and had even been a deputy sheriff for a short time in a wild town in Arizona. If he was feeling anything, he decided, it was as if he had been dangling at the end of a string and suddenly the string had been cut. But he wasn't as devastated as he had once imagined he would be if such a thing should happen. He was just dispassionate about the whole situation.

He folded the paper, put it in his pocket and opened the second telegram. He read it quickly and crushed the paper in his hand. Now he did feel something. Alex, his friend of many years, had lost his own fortune and had killed himself.

"Oh, Christ!" Kain spoke aloud in a breathless, regretful voice. Why would a man kill himself over money? Alex had everything, a beautiful wife who loved him, children. He could have started over.

Kain smoothed out the paper so he could read the words again. He reviewed the first part slowly, sorrowfully, then moved on to the last line. SEE RANDOLPH IN DENVER STOP PROPERTY NEAR JUNCTION CITY NOT AF-FECTED. The telegram was signed by Alex's assistant.

On the way back to the hotel, Kain felt the full pain of sorrow. Poor Alex. Poor son of a bitch! He wondered if there was anything he could do for Ruth and the kids. He decided not. She had her family, and besides that Kain was flat broke. No, not flat broke. He owned a whorehouse. If he hadn't felt such sorrow over Alex's death he would have smiled.

The year before he had bought the property from Mary Malone when she and Case had decided to go back to Texas. For years the place, located about five miles from town, had been simply known as The House. It was a quiet place and men went there from miles around for an evening of pleasure with one of the three whores in residence. Mary served drinks or tended the sick or wounded. A man was never turned away unless he was drunk or abusive. Mary's husband had died after Adam Clayhill, a powerful, land-hungry rancher, brought in gunfighters and had run them off their claim along with a half dozen other settlers. Mary had bought The House and had run it until she married Case Malone. Then a woman named Bessie Wilhite took over. Last year Bessie herself had married and had moved to Cheyenne. Since that time the place had been boarded up.

Kain wondered what had happened to the skinny, mouthy whore named Minnie who had been at the house for five or more years. Wherever she was, he decided, she would make out all right, she was a survivor. His lips quirked in a half grin when he thought of how she hated that greedy Adam Clayhill and how she had taunted him whenever she got the chance.

Kain went straight to his room when he reached the hotel. It was ironic, he thought, that everything he owned was right back there in Adam Clayhill's territory. Clayhill had gone East, married Kain's widowed mother and brought her, his sister Della, and him to the Colorado Territory. Kain had been fifteen at the time, but he realized right away that his mother had made a dreadful mistake. He and Adam despised each other, so after a few months, Kain had gone back East to where his uncle lived and finished his education. He had kept in touch with his mother until she died, but after that he had made only two trips to Junction City. He tried not to think about Della. There had never been anyone in their family to equal Della. She had been a beautiful, completely unscrupulous girl, and now she was the madam of the most expensive brothel in Denver. He suspected that she had also been old Clayhill's mistress at some time. Long ago Kain had relegated his sister Della to a special place in his mind —the place where he put unpleasant things he didn't like to think about.

Clayhill, that wicked old bastard. Kain wouldn't be surprised if someone had killed him by now. Kain's thoughts turned to Logan Horn, the old man's son by an Indian woman. A few years back the old man had hired gunfighters to kill Logan. When that didn't work Adam had trumped up a charge and tried to get Logan hanged for raping Della. Now Logan was a prosperous, if not well-liked rancher. If he hadn't had Indian blood in him, he would more than likely be a candidate for territorial governor. And then there was Cooper Parnell, the old man's other bastard son by sweet, gentle Sylvia Parnell. Cooper was the spitting image of the old man, but there the resemblance ended. Cooper despised Clayhill for the way he had left Sylvia pregnant and alone. If old Clayhill provoked him, Cooper wouldn't think twice before killing him.

Kain remembered the last time he had seen Adam Clay-hill. He and a young friend, a spunky kid named Fort Griffin, had dumped the dead bodies of two of Clayhill's henchmen on his doorstep. The old man had sent those roughnecks to kill Griffin because Griff refused to be run off the range. The old son of a bitch hadn't batted an eyelash when he saw the corpses. He even acted as if he were glad to see Kain and had the gall to ask him to come work for him. Kain shook his head at the memory. The old man was rotten through and through, but he had guts.

That had been two years before, and Kain had promised himself then that he would keep as much distance as possible between Clayhill and himself. Now he would have to go back to Junction City and decide what he was going to do about The House and the several thousand acres of land that went with it.

He wasn't too bad off, he decided after he sorted through his belongings. He had over four hundred dollars in cash, a pair of Smith & Wesson .44 Russian pistols, the best gun built, a small palm pistol, a good Winchester rifle, a double-barreled shotgun, and Big Red—as good a horse as any he'd ever ridden.

Suddenly Kain wanted to get out of his city clothes. He

stripped naked and started to dress. After he put on a pair of buckskin breeches and a pullover buckskin shirt, he strapped on his gun belt. Then he began to pack, starting with his bedroll, then extra trail clothes. When he finished, he bundled up a pile of discarded clothes and left the room. The desk clerk looked at him when he passed, then took a second look before he recognized him as the well-dressed man in the broadcloth coat and fancy vest who had checked in several days before.

Kain shouldered his way through the crowd loafing in front of the general store and paused in the doorway to allow his eyes to adjust from the bright sunlight to the darkened interior. The store was packed to capacity with all manner of goods needed to sustain life on the frontier. He made his way to the counter through a maze of barrels, grain sacks, crocks, stacks of rope, leather goods and tools.

"Howdy," he said to the white-aproned clerk, and dumped the bundle on the counter. "If you can use any of this stuff I'll take the money in trade."

The clerk shook out the frock coat, the elaborately stitched vest, white silk shirts, tapered-leg trousers and custom made shoes.

"I can't give you what they're worth."

"I know that. What are they worth to you?"

The clerk named a price and Kain nodded in agreement. He began to set items down on the counter, a large granite cup with a pouring spout, skillet, a gray granite plate, a spoon and a fork.

"Add coffee, salt, rice, beans, bacon, dried beef, and some cans of peaches," he told the clerk.

"Headin' out, are you?"

"Thinking about it." Kain's hand brushed a long whip lying on the counter. He picked it up and looked at the workmanship. "Someone around here make this?"

"Naw. A young lady brought it in a few days back."

"Did she bring some quirts, too?"

"Sure did, but they're gone. This is all I've got left. Want me to add it to the pile?"

Kain thought for a minute. He didn't have any use for a whip and from now on had to be close with his money, but what the hell. He would take it as a present for Lorna, Cooper Parnell's wife. She was the best he had ever seen with a bullwhip. He added it to the pile on the counter. He really didn't need it, he told himself, to remind him of the woman with the fierce blue eyes.

That morning he had walked to the end of Front Street. The lot where her wagon had been was empty. He had chided himself then for feeling disappointed, and he chided himself now for thinking about her. There was no room in his life for a woman right now, not even one who sent excitement coursing through him as that one did. He'd not been able to sleep for thinking about her and wondering if her hair was light or dark. She must be blond, he had decided, because her skin was so fair. Many years had gone by since a woman had made such an impression on him. He was attracted by her fiery spirit, he told himself. He grinned, thinking about the way she had swung that shovel. Oh well, he thought, she was probably well on her way to Wichita or Kansas City by now.

Before he went back to the hotel, Kain walked by the stable. If there was anything in the world he loved it was the big, red sorrel that had been his constant companion for the last five years. The horse whinnied a greeting as soon as Kain walked down the aisle to his stall.

"Hello, Big Red. Are you getting tired being couped up in this barn? It's a mite better than that boxcar you rode in from Kansas City. I know how you hated that."

Kain crawled through the rails and ran his hands down each slender leg, and lifted each of the horse's feet. He looked closely at each shoe and dug around it with the tip of his knife before setting it down. When he finished he patted the horse on the rump.

"You're in fine shape, Big Red. Tomorrow we'll leave this stink hole and you can stretch your legs. We're heading for Denver, boy. It'll be kind of nice being out on the trail again, just you and me." Kain filled the feedbox with a scoop of grain. "Eat up, big man. It might be a while before you have grain again. I'll be back for you tomorrow and we'll head out."

Suddenly a pain knotted Kain's stomach. He leaned against the stall rails and panted. He began to sweat. Damn! For several weeks now, off and on he'd had the pain. This was the worst one yet. A doctor in Kansas City had told him he had worms. The concoction he had given him to kill them tasted so vile that Kain had taken half of it and tossed the rest out the train window on the way to Dodge City. Now he wondered at the wisdom of his impulsive action.

The pain passed, but left him shaken. He stood still and waited, hoping it was over. He'd never known physical pain and this pain robbed him of his strength. He resented it. Right now all he wanted to do was lie down and sleep. He felt his stomach. It was sore, but the pain had gone.

Once he was back at the hotel, Kain stretched out on the bed. He had a sudden yearning for Colorado and tried and true friends such as Griffin and Cooper. He thought of Lorna and her beautiful voice, and of Mrs. Parnell. A picture of Vanessa floated into his mind, but it was an incomplete picture. He wondered, once again, what she would look like without that damn bonnet.

Vanessa sat beside Ellie on the wagon seat with one booted foot on the rail in front of her. She shifted the reins so she could pull her hat down tighter on her head. From a distance she looked like a young boy in the breeches and shirt, and that was just what she wanted folks to think she was. She wore her hair braided in a tight coronet that fit snugly into the crown of one of Henry's old broad-brimmed hats that came down over her ears. Ellie had been horrified when Vanessa had first put on the pants, but after a few encounters with passersby, she saw the wisdom of the disguise.

Vaness liked the freedom the breeches afforded her when she climbed up onto the wagon seat, or rode astride, although she had been wearing a split riding skirt for years.

The first few days after they had left Springfield, Vanessa had thought her arms were going to be pulled from their sockets, and she often had to exchange places with Henry, who rode the horse alongside the wagon and kept an eye on the extra mules tied behind. But now her arms had developed muscles, and the reins in her leather-gloved hands no longer caused blisters.

As the day wore on, Vanessa looked behind from time to time to the wagon that had pulled onto the trail to follow them when they left Dodge City. It stayed a mile or so back and made no attempt to catch up. She and Ellie talked about it and wondered if it was carrying a family going west or a rawhider going out to find the buffalo herds. They met several wagons going toward Dodge City, but the only people who passed them were a troop of soldiers. The captain leading the platoon had tipped his hat to Ellie and kept his men well out to the side so as to not stir up the dust until they were far ahead of them.

That night they pulled off the trail and camped beside an abandoned soddy. There was a pole corral of sorts, and after Vanessa and Henry set a few crossbars right they turned their stock inside. After that they explored the soddy like curious youngsters while Ellie prepared the evening meal. The soddy was dark and smelled musty, and Vanessa wondered how anyone could have lived there.

"I found some pieces of blue glass," she called out to Henry just before she heard the angry rattle of a snake. "Oh! Henry, let's get out of here!"

They bolted for the door.

"What was it, Van? I saw some spoons and things."

"Snakes." A cold shudder ran down her back. "We'll not do that again, Henry. Stay out of places like that, hear?"

"Oh, golly, Van. I never saw anything."

Ellie was shaking out the cloth she insisted on using on the fold-down table when a man approached their camp and stopped some fifty yards off, his hands held up. Vanessa recognized him as the old man who had witnessed the fight and had spread the word about the pies. Nevertheless she sidled over to where she had leaned the shotgun against the wagon.

"Howdy," he called. "Is it all right if I come in?"

"Of course it's all right. Evening to you." Ellie, always gracious, greeted him as if he were stepping into her home. "So you're the one who's been behind us all day."

"Yes'm." The man's eyes went from Vanessa to Henry and back to Ellie. He plainly didn't know to which one he should address his remarks. Ordinarily he would have spoken to the man, but in this case he was sure the young woman in the breeches was the one who made the decisions. She hung back, so he spoke to the neat woman with the white apron and the soft light hair piled on top of her head. She was a sightly woman, he thought, but not one suited for life on the trail.

"Ma'am, it 'pears we're both headed west. I'm awonderin' if'n it would set with ya folks if'n I—we strung along with ya. Seems like we'd be a heap better off than goin' it by our ownselves."

"Who's with you?" Vanessa asked bluntly.

"Ah, my girl, is all."

"Where are you headed?"

"Denver or thereabouts. I thought to do me a little placer minin'."

"Is your outfit in good shape? We don't want to tie up with someone we've got to wait on."

"Yes'm. I keep thin's in top shape. I done me some wagoneerin' and some blacksmithin' in my day. I might even be a help to ya'll, too." His eyes wandered over the caravan and he shook his head in wonder. "That's a might fine outfit ya'll got. I don't know as I ever seen finer."

He looked toward Henry, then back to Vanessa. She could read his mind, as she had read the minds of a hundred other men who had looked at her cousin. Dummy, he was thinking. Two women and a dummy had no business on the trail.

"We've been doing all right," she said sharply.

The man stood first on one foot and then the other. The girl's words seemed to close the door on the subject of the two wagons traveling together. He twisted his hat around and around in his hands.

"Name's Wisner, ma'am. John Wisner. Late of the Cimarron country down in Indian Territory."

"I'm Vanessa Cavanaugh. This is my cousin, Henry Hill, and my aunt, Mrs. Hill."

"Howdy." The old man bobbed his head at the women and held out his hand to Henry. That gesture was what decided Vanessa to allow him to join them.

"Glad to make yore acquaintance, young fella."

Henry stepped up and seized the man's hand. He was like a friendly puppy, but he had learned to hang back until someone made a friendly overture.

"Howdy." He grinned happily.

"We'll be glad for your company, Mr. Wisner. We like to leave at first light, travel while it's cool and stop for awhile in the middle of the day if we can find a cool place," Vanessa said flatly, leaving no room for argument.

"That'll suit us fine, ma'am. Do ya mind if'n I call the girl over? I don't know if she'll come, she's mighty shy 'bout meetin' folks."

"Thunderation!" Ellie exclaimed. "There's no call for her to be shy with us. We're just plain folk."

"Ma'am, she ain't been with folks much." The old man went a few paces back from the campsite and yelled, "Mary Ben! C'mon over here 'n meet these folks." He waited a moment and called again. "Mary Ben!" There was no answer. "I guess she ain't acomin'. I see you folks is fixin' to eat. I'll jist mosey on back and maybe after a while I can get 'er to come over."

"Landsakes," Ellie said after the man walked away. "Should we have asked them to supper?"

"Of course not. Just because we'll travel together doesn't mean we have to be social." Vanessa took off her hat and tossed it up on the wagon seat. She put a dipper of water in the washpan, washed her hands and splashed some on her face. "We'll water the stock out of the barrels tonight, Henry. Tomorrow night we'll try to camp closer to the river."

"How come the girl wouldn't come over?" Henry asked when they sat down to eat.

"Her pa said she was shy. He said she'd not been around folk much." Ellie shook her head sorrowfully. "Maybe she's been living far out on the prairie someplace. Will you say grace tonight, Henry?"

Henry bowed his head. "Thank you, Lord, for helping us get through this day, and bless this food."

"Pass the biscuits to Vanessa first, Henry," Ellie chided gently when he helped himself first.

"Yes, ma'am. I forgot. I sure wish we could have found a dog back in Dodge."

"We'll get one the first chance we get," Vanessa promised.

"We won't get one now till we get to Colorado," Henry said like a disappointed child. "Mr. Wisner has a dog."

"Good. I hope it's friendly. Well," she said and smiled, "not too friendly. If it's too friendly it won't be worth a hoot as a watchdog."

When Ellie cooked the evening meal she always cooked enough food for the noon meal the next day. After supper she packed the food in a basket and set it in the wagon.

Vanessa helped clean up while Henry watered the stock. All three had their chores. It was a routine that worked well.

"Sometimes I wonder if we've done the right thing," Ellie said when they had settled down beside the dying cookfire. "It's so . . . big." Her gesture took in their surroundings. "I had no right to bring you and Henry into this. Adam Hill could be dead. He didn't answer my letters."

"Oh, Aunt Ellie! Don't look on the dark side. You know how mail is in this country."

"I'm thinking there may be other kinfolk. My Henry said his brother was one of the most important men in the territory. He said he owned a big ranch and most of the town . . ." Ellie's voice trailed off.

"Now stop worrying. We discussed it. Henry and I agreed it was the best thing to do. We were in a rut in Missouri. It's been good for all of us, especially Henry. He's learned a lot and so have I. We've seen a whole new way of life out here and we've enough money to get us a start. Finding that Henry has kinfolk will be an extra bonus, but we'll certainly not depend on them for our living."

"I know you wanted to come, but it's one thing to sit in a comfortable house and talk about going west and something else when you are doing it." She looked westward, toward the stretch of open plain. "I can't help but wonder what's waiting for us out there."

"Whatever it is, it can't be worse than Dodge. Don't worry, Aunt Ellie, dear. We've managed just fine up to now."

"Dodge was the jumping off place. From here on it's a wild and lawless land."

"'The Lord takes care of those who take care of themselves,'" Vanessa quoted. "With that shotgun and rifle I plan to do just that."

Henry had been listening quietly. He didn't like the worried tone of his mother's voice. His slow thinking mind tried to sort out what was bothering her. At first the trip was exciting; but now that the newness had worn off, there were times when he was bewildered and longed for the farm and the familiar everyday things; the cows, the sheep, the warm coziness of the barn, and old Shep. But Vanessa had said all that was behind them and they had to look ahead. She said they would have a new home in Colorado and that he was the man in the family and he would have to work hard just like he had in Missouri. He could do that. He could work hard, and he could take care of his mother and Vanessa.

Henry placed his hand on his mother's shoulder and looked up at her. His face was that of a man, a handsome man. But his eyes were the wide, worried eyes of a child.

"Don't worry, Mama. I'll take care of you, and I'll take care of Van, too."

"I know you will, dear." There was a breathless sob in Ellie's voice that only Vanessa recognized.

The old man and the girl were moving around their breakfast fire when Vanessa and Henry went for the mules. When the moved out at dawn the Wisner wagon fell in behind. Daylight found them on the trail that ran parallel with the Arkansas River. The day was warm, but a cloud bank in the southwest promised a rainstorm before the day was over.

At noon they pulled off the trail toward the river. Vanessa and Henry unhitched the mules and took them down to drink. On the way back they passed Mr. Wisner leading his team to the water, and caught a glimpse of a dark-haired girl in a faded and patched calico dress that barely reached the tops of her high-laced shoes. She moved to the back of the wagon as they approached. A big yellow dog lay beneath the wagon and eyed them but didn't move. After they passed Vanessa glanced over her shoulder and saw the girl peeking at them from around the water barrel.

"We'll have plenty of time to get acquainted," she assured Henry when he lagged to look at the dog. "Right now I'm hungry."

The man and the girl kept their distance through the nooning, and when Henry drove the team out onto the trail again, they fell in behind and moved up close because the southerly breeze blew the dust cloud made by the wagon ahead away from them. Vanessa rode out ahead astride the saddle horse.

The country slid away behind them. It was big, open and grassy as far as the eye could see, and to the south was the Arkansas River. It was lonesome country. Since noon Vanessa had seen nothing but a lone buzzard, a roadrunner, and a snake that slithered across the trail. Here the gigantic herds of buffalo had roamed for hundreds of years. Here the rawhiders had come to slaughter them by the thousands. Buffalo were different from cattle; they moved constantly, allowing the grass to grow back, and they left chips for travelers to use for campfires.

Vanessa studied the country ahead and reckoned that by evening they would reach the Cimarron cutoff. That notorious stretch of the trail was a shortcut going south across Indian Territory, used by those brave souls who thought the risk of attack by marauding Indians and bands of cutthroat outlaws was worth the two hundred miles it saved to Sante Fe.

She worried a bit about the weather. Today was the first of September. Back in Missouri they would have two months of good weather before winter. Here there was more brown in the grass than green, and the cottonwoods along the riverbank had a tinge of yellow to their leaves. That could be due to a dry season, Vanessa thought. Nevertheless, she felt they needed to make every day, even every hour count if they were to reach Junction City before winter set in.

When she saw the three horsemen come out of the trees along the river and walk their horses toward the trail, she dropped back beside the wagon and held out her hand for the shotgun. Ellie handed her the gun, then reached under the seat and placed the rifle between her and Henry. It was a plan they had worked out and used several times before. Henry had never shot the gun, but no one knew that except Ellie and Vanessa.

"Don't say anything, Henry," Vanessa cautioned. "And don't stop even if they get onto the trail ahead of you. Just whip up the mules and go ahead. They'll get out of the way."

"I will, Van. I'll do just what you tell me to," he said, but he had a worried frown on his face.

The trio drew up beside the trail and waited for them. Vanessa cocked the shotgun and let it lie across her lap. One of the men wore a flat-crowned black hat and had on a black vest over a dark red shirt. He was lean and dark and clean shaven. One was sandy-haired and looked no older than sixteen. The other man was thick in the middle, his clothes were filthy and he had a tobacco stain running down the side of his mouth. All three had bedrolls tied on behind their saddles.

"Howdy." It was the heavyset man who spoke.

Vanessa nodded and rode on past them. She could feel their eyes boring into her back and had to suppress the desire to turn and look at them. She listened intently, and knew the instant they put their heels to their horses to follow her. Long ago she had planned what she would do in such a case. She had to act decisively and catch them by surprise. She was an excellent rider and knew her horse well. She gigged him so he turned on his hindlegs and set down directly in front of the three riders, the shotgun lying along his neck. She said two words.

"Back off!"

The men pulled up.

"Ain't friendly, huh?" The heavyset man's nose was big and veined, and his eyes were small and piggish. He was a wide man and the sleeves of his dirty shirt were rolled halfway to his elbows. His hat was too small for his big head, and Vanessa could smell his unwashed body from ten feet away.

"No."

Henry had stopped the wagon about fifty yards ahead, and the Wisner wagon had stopped a good hundred yards back. Vanessa faced the men between the two wagons.

"Got any tobaccy to sell?"

"No."

The dark man had the blackest eyes Vanessa had ever seen. He turned his head to look at her with both of them, the way a snake would do. His clothes were clean, his boots good, and his gun was tied down. He sat quietly watching, but she knew he was the dangerous one. The other was a shifty-eyed kid whose brows grew together over his nose. He had a constant grin on his face.

"Yo're shore a purty little thin'." The big man spit, then grinned at her with snuff-stained lips. "Ain't she a purty little thin', Tass? We ain't seen nothin' purtier since we seen that little filly dancin' bare naked on the bar in Trail City."

The dark man took his time answering, and all the time his black eyes never blinked.

"That whore don't hold a candle to her." His voice was soft and silky and rolled out through lips that barely moved. It was a voice Vanessa didn't like. His hair, as black as his hat, was shiny and grew down in front of his ears, framing his narrow dark face. His features were fine, but his high cheekbones stamped him as a half-breed. The dark man's horse began to move slowly forward, one step at a time.

"Come any closer and I'll blow you out of the saddle," Vanessa said confidently and in a conversational tone.

The horse stopped and the dark man's face broke into a smile that didn't seem to affect his eyes; they stayed open and unblinking. "Ya got a man?"

Vanessa ignored his softly spoken question.

"Ya got a man?" he asked again. Silence. "Well, it makes

no never mind if'n ya got a man or not. You 'n me are agoin' to get mighty friendly afore long."

"I doubt that," she retorted in a cool, lofty tone. "Now ride out."

"Do ya think to hold off all three of us with that shotgun?"

"No. Just you. It'll not matter to you what happens after the first shot. You'll be splattered all over that horse."

The man threw back his head and laughed as if what she had said pleased him. "C'mon," he said to the other two. "Leave *my* woman be . . . for now."

He lifted his hand in a salute, wheeled his horse and rode toward the river. The other two followed, the kid looking back over his shoulder and laughing.

Chapter Three

Vanessa rode back to speak to Mr. Wisner when the wagons began to move again.

"Ma'am, I hung back cause I didn't want to let 'em get us bunched up."

"You did right, Mr. Wisner. I don't think we've seen the last of them. We'd better make camp together tonight."

"I was athinkin' that, ma'am. If'n ya don't mind me sayin' so, we ort a pick us a spot in the open."

"I don't mind at all. I appreciate your suggestions."

The girl on the seat beside the old man kept her face turned away. She was small but full grown. Her breasts were rounded and strained the bodice of the dress that was too small. Her hair was brown and curly and brushed straight back from her forehead without a part. It was tied at the nape of her neck with a string.

"This here's Mary Ben. Say howdy, Mary Ben," Mr. Wisner nudged the girl gently with his elbow.

"Howdy."

Vanessa barely heard the girl's greeting, but she leaned forward in the saddle so she could look into her face. "Hello, Mary Ben. I'm Vanessa. We'll get acquainted later."

"It'd be good to water the teams afore we make camp." The old man's eyes moved constantly, scanning the area on each side of the trail.

"Have you been over this trail before?"

"Once or twice. If yo're willin' to press on there's a openin' to the river on ahead where we can drive down, then it'd be best to back off aways 'n make camp."

"All right. I'm glad you're with us, Mr. Wisner."

Vanessa rode ahead and told Henry and Ellie the plan, then watched for John Wisner's signal to turn toward the river.

It was almost dark by the time they made camp and staked out the stock. The prairie grass was pale gold in the dusky light, and there was the smell of the sun-ripened grass and cool river water on the breeze that came from the south. Firelight flickered between the two wagons and soon a trail of wood smoke drifted upward and bacon sizzled in a pan.

Mr. Wisner walked around the end of his wagon with his hand firmly grasping Mary Ben's arm. The girl had a pained, frightened look on her face, but the determined old man was urging her forward.

"Ma'am," he said to Ellie, "this here's Mary Ben."

Ellie took in the situation at a glance. "Hello, dear," she said as she continued working. "Now, if you'll give us room around this fire, Mr. Wisner, Mary Ben and I will have some supper ready in no time at all. Mary Ben, fetch that plate from the table and dish up this bacon. I'll fry us a mess of eggs tonight. I've got to use them up before they get too old."

The old man backed off. He watched anxiously for a moment, then went to his wagon. He returned with a large-mouthed crock with a cork stopper in the top and set it on the table.

"You folks got a likin' fer honey? Me'n Mary Ben got us a bit awhile back," he announced shyly.

For the first time in months Ellie didn't insist on getting out the table and eating on a cloth. She filled a plate for each and they ate hurriedly. Neither the girl nor Henry said a word while Vanessa, Ellie and John Wisner talked of keeping watch through the night. Henry was interested in the dog. He watched it and glanced shyly at the girl. The big yellow dog lay beneath the wagon, his eyes seldom leaving Mary Ben. She sat down on the ground beside him and fed him bits from her plate from time to time.

Henry cleaned his plate, set it on the box where he had been sitting and went to where the girl sat beside the dog. He hunkered down beside them and held out a piece of bacon he'd saved from his own meal. The dog ignored it. The girl reached over and took the meat from his hand. She held it out and the dog carefully took it from her fingers. Henry smiled and reached out to scratch the dog's ears.

"Don't touch him," Mary Ben said sharply.

"Why not? I'll not hurt him." The girl glanced at him and then away. "My name's Henry." Mary Ben placed her plate on the ground, folded her hands in her lap and looked down at them. "What's his name?" She didn't answer. Puzzled and disappointed because she wouldn't talk to him, Henry asked, "Does he have a name?" Mary Ben twisted her hands in her lap and refused to look at him. Doggedly, he persisted. "I had a dog named Shep, but he was killed in Wichita. If he doesn't have a name why don't you call him Shep?"

"His name is Mister."

"Mister what?"

"Mister nothin'. Just Mister." She looked at him and Henry smiled.

"I like that. Will he let me pet him?"

Mary Ben continued to look at him, her face still, her

eyes large and questioning. He wasn't like any man she had met before. He was clean and he didn't grab at her. He seemed to be as unsure of himself as she was, and he was anxious to please—like a youngster in a grown man's body. Her shyness began to dissolve and the tension eased out of her. The shoulders that she had held so straight relaxed, and her hands that had been clenched together fell apart. An awareness of Henry's simple nature crept into her mind, and her eyes softened and became misty. This man was no threat; he was as nervous and shy around folks as she was. Lips that had been pressed firmly together softened and tilted upward. Eyes as velvety brown as a fawn's smiled into his.

"Give me your hand so he can smell it." She spoke in a low husky whisper and Henry held out his hand. She shyly reached for it and held the back of it to Mister's nose. The dog sniffed, looked at her and sniffed again. "He's a friend, Mister," she said softly, then placed Henry's palm on the top of the dog's shaggy head. A big smile slashed Henry's brown cheeks as he stroked the dog's head. "I think he likes you," Mary Ben said.

"I like him. And I like you, too, Mary Ben," Henry replied with simple honesty.

Ellie had been watching her son as he tried to make friends with the girl, praying he wouldn't be rebuffed. It had happened so many times, and his hurt was her hurt. Relieved when they began to talk and pet the dog, she turned her attention back to what Mr. Wisner was saying.

"Ya got to be careful with yore fire, ma'am. Ain't nothin' awfuller than a prairie fire. I ain't been in but one, but it was a ripsnorter. There jist ain't no place to go when yo're on the prairie 'n fire comes down on ya."

"What in the world did you do?" Ellie asked.

"Why, ma'am, I turned the team loose, rolled my water barrel out from the wagon 'n jumped in. That fire come aroarin' like a tornado. Yes siree. Twas all over in five minutes. Lost my tucker, but not a hair on my head. I was plum tickled 'bout that."

"You were lucky you had water in the barrel."

"Yes'm. 'Nother thin' we gotta watch out fer is wolves. They ain't likely to corner ya or brin' down a mule here cause there be small critters around fer 'em to eat, but ya ain't ort to be roamin' around outside camp."

"We'll not be doing that," Vanessa said firmly. "We've got those two-legged wolves to worry about now."

"Will the young feller . . . ah, take a watch?" John asked hesitantly.

"No," Ellie said quickly. "But Vanessa and I will."

"Mary Ben 'n the dog can stand a turn. Nothin'll come up on Mary Ben 'n the dog without her aknowin'."

"How old is Mary Ben?" Vanessa asked.

"I don't rightly know, ma'am. Some'eres around sixteen, seventeen, I reckon."

Both women gave the wiry old man a puzzled look, but he didn't say anymore, and they were too polite to ask why it was he didn't know his daughter's age.

They broke the night watch into four two-hour shifts. Ellie would take the first one, then Mary Ben, then John. Vanessa would take the last shift. The rainstorm that had threatened all day became a reality. The wind came first and began scattering the embers of the cookfire. Henry scooped dirt over them, then hurried to the wagon as the rain came down.

One of the double doors at the back of the caravan was a split door. Ellie folded back the top half and sat looking out into the night. An occasional flash of lightning lit up the camp and she could see the wind whipping the canvas top of the Wisner wagon. Henry was stretched out on the floor beneath Vanessa's bunk, and Ellie could hear him snoring peacefully.

It had taken Ellie ten years to become reconciled to the fact that her son's mental capacity was impaired. He hadn't walked or talked until two years after Vanessa walked and talked, and it was so terribly hard for him to learn to read simple words and write his name. Had it not been for Vanessa's companionship, he would not have advanced to the stage he was in now. His cousin had been wonderfully patient with him. Several years before she had discovered he had a skill and ease in using his hands and enjoyed working with leather. She had traded medical services and medicine to a neighbor to teach him how to make whips and quirts. Soon Henry's work was even better than his teacher's and the association had ended.

When they left Missouri they had brought with them several tow sacks of cut, rolled hides that had been run through the splitting gauge to remove the hair. They had had to leave behind the grindstone Henry used to sharpen his knives because it was so heavy, but they planned to buy another when they reached Colorado. It had been a big boost to Henry's confidence to know that he excelled in something.

Lightning flashed and Ellie saw Mary Ben climb out of the end of the Wisner wagon with a slicker over her head. She crawled beneath the wagon and sat down beside the dog. Ellie knew she was free to go to bed, but still she sat looking out into the night.

She thought of her husband and closed her eyes. Once again she saw his handsome blond head, his laughing eyes, and felt his soft mustache against her face. Within two glorious days he had swept her off her feet with sweet and persistent courting. They married and had what were the happiest weeks of her life, followed by utter despair. She never fully believed that he had deliberately deserted her as some of her friends suggested. The years had passed terribly slowly, and then she received the horrible news about his death from his brother in Colorado. But he had left a part of himself with her—their son, Henry.

Ellie sighed and sought her bed. She regretted nothing. What she hoped and prayed for was that there would be a

place for her son where he could work for his keep and have
kin nearby to care about him. It saddened her to know that
he would never know the fulfillment of such a love as she
had known.

Vanessa was awake when John tapped on the end of the
wagon to let her know it was her turn to stand watch. She
took the shotgun, wrapped a shawl around her shoulders and
stepped out of the wagon. The rain had ceased and the air
was crisp and cool. She sat down on a box so she could look
toward the river and the darkness closed in around her. Her
hair was braided in one long, loose braid, and the damp air
had caused the tendrils to curl tightly on her forehead and in
front of her ears. She brushed them back from her face, then
buried her hands in the shawl. The night was quiet. Nothing
moved, as least nothing she could see or hear. Her mind
wandered to her home in Missouri, and she wondered if the
people who had bought the farm had cut the dense growth of
raspberry bushes. She thought about the lights along the
streets in Springfield and people sitting in their porch
swings. It was all so far removed from this quiet spot that it
seemed to Vanessa they were alone in the world on an island
of floating grass.

Far off a coyote howled, then another. It made her think
of the thin-faced man with the black eyes. Vanessa felt herself go cold. She didn't want to think of him. There was
something about him that frightened her, something evil and
dangerous, as if he had no regard for any living creature who
stood in the way of what he wanted. He had looked at her as
if he were looking right through her clothing. She shuddered
again as she remembered his words and the positive way he
had spoken them. Leave *my* woman be . . . for now, he had
said.

She heard the coyote howl again, or was it a wolf? She
heard the dull thud of the stock pawing the wet sod. There
was no other sound and the time passed slowly. The clouds

drifted away and a few stars came out. The breeze came up and rippled the canvas on the Wisner wagon.

"Quiet night."

The voice made her freeze with fear. She had heard nothing, seen nothing. Yet the voice reached her from the darkness directly behind her. She made a grab for the shotgun and a large, strong hand caught her wrist.

"Don't be scared. I'm not one of them you're looking out for." He released her hand, but stood close behind her, his other hand on her shoulder pressing her down. "I'm mighty glad you're not a screaming woman, Vanessa."

"Who are you?" Fear almost choked her.

"Remember that puffed-up jackass back in Dodge?" There was laughter in his voice. "The one you ran off with the shotgun after you clobbered the boy with the shovel?"

"I remember. What are you doing here?"

"I came to tell you your mules are gone."

"What?" She jumped up and whirled to face him. All she could see was a dark shadow against the wagon.

"Don't get all het up and go off half-cocked. I passed a camp over by the river and saw three horses and four mules. I figured the mules were yours."

"You've been following us!"

He chuckled. "Yes and no. I saw your outfit this afternoon. There's no mistaking that wagon. I doubt there's another like it this side of the Mississippi. I couldn't believe you were stupid enough to strike out with only one other wagon."

"So you tagged along to see what happened," she said caustically.

"I'm in no hurry so I lagged behind a bit. I saw you meet up with some real fine...ah, gentlemen. I smelled the bacon you had for supper and saw that there were three women and two men in your party. I figured to leave early and go on ahead of you. Then I saw the mules. Tell me,

Vanessa, what the hell are you folks doing out here by yourselves?" There was harsh impatience in his voice now.

The familiar way in which he used her name made her temper flare. "That is none of your damn business, sir!"

"I didn't expect a civil answer from you. Do you have any coffee?"

"No, and I'm not making any. I'm going after those mules."

"You're doing no such thing. You're not doing anything until I've had my coffee."

"Well! I'll not have a . . . a sneaking nighthawk coming in here telling me what to do!"

"Vanessa?" Ellie stepped down out of the wagon. "Who's out there?"

"It's all right, Aunt Ellie. It's that—"

"It's the puffed-up jackass from Dodge, ma'am."

"Stop saying that!" she hissed, and his chuckle made her clench her teeth in barely suppressed fury.

"Landsakes! What's going on!"

"Vanessa's in a stew because I slipped up on her," Kain said. "I made enough noise to wake the dead. I thought sure she'd turn around and shoot me, but she sat there and let me walk up on her. I'm not surprised they stole the mules right out from under her nose."

"Stole the mules? Oh my goodness! What will we do?"

"I've not decided. I'll have to study on it. Name's DeBolt. Kain DeBolt."

"How do you do?" The polite lady, under any circumstance, Ellie offered her hand. "I'm Mrs. Hill, and this is my niece, Vanessa Cavanaugh."

"Vanessa and I have met."

"Did I hear ya say the mules is gone?" John Wisner's voice preceded him out of the darkness.

"Two black, a gray and a brown," Kain said.

"Our mules!" Vanessa blurted angrily.

"Of course. The thieves figured they'd kill the men when they went to get them."

"Kill the men! Why on earth would they do that?" Ellie asked.

"For you women. Your fancy outfit is worth something, but three women are worth more. There would be one for each of them and when they tired of you, they could always sell you to rawhiders or plains scavangers. They took the mules so the men would come armed. Nobody much asks questions out here, but that army platoon that passed could be somewhere up ahead. They'd just say the men rode in shooting, made a fight of it and they had to defend themselves."

"Oh my goodness!" Ellie was shocked by his blunt words. Her hand grasped the side of the wagon for support.

"I'd appreciate a cup of coffee, Mrs. Hill."

Ellie breathed deeply, squared her shoulders and moved to a compartment beneath the wagon bed and took out dry kindling. "Do you think it's all right to build a fire?"

"They'll not expect you to discover the mules are gone until daylight."

"Why didn't the dog make a fuss when *he* sneaked in here?" Vanessa demanded.

"Mary Ben's the only thin' that dog cares for, ma'am," John said regretfully. "Long as she ain't bothered, he'll not do nothin'."

"Fine watchdog he is!"

John started a small fire. Ellie filled the blackened coffeepot with water from the barrel, added coffee, and set it on the grill over the flames. Vanessa stood back out of the light. She looked often at Kain DeBolt as he stood talking to John. In the faint light she could tell that he was dressed in buckskins, wore knee-high moccasins, and had a gun belt strapped around his slim hips. His hat was pulled low over his eyes, and his face was turned toward her. Damn him! He was watching her.

Henry came out of the back of the wagon, yawning and scratching his head. "Is it time to hitch up?"

Vanessa went to him before he reached the circle of light and urged him back against the wagon. "The mules are gone, Henry. Those men we met yesterday stole them."

"Well, golly! I didn't think they were very nice fellows anyway. They looked mean. Is he one of them?" he asked in a low voice, but it carried in the stillness.

"I don't . . . think so." Vanessa made sure her voice carried across the camp. "But you can't trust anyone you meet up with out here in this accursed land."

"Henry, come meet Mr. DeBolt." Henry moved obediently toward his mother. "My son, Henry." There was always pride in Ellie's voice when she introduced her son.

"Howdy, Henry." Kain held out his hand.

Henry took it, mumbled a word, and stepped back into the shadows beside Vanessa. He could tell that Vanessa didn't like this man, so he didn't like him either.

Vanessa stood silently beside Henry for a moment, then slipped into the caravan. She pinned her hair up on the top of her head, put on Henry's old hat and pulled it down over her ears. Kain DeBolt was too smooth and it bothered her. As a matter of fact, everything about him bothered her a lot. He was so damn sure of himself. The way he laughed at her infuriated her. She wanted to cry when she thought of the mules. Had they been stolen while she sat there daydreaming? The possibility of their being taken by white men hadn't occurred to her. Indians, perhaps, but not white men.

One thing was sure, she thought. They couldn't stay where they were and they couldn't move without the mules. They had to get them back since they couldn't pull the wagon to Colorado with one saddle horse. Maybe she could ride ahead and find the army patrol. The more she thought of it, the more she realized that was the only hope they had. She would have to do it and she might as well get started. She stepped out of the wagon to tell her aunt her decision.

Kain was squatting on his heels with a cup in his hands, talking to Ellie. Vanessa approached the fire and held out her cup. His hat was lying on the ground beside him. He looked younger without the hat until he turned to look up at her and the light fell on the scar across his cheek. Vanessa quickly looked away, but the picture of him stayed in her mind. Until he smiled he looked almost as sinister as the dark-eyed man. But when he smiled it made all the difference. He grinned at her with his lips and his light, fawn colored eyes. She turned her back on him and spoke to her aunt.

"The only hope we have of getting our mules back is to reach that army patrol up ahead. I'll ride out and try to find them."

"You'll do no such thing."

Vanessa turned slowly, disbelievingly, when she heard those softly spoken words. Kain was still squatting beside the fire. His eyes caught and held hers. He wasn't smiling. Silence pressed down on the entire camp as the two did battle with their eyes.

"If you said what I think you said, you just watch me," Vanessa said through lips stiff with anger. "We've got enough trouble here without you adding to it, so ride out, mister."

Kain stood, his face rigid with impatience and anger. He would have given a year of his life to be able to throw her across his lap and spank her bottom.

"You'll have more if you ride out of this camp by yourself, you stubborn, muleheaded little brat. In an hour's time you'll find yourself flat on your back in the grass, and when those woman-hungry drifters get through with you, if you're still alive, you'll wish you were dead!"

"Well I never! You don't have to be so crude!"

"Crude? For God's sake! Who do you think took those mules? Sunday school boys? They're cutthroat drifters, out-laws, the scum of the Plains. They want women! And here, in this camp, is a woman for each of them. Get some sense in that stubborn head of yours and stop acting like a balky mule."

"You hadn't ought to talk to Vanessa like that." Henry came to stand beside her and Vanessa looked up at him in dismay. He had squared his shoulders and was trying to look Kain in the eye, although she could feel the hand on her arm trembling violently.

"I'm not being disrespectful, Henry," Kain said gently but firmly. "I had to speak plainly so she'd realize I will not allow her to go off on a wild goose chase that could get her killed or . . . worse."

"I don't want her to get hurt, either." Henry's voice dropped to a whisper.

Surprised by Henry's defense and Kain's understanding of what an effort it was for him to speak up, Vanessa was silent for a moment. And when Henry backed down, an overwhelming desire to hit Kain made her clench her fist and bite her lower lip. He had won Henry over to his side! She was losing control. This . . . puffed-up jackass was taking over.

"*You* won't allow?" Vanessa focussed on what irritated her the most.

"*I* won't allow," Kain answered evenly. "Now climb down off your high horse, Vanessa, and behave yourself. I have to get going if I'm going to get those mules back."

"How do we know you're not one of them?"

"You don't. But I'm the only hope you've got."

"He's right, dear. Please listen." Ellie stood on the far side of the campfire, her hands wrapped in her apron and a worried look on her face.

"Saddle up, Henry. You'll have to help me bring the mules back if I get them."

"He's not going with you," Vanessa said quickly. "I'll go."

Kain ignored her. "You can handle the mules, can't you, Henry?"

"Yes, sir."

"I tell you he isn't going!"

"No, Mr. DeBolt," Ellie said worriedly. "Henry . . . has never shot a gun."

Kain looked from one woman to the other and then to Henry. Henry hung his head and looked away. Kain muttered something under his breath that sounded like a string of curses.

John spoke, breaking the awkward silence. "Young feller, I'd be obliged to go with ya."

"I was counting on you staying in camp and looking after the women, Mr. Wisner. I was also counting on Henry to bring the mules back if I got pinned down."

"Mary Ben can shoot a rifle good as any man I ever did see. With Mary Ben they be as well off as if it was me here."

"I want to go, Vanessa. I want to help." Henry was shaking her arm to get her attention.

"Henry! It will be dangerous."

"Saddle the horse, Henry," Kain said quietly and waited until he walked out into the darkness. Then he spoke to Ellie. "John will go with me, and Henry can bring back the mules. He'll be all right. I left my horse back in the trees. I'll get him."

"Who does he think he is?" Vanessa sputtered after Kain left. "He just comes waltzing in here and takes over."

"Ma'am," John had turned away, but came back. "I been all up 'n down the cattle trails from the gulf to Kansas, 'n I seen men aplenty. This one knows what he's about. Them's three bad fellers we come up against. We be mighty lucky DeBolt came along."

"He's right." Ellie rolled and unrolled her hands in her apron. "Oh, I wish we'd never come to this godforsaken land."

"If Henry goes, I go," Vanessa announced stubbornly before stalking off in the darkness.

She was mounted behind Henry with the shotgun in her hand when Kain rode into camp. He eyed them for a long moment, as if that was what he expected. John spoke to Mary Ben, picked up a big buffalo gun, checked the load, and climbed up on one of his horses. He rode Indian fashion with only a blanket between him and the horse as if he'd been doing it all his life.

"Does she know how to use a gun?" Kain nodded toward Mary Ben. "And would she use it if she needed to?"

"You can bet yore life on it." John rode to the far side of the camp and let loose a stream of tobacco juice before he spoke again. "Ma'am, ya'll be all right with Mary Ben. She'll do what's got to be did. She been down the trail 'n cross the creek."

Kain's eyes sent a silent message to Vanessa that she interpreted to mean, "He'd much rather have Mary Ben along than Vanessa." She tilted her chin defiantly and glared at him.

"Come on. Let's get at them before they know this is all they're up against." Kain led off and John followed with Henry and Vanessa bringing up the rear.

Vanessa, snug against Henry's back, could feel his excitement. She wondered why in the world Aunt Ellie had permitted him to go. Henry was her whole world. If anything should happen to him it would kill her aunt. It would kill her, too, she thought and hugged him close.

"You be careful, hear?" she whispered.

He didn't answer because Kain had stopped his horse and they had moved up beside him.

"The camp is just ahead, Henry. John and I will ride in. You stay back until I tell you to get the mules. Understand?"

"Yes, sir."

"And you stay out of sight," he said to Vanessa.

Fifty yards from the camp he held up his hand and Henry halted the horse. He pointed his finger. Henry slid off the horse and went silently through the brush to the spot where the mules were tied to a line strung between two trees. Kain and John walked their horses to the edge of the camp. Light streaked the eastern sky. Birds chirped noisily and fluttered in the willows that grew beside the river. The horses and mules, not used to being together, added to the noise by stamping and blowing gusts of breath through quivering lips.

The men by the fire didn't hear anyone approach until a horse whinnied a greeting. They looked up, and the heavyset man jumped so quickly to his feet that he dropped his coffee cup in the fire. There was a short hissing sound when the liquid hit the flames, and then quiet. They stood waiting, their eyes going from the man on the sorrel to the old man riding bareback.

"Our mules got loose in the night. I reckon you caught them and are holding them for us," Kain said. "We're much obliged. We'll take them off your hands."

"Ya will, huh?" The fat man wiped his greasy hands on his shirt and looked nervously at the thin, dark man in the black vest. "Wal, now, I'm athinkin' we ort a study on that a bit. Finders is keepers is what I hear. Ain't that right, Tass?" The thin, dark man stood stone still, his coal black, unblinking eyes on Kain's face. The light-haired kid grinned, showing missing teeth. Kain knew exactly what the kid was thinking: they'd be easy pickings because there were only two of them against three.

Although the fat man was doing the talking, Kain knew instinctively the breed was the one to watch. He wore his gun tied down and his right hand was ready. He had that still look about him that spelled trouble.

"The mules belong to the folks back there. We're taking them back."

"Are you?" The dark man spoke for the first time. His face was tight and his lips barely moved. "We've got the number on you. That means we keep the mules till the woman comes to get 'em."

"She's here." Vanessa spoke from somewhere behind Kain. "Now it's three on three."

An oath sprang to Kain's mind that he dared not voice. The damn fool girl would mess around and get them killed. He shoved his anger to the back of his mind. He couldn't allow it to tighten him up.

"No," Kain said, choosing his words carefully and looking squarely into the dark eyes of the man who stood tensely, as if coiled to spring. "It's just you and me."

Tass' thin lips tightened, honing his already sharp features. He had not expected that. There was quick calculation in his eyes. The stranger was mounted, he was on the ground. But there was the old man with the buffalo gun.

"What does that mean?"

"It means we take the mules and ride out. It means if you make a move to stop us, I'll kill you."

The breed was bothered by Kain's confidence but was still sure enough of himself to stand his ground. Kain waited to see how long it took for the man's sand to run out. The more bothered he was the better Kain's chances. The breed was a killer. Kain had seen his kind before; quiet like a snake, but when he struck he meant to kill. How many men had he shot in the back, and how many men had he killed face-to-face?

"Vanessa, you and Henry get the mules."

Kain heard her turn her horse. The breed's ink-black eyes darted from him to the girl and back. His nostrils flared, but otherwise he didn't move a muscle.

"Like hell," the fat man yelled suddenly.

Vanessa's horse jumped nervously and squealed when she drew up on the reins. The fat man thought this was his chance; his hand swept down. It was the last thought he would ever have. The buffalo gun boomed. The force of the shot flung him back like a rag doll, and when he landed there was scarcely anything left of his head.

Kain's gun was out and covering the other two, who

stood in flat-footed astonishment, caught that way, unmoving, not wanting to move. The gruesome sight of their companion's headless torso had taken the fight out of the young one. The skin on his face had turned a pasty yellow.

"Get out of here," Kain snarled at Vanessa and she went.

John calmly rammed another charge in the buffalo gun, then cocked it and pointed it at the men.

"I'm aready," he said calmly. "Ya want that I blow 'em to hell, too?"

"It's up to them," Kain said matter-of-factly. "If they don't shuck the guns by the time I count to three, go ahead."

"I ain't sure I know past one," John said innocently.

The men unbuckled their gun belts and let them fall to the ground. The kid seemed to notice for the first time the splatters of the fat man's blood on his pants. He gagged repeatedly, then bent over and vomited. The dark man seemed unmoved by the grisly sight and kept his eyes on Kain's face.

"Keep them covered, John, while I collect the guns." Kain got down out of the saddle, picked up the gun belts and the gun the fat man had dropped. He collected three rifles and bashed them against a tree until the barrels were bent. "You birds will be busy for a while burying your friend, so you won't need your horses. We'll borrow them for a spell." He walked over and cut the horses loose from the line. "Unless you want to join your fat friend, keep a distance between yourselves and those wagons."

Kain mounted and drove the horses out of the camp ahead of him. John followed slowly, watching the men over his shoulder.

Primer Tass watched the old wolf with the buffalo gun ride out and congratulated himself on his self-restraint. Unlike the stupid, fat Dutchman, he would live to even the score with the gringos. They would wish they were dead a hundred times before he was through with them. The kid and the Dutchman had both wanted the girl who rode with the old man. He'd have the spunky woman! She was just what he'd always looked for and had known he would find some day. She was fresh and spirited and would fill his days and his nights with excitement.

All his life Tass had taken leavings; leftover clothes, leftover food, leftover, used-up women. His own mother, part Comanche and part Mexican, had been used up by his father, an old white son of a bitch, by the time Tass was old enough to know who he was. But he had fixed the old bastard with a knife in his throat when he'd tried to use him after his mother died. This time it would be different. Someone would get *his* leavings.

Tass had thought of nothing but the woman since he had seen her. He thought of the way she had warmed him the day before when she sat on her horse and looked just at him, and the way she'd sassed him back. She reminded him of a little wildcat, and he was sure she'd fight like one. He would watch and wait, and when the time was right, he would take her and head for the wild, desolate country in Mexico. On the way he would break her like he would a wild mountain pony. Just thinking about it excited him. He'd tame her with his quirt and fists until she lay naked and willing beneath him, legs and mouth open to welcome him. He would teach her what he wanted her to do, then he'd devour her day and night until he got his fill.

His mind told him to stop thinking about her. Soon, and for as long as he wanted her, the woman would be his. He was in no hurry. It was a long way to Denver or Santa Fe or wherever the woman was going. He would follow slowly, take his revenge on the gringos, then take her.

Chapter Four

Ellie and Mary Ben were waiting at the edge of the camp when Vanessa and Henry rode in with the mules. Mary Ben, shading her eyes with her hand, looked behind them toward the river.

"Mr. Wisner's all right, Mary Ben."

"And Mr. DeBolt?" Ellie asked.

"He's all right, too, Aunt Ellie. Mr. Wisner killed one of them," Vanessa blurted, still shocked by the sudden violence.

"Killed one? Oh my goodness!"

"Let's get hitched up, Henry." Vanessa feigned composure, for she did not want her aunt and cousin to see how unnerved she was. She had seen death many times in her life and had come to accept it for the old, the sick and the injured. But never had she seen such sudden violent death as she had just witnessed.

They were ready to leave camp when John Wisner rode

in. He went to his wagon and handed the gun up to Mary
Ben, then slid from the horse and hitched him alongside the
other horse Mary Ben had backed into the traces. He didn't
offer an explanation for Kain's absence and Vanessa didn't
ask. When he climbed up on the seat, Vanessa set the team
in motion and moved out onto the trail.

The horizon ahead seemed to melt into the sky. Nothing
moved except the long grass bending in silver ripples before
the wind. Vanessa's eye swept the country. It was vast,
empty and still. They were deep in the prairie, which was
broken only by the river to the south of them. It was quiet
there. Quiet beyond anything she had imagined.

They were at least three miles from the camp before Ellie
brought up the subject of Kain DeBolt. "I wonder where he
is?"

"Who?" But Vanessa knew who she meant.

"Mr. DeBolt."

"He drove off their horses, Ma." Henry rode beside the
wagon on the saddle horse. "He just went in there and told
them we were taking the mules. He told me what to do, Ma,
and I did it." There was pride in his voice. "I like him. I
hope he comes back. You don't care if I like him, do you,
Van? He got our mules back."

"Of course not. You've got the right to like whoever you
want to."

"I hope he comes back, too. I'm afraid now. I just never
imagined it would be like this." Ellie's eyes swept the wide
horizon ahead and on each side of them. "Just look at all that
space, and we're right in the middle! Anything could happen
to us out here and there's nobody to help."

"We've got Mr. Wisner and Mary Ben. And you've got
me." It bewildered Henry to see his mother so worried.

"Yes. I've got you and Vanessa. The two of you are my
life, and I'm so afraid for you."

They had been on the trail about an hour when they met a
group of horsemen headed for Dodge City. Ellie drew in a

frightened breath as they approached and gripped the side of the wagon seat. Vanessa placed the shotgun across her lap and watched them carefully. The men eyed the women curiously, tipped their hats and rode on. Ellie kept looking back as if she expected them to turn and follow. Just before they reached the Cimarron cutoff, they met a wagon filled with hides. The driver snatched his hat from his head when he saw Ellie and pulled his team to the side of the trail so they could pass.

There was no sign of Kain DeBolt.

At noon they stopped to eat, watered the teams and let them graze for an hour, then hitched up and went on. Four horsemen overtook them in the middle of the afternoon. They swung wide of the wagons. Vanessa thought one of them could have been the young bully she had hit with the shovel back in Dodge City. They were dirty, tough looking men. She was relieved when they went on ahead and soon became a dancing speck on the horizon.

By evening Vanessa was sure it had been the most miserable day they'd spent since leaving Springfield. Most of the time Henry had ridden beside the Wisner wagon. He was enjoying the novelty of having someone new to visit with. Ellie, awash in guilt for being instrumental in bringing Vanessa and Henry into this lawless country, was wrapped in her own thoughts. Vanessa realized how close to death they had all been this morning and wondered if they should turn back or keep going.

Kain DeBolt had been in and out of her thoughts all day. They had exchanged only a few words, yet his face stayed in her thoughts with the memory of his voice. No man had ever disturbed her like that before, and she was irritated by it, fighting the feeling. She understood herself very well, and she was perfectly aware that something had happened that day in Dodge City when she had looked at him. Just what it was she didn't know, but a connection had been forged between them. Even now, just thinking about it, she was conscious of a strange sensation tingling along her nerves. He had made no effort that day to mask the look of interest in his eyes. It was the look a man gave to a woman he wanted. She had seen that look in the eyes of men before but it had never affected her like the look Kain had given her.

He was different, the kind of man who in the proper clothing would fit in anywhere. There was something that went beyond the handsome darkness of his face, his tawny eyes, his lean strength or the hard, strong maleness of him. The scar across his cheekbone only added to the mystique that surrounded him. He was a doing man, as they said back in Missouri. He had taken an enormous personal risk to get their mules back for them. She wondered if she would ever get the chance to thank him.

Kain drove the horses a good five miles back down the trail, then stung each one of them on the rump with the whip and sent them galloping off in different directions. He was sure of one thing: it would be many days before the breed and the kid rode those horses.

He was sick. He sagged in the saddle and closed his eyes against the agonizing, gut wrenching pains turning his stomach inside out. The pain hadn't bothered him much, except for a little gnawing now and then, since he'd left Dodge City, and he had come to believe that whatever had ailed him had passed. Early that morning he had eaten a can of peaches, not wanting to take the time to cook breakfast. The damn peaches could have been tainted, he thought. They sure were not sitting right in his stomach.

He turned his horse to the river and at the end of an animal path he found a maze of boulders and a dense outgrowth of brush. He got off his horse and sat down on a boulder and waited until the pain let up a bit. The warm sun felt good on his back. He sat there, hunched over, and wondered if Vanessa realized she had come to within an inch of getting him killed. His anger at her disregard for his orders had been eating at him all morning. If he had batted an eyelash, the breed would have drawn on him, with the advantage of being on his feet. John Wisner was a trail-wise old wolf, Kain thought. He had known instinctively that John would watch the other two when it seemed the fight would come down to Kain and the breed. Vanessa had set the play in motion and the fat man's luck ran out.

Thoughts of Vanessa were suddenly driven from his mind as his stomach convulsed again. Kain had never had a serious illness in his life and had always been able to rely on his strength. He was not accustomed to a feeling of weakness and he could do without it now. He had a long way to travel. The pain twisting his vitals caused the sweat to roll from his face and saliva to flood his mouth. He sat very still, breathing hoarsely, fighting the sickness in his stomach.

A jolting pain seized him and doubled him up. He fell to his knees and retched violently. Frightened by the terrible pain, he stayed there, his head hanging, not caring that moans were coming from his lips. When he was finally able to open his eyes, he saw blood mingled with his vomit.

Fear of a different kind seeped into his mind. He remembered the Arizona town where he had been a deputy, and the sheriff who had a cancer in his stomach. He had suffered terribly and vomited blood. Kain broke out in a cold sweat. Christ almighty! Would it be his fate to die a little bit each day, screaming his life away in agony as that man had done? He was frightened now—more frightened than he'd ever been in his life. The last thing he wanted was a long, painful death out here where no one knew him or cared.

Kain sat quietly for a long while, and the gnawing in his stomach lessened to just an uncomfortable feeling. He thought of the doctor in Kansas City who had examined him, left him waiting for fifteen minutes, then invited him into his brand-new office to tell him he had worms and sell him a bottle of worm medicine. Maybe he knew that he had a cancer and just didn't have the nerve to tell him. No, he thought, it was more than likely the young doctor hadn't known what ailed him, but thought he had to tell him something in order to collect his fee.

He considered going back East to see another doctor but then thought of the sheriff who had wasted his strength traveling to see every doctor within five hundred miles. Some of the doctors had told him his stomach trouble was caused by drinking alkaline water and a few said that someone was poisoning him. One even said that his kidneys were leaking into his intestines and sold him ten bottles of kidney medicine. Finally, an army doctor told him he had cancer which was eating a hole through his stomach and that there was nothing he or any other doctor could do for him. He was going to die.

Hours passed and Kain became partly reconciled to what was happening to him. He knew with certainty that he would not put himself through the torture the sheriff had endured by going from doctor to doctor. He remembered, with clarity, everything the sheriff had told him about his illness. The symptoms the sheriff described were exactly the same as his own. He wondered how much time he had. Weeks? Months?

He was reasonably sure there would be time to get to Junction City. He would see Cooper and Griffin and do what had to be done about The House, and the land. One thing was sure: he'd see to it that Della or Clayhill wouldn't get their hands on it.

Della would be glad to know he was no longer rich. The last time he had seen her she had cursed him for not giving her money for a trip to Europe. She said she was going to inherit from Clayhill and would pay him back. He had turned her down because he wanted to sever all ties with his sister. She cared nothing for him. He remembered the pain she had caused their mother from the day she had realized women were different from men. Long ago he had come to the conclusion that Della loved men and what they did to her. She had no scruples, and went about taking what she wanted regardless of whom she hurt in the process.

Kain's thoughts turned to Vanessa. She awakened something in him that no other woman had ever even stirred—something that left him restless and excited. He remembered the clear, honest way she had looked at him, the graceful movements of her soft body. He liked the proud lift of her chin, liked her blue eyes. There was quality to Vanessa, like a slim and handsome thoroughbred. She was the most feminine woman he'd ever met, yet spunky beyond all reason. Why had he not met such a woman years ago? Now it was too late.

He wondered about Henry and what there was about him that seemed familiar. It was as if he had seen him before, but he knew that was impossible. He had never been in the Springfield area. The boy could be no more than twenty and was what people would consider simpleminded. He was not a half-wit, Kain was sure. He had at least obeyed orders this morning, which was more than his cousin had done. Mrs. Hill and Vanessa had overprotected him until he hadn't developed to the limits of his abilities. Someone should have taught him how to use the rifle and fight his own battles. No man should suffer the indignity of being beaten to the ground without fighting back.

Hell, he thought, it had been in the back of his mind since he talked to Mrs. Hill that morning to see them to Denver. His plans had been to turn north at the Big Sandy, bypassing Denver and going north to Greeley, then over to Junction City. It was a shorter route, dangerous for a white man because he would pass through the vicinity of Sand Creek where the infamous Colonel Chivington and his troops had slaughtered hundreds of Indians: old men, women and children. But now he would go on to Denver, see a doctor there and get a supply of laudanum to use later on when the pain became unbearable.

Kain was surprised at the peace within him. He had never

given much thought to dying, not much thought to living either. He had been in a few tight spots, killed a few men when he had to, and avoided trouble when he could. He never drew down on a man unless his own life was in danger. He was a loner, making a few friends here and there, but never settling in one place long enough to establish roots. Now he wondered at the emptiness of his life. His mother was the only person who had ever loved him, and she had lived for only a short time after she married Adam Clayhill and moved west with him.

Fort Griffin, the young man he had picked up in Santa Fe and trailed with for a couple of years knew him better than anyone else. He supposed that if he loved anyone it was Griff, and maybe Griff loved him in his own way. They were an unlikely pair to team up. Griff was a young, penniless drifter who had come to his aid during a barroom brawl. They had backed out the door side by side and made a run for the mountains with four Mexican desperadoes trailing them. Griff was a wild, tough kid, but lonely and scared beneath his quiet and confident exterior. Then Griff had met Bonnie, a little abused waif with two arms but only one hand. They had married and were so happy it was a real pleasure to watch the two of them together. They were the only two people in the world aside from Cooper Parnell and his wife who would take on the burden of caring for him if he should ask them. But of course he wouldn't. When the time came and he couldn't do for himself, he'd end it with his six-shooter.

Thinking of Bonnie and Griff brought on a feeling of regret. He had never felt a love such as they knew. Kain had known many women and had loved none of them. Always he would leave them, and while he would often remember, he would never feel the urge to go back. He wondered how it would be to make love to a woman who was totally his, who had the look of love in her eyes just for him, not for the amount of money he would leave her. Vanessa was the kind of woman who would love a man wholeheartedly or not at all.

"Vanessa, Vanessa," he murmured. "I've got to stop thinking about you in that way."

The red horse, cropping the grass around the boulders, lifted his head, perked his ears, and gazed fixedly toward the trail. Kain got to his feet, moving slowly, fearful the pain would return. Soon his ears picked up what Big Red had heard a full minute before, hoofbeats on the hard-packed trail. Well concealed, he watched four riders pass. They were tough, dirty men. One was a small man with a thin face and straw colored hair—the kid Vanessa had hit with the shovel.

Kain leaned weakly against his horse while questions dogged his mind. Was it a coincidence the kid was on the trail behind Vanessa's wagon or was he deliberately following it? He mulled it over in his mind and decided that if the kid was following, he would not do anything in broad daylight, not with old John Wisner riding shotgun with that powerful buffalo gun.

The air was very still, the sky impossibly clear. Kain patted Big Red, and the horse nuzzled his hand affectionately. The thought came to him that he would ride out of this place a much different man than when he rode in. He considered that for a moment, then shrugged his broad shoulders. Life was uncertain and death was sure for all. His end would just come sooner than he had expected.

Kain was hungry, but afraid that if he ate the terrible pain would return. After a few minutes he realized he would have to risk it and dug into his pack for the last of his soda crackers. He ate them slowly, then mounted his horse and rode out.

The sun was down. Vanessa went for a short distance after they crossed a dry creek bed before pulling the mules to a halt. John drove his wagon alongside hers.

"Not here, ma'am. There's a better place on down aways."

Vanessa waved him on and followed. John turned down the dry creek bed. There was a fold in the ground where a trickle of a spring ran down to the creek and made a small pool.

"Ain't nobody agoin' to see us here till they're right up close," John explained. "Ain't no use tellin' folks where we be."

"Do you think Mr. DeBolt is all right?" Ellie asked.

"Him? He'll make out. He's makin' sure them horses is scattered to hell 'n yonder. That breed'll be madder 'n a stepped-on snake. I ain't met a mean breed yet what wasn't as sneakin' as a snake. He be wily as a wolverine, 'n if'n ya ain't careful he'll poke a knife in yore back shore as shootin'. Kain ort a killed him. He's gonna have to anyways."

"Oh! I do hope not."

"That's how tis out here, ma'am. Ya got to do what ya got to do." John took off his hat and tossed it up into the wagon seat. "We'd best share a fire agin tonight, cook what we got to, then dowse it 'n set back."

Vanessa and Henry unhitched and Mary Ben began to build a fire on a flat shelf beside the spring.

"Do you think we'll be . . . bothered?" Ellie asked.

"I ain't aknowin' that, ma'am. It jist don't make no sense to not be ready if we are."

"Mr. Wisner, does it bother you that you killed a man today?"

"No ma'am. I ain't never liked that Dutchman, no way."

"You knew him?" Ellie was shocked.

"I sort a knowed him. He was low caliber 'n meaner 'n all get out. Ain't nothin' lower 'n a man who'd kill his own woman. It's said it's what he done. I ain't never heard a him shootin' it out face-to-face. Backshooter is what he was." He glanced at Ellie's white face and cursed himself for his blabbering tongue. "If you're afigurin' on eatin', ma'am, you'd best get at the fixin' of it."

"Yes, of course, Mr. Wisner. We appreciate your help, and Mary Ben's, too. I don't know what we'd have done without you." Ellie went to the side of the wagon and unhooked the lid of the chuck box. It was hinged on the bottom and when let down became a table. She took out an iron pot with a bail and began to peel potatoes for soup.

John noticed her trembling hands. The woman had sand, he thought. Sand and grit, but she was scared half out of her wits.

"Mary Ben's right good at givin' a hand, Mrs. Hill. 'N we got vittles in the wagon."

"She was worried about you today."

"Yes'm, I 'spect she was."

Morning came and Vanessa was tired, more tired than she had been since leaving Springfield. They had divided the watch as they had done the night before, with her taking the early morning hours. She had half expected to hear Kain's voice coming out of the darkness and was reluctant to admit her disappointment when he hadn't come. All had been quiet except for the familiar night sounds. And when the birds began their flutter and chirping in the trees above the wagons, Vanessa rapped on the door to awaken Ellie and Henry.

Ellie was nervous and jumpy but quiet. She sat on the seat beside Vanessa when they pulled out on the trail. Vanessa was beginning to worry about her. She had scarcely eaten the night before, and that morning she had only nibbled on a cold biscuit while the rest of them had eaten cornmeal mush and honey. Even Henry was quiet; his moods often reflected those of Vanessa and his mother. He watched them anxiously, hoping they would smile.

The orange globe rising over the eastern horizon predicted a bright, clear day. A few fluffy white clouds drifted overhead, birds called and flitted in the grass, a flock of crows flew up when they passed, then settled once more on their morning feast. Behind them the sun, when it fully emerged, threw their long shadows before them across the rippling grass. Ahead of them the land lay empty.

"I don't understand why Mr. DeBolt didn't come back," Ellie said after almost an hour's silence.

"He may have gone back to Dodge." Vanessa didn't believe that, but she wanted to keep the conversation going. It made the time pass more quickly.

"No, dear. He wouldn't have turned back. He's out there somewhere. Maybe those men found him—"

"That isn't likely. He took their horses and left them afoot."

"I wish he'd come back. I liked him, and I liked the way he treated Henry."

"I liked that too, although at first I was afraid for Henry to go with him. But Henry did just fine and he was so proud that he'd helped."

"I know. If his father had lived he would have had a strong man to guide him, and Henry might have been different. I'm afraid, Vanessa. I'm afraid of what will happen to him in the years ahead."

"Henry will always have a place with me, Aunt Ellie. You know that."

"I know, dear. But you will marry someday and have a family of your own. Your husband may resent Henry. I'm so hopeful Henry will have male kin who will look after him."

"You're still young, Aunt Ellie. You're not yet forty years old. You've devoted your life to Henry and me, and you act as if your own life is over. I've seen men look at you a second and third time. You should have married and had more children."

"Oh, no! I never even considered another man after I lost my Henry. If you could have known him, Vanessa, you

would understand. He was so handsome, so... in command. Why, he would walk into the hotel dining room and
everyone would jump to wait on him. In the shops the clerks
would leave others standing in order to serve him. He was
that kind of man, sweet and generous, and he made me feel
like a queen. I've thought about each of the thirty wonderful
days I was with him. I met him the second day he arrived in
Springfield. He was a banker from Chicago, and he had
business with the bank president. I was waiting for a friend.
We talked and three days later were married."

Vanessa had heard the story of how Ellie had met Henry
Hill many times. She listened now while Ellie's voice softened as she told of the picnics and the walks in the park with
her lover. She told about his renting a buggy and driving to
the preacher's house. After the ceremony he had told the
minister to send the marriage certificate to the hotel. The
desk clerk had given it to Ellie and it was one of her most
treasured possessions. Ellie described the lovely room they
had shared after their wedding, and then her voice became
dreamy as she remembered.

The day passed uneventfully. Henry drove the Wisner
wagon late in the afternoon and John rode the horse ahead to
find a suitable place for their night camp. When he returned
he guided them to a place along a dry gully that carried
water to the river during a hard rain.

By the time they stopped for the night Vanessa had a
sharp pain between her eyes from facing the setting sun. As
soon as she pulled the mules to a halt she discarded her hat,
shook her head and massaged her temples with her fingertips. The unbrushed tangles of curly, coppery hair drifted
down around her face and over her shoulders in a glistening
mass. The cool air felt so good as it touched her scalp that
she threaded her fingers into her hair and lifted it time and
again, until it floated about her face like a bright, fiery
cloud.

* * *

The man concealed in the dense growth of brush that lined the gully could only stare. Kain had kept the wagons in sight for the past two days, and that afternoon he had kept pace with them along an animal path that ran parallel with the river. When he saw John ride out on Henry's horse, he rode ahead to meet him, and together they had discovered this camp site. Kain asked John not to tell the others yet that he was trailing them; he still had some scouting to do.

Now as Kain watched Vanessa he was aware of two things. That this was the most alive woman he'd ever met, and that something new and strange was making his heart pick up speed and sending a tingling sensation racing over his skin. She was pretty, even beautiful, but more than that, she wasn't one of those females who were all ruffles and flutters. She was a self-reliant woman who knew who she was, and one, Kain thought, who wouldn't be shocked to the roots of her being by sex.

In all his travels, he not seen such glorious hair on any woman, and he had thought he had seen the beauties of the world. Now he understood the reason Vanessa wore the bonnet in Dodge City and the old hat on the trail. Her beautiful face, long, supple, swaying body, and glorious hair would stop most men in their tracks. He imagined she had come to dislike the attention, and that was probably the reason for the hostility the day he had bumped into her in Dodge City.

Just looking at her made his heart stop, then race so wildly he found it necessary to draw deep gulps of air into his lungs. He knew with a certainty that he was in love with this woman; completely, utterly, ridiculously in love for the first time in his life. Following that realization came an eruption of regret so acute that for a moment it stupefied his mind. When the feeling passed, Kain DeBolt, self-assured man of the world discovered he had tears in his eyes.

Love had come too late.

* * *

Vanessa dipped water into a pan and carried it into the caravan to wash the day's accumulation of dust from her body. She used the same water to wash her shirt, then sat quietly brushing her hair and thinking about the man who had appeared out of the darkness to tell her the mules were gone. What had happened to him? It had been two days since he had left them. An emptiness flowed through her at the thought of never seeing him again. She stopped brushing and sat staring at the hairbrush, idly picking out the bright red hairs caught in the bristles. Why had he come to help them in the first place? Why was he staying away now? Vanessa shivered without knowing why.

Ellie, with Mary Ben's help, had a thick stew bubbling in the iron pot suspended on a cross beam over the fire by the time the stock was watered and staked out for the night.

"What are Mr. Wisner and Henry doing?" Ellie asked when Mary Ben returned to the cookfire with an armful of small sticks, the yellow dog trailing at her heels.

"I told him there's a rabbit run back down there where the brush is caught on a windfall. He's down there showin' Henry how to set a snare. We'll have us a rabbit or two by mornin'." Mary Ben knelt and fed a few small sticks of wood into the fire. "I'll get us more wood. Ain't no use wastin' the daylight." The dog had flopped on his belly, but got quickly to his feet and followed her out past the wagons to where a brush pile blocked the dry creek bed.

Ellie stirred the stew. That was the longest group of words she had heard Mary Ben put together at one time. The girl never spoke unless she was asked a question, and until now her answers had been one or two words. Ellie watched her approach with another armload of wood. She was small and sturdy. A softly rounded girl with smooth, sun-browned skin, straight dark brows and curling eyelashes. Her thick, brown, wavy hair, tied back with a thong, came to the middle of her back. The dress she wore had patches on top of patches and was far too small for her. Ellie wondered how she could arrange to give her a dress without it appearing to be charity.

"That dog never takes his eyes off you, Mary Ben. I've never seen the like."

"Yes'm. He likes me. I like him, too."

"I've been wanting to ask you why he didn't make a fuss the other morning when Mr. DeBolt came into camp."

"I told him not to."

"You knew he was out there?"

"Yes'm. But I knew he wasn't one of them others."

"Well, for goodness sakes! How did you know that?"

"Cause I knew they'd come 'n took the mules. I told Mr. Wisner 'n he said there wasn't nothin' to do right then but wait it out, cause if he made a fuss them fellers would shoot up the camp."

"Well...I swan to goodness. Mr. DeBolt could have been somebody just as bad."

"No, ma'am." Mary Ben shook her head. "Mr. Wisner knew he wasn't no bad man. He'd been trailin' us most all the day 'n Mr. Wisner'd been lookin' at him in his glass. He said it was him who'd stood up to that little old bast—to that man in Dodge who beat Henry."

Ellie was dumbfounded. All this had been going on and she had been unaware of it. Suddenly she wanted to hug Mary Ben, and she did. She put her arms around her, gave her a quick hug, and kissed her on the cheek.

Mary Ben stood as if in shock. She neither drew away nor responded to the gesture. When Ellie's arms dropped from around her she didn't move. Ellie stepped back and saw the bewildered look on her face and suddenly realized that a gesture of affection was unknown to the girl.

"Bless you, child. It was a lucky day for us when you caught up with us. I'm so glad you did."

"Luck didn't have nothin' to do with it," Mary Ben said slowly. "Mr. Wisner seen ya was moving out. He said ya didn't have no trail sense or ya'd not be strikin' out all by yore ownselves, 'n ya'd be in a heap of trouble. He said he'd been athinkin' 'bout us goin' west, 'n we'd just pull out 'n string along with ya folks."

"You mean . . . Mr. Wisner was worried about us and came after us?"

"Yes'm. Mr. Wisner said ya was fine ladies 'n ya'd not last out here a'tall. He said that Henry wasn't . . . that Henry needed somebody to tell him what to do."

"Well, I do declare! My, my, wasn't that nice of him? I just never heard of such a thing. We're very grateful to have you and your father with us."

"Ma'am, he ain't my pa."

"Oh, my!" Ellie's hands twisted in her apron. She hadn't thought it strange at all for Mary Ben to speak of her father as Mr. Wisner. Many women referred to their husbands in that formal manner. *Husband?* "Oh, my goodness!" Ellie said again, and her hands dropped the apron as she stared at the young girl.

Mary Ben was puzzled. She didn't understand why Mrs. Hill stared at her so strangely. Had she done something wrong? Did this mean Mrs. Hill didn't like her anymore? It had gotten so easy to talk to her she just talked and talked. She'd been running off at the mouth. That's what it was, she realized, and Mrs. Hill didn't like it. She clamped her lower lips between her teeth and her brows drew together in a worried frown.

Ellie saw her distress and the way her body tensed as if to turn and run. The shy little creature was very perceptive. The distaste she had felt at the thought of this child being the wife of that grizzled old man—regardless of how kind he had been to them—had run rampant across her face and the girl had seen it.

"I'm just surprised, Mary Ben." Ellie smiled, although she didn't feel like it. She was desperate to put the girl at ease again. "I'd just taken it for granted Mr. Wisner was your father. But many young girls marry older men."

"We ain't married, but I would've if he'd awanted me to. Mr. Wisner's the best man I ever knowed."

"I see." There was a silence while Ellie jabbed a fork in the stew. "Well . . . the meat's done, we can eat anytime. Here come the men. Set out the plates, Mary Ben, and I'll call Vanessa."

The daylight disappeared while they ate, replaced by the tongues of color licking up from the glowing logs of the campfire into the surrounding darkness. Vanessa and Ellie sat on chairs and Henry and Mary Ben on the ground with the yellow dog between them. John sat on a log well back from the campfire. He and Henry took second helpings, and Ellie lifted the iron pot and what was left of the stew away from the fire and covered it.

Vanessa listened to the crackle of the fire. The warmth was inviting and the smell of the smoke was pleasant. She watched Henry and Mary Ben. Henry had never seemed happier. It scared her a little to think that maybe he was getting too fond of Mary Ben. Sometimes she had to stop and think that he was a man with physical urges the same as any other. The girl looked at him often when he wasn't looking at her. Vanessa couldn't blame her for that. Henry was an extremely handsome young man. Having grown up with him, she seldom thought of that, either. She would have loved him just as much if he had been fat and ugly. It was his sweet nature that was so endearing.

Vanessa had to admit that Mary Ben was wonderfully patient with Henry. She answered his questions and didn't talk to him as if he were a child, like some people did. She seemed to be more at ease with Henry than with her and Ellie.

Mary Ben's eyes strayed often to Vanessa. They had exchanged very few words. Mary Ben shied away from her, not knowing what to say. Even in shirt and pants she was the prettiest woman Mary Ben had ever seen. The firelight shone on her hair, reminding Mary Ben of a bright new penny. She looked down at her own faded, patched dress and the toe peeking through the end of her shoe. She had always been too busy trying to get enough to eat or stay out of the reach of men who tried to grab her to worry about how she looked. Just to be decently covered had been enough.

Mister raised his head and stared into the darkness. Mary Ben placed her hand on his neck and felt him shiver. The dog lowered his sagging jowls to her lap, his eyes riveted to the spot in the darkness at the end of their wagon. He continued to shiver as she stroked his head.

John got up and carried his plate and cup to the pan of water beside the fire. Mary Ben made a small hissing sound to get his attention as he passed. She patted Mister's head with one hand; the other hand fluttered up to push back her hair, a finger pointing toward the darkness beyond their wagon. The old man made no sign that he'd gotten the message.

"Them vittles was mighty larrupin' 'n plumb fillin', ma'am. I'll mosey on out 'n see to the stock. Mary Ben, I reckon ya ort a turn in."

Vanessa turned to look at the girl when she got to her feet. Mary Ben stared straight into her puzzled eyes, then rolled hers in the direction she had indicated to John. Comprehension dawned and Vanessa stood. Her knees began to tremble, then spread to the muscles in her legs as tension came over her. Would they never know peace again?

"What? Who?" she mouthed.

Mary Ben lifted her shoulders. "Somebody." She bent down and pulled some of the larger sticks of wood from the fire and the blaze died down.

"We don't even take time to visit," Ellie said disgustedly, and carried the dishpan to the shelf on the side of the wagon.

Henry was disappointed. He had looked forward to spending the evening with Mary Ben. He threw the rest of his coffee in the fire and stood up. It suddenly occured to him that something had happened and they were not telling him. Vanessa was whispering to his mother, and she had a frightened, serious look on her face. Why didn't they tell him what was going on? He moved a step closer to Mary Ben and looked down on her bent head.

"What's going on, Mary Ben? Why did John tell you to turn in?"

She looked up into his face and saw the confusion in his eyes. "Mister heard somebody prowlin' around 'n Mr. Wisner's gone to see about it," she whispered. "He said for me to turn in cause it ain't a good idey for us all to be bunched up this a way. I'll go to the wagon, 'n it'd be good if ya sit right here till Mr. Wisner comes back."

She searched his eyes to see if he understood. Seconds passed. She held her breath for fear he'd repeat in a loud voice what she had said. Then the confused look faded from his eyes and a smile began to twitch at his lips. The corners of his eyes crinkled. He was breathtakingly handsome. But it was much more than his looks that made Mary Ben's heart flood with a happiness that shone in the brilliant smile she returned. For just an instant they were united in an understanding that included just the two of them.

A surge of pleasure rushed through Henry when he saw her smile. Mary Ben liked him! She told him things. Suddenly he threw an arm around her shoulders. The hug he gave her was a wholesome, friendly gesture, but Mary Ben didn't understand that. She froze. Touching to her was grabbing, pinching, and wanting to pull her clothes off.

Henry's arm dropped from around her and his large hands gripped her shoulders without his knowing she was on the verge of panic.

"You be careful, hear? Don't worry. I'll be right over yonder where I can watch your wagon. I'll not let anybody hurt you, Mary Ben," he told her, his voice suddenly thick.

She nodded, unable to speak over the lump that rose in her throat.

Chapter Five

It was a still, moonless night. Vanessa sat on a box at the end of the wagon and Henry sat on the ground beside her. He had insisted on standing watch with her and she was glad for his company. Ellie had taken the first watch after John returned. He reported that he had seen and heard nothing unusual and said that he would bed down near the stock.

They had talked for awhile; now they were silent and slowly the minutes went by. Vanessa's hand slid up and down the barrel of the shotgun leaning against her thigh, and she began to speculate on how it would feel to shoot a man. She was startled to realize that she had come to accept the idea with no accompanying sense of guilt. Was the hard land making her hard too, or was her attitude born of the instinct to survive? No matter, she told herself. She would do what she had to do to protect herself, Ellie and Henry.

"Vanessa, are you ever going to get married?"

In the stillness that enclosed them after Henry's whispered words, Vanessa swallowed her surprise so she could answer calmly.

"I don't know. I've not met anyone I want to marry. Are you trying to get rid of me?"

"I bet Mr. DeBolt would marry you."

"What makes you think that?"

"You're pretty. I never thought about you being pretty until we come on this trip. Most women are ugly and frown all the time. They wear dirty aprons and their hair slicked back tight. You and Ma are pretty, and you smell nice, too."

"Thank you."

"I think Mary Ben's pretty. She likes me and talks to me."

"I noticed that. Henry. . ." Vanessa turned to look at his shadowy face. There was nothing pretentious about Henry. His thoughts and feelings were uttered honestly as they came to him. His trusting acceptance of whatever advice she gave him made her choose her words carefully. "I don't think Mary Ben has had many friends. You and Mary Ben can be friends, but that doesn't mean she thinks of you as a beau."

"You mean she don't want to be my sweetheart?"

"I mean that . . . it takes time to get to know someone that well, and they'll be leaving us in a week or two."

"I didn't know that. Why can't they go with us to Junction City?"

"Because Mr. Wisner wants to go to Cripple Creek and look for gold."

"Mary Ben could come with us."

"Her place is with her father. I'm sure she wants to be with him."

"Mr. Wisner's not her father."

"Well, for goodness sake! How do you know that?"

"Mary Ben told me when I was driving their wagon. Mr. Wisner found her down in Indian Territory. She was all by herself, just her and Mister."

Vanessa was silent while she absorbed the information.

She was sure that Henry was feeling something more than friendship for Mary Ben. She and Ellie had talked about the possibility of Henry falling in love, but now that it could be happening, she didn't know how to deal with it. He couldn't take care of himself much less a wife. And if there were children—

Without a hint of a warning someone was beside her. Before she could even gasp, a hand jerked the barrel of the shotgun from her grasp.

"Whoa, now. I don't want you to shoot me, Vanessa."

It was him! Vanessa's heart flooded with relief and then with anger because he had startled her.

"What are you doing here?" she hissed.

"That's a fine way to greet me."

"Why are you always sneaking around? Where have you been?"

"Why? Have you missed me?" She didn't answer and he chuckled. "How are you doing, Henry?"

"Fine, Mr. DeBolt. You sure don't make any noise. I didn't hear you either."

"You and Vanessa were so busy talking you wouldn't have heard a herd of wild horses."

"Were you out there spying on our camp tonight?" Vanessa felt the heat on her cheeks and a fluttering in her stomach.

"I wanted to talk to John."

"Then why didn't you come in and talk to him?"

"You ask a lot of questions. Henry, does she ever shut up and listen?"

"Sometimes."

"Well, she'd better listen now, because she might have some company before morning. There's a bunch of slack handed drifters camped about a half mile down the draw, Vanessa. One of them is the kid you worked over with the shovel in Dodge. They passed you yesterday and they know you're here."

"Well, for goodness sake! That doesn't mean they'll bother us." Vanessa hated him for making her so tense and nervous.

Kain ignored her outburst. "I thought they would turn south and take the Cimarron cutoff. They still plan to do that, but that young bully wants to get even with you first. He's talking up the idea that because of your fancy rig you may have a lot of money. He's thinking they'll waltz in here and hold you up."

"How do you know? You—" She stopped because she was having trouble breathing. She took a deep breath. This man was overwhelming. She desperately needed to be delivered out of his presence, and she wondered where miracles were when she needed them.

"My sneaking ability comes in handy. As a matter of fact, I consider myself a first-class sneaker. I sneaked up on their camp and heard them talking. I've talked to John and here's what we're going to do: We'll let them come in, then we'll bash a few heads."

"Why don't we just shoot them?" she hissed angrily.

"My, you're bloodthirsty. I'll not shoot them if I don't have to. No. This situation calls for head bashing. Want to join the fun, Henry?"

"Yes, sir!"

"You leave Henry out of this!"

"That isn't for you to say, Vanessa. It's up to Henry."

"Damn you! Who the hell do you think you are coming here and ordering Henry around?"

"Don't swear, little red bird. I'm not ordering Henry, I'm asking. Henry gets enough orders from you."

"Well, I never!"

"Vanessa?" Ellie called. "Who's out there?"

"Kain Debolt, Aunt Ellie."

"Well, isn't that nice. Do you want coffee, Mr. DeBolt? Or something to eat? We have beef stew."

"No, thank you, Mrs. Hill." He bent toward Vanessa. "At least your aunt likes me!"

Even in the dark, Kain could see her white face and shining hair. He didn't understand himself at all. There was something in the tension charged atmosphere when he was near this woman that compelled him to irritate her and act the fool. He had never been like this with anyone else. He was purely crazy, he thought. She threw his mind completely out of circuit. He would have to be careful of her, he warned himself. He wanted to reach out and slide his fingers along her cheek and into her hair. Vanessa, Vanessa, sweet woman-child... The way he felt this minute downright scared him.

"Mrs. Hill?" he called. "Can you keep this little red bird in the wagon and out of trouble for the rest of the night?"

"Well... what... damn you!"

"Mind me this time, Vanessa, or I'll give you something to sputter about. You need a strong hand to hold you in line and curb your rebellious nature."

Vanessa drew in a deep breath. Her temper was on the verge of exploding.

"Oh my goodness!" Ellie climbed down out of the wagon looking like a ghost in her long white gown. "We'll be glad to do as you say, Mr. DeBolt. Won't we, dear?"

Kain chuckled. "Vanessa would rather swallow a toad than do as I say. But no matter. She'd better do it... this time. You ladies stay in the wagon. If we need you to rescue us, we'll call you. Won't we, Henry?"

Henry laughed, and it added to Vanessa's irritation as she followed her aunt into the wagon. "That man sets my teeth on edge, gets my back up, and makes my blood boil! He's so damn sure of himself. He's got Henry thinking he's the greatest thing since fire! If anything happens to Henry I'll shoot him!"

"Somehow I think he's trying to help Henry. I'm thinking

maybe we've been wrong, Vanessa, in not forcing Henry to take more responsibility."

"It's too dangerous to start teaching Henry that now, Aunt Ellie. And I'm not going to sit here twiddling my thumbs. This wagon and what's in it is all we have in the world, and I'm going to be out there protecting it."

"Please be calm, dear. Mr. DeBolt said you should stay in the wagon."

"I'm not taking *his* orders. You may think every word he says is pure gospel, but I don't."

"He just . . . well, he just seems to know what he's doing, and he's trying to help us. He's like Mr. Wisner. If we get out of this awful country it will be because of them." There was a pleading note in Ellie's voice, and Vanessa had to harden her heart against it.

"I'm going out. Here's the rifle. Don't shoot unless some-one is forcing his way in." Vanessa opened the door and eased herself out into the darkness.

She moved cautiously along the side of the wagon as silently as a shadow, then ventured out away from it and pressed herself against the trunk of a tall oak tree. The camp was still except for the usual night sounds. An owl hooted nearby, and from far away came an answer. Vanessa drew cool air deep into her lungs, air touched with the faint scent of the wet ashes of their campfire.

It seemed to her that hours passed while she waited and listened. Where were Henry and Kain? Where was Mr. Wisner? If the robbers come she would not panic, Vanessa told herself. Someone had said that panic only filled an empty mind. She would think of something—anything. But she wouldn't waste another thought on that conceited, arro-gant, know-it-all, Kain DeBolt. She still had to thank him for getting their mules back. He'd probably throw her thanks back in her face. The idea of him having the gall to ask her if she had missed him! Well, his charm might work on Henry and Aunt Ellie, but it didn't work on her!

And then she heard it, the soft sound of footsteps muffled by the thick grass. Warning herself that she must be careful not to hit the wrong man, she gripped the barrel of the shotgun in her two hands like a club. A movement to the side caught her eye. It stopped and she saw the outline of a man in a wide-brimmed hat. He was too short to be Henry or Kain, and too thin to be Mr. Wisner. She concentrated all her attention on the shadowy figure as it approached and stopped on the other side of the tree. Whoever it was had the rancid, unclean odor of one long unbathed.

Vanessa slowly drew the shotgun back. Anger washed over her like a tidal wave. The low life, chicken-livered sidewinder! He was here to take their money. If he thought they would be easy victims of his thievery, he would soon find out how mistaken he was. The man was unaware of her, but so close she could hear him breathing. Realizing he would discover her any second, she swung the butt of the shotgun at his face with all her strength.

The wooden stock struck with a dull smack. The man cried out and staggered back. She followed and swung again. This time the blow caught him on the side of the head. He grabbed for the gun she was using as a club, but she jerked it away and jabbed at his face.

"You sneaking polecat!" she shouted and struck out wildly. "Snake! Robber! Dirty stinking dog!" He grabbed for the gun. It slipped from his hand and she brought it down with a chopping motion. It missed his head and struck his shoulder. He lost his footing and fell.

"You dirty little swine! I ought to beat your head in!" Vanessa continued her attack, aiming for any part of his body. He grabbed her pant leg and she kicked him in the face.

"Stop it! You damn hellcat! Ah, shee . . . it!"

Suddenly she heard a shot, a deafening roar, and saw a flash of flame. She reeled backward to regain her balance, panting for breath. *The damn little weasel had shot at her!*

Kain's strong arm swept her aside and his tall form loomed over the man on the ground. He kicked the gun from his hand.

"Hold him, Henry!" he commanded.

Henry fell on top of the man who was struggling to rise.

"Vanessa! Are you all right?"

"I . . . hit him. With this."

"Goddamn it, I told you to stay in the wagon." Kain seized her by the arms and shook her. "Don't you ever do what you're told? You could have been killed."

"But I wasn't!" She jerked away from his grasp.

"Vanessa! Henry! Oh, my God!" Ellie came stumbling out of the wagon. "Are you all right?"

"We're all right."

"Thank God! Oh, thank God! I was so scared."

"Somebody light a lantern. Hold on to that bastard, Henry. His three friends will have headaches in the morning and I'm thinking he'd rather have one than what he's got."

"Oh, Henry!" Ellie's eyes were fastened on her son. She pressed her balled fist to her mouth. She had never seen him use physical force on another person.

Mary Ben came out with a lantern and the light shone on the bloody face of the young bully who had fought Henry in Dodge City. His nose was obviously broken, his lip split, and one eye was rapidly swelling shut. Blood ran from a gash on his cheekbone to his chin. He rolled his head from side to side and whimpered with pain. Henry sat astride him.

Vanessa was startled when she saw the boy's face. She had done that? What sort of person was she becoming?

"I hit him too hard!"

"Not *too* hard." Kain grinned. "But you sure whacked him a good one. There's blood on your gun butt."

"I didn't know. I didn't realize—"

"The poor boy's nose is broken," Ellie moaned.

"Poor boy?" Kain snorted. "The bloody little bastard came to rob you. He deserved anything he got. I should break his damn leg to teach him a lesson. Let him up, Henry."

Henry stood and the young man rolled to his knees, picked up his hat, and got slowly to his feet. He looked around on the ground for his gun, saw it, and went to pick it up.

"Leave it," Kain said sharply. "Hightail it out of here. You'll find your gun as well as your friend's after we leave here. I won't send a man down the Cimarron cutoff without a gun. But if you bother these folks again I'll bury you. Understand?"

The boy's eyes blazed with hatred as he looked at Vanessa. His lips formed curses, but no sound came from them.

Kain followed him to the edge of the camp and watched him stagger off into the darkness. When he turned his eyes went to Vanessa and stayed there.

Her head was tilted defiantly, her red mane of hair glistening in the light from the lantern. She watched him, her eyes lit with the fire of her hostility. Dear God, she was lovely! The hunger to be with her had been with him for the past two days and he had had to force himself to stay away. Tonight his painful restraint had broken. He should have taken John's advice and his buffalo gun, and scattered the thieves before they reached the camp. The damn kid had shot at her! God help him if he had hit her!

"You did well, Henry." Kain's words were not related to his thoughts. "You could learn to be a real good sneaker. You got the right touch for head bashing, too. Just enough force to knock them out and give them a hell of a headache."

"Ma, John got one, and me and Kain sneaked up behind the other two. We each hit one." Henry was delighted with his part in foiling the robbery. "We were coming to get the other one when we heard Vanessa yelling."

Vanessa's furious eyes met Kain's. "You think this is some kind of game, don't you?"

Kain looked at her in silence. Her blue eyes shimmered

moistly with her anger. When he finally spoke it was lazily, as though he were thinking aloud.

"Pretty little red bird. If someone doesn't clip her wings she'll not live to get to Denver."

"It'll not be *you* to do it!" she exclaimed.

"Mr. DeBolt, can I speak with you?" There was a cool determination in Ellie's voice.

"Yes, ma'am. But can it wait a little bit? I've got something to say to Vanessa." While he spoke his eyes never left Vanessa's face.

"You'll not leave until I can talk to you?"

"No, ma'am. You can count on it." He waved his hand toward the outer circle of the camp. "I don't think you want your aunt and cousin to hear what I've got to say to you, Vanessa."

Her first compulsion was to defy him; she trembled with the force of it. Kain gave her a menacing look, and with a toss of her head, she pivoted and walked proudly and stiffly to the edge of the camp and into the darkness.

A seething anger stopped her before she took many steps, and she turned to face him. His grip on her arm set her feet in motion again, and she was propelled over the uneven ground. When they finally stopped the glow of the lantern and the outlines of the wagons were but dim images. She tried to pull her elbow from his grasp, but his fingers tightened.

"Let go of me, damn it!" Thoughts whirled about her brain like wind whipped tumbleweeds.

Kain looked at her in silence. Her face was a blur in the darkness. "I should turn you over my knee and spank your behind." He spoke softly in spite of his anger.

"While you reconsider such an outlandish notion, release my arm," she snapped, "unless you intend to break it—to teach me a lesson."

He laughed. Dear God, she was lovely! In the faint light her face was starkly white under the cloud of glowing hair, and he was again struck by her beauty and the slender reach of her full-bosomed body. He was aware of an involuntary arousal, and conscious of the hard pounding of blood through his veins and a simultaneous shortening of his breath.

"If I let go, will you run back to the wagon?"

"I might!"

"Vanessa! I'm the one who should be angry. I told you to stay in the wagon. You came to within an inch of getting yourself killed tonight. And that morning when we went to get the mules, I told you to stay out of sight. What did you do but come in right behind me. I had no idea you were there. What am I going to do with you?"

"Nothing! I'm not your responsibility. I thank you for what you've done for us. Good-bye." She stepped away, but the hand on her arm pulled her back.

"Not so fast!" His patience snapped and he spoke in a firm, irritated voice. "You may not give a damn, but if I had batted an eye that morning by the river, the breed would have killed me, or tried to. I had no idea you were behind me. I know I won't . . . live forever, but I'm not anxious to be finished off by a bullet from a gunslinger."

The harshness in his voice knocked all the composure out of her. She rolled her head back and forth and said woodenly, "I'm sorry. I was merely trying to help. They were our mules."

"Yes, they were. And it was your money the thieves were after tonight, but you'd be just as dead if that bullet had hit you or if that shotgun you were using as a club had gone off. Did you think to unload it?"

"I was protecting what was ours," she said stubbornly, but her voice lacked the sharpness it had held before in spite of her determination to keep her anger as a shield between them.

"If I let go of you to light a smoke will you run away?"

"Run? Why should I run from you? Am I your prisoner?"

"No." He rejected this with a slow shake of his head. And then said, as if to himself, "But I may be yours." He drew in a deep breath and his hand dropped from her arm. He fumbled in his pocket for his tobacco pouch and began to roll a smoke. His eyes left her face only to glance occasionally at what his shaking fingers were doing.

The match flared and he held it between cupped hands until it blazed, then raised it to the cigarette in his mouth. The light outlined his face and turned it into a bronze mask.

Vanessa's eyes clung to his smooth skin, straight brows and thin, high-bridged nose. He was too handsome, far too handsome, despite the jagged scar that slanted across his hard cheekbone and disappeared into his thick brown hair. His gold-tipped lashes lifted and his amber eyes looked into hers. Oh, God! Why did she have this feeling of rightness when she was with this . . . stranger?"

He blew out the match. "What were you thinking, little red bird, when you looked at me with those beautiful eyes?" His hand came up and his fingers gently fondled her cheek and looped a strand of hair behind her ear. Vanessa caught her breath sharply. It was an action she hadn't expected. She tried to move away, but he held her with his words. "Don't go."

"I should get back. Aunt Ellie . . ." Her voice grew weaker and then ceased altogether. She brushed her hair from her forehead with the palm of her hand.

"Stay and talk to me."

"What about?" His gentle request also caught her unaware. Their constant sniping at each other was tiring, and her heart was beating twice as fast as it should have been. She let out a sigh.

"Tired?" Kain asked. Long, slim fingers carried the smoke to his lips. He drew deeply on the cigarette and the end flared briefly.

"Not as much as I was at first."

"Where have you come from? Where are you going?" He

asked the first thing that came to mind, although he knew they were going north of Denver.

"Why do you want to know?"

"I have a feeling your aunt is going to ask me to ride along with you."

"Yes. She's terribly frightened out here."

"And you?"

"I've no time to be scared."

"That breed wants you. He isn't the kind to give up."

She flinched, and her eyes closed for an instant. "He just wanted what was handy. If he comes near me again I'll fill him with buckshot."

"Have you ever shot a man?"

"No, but I could . . . if I had to." She turned her head and looked back toward the wagons. Kain looked down at her clearly etched profile. He marveled that she could be so distant and seductive all at once.

"I believe you," he said very quietly.

Looking into his eyes, Vanessa voiced the question that came to her then. "Are you going to stay with us?"

"Do you mind?"

"Why should I? Mr. Wisner thinks we'll catch up with a train going to Denver in a few days."

"Is that where you're going?"

"That's where Mr. Wisner and Mary Ben are going. We're going north to Greeley, then west."

"West? West to Junction City?"

"Have you been there?"

"A time or two. Why are you going to Junction City?"

"Aunt Ellie has a brother-in-law there. She wants Henry to be near his kin."

There was a long silence while Kain's thoughts raced and collided in wild disorder. Henry had reminded him of someone that first day he had seen him. Earlier that night, the way he had laughed had a familiar ring to it. Could it be?

Was it possible that Henry was related to Cooper Parnell or Adam Clayhill?

"Who was Henry's father?" he asked quietly.

"Henry Hill. He lived in Chicago. We should go back. Aunt Ellie wants to talk to you and we need to get some sleep." She looked back toward the wagons. He did not speak or move. She sensed his eyes on her, willing her to look at him.

"Will you walk out and talk to me again?"

Happiness surpassed her surprise. "Will you ride out if I don't?"

"No. I'm not trying to bribe you. I wouldn't want you to come if you didn't want to."

"Do you think we could talk, without quarreling?" Laughter quivered in her voice.

His hand came out and stroked the hair falling over her shoulder. "I don't know, my fiery redhead. We may quarrel, but even that's better than not talking at all." He paused, then said in a different tone, "I've never met a woman as fascinating as you."

He felt laughter shake her. "Don't you mean irritating?"

"That too."

Kain searched her face and found her smiling radiantly at him. For a long moment he stood there looking at her. Then reason dissolved the hunger to wrap her in his arms and kiss her, to know the joy of having her body pressed against him, her firm breasts against his chest, small round buttocks in his hands. He gripped her elbow and urged her toward the wagon before his torment broke his control.

Suddenly he was determined to cram a lifetime of happiness into the few short weeks it would take to reach Junction City. He would see her and the Hills settled, and after that he would simply disappear.

The thought of her in the years to come with another man was like a knife turning in him. His fingers tightened on her elbow as they walked silently back to the camp.

Chapter Six

Ellie wasted no time getting right to the point.

"I'm frightened, Mr. DeBolt. I—we didn't realize this was such a rough, harsh land. We can't cope. We simply can't cope! Oh, Vanessa and Henry can manage the wagon, the mules and all, but it's this . . . lawlessness." Her voice shook and nearly broke. "I have a little money. The farm was Vanessa's, and . . . we plan to use that money to start a small bakery if Junction City doesn't already have one. All I have is money from dressmaking and nursing the sick. It's yours, every cent of it, if you'll see us to our destination."

In her anxiety to have Kain travel with them, Ellie was unaware that she was disclosing the very thing that had been a shame to her. All of these years she and her son had lived on her brother-in-law's charity. It was true that she had raised his daughter and cared for his home, but it was charity nonetheless.

"I don't want your money, Mrs. Hill, but I could do with

a meal now and then. A constant diet of beans and sowbelly is hard on the stomach," he admitted with a dry smile.

"I *can* cook. It's one of the things I do best."

"I'm glad to hear it."

"You'll stay with us?"

"My being with you won't guarantee your safety."

"Oh, I know that! But I'll be ever so grateful to have you along. And, Mr. DeBolt, don't be offended by Vanessa's sharp tongue. She's worried and frightened, too, but she doesn't want me and Henry to know it."

"I'm surprised that a woman as beautiful as Vanessa is unmarried."

"She had plenty of beaus back in Springfield. One of the wealthiest men in the county wanted to marry her. I'm afraid that . . . Henry and I were a liability to Vanessa."

"How is that?"

"Vanessa's mother died shortly after she was born. Vanessa thinks of me as her mother. She and Henry are like brother and sister. People can be . . . unkind about Henry, and Vanessa will not tolerate that."

"Did she love that man?" Anxiety tore through him, choking his voice.

"She said she didn't." A girlish spurt of laughter broke from Ellie's lips. "She said he made her want to . . . puke."

Kain smiled and stroked the stubble on his chin. "Sounds like something she would say. Mrs. Hill, Vanessa said that Henry has kinfolk in Junction City. I've been there a time or two. Maybe I know the party you're looking for."

"Good heavens! Wouldn't it be grand if you did? Do you know Adam Hill? My husband, Henry, who died before young Henry was born, told me about his brother in Colorado. He said he was an important man and owned the largest ranch in the territory. It was Adam who wrote me and told me that friends of Henry's had notified him his brother had been killed. I had written to him to see if he knew what happened to Henry. I guess Henry's friends in Chicago didn't know about me."

"I don't know anyone named Hill, though I'm not saying there aren't some there. Is that the only time you heard from your husband's brother?"

"Yes. I guess you think I'm foolish to go there on the strength of that one letter. But Henry told me such wondering things about his brother. Young Henry is the image of his father, and so I thought perhaps his uncle, if he is still living, or cousins, would take a liking to him."

"Speaking of Henry, he should know how to shoot a gun and how to defend himself, Mrs. Hill."

"Oh, I know, but . . . Henry is limited as to what he can do. I appreciate—"

"Perhaps he hasn't reached that limit yet. Forgive me for being blunt, but it seems to me you and Vanessa have sheltered him too much."

"We were afraid—"

"Afraid to give him responsibility? I can understand that. He obeyed orders tonight. In that respect he's more responsible than Vanessa."

"I've been thinking about that. Henry has never known the companionship of a man. If his father had lived . . ."

"You'd better get some sleep, Mrs. Hill."

"Yes, I will. Thank you, Mr. DeBolt."

"Kain, ma'am. I'd be pleased if you called me Kain."

Kain stretched out on his bedroll well back from the wagons, rested his head on his folded arms and looked up at the stars. His mind was too busy to record the sound of a coyote calling to his mate or her answer echoing in the stillness. He was filled with a quiet unrest as his thoughts raced. Was it possible that Adam Clayhill had a brother who had called himself Henry Hill? Adam was a common enough name and so was Hill. It was the fact that Henry looked so much like Cooper, Adam's son, that set Kain's mind to wondering if Henry Hill could have been Henry Clayhill. But, he reasoned, Ellie said she had had a letter from Adam Hill.

Kain turned restlessly in his bed. If Adam Clayhill were Henry's uncle, Mrs. Hill would find no sympathy for her son there. Adam was the most ruthless and bigoted man he'd ever known. If he despised his own son because of his Indian blood, he would heartily despise this naive young man with a limited intelligence.

Henry looked enough like him to be his nephew, Kain thought. He also looked enough like Cooper to be his brother. The Clayhills seemed to have strong family characteristics. Logan Horn, Adam's Indian son, had said Adam Clayhill resembled his brother who had raised Logan. Poor Mrs. Hill. She and her son should have stayed in Missouri. On the heels of that thought came another: if they had, he would not have met Vanessa.

His reverie turned to her and the way she had smiled at him earlier. Her warm gaze had reached some longing deep within him, secret even from himself. Nothing in his life had geared him for love, for home and family. He had thought about it sometimes as he went his lonely way, but always as something other men had.

With a woman like Vanessa to love, protect and build a life around, a man would be king. But why think of that now? It was too late.

The succeeding days would have been the happiest of Kain's life if not for the shadow of death that hung over him. He did not feel like a dying man. His mind had accepted the verdict and filed it away in some secret part of his brain so that it didn't keep him from enjoying the warmth of the sun or the taste of the cool night wind. He felt better than he had in weeks and the pains did not bother him so much. Once, when they came suddenly, viciously, he rode away by himself, retched, and found blood on his lips. While he waited to get his strength back, the lonely spot in his heart ached for warmth, for love.

Each morning he woke with a sensation of excitement about another day to spend with Vanessa. Sometimes they rode together, and at other times he rode beside the wagon while Vanessa drove the team. It seemed as if they had, by mutual consent, dropped their rapiers and were now able to engage in light conversation. Kain and John chose the campsites, and Vanessa seemed to be pleased to relinquish some of the responsibility.

Each evening, while Ellie and Mary Ben prepared the evening meal, Kain spent time with Henry. First he taught him how to break down the rifle and clean it. Then he taught him how to load and shoot it. Kain was painstakingly patient and discovered that Henry's mind grasped the mechanics of the weapon much faster than it did the actual aiming and firing of the gun.

One evening, while out of sight of the others, Kain suddenly turned, hooked his foot behind Henry's knees, and threw him to the ground. Stunned, Henry looked up at him with eyes filled with disappointment.

"What did I do, Kain? Why are you mad at me?"

"I'm not mad." He reached for his hand and hauled him to his feet. "I just wanted to show you how fast you can knock a man off his feet if you know how. Do you want to learn?"

"I don't like to hurt people."

"That bully back in Dodge was trying to hurt you. Didn't you want to fight back?"

"I didn't know how."

"I can show you."

"Do you think I can learn?"

"Of course you can. You can learn to do anything you want to do if you try hard enough."

"I don't like to fight."

"I don't either, but if someone picks a fight, I fight back

and try and get it over with as soon as I can. There are several places where you can hit a man that will lay him low. Here, I'll show you."

At first Henry was reluctant to use his strength against Kain, but after several sessions he began to enjoy the bouts. The first time he hooked Kain behind the knees and threw him to the ground, Henry whooped with laughter.

Four days after Kain started riding openly with Vanessa's party, they came to the forks of the Arkansas River and Big Sandy Creek. A train of six wagons taking the Big Sandy route to Denver were camped there, farmers from Ohio seeking new land. The train moved out the next morning in spite of John's warning about Indian trouble in that area.

"Damn know-it-alls," John snorted as he watched them pull out. "They'll get them women 'n kids killed is what they'll do."

"Maybe," Kain said. "But what can you do?"

"Nothin'."

Kain had taken an immense liking to the gray-haired old man who had spent his life on the Plains. He was a thoroughly skeptical old wolf who let his sight and his instincts ferret things out, and then acted according to what was necessary at the time.

"What made you strike out after the Hills and Vanessa, John?" They were each leading a span of mules to the water. Henry and Mary Ben were behind them with John's team.

"Well, now, it was jist a idey I had. I knowed they was nice folks, quality folks. I knowed they'd no more trail sense than a pissant. More than that I figgered twas time Mary Ben met up with some quality womenfolk."

"How long has she been with you?"

"Two, three year, I reckon. Some fellers told me a wild gal was alivin' in a cave down 'long the Canadian River. I figgered I ain't ne'er seen no wild gal 'n I'd jist mosey on down to get me a look-see. What I found was a scared little

ole gal what was pert near starved to death. 'Er pa'd run off
'n left her 'n her ma. 'Er ma'd died. The poor little mite
buried 'er all by 'er ownself. It was plumb pitiful. She'd
been ahidin' out from drifters 'n the like. It took me a spell
jist to get in talkin' range. I put out some grub n' them
vittles was mighty temptin' to the youngun. I couldn't leave
'er or jist set 'er off somewheres. She been with me since."

"It seems like she and Henry have taken to each other,"
Kain said after a spurt of soft, girlish laughter came from
behind them.

"I ain't ne'er heard her laugh till jist lately. It's plumb
purty to hear," John said proudly. "She's agoin' to hate lea-
vin' these folks." He watched the mules slurp the water
thirstily.

"Did you have it in mind to ask them to take Mary Ben?"

"No. I ain't had no notion to do that. It'd be a horse of a
different color if'n they was to ask. I do get to worryin'
'bout her some. She'd had it hard, awful hard. She don't
know nothin' a'tall 'bout town livin'."

"Are you thinking to kick the bucket pretty soon, old
man?" Kain asked with a teasing grin.

"I aim to put it off long's I can," John answered
staunchly. "Still, it'd be peaceful on my mind if'n Mary Ben
had folks who'd look after 'er."

"How would it set with you to come along to Junction
City?"

"I give it thought when twas said the womenfolk was
agoin' there. Ya reckon there'd be work?"

"I thought you wanted to try your hand at panning for
gold down along Cripple Creek?"

"Naw! Why'd I want to freeze my arse off fer a nugget or
two 'n pay it all out fer beans 'n bacon? 'Sides, a gold camp
ain't no fit place fer Mary Ben."

Kain sent a smooth stone dancing across the sunlit water.
Everyone needed someone, he thought. This rusty-voiced

old man needed something to love and care for, and he had found it in the young girl who had no one.

"I know a few people near Junction City. Mary Ben would find a welcome. You too, old man, if you can make yourself useful around a horse ranch."

John took off his hat and scratched his head. "It's what I'd hoped fer."

"It won't take much more than a week to get to Denver. And another week to Junction City if the weather holds."

"If'n we don't have no breakdowns. I'm athinkin' the Hill's wagon'll need a rim in a day or two."

Kain felt a warning pain in his stomach and his mouth filled with saliva as sickness rolled over him. He stood still, breathing hoarsely, dreading the agonizing pains that were sure to follow.

"I'm going to ride out for a little bit, John," he said when he was sure he could speak casually. "Henry," he called, "I'd be obliged if you'd take the mules back to the wagon and hitch them up. I'll be back soon."

Without waiting for an answer, Kain walked quickly to where he had tied his horse, mounted and rode back down the trail, then into a thick stand of willows and cattails that grew along the creek. He clenched his teeth and closed his eyes against the pain that knifed through him. He pulled Big Red to a halt and waited, hoping the pain would let up and he wouldn't retch. He didn't move for a long while and his breathing eased. The pain subsided, yet he waited. Sweat beaded his forehead and he wiped it away with the sleeve of his shirt.

This was the first attack he'd had in several days. He had felt better lately, and he was sure this was due to the good food Mrs. Hill prepared, stews, rice, beef or rabbit broth with dumplings. Greasy food upset his stomach, so he steered clear of it. Kain thought back to the morning meal. He hadn't eaten much. Although he was almost always hungry, he hesitated to eat more than a few bites at a time.

Now, he realized, he would have to eat in order to keep up his strength. This feeling of weakness scared him.

Big Red's ears perked and twitched seconds before Kain heard hoofbeats. When he heard the approaching horse turn from the trail and come toward the willows, he turned Big Red in order to face whoever was coming. He shifted the reins and dropped his hand to his thigh near his gun.

Vanessa came toward him, bending her head to keep the willow branches from dislodging her hat. She was unsmiling. Her blue eyes questioned his, and her face expressed concern.

"Kain? Is something wrong? I saw you leave camp and—"

His slow smile altered the stern cast of his face. "Nothing is wrong. I saw movement down here and figured to get some fresh meat. But if there was a deer here, it's probably halfway to Texas by now."

For a moment Vanessa gravely studied him, her brows lifted in puzzled arcs. "You look pale, and white around the mouth. Are you sick? Aunt Ellie says you don't eat enough. She thinks you don't like her cooking."

"I'll have to set her straight on that. I'm all right. I've had a little trouble with my stomach. I think I got food poisioning back in Dodge. Are you driving today or is Henry?"

"They've already started. If you got some tainted food back in Dodge, you should be over it by now."

"Are you a doctor?" he teased.

"No," she said slowly and lowered her gaze to her hands, suddenly uncomfortable under his direct eyes. "But my father was. I learned a lot from him."

"How are you at digging out bullets?"

"I've done it," she said simply.

"You might get a chance to do it again if that cold-eyed breed catches up with us."

"Do you think he will?" she asked almost fearfully.

"I'd not bet that he won't. It was a blow to his pride to

have to back down in front of you. Pride is all a man like that has. It'll force him to do something to redeem himself in your eyes."

Vanessa's face mirrored her distaste. "I'm sorry about that morning. I didn't know—"

"You don't understand, do you? Out here, Vanessa, a man would die for a woman like you."

A faint run of color laid its fleeting change across her face and she gave a short laugh. "Are women that scarce?"

"Women are scarce," he admitted. "And the odds against finding a young, beautiful woman are mighty slim."

A smile continued to lengthen her lips. "I think I just had a compliment."

"There's no doubt about it." She caught the brilliant flash of his smile and heard his hearty laugh as he put his heels to the stallion.

"We'd better catch up. Aunt Ellie will think we're lost." Her laugh was a free and warm sound.

"I'd hoped we could make twenty-five miles today." Kain followed her out of the willows and onto the trail. He held Big Red down to a fast walk so it would take longer to reach the wagons. Vanessa rode beside him, her feet lightly resting in the stirrups.

"Where did you learn to ride like that?" he asked.

"My father was a mighty particular man where horses were concerned—not to mention the way they were ridden. He almost killed me before I sat a saddle to suit him."

"He knew what he was doing."

Vanessa said nothing for awhile, then she said above the rhythmic thud of hooves, "He knew a lot about a lot of things." There was a note of sadness in her voice.

"Tell me about him."

She gave him a measuring glance. "He was a wonderful man, a dedicated doctor. He had helped so many people, saved many lives, but could not save his own. The war killed him. He drank himself to death after he came home."

"I'm sorry."

She shrugged her shoulders. "It's been three years."

On mutual impulse the horses broke into a measured canter, carrying them closer and closer to the wagons. At first Vanessa permitted herself only darting glances at Kain, but as he became more and more engrossed in his thoughts, she held her eyes fixed on him, studying him from boot to hairline. Something had happened to her that day in Dodge City when she had looked into his tawny eyes. The attraction had stayed with her. It was one that she felt deeply. There was a kinship between them that had not existed between her and another man.

He watched her without speaking.

Finally he broke the silence with her name. She barely noticed what he said, her gaze was fixed on the movement of his lips.

"Vanessa," he said again. "Vanessa. The name suits you."

"Aunt Ellie said my mother read a story about a red-haired siren named Vanessa, and when I arrived with red hair that was the only name she could think of."

"I don't think I've heard it before. I like it. I like your hair, too. It's . . . it's magnificent."

She laughed, her eyes wide and sparkling. His eyes feasted on her face, the graceful tilt of her head, her laughing mouth.

"I know it's hard to find a word to describe it," she said teasingly. "You're too kind."

"I'm not being kind. You don't know how beautiful you are, do you?" he said enigmatically, and was more personal with his voice than before.

Color flooded her cheeks and she dropped the reins on the mare's neck and ducked her head in a show of fastening her already securely anchored hat. They rode in silence and had almost reached the wagons before either spoke.

"Hold back a moment, Vanessa. I want to talk to you

about Mrs. Hill and Henry. What do you know about Henry's uncle, Adam Hill?"

"Nothing, really. Aunt Ellie wrote to him many times and finally got a letter from him when Henry was two years old. She had been trying to locate her husband in Chicago and her letters had been returned. She thought he had deserted her, but then she found out he had died a hero and now she idolizes his memory."

"Have you ever heard the name Clayhill?"

"No. Why?"

"There's an Adam Clayhill in Junction City who has a son that looks a lot like Henry. If he's the brother-in-law your aunt is seeking, she'll not like him. He's a real tyrant."

"Do you know him?"

"I know him." He gave her a long thoughtful look. "He was married to my mother."

"Was?"

"She died quite a few years ago." They rode along quietly for a little while. "I'll not say anything to Mrs. Hill about Adam Clayhill. I could be wrong."

"Aunt Ellie has a picture of Henry's father. Henry looks a lot like him. She said Adam Hill will know Henry is his nephew because he has his father's crooked forefinger. The bent finger is a family legacy passed down for generations."

Something that was almost a scowl changed Kain's expression, and when he looked at her his eyes were thoughtful. "I'm afraid Ellie is in for a disappointment, but there's no point worrying her about it now."

Kain frowned to remember those times Adam Clayhill's crooked finger had stabbed him in the chest as he swore at him for doing something he disapproved of. The loneliness he had felt as a callow youth had been even more painful than the loneliness he felt now. He shook his head, sadly remembering those long-ago sessions and the man he despised above all others.

"Aunt Ellie is worried about what will happen to Henry

later on. I've told her that he'll always have a place with me, but she feels that's unfair. She's of the opinion that it's the duty of the male members of the family to look after the females and the weak." She gave a little laugh, then sobered. "She's had to endure so many disappointments. I hope that Henry's uncle—and cousins if he has any—will not be unkind to him."

"If Henry's uncle is Adam Clayhill, you can count on him being unkind—downright mean will be more like it."

"Poor Aunt Ellie."

"How about you, Vanessa? Was it hard for you to leave your home and come west?"

She thought for a moment before she answered. "Yes and no. I hated to leave Papa and Mama's graves and the house he built for her. But it was best for all of us to start a life in a new place. Places change, people change. Neighbors Papa thought were his friends and people he had doctored without pay turned against him when he came back from the war a shattered man. He was called sawbones, butcher, and things even worse. There were stories about surgeons who cut off arms and legs and fed them to the hogs. Some of the men who returned without limbs blamed the doctor. Papa drank a lot, and when he was drunk he would try to defend what he'd done, and he'd become belligerent..."

"I can understand that," Kain said.

"Ozark hill folk are suspicious, and many of them are narrow in their thinking," Vanessa said with a deep sigh. "Some were sure that Henry was Papa's son, and that God punished Papa by making Henry simpleminded. I guess Aunt Ellie and I needed a reason to pull up stakes and leave."

"I'm glad."

Kain said the words simply, and Vanessa turned to look at him. She was surprised to see a deep sadness in his golden brown eyes, and a flood of tenderness and longing swept through her body. The smile she gave him had warmth, almost affection.

On seeing that smile, Kain felt the full pain of his regret. If only he could lean over and lift her from the saddle to sit across his thighs, if only he could tell her she was everything he had ever dreamed of, and that he wished to spend the rest of his life with her. If only. . . .

Chapter Seven

The two wagons reached Fort Lyon in the early afternoon of a windy day, and camped a half a mile down the trail from where dozens of wagons dotted the campground. Kain thought it best, and John agreed, that they keep to themselves as long as they had decided to travel alone. They could make faster time, and time was important now that the nights were getting increasingly cooler and the elevation higher. With most of the afternoon at their disposal, the women took the opportunity to do their washing, and John repaired a wheel on the caravan. Kain and Henry rode to the fort with a list of supplies written in Ellie's neat hand.

A town of sorts had sprung up around a stage station outside the fort. Wind and weather had taken a toll on the unpainted structure, reducing it to a nondescript gray. Several more buildings were in the vicinity, a saloon, a post office and a general store. The store was a low building with an awning supported by posts sunk into the ground. Three or four loafers squatted on their heels under the awning that fronted the store, and tired, dusty horses crowded the hitching rail. Kain and Henry moved on past the store and dismounted in front of the stage station. They tied their horses to a sagging rail, and Kain led the way back to the store. He eyed the men on the porch without seeming to before going inside. Henry followed on his heels as he made his way through a clutter of goods to the counter that supported a huge scale with a brass scoop and an elaborately painted, big-wheeled coffee grinder.

The man behind the counter looked as if he could wrestle a bear and not work up a sweat. He also looked as if he rarely washed or shaved. His sandy walrus mustache was stained by snuff or tobacco, and his high, thick shoulders were stooped, crossed by suspenders over a faded, red flannel undershirt. He had a double-barreled shotgun on a shelf behind him, as if he expected every man who came through the door to give him trouble.

Kain took the list from his shirt pocket and handed it to the storekeeper. He snatched it from Kain's hand with a snort, scanned it, then looked up with hard suspicious eyes.

"Let's see the color a yore coin." Kain took a gold piece from his pocket and bounced it on the counter. The man looked at it, but let it lie. "It'll do," he said and reached for a can of baking powder. Silently and swiftly, he went about the task of filling the list, setting each item on the counter with a loud thump as if he were angry.

Henry had wandered to the back of the store but soon was back tugging on Kain's sleeve. Kain followed him to a shelf that held several spools of ribbon and a stack of dusty straw hats trimmed with flowers and bits of lace.

"I got a dollar, Kain. Do you reckon I could buy something for Mary Ben? She doesn't have any ribbons or things like Ma and Vanessa." He fingered a length of pink satin ribbon and watched Kain's face anxiously.

"It would be right nice to give Mary Ben a present. What do you have in mind?"

"I could get her a hat, or some ribbon."

Kain looked at the dusty hats. He suspected that most of them had been brought in by travelers and traded for goods when they ran out of cash.

"Women kind of like to pick out their own hats, Henry. I think she'd like the ribbon."

"She could tie it in her hair. She's got awful pretty hair."

"Maybe you should get some for your mother and Vanessa, too."

"I'm going to get this for Mary Ben." Henry took the spool of pink ribbon from the shelf. "Why don't you get the blue for Van, Kain? She likes blue."

"All right. Now pick out one for your mother." Kain was suddenly pleased with the suggestion and the fact that Henry had coupled him with Vanessa in somewhat the same way he had matched himself with Mary Ben. It had been obvious to him for some time that Henry had strong feelings for the young girl.

"Mama likes pink," Henry said with a puzzled frown. "But I wanted to give Mary Ben the pink."

"Then get something else for your mother. Ladies like things that smell good."

"Yeah!" Henry said buoyantly. He selected a bar of scented soap, then carefully scrutinized the bottles of toilet water and chose one painted with small pink flowers. "Do I have enough money for all this, Kain?"

"I'm sure you do, but if you don't, I'll lend you some and you can pay me later."

Kain took the bolt of blue ribbon with him when he returned to the counter and requested the clerk to cut off a couple of yards.

Henry had more than enough money to pay for his presents. The clerk grunted and handed them to Henry after

Kain asked him to wrap them separate from the other purchases.

They were almost ready to leave when the door swung open and four men came in. Kain glanced at them briefly and saw trouble. Two were young rowdies, loudmouthed and swaggering. One looked as if he might have been run over by a freight wagon. His nose wasn't exactly centered in his face, he had bruised and cut cheeks and a dark circle around his eye. It was the kid Vanessa had worked over, first with the shovel, and then the butt of her shotgun. The other two men were older. One was a Mexican.

"Hey," the kid yelled. "Jist looky what's here! If'n it ain't the dummy what likes to bash heads 'n the dude who thinks his shit don't stink." The kid came toward the counter and elbowed Henry out of the way. "Get outta my way, dummy. Gimme some shells," he demanded of the storekeeper.

Anger rose up in Kain. Was it anger because Henry let this cocky, little bastard push him out of the way or because this tough kid was going to live when Kain knew he was going to die? He decided the reason he was going to hit him wasn't important—he just knew he was going to.

"The clerk's waiting on us you little shithead," Kain said roughly. "Take your turn."

The kid turned like a spitting cat. "Who do ya think yo're callin'—"

He never completed the sentence. Kain's fist lashed out and struck viciously. The punch caught the rowdy flush on his chin. He hit the floor as if struck down by a mallet.

Kain looked across the fallen man to the three who were with him. "There's more if you're dealing yourselves in."

The young drover looked down at his fallen companion with something like disgust on his face. "You *are* a stupid shithead!" he said to his friend. "You ain't got no more sense 'n a pissant."

"Ya hit hard," one of the older men said from just inside the door. "How are ya with a gun?"

Kain didn't answer immediately. He looked the man up and down, his amber eyes fierce and probing. "You're wearing one. If you want to know, you'll have to pay to find out." He spoke with deceptive mildness.

"Jist askin'." The careful way the man used his voice revealed his awareness of the ticklish situation in which he found himself.

There had been no move from the kid on the floor. "Is he dead?" The younger man prodded him with the toe of his boot.

"I doubt it," Kain said dryly.

"Get 'em outta here," the man behind the counter said in a loud and commanding voice, his words followed by the unmistakable sound of the shotgun behind cocked.

The Mexican walked over, lifted the boy's head and let it fall back to the floor with a thump. The boy blinked, rolled his head and groaned.

"Ya'd better take his gun," the clerk said. "Son of a bitchin' kids ain't got no sense a'tall. Think they be all balls 'n rawhide."

"Let him keep it," Kain said. "If he pulls it on me I'll do what I have to do."

The Mexican pulled the boy to his feet. He blinked, put his hand to his jaw, then stared around him, suddenly remembering. He stood swaying uncertainly.

"If you've got it in mind to use that gun," Kain said coldly, "get at it or get the hell out of here."

He looked at Kain for a moment, trying to focus his blurry eyes, then turned and stumbled toward the door. Kain followed and watched until the four rode away. He went back to the counter.

"Ya don't take much proddin', do ya?" The clerk put the shotgun back on the shelf.

"Not from a mouthy asshole like that. That's the third time I've had a run-in with the little bastard. The next time I'll break his damn neck." He glanced over his shoulder.

Henry was still watching out the door. "You got any laudanum?" Kain's eyes met the clerk's squarely.

"Only fer sick folks." He fixed his gaze on Kain's face.

"I'm not an addict, if that's what you're thinking. It's for a man with a cancer."

He looked at Kain for a long moment, then nodded. "It's reason enough." He went to the end of the counter and opened a padlock with a key he took from his pocket. He returned with a small bottle wrapped in paper and handed it to Kain. "Five dollars."

Kain put the bottle in his pocket, dropped a gold piece on the counter and picked up the supplies. The buzz of voices on the porch stopped when he and Henry walked through the door. Kain's sharp eyes scanned the dusty street. The four riders were nowhere in sight. The only movement was a dust devil dancing in the distance and tumbleweeds rolling aimlessly toward the open prairie.

"I just didn't know what to do, Kain. I just didn't know what to do," Henry said with a worried frown when they had left the town and were walking the loaded horses toward camp.

"As it turned out you didn't have to do anything. But if the chips were down, I was counting on you to take care of the other kid while I got the two at the door."

"You mean you'd shoot them?"

"That would depend on whether or not they were going to shoot me."

"But, Kain, I don't know if I could have helped any. That other fellow had a gun, too."

"If you had spun around real fast and swung your foot, you could have kicked him in the balls with the toe of your boot. He'd have doubled up and forgotten all about the gun, and you could have knocked him out with a blow on the back of his head. Remember? I showed you how to do that. Always do what they least expect you to do and you'll have the advantage."

"That would've hurt him something awful."

"He'd have done the same to you, Henry."

"I know. I've never had a friend like you, Kain. I'm glad we left that old farm. I've got you for a friend and I've got Mary Ben. Kain?" His voice dropped as if he feared someone would hear him. "Can I ask you something?"

"Sure, Henry."

"Sometimes when I'm with Mary Ben," he looked Kain full in the face without a trace of embarrassment, "I want to kiss her awful bad, and I get all hard and have a terrible ache . . . you know where. I just have to go off by myself until it quits. Ma told me a long time ago when I was little that I mustn't touch it when it gets big like that. She said it made people go crazy. I've been worrying about it, cause I did it . . . once."

"Don't worry about it, Henry. I've heard it said that people go insane if they—ah, touch their privates, but if it were true there would be an awful lot of crazy people in the world."

"Do you ever wake up at night like that?"

"A time or two."

"What do you do?"

The question jolted Kain, and he thought over several answers before he selected one.

"I usually turn over on it and try to go back to sleep."

"Do you ever get that way when you're with Van? You like her, don't you? I've seen you looking at her a lot."

"Yes, I like her. She's a beautiful woman and sometimes I ache to mate with her. It's natural for a man to feel like that when he's around a pretty girl that he likes."

"What do you think Mary Ben would do if I kissed her?"

"I don't know. Maybe you should ask her."

"She's nice. I'm glad they're going to Junction City with us. Mary Ben said she'd help Ma and Van with the bakery if they wanted her to."

They rode silently for awhile. In one way Kain was glad

Henry's questions had stopped, in another way he was glad that their relationship was so open Henry felt free to ask him things he felt he couldn't discuss with his mother or Vanessa. As long as they were on the subject of sex, Kain thought, it was a good opportunity to bring up a subject he'd never talked about before, but something he thought should be impressed on this simple, naive boy in a man's body. Knowing he had to put what he wanted to say to Henry in the simplest terms, he thought out carefully what he wanted to say.

"Henry, you say you want to kiss Mary Ben?"

"Yes, I do. I put my arm around her once, but she pulled away like she was scared."

"She might have been mistreated by a man at some time. Women aren't as strong as we are and must be treated gently. Go easy with her at first. Hold her hand and ask her if you can kiss her. Never force yourself on a woman, Henry. If she says no you back off. Understand?"

"I think so."

"Men have strong urges that are hard to control sometimes. God made us like that so that there would always be people on the earth. That doesn't mean that we force a woman if she isn't willing," he added hastily. "If you do it's called rape, and a man can be hung for doing it."

"I'd never do that to Mary Ben."

"I didn't think you would. But it's something we men must keep in mind when we're with a woman."

"Does it hurt, Kain? I mean, does it hurt when you do it to a woman so she'll get a baby? I've heard mares squeal something awful when a stallion rams it in her."

Henry's watchful eyes prevented even the slightest smile to spread Kain's lips. This was by far the strangest conversation he'd ever had. He wondered vaguely if these were the things a father told his son. No adult had ever discussed sex with him. He had learned first from his classmates, and later from courtesans.

"It may hurt the woman the first time, but after that she can receive you without pain. It isn't at all like putting a stallion to a mare. The man must kiss the woman, pet her and make her want him to . . . complete the act."

"Does it hurt the man, too?"

"No. In fact, it's very pleasant. If a man and a woman love each other, it's something that they both want to do. It's one of God's greatest gifts."

"I'm glad you told me. I wonder if Mary Ben knows about it. Do you think I should tell her? I want to do it with her someday."

"I don't think you should talk to Mary Ben about it just yet, Henry. John looks after her as if he were her pa. Let's wait and see if it would set easy with him if you courted her."

"Why would he care?"

"Well . . . she's awfully young."

"I'm going to ask Mary Ben if I can court her," Henry said determinedly. "If she says I can, I'll ask John. I'll give her the ribbon and the toilet water, and I'll ask her. Van doesn't have a beau, Kain. You should ask Van if you can be her beau."

"That's a good idea, Henry. I might do that."

If it were only that simple, Kain thought as he prodded Big Red into a lope. Since the encounter in the store he'd felt an increasing uneasiness in his stomach. The last thing he wanted to do was to be sick in camp. He wanted to hurry and get there so he could drop off the supplies and go downriver with the excuse of taking a bath.

Vanessa finished spreading the wash on the bushes to dry and watched Kain take his pack from the back of John's wagon, remove clean clothes and ride off back down the trail. She shifted her body to free the sticky shirt from her back. The day was unnaturally warm for this time of year and Vanessa longed to go to the river and bathe. She went to the wagon where Ellie was putting away the supplies.

"Let's go take a bath, Aunt Ellie. When the sun gets low it cools off too fast."

"You go ahead, dear. I'll come down later. Take Mary Ben with you."

"Mary Ben won't come with me. I've asked her before. I think it's because she doesn't have underclothes, Aunt Ellie. Or if she does, she doesn't want me to see them."

"Oh, dear. I hadn't thought of that. Poor shy little thing." Ellie clucked her tongue sorrowfully.

"She isn't as shy as she was a first, but she still won't say over a few words to me. She's more at ease with Henry, and they spend a lot of time together."

"I've noticed," Ellie said with a worried frown. "Henry seems to be taking hold of things more, though. I don't have to prod him so much. I think he's trying to impress Mary Ben. He likes her a lot, Vanessa. Maybe too much, and I don't know what to do about it. It's something I hadn't counted on."

"They're like two little kids, playing and laughing and whispering secrets to each other," Vanessa said wistfully. "I don't think Mary Ben's had much to laugh about."

"What should we do, Vanessa? Henry wouldn't understand if I told him not to spend so much time with her."

"No, he wouldn't understand. He would think he'd done something wrong and was being punished. Mary Ben is the first girl who has been friendly with him. The girls back home were meaner than dirt to Henry," Vanessa said, her remarkable eyes flashing with indignation.

"But what if . . . He might—"

"What if he wants to . . . make love to her? It would be up to Mary Ben to put a stop to it. Henry wouldn't force her. It isn't in him to hurt anyone or anything."

"But what if she wants him to? Mary Ben might not realize the consequence."

"Mary Ben hasn't been sheltered like the girls back home, Aunt Ellie. I'd bet there isn't much about men she doesn't know—bad ones, that is."

"Do you suppose Kain would talk to Henry?"

"I'm not going to ask him to!"

"I will. I like that man. He's quality. I was hoping that you and he—"

"No chance of that. He's not the settling kind." Vanessa snatched up a towel and a bar of soap and started toward the river. After a few steps she turned, walked back and picked up a bucket. "The river is icy cold. If there are still coals where we had the wash pot I'll heat some water."

Sunlight filtered through the branches and made speckled patterns on the ground. Vanessa watched them idly as she walked toward the river. As always when she was alone, her thoughts went to Kain. Was it her imagination or had he been avoiding her of late? They hadn't been alone for several days. Each time she made an attempt to ride beside him he seemed to have a reason for dropping back to talk with John. Several times she had caught him watching her, but he no longer teased her like he had when they first met.

Ellie, with her gentle questions, had started him talking one evening. He had been all over the world, even to places she hadn't heard about. She had sat back in the shadows, listening and watching the firelight flicker on his dark face. Each time he had looked at her with those honey colored eyes, she sensed a certain tenseness in him. For the dozenth time she recalled the touch of his hand on her cheek and the way his fingers had stroked her hair the night he was so angry because she hadn't stayed in the wagon. His touch had sent the most extraordinary sensation through her body. He'd made no attempt to touch her since. Why couldn't she get him out of her head?

Vanessa reached the riverbank, filled the bucket and carried it to the red coals in the circle of stones. She dropped a few handsful of grass on the coals, and when it blazed she fed small sticks to the hungry flames. Her mind kept straying back to Kain. Why had he ridden away without a word? He acted as if he were a man with a lot on his mind.

When the water in the bucket was warm she lifted it from the fire and removed her shirt. She ran the warm, soapy cloth over her neck and shoulders and down her arms, and thought, longingly, of a big tub of warm water. A full bath was the thing she had missed the most during this trip. After she washed and dried her upper body she slipped the shirt back on, wishing she had brought a clean one with her. She removed the pins from her braid and put them in the pocket of her shirt before she unbraided the long rope of fiery hair. When it was spread over her shoulders, she massaged her scalp and raked her fingers through the curly mass, glorying in the sense of freedom the gesture gave her.

The man concealed in the thick willows that grew along the river bank watched in fascination. He had caught glimpses of her several times during the past week, but he had not seen her this close. She was paler and thinner than he remembered, but a thousand times more enticing. The closer the bone the sweeter the meat, he thought as his black eyes raked her slender figure. Her waist and hips were so lithe and slender that in contrast her breasts were startlingly soft and emphatic. Primer Tass stood as still as a stone, but blood raced to the seat of his lust and his fevered flesh leaped upward. That fiery hair! He had never seen anything like it. His brain stopped; his heart was not beating; he was there, alone with her.

Primer Tass' feet began to move and he was out of the willows and standing not six feet behind her when she turned. He had not meant to reveal himself. He wasn't ready to make his move, but his need for her to know that he was there and that she was his woman overrode his judgment.

Vanessa froze with terror. It was as if the man in black had sprung from a nightmare. He had the same dark face and flat expressionless eyes as when she'd last seen him. Her frightened mind registered the fact that he was not a big man, he was not much taller than she. That he moved quietly and quickly was evidence since she had heard nothing. What a fool she was for coming down here without a weapon to defend herself. He stood looking at her with those dull, black eyes. She wanted to run, but she'd have to turn her back on him, and she'd be damned if she'd give him a chance to pounce on her.

"Ya waitin' fer me?" His voice was as oily as she remembered, oily and smooth.

"Waiting for *you*? I don't know you. I want nothing to do with you. Get away from me."

"Ya got the purtiest titties I ever did see."

Her eyes widened, and her mouth opened only to snap shut again. Then her fright turned to anger and blossomed into an outburst.

"How dare you spy on me! You nasty, vile, stinking piece of horsedung!"

"Ain't nobody got more right ta look at yore titties 'n me. I done told ya I took ya fer my woman."

"I'm not your woman! Get that through your thick skull right now. And get the hell away from me."

His laugh was guttural, and his eyes took on a feverish glow. "Spunky, ain't ya? I like that."

"Come near me again and I'll blow your stupid head off."

"I'd not be much good to ya dead." With his eyes on her face he ran his hand down over his lower stomach and outlined the elongated hardness that was causing his buckskins to protrude. Without wanting to, her eyes followed his hand, and her face flamed. He laughed again. This time it was a throaty, pleased chuckle. "Jist alookin' at ya gets me all het up 'n ready fer ya." The black eyes fastened to her face were like two bottomless, evil pits.

Vanessa was speechless with horror and outrage. She longed to smash his hateful face, but more than that she longed to turn and run.

"Ain't ya got nothin' to say 'bout it, purty woman?"

"I've got plenty to say and I mean every word of it. Come near me again and I'll blow a hole in you big enough to drive a wagon through! Now go and leave me alone. If Kain knew you were here he'd kill you right now!"

"Are ya aworryin' 'bout me?" He stood with his thumbs hooked in the strap of his gun belt. "I jist wanted to make sure ya knowed I laid my claim on ya that first day. The fat Dutchman 'n the kid thought they'd get a go at ya, but I'd a killed 'em first."

"You've no claim on me, you stupid, ignorant lout! I could horsewhip you for even thinking it. I wouldn't have anything to do with you if you were the last man on earth. You're everything I despise in a man."

"That's the kind a talk I like from my woman. We'll hitch good . . . when the time comes. Ya'll be wantin' it same as me when I get ya off in the mountains 'n show ya how tis. I'm aimin' fer us to have us a mighty fine old time out there all by our lonesome. Ya can do all the hollerin' 'n scratchin' 'n fightin' ya want. It'll jist make it better."

He leaped toward her. He moved so fast she was caught off guard. She turned to run, but managed only a few steps when his hand tangled in her hair and jerked her back against him. Before she could scream his hand clamped over her mouth, and he dragged her into the thick willows. A fresh flush of fear raced through her body.

"Ya'll keep quiet now, cause I could squeeze the life outta ya afore ya knowed it. I don't want to, but I will afore I let ya brin' the gringos down on me." His hand moved from her mouth to her throat and his fingers tightened.

"I won't . . . I won't scream. Kain will kill you if he catches you here," she managed to say.

"The gringo ain't your man. If'n he was he'd be fuckin' ya ever' night, like I'd be adoin'. I been watchin'. But it don't matter none. I'm goin' to kill him," he muttered against her ear. The hand on her rib cage moved up to her breast. His fingers closed over her soft flesh and he rasped, "I love titties. I like to bite 'em, lick 'em, nuss 'em." his thumb and forefinger pinched her nipple. "It ain't big. It ain't been nussed, has it?"

Pain and terror knifed through her. Unmindful of his threats she began to struggle. His fingers moved up to her jaw and he jerked her head around. He attacked her mouth with brutal, wet kisses, and all the while his arm held her back against his chest. Finally he lifted his head. She felt faint and sagged against his arm. Her stomach rolled and bile rose in her throat.

"Ya like that, do ya? It ain't nothin' to what it'll be. I can show ya thin's that'll make ya so hot fer me ya'll chase me all o'er them mountains a tryin' to get me."

Her eyes blazed. She would have spit in his face if not for the fingers that clamped her chin and dug into her cheeks.

"Wait fer me. When I get thin's fixed, I'll be back fer ya." His arm fell way, but his fingers on her cheeks tightened. A long, thin knife appeared in his hand and she made a frightened sound and tried to jerk away. "Jist hold still. I ain't agoin' to hurt ya none if'n yore quiet. I jist got to have this. I jist got to." He grabbed a handful of hair at the top of her head and the knife began sawing through it.

"No!" The protest came from her choked throat.

The pull on her scalp was so painful it brought tears to her eyes. Finally the pressure stopped and he held out a two-foot length of gleaming copper hair. He smoothed it and carefully wrapped it around his hand. He was smiling. Vanessa's hand went to the top of her head. Not over an inch of hair covered a large patch on her crown. Her mouth formed a soundless cry of rage.

"I ain't never seen white skin like yores or hair like this here. I'll be akeepin' ya jist fer me 'n not let nobody else have ya—if'n ya behave yourself."

"Vanessa!" Ellie's voice came from beyond the willows. "Are you down here? Vanessa!"

The tip of the knife sliced the top button from her shirt, then was suddenly beneath Vanessa's chin and held her silent. "I'm goin' to have me this, too. Ya listen up good. Tell the gringo Primer Tass was here. Tell 'em I'll be waitin' up the trail 'n I'll drop him from any hill or clump a tree he passes. Then it'll be jist you 'n me."

"You'd shoot a man in the back?"

"Shore. What's him to me?" He laughed openly at her. "I killed men I knowed better 'n him. Ain't no man standin' atween me 'n a woman I want."

"You're an animal!" Vanessa croaked. "I'll never go with you. If you force me I'll put a knife in you the first chance I get!"

To her amazement he laughed. "I warn't mistook 'bout ya. Ya'll come when the times right, 'n ya'll fight ever step of the way, won't ya, Vanessa? That's yore name, ain't it? Vanessa."

He said her name again as though trying to taste it. "Now mind I'll be watchin' ya, same as I been doin'. Ya can tell these folk I been here, it don't matter none. I'll jist be up ahead, 'n pick that bastard off with a shot in the head. Ain't no way he can be ready fer me," he concluded blandly. He watched her the way a snake watched a small frog or an insect, his black eyes still and staring. "I got to be aleavin' ya, but I want me a little kiss first."

"Vanessa?" Ellie's voice sounded anxious.

As soon as his mouth was near enough, Vanessa sank her teeth in his lip with all her strength. He grabbed her hair and twisted until she let go. Blood ran from his lip and down his chin, yet he smiled.

"Does hurtin' make ya hotter? I knowed women like that." His voice was a mere purr of a sound.

He jerked on her hair so hard that tears sprang to her eyes and she stumbled back, falling against a tree trunk. When she turned to look, he was gone.

"Vanessa!"

"I'm here, Aunt Ellie." She got quickly to her feet and pulled up the tail of her shirt, wiped her eyes and scrubbed her mouth, then straightened her clothes and pushed the hair back from her face. Her stomach churned as if she was about to be sick. She felt herself go ice cold. The next second she was burning hot. She was trembling from head to foot, but she made an effort to keep her voice steady. "I'm in the bushes. I'll be there in a minute." She took deep breaths to calm herself, then walked out from behind the willows, adjusting the belt that held up her britches.

"It scared me for a minute when you weren't here," Ellie said with a little laugh.

"There are times when a body's got to go to the bushes." Vanessa kept her face turned away. A gust of wind from the river whipped her hair. "It's getting cold. I'll finish washing in the wagon." She leaned over, away from her aunt, whirled her hair into a loose roll and pinned it to the top of her head.

"I thought you'd have your hair washed by now and I'd pour water over it to rinse out the soap."

"I decided to not wash it today. It would take a long time for it to dry." It was a lame excuse, but the only one Vanessa could think of. "Let's go back to the wagons, Aunt Ellie. This place gives me the creeps."

"Is something wrong? Why, heavens! You're nervous and jumpy."

"I—I thought I heard someone back there sneaking around." She picked up the bucket and dumped the water on the coals. "I shouldn't have come down here without the gun." She started back through the trees and Ellie followed.

"Could it be Indians?" Ellie looked back over her shoulder fearfully.

"I don't think so. It was probably someone from the campground."

Vanessa's knees were weak and trembling, but she was not too rattled to think clearly. With mounting distress she silently acknowledged that there was no place where she was absolutely safe from Primer Tass. She could never be alone again as long as that man lived. He was a beast! She had suffered indignities from him that no decent woman should have to endure, the way he handled her breast, his foul talk. . . .

She would have to tell Kain, she thought. Kain had to be warned. Tass said he would be waiting up the trail . . . to kill him and take her. Oh, Kain! Oh, darling!

Chapter Eight

"Mary Ben? Are you in there?" Henry stood at the end of the Wisner wagon.

"No, silly. I'm over here."

Henry turned and saw Mary Ben standing at the edge of the camp beneath a large oak tree, its branches cut off so as to not tear the tops of the wagons. She was laughing at him.

"Silly?" He went toward her. "Are you calling me silly, Mary Ben?"

"Silly! Silly!" she shouted and struck off through the trees, running lightly. Her joyous laugh and the old yellow dog trailed her. When she was sure she was out of his sight, she hid behind a large tree trunk. Henry passed her hiding place, although he knew she was there, then turned and caught sight of her skirt as she darted to the other side.

"Now you quit hiding from me, Mary Ben." A giggle answered him. "Come on out or I won't give you the present I bought you."

"Present?" Her surprised voice came from behind the tree.

"Yes, but I'm not going to give it to you if you don't come on out and be nice."

"I don't need no present, Henry, 'n I ain't agoin' to be nice, so there!" She flattened herself against the tree trunk and held her hand over her mouth to stifle the excited giggles that bubbled up in her throat.

Henry sneaked up to the tree, reached around and grabbed her shirt. "I got you, Mary Ben! You're no good at hiding. I knew you were there all the time."

When she started to run Henry jerked on her skirt and she sat down hard on the ground. Her eyes shone up at him and she burst out laughing. Henry threw himself down beside her, his eyes fastened to her face. He didn't think he'd ever seen anything prettier than Mary Ben laughing. The yellow dog decided the game was over. He flopped down and rested his jowls on his paws.

"Ain't it fun, Henry? I ain't never had fun like this. I ain't never played with nobody. It's just like we were little younguns again."

"I played with Vanessa when I was little, but nobody else wanted to play with me." He smiled. There was no self-pity in his voice. It was a statement of fact.

He took off his hat, set it on the ground beside him, and wiped his brow with a red neckerchief. They sat quietly, looking at each other as if the two of them were alone in the world. Mary Ben loved to look at him. He was so handsome and clean, so . . . gentle. He didn't leer at her as other men did. He said things as they came to him, honest and straight out. From the first she had known he was different from anyone she'd ever met before. He was like a small boy in a grown man's body. She wished for his sake that he could be more like Mr. DeBolt, but not for hers. She loved him just as he was, and if she had her way she'd stay with him forever.

"I got something for you. I saw it at the store and Kain said I had enough money to buy it." He took a package from the inside pocket of his vest and placed it in her lap. He was looking at her with a nervous smile and such tender concern in his eyes that she wanted to cry. "Open it," he urged. His face lost the smile and his eyes became anxious.

Mary Ben looked down at the package, then up at Henry. Her eyes filled with tears. "I ain't never had a present afore. I ain't never had nothin' wrapped up." She picked it up with both hands and held it to her breast. "I jist want to hold it a minute afore I open it."

"Don't cry about it!" Henry peered down into her face and a small distressed sound came from his throat. "Ah . . . Mary Ben, please don't cry. Smile again. Please," he begged. "I got the present to make you happy."

"People cry when they're happy, silly." She sniffed and smiled into his eyes.

"They do no such thing."

"Yes, they do to, Henry Hill." She carefully unwrapped the paper and the length of pink ribbon and the bottle of toilet water spilled out into her lap. "Oh, my goodness!" she said in an awed voice, lifting the toilet water in one hand and the ribbon in the other. Her eyes became round with surprise and pleasure. "Oh, my goodness gracious me!"

"Do you like it?' Henry asked anxiously.

"Like it? Oh, Henry! I ain't never had nothin' so fine."

"The ribbon will be pretty in your hair, or you can put it on a dress. Do you want to smell this? I'll open it." He took the bottle from her hand, pulled the cork plug, and waved the open bottle beneath her nose. "Doesn't it smell good? Ma and Vanessa put some on their fingers and rub it on their necks and behind their ears. Want me to show you?" Without waiting for an answer, he put a generous amount of the scented water on his fingers and gently spread it on her neck and up under her hair. "You're pretty, Mary Ben. You're so . . . pretty. I never saw a girl as pretty as you," he said softly.

"I ain't neither pretty," she said shaking her head and hoping he'd deny it. "Vanessa's pretty. She's the prettiest thing I ever did see."

"Van's pretty," he admitted, "but you're prettier. You're hair is soft and shiny." He lifted his hand and his fingers lightly touched the tendrils at her temples. "I like the way it curls and hangs down your back. You're eyes are pretty, too. They're like the brown-eyed daisies we have back home. I think about you all the time, Mary Ben," he whispered, looking straight into her eyes.

"I think about ya too, Henry."

"Can I ask you something?" He replaced the cork in the bottle and laid it in her lap. His hand clasped her's tightly. "Kain said I ought to ask before I did anything. He said if you said no, I was to back off. He said to never force a woman. I'd not ever hurt you, Mary Ben."

"I know ya wouldn't, Henry. Yo're the kindest man I ever did know. Ya can ask me anythin'.' "

"Can I kiss you? I've been wanting to for a long time, but I won't if you don't want me to."

"I ain't never kissed nobody. I don't know how.' "

"I'll show you. I've kissed Ma and Van on the cheek. But I want to kiss you on the mouth, Mary Ben, like you was my girl."

"I don't care if ya . . . do."

Mary Ben felt her breath catch in her throat when his fingers lifted her chin, felt her insides warm with pleasure as his lips softly met hers. She closed her eyes and allowed herself the pure joy of feelling his nose against her cheek and the rough drag of the whiskers on his chin. His mouth was warm and moist, and his breath fresh. She didn't even think of the panic she'd felt when men had tried to grab her and kiss her. This was different, so different. Such a lovely feeling unfolded in her midsection and traveled slowly through her body. She wanted it to go on and on. His mouth moved against hers ever so slightly with delicious provocation. Gently, as if she were something so fragile she would break, his lips moved over her cheeks, her brows, and touched her closed eyelids. They returned to her lips which opened under the pressure, and she leaned against him, her arms finding their way around his neck as his arms held her gently against him. A surge of pleasure rushed through her, and she heard a soft moan, not knowing if it came from her or Henry.

He lifted his head immediately. "Was I too rough? Oh, my pretty, sweet Mary Ben, I didn't mean to hurt you!"

"Ya didn't!" She reached for his face with her hands and stroked his cheeks with her palms. "Ya didn't hurt me a'tall, Henry. I jist didn't want ya to stop."

"Does that mean you like for me to kiss you?"

"I like it a lot."

His arms tightened and he hugged her to him fiercely. "I'm glad! I liked it, too. I like everything about you, Mary Ben. I like to hold you and feel your arms around my neck. It makes my insides all fluttery," he said with a nervous little laugh. "I want to court you. If you want me to, I'll ask John if I can."

"Court me? Oh, Henry! What would yore ma say? She won't want ya courtin' such as me."

"Why not?"

"Cause . . . cause—well, I ain't nobody. I can't write my name or do sums or nothin' like that."

"I can do sums. And I can write your name for you," he said anxiously.

"But courtin' leads to . . . leads to—"

"It leads to a weddin'. I know that. If we were wed we'd never have to leave each other." He held her away from him and looked down into her eyes. There was an intense, almost desperate look on his face. "Tell me truthful and honest to goodness, Mary Ben. Do you think I'm a . . . dummy? Is that why you don't want me to court you?"

"Henry Hill! Don't ya ever say that again! Hear? Ya ain't no dummy! Ya ain't no dummy a'tall! Yo're the nicest, sweetest thin' in the whole wide world. I'm jist worried is all. I ain't good enuff fer ya."

"It's me that's not good enough for *you*. I'll take care of you the best I can. I'm learning things from Kain. He's showing me how to fight and how to use the gun. I could do anything if you were with me and telling me what to do," he whispered, distress lines creasing his brow. He stared deeply at her stricken face and saw the sparkle of tears come to her eyes.

"I'm scared a what yore ma 'n Vanessa'd say. Look at me, Henry. Look at my dress and my shoes. I ain't never lived in a house in my whole life—it's always been a dugout or a wagon. I killed a man down in the Territory. I might a killed two of 'em. They was after me 'n I shot 'em. There was jist me 'n Mister fer a long time, till Mr. Wisner come." She bowed her head and rested her forehead on his shoulder. When her voice came again it was muffled against his shirt. "I can't hardly talk to decent folk. Yore ma and Vanessa are fine ladies. They'd not want me wed to ya."

"I'll ask them. I'll tell them I want to court you and wed you and be with you forever. Ma wants me to be happy. She tells me, 'be happy, Henry.' I'm happy when I'm with you. It's like I can do anything. It's like I'm as smart as anybody." His voice vibrated with tender emotion and his lips quivered against her brow. "I don't want you to ever go away."

She pressed her face against his shirt, not wanting him to see the tears that filled her eyes on hearing his tender words. She was aware of the heavy beat of his heart and his warm breath on her ear. He rocked her in his arms as if she were a small child. Her lips found the pulse that beat at the base of his throat. This gentle man had given her more tenderness during the few short weeks she had known him than she had received in all her seventeen years. A feeling of faintness seemed to sweep over her. She wanted to cling to him, to give him love, to shield and protect him always.

His arms held her firmly but gently. She nestled in the warm protection of his embrace and heard him croon softly, "Don't you worry, Mary Ben. I'll take care of you."

They sat for a long while in the quiet woods while the squirrels raced through the branches overhead and scolded the yellow dog as he lay watching the man who held his mistress in his arms, stroking her hair.

Vanessa was gathering the dry clothes from the bushes when she saw Kain riding toward camp on the big red horse. Her relief was so intense that her knees trembled. As mealtime approached and he hadn't returned, she had become so worried that Primer Tass had found him she had been sick to her stomach.

Kain rode on past her with only a brief nod of his head and dismounted behind the Wisner wagon.

Her mind was temporarily distracted from Primer Tass and all his visit implied when Henry and Mary Ben came out of the woods, hand in hand. Her hair was tied back with a new pink ribbon and Henry had a shy smile on his face. Vanessa watched Ellie anxiously, saw her look at the couple and then down at the biscuit dough she was pinching off and putting in the pan to bake.

"Look, Ma." Henry pulled the reluctant girl to where Ellie stood beside the workbench. "Don't Mary Ben look pretty with the new ribbon in her hair?" Mary Ben hung her head and refused to look up.

"Mary Ben is pretty with or without the ribbon." Ellie glanced at the shy girl.

"I think so, too," Henry said with all the honesty of his simple nature as he smiled down at Mary Ben. The girl's head was bent so low her chin was resting on her chest. "I bought a present for you, too, Ma. I bought you some soap. Doesn't it smell good?" He held the bar beneath her nose.

"Why, thank you, Henry. That was very sweet of you. Yes, it does smell good." Ellie smiled up at her tall son. "Lilac, isn't it? I can't take it right now, I've got my hands in the biscuit dough and it's almost supper time. Put it there by the wash dish and I'll put it away later."

"Let go my hand, Henry," Mary Ben whispered and tugged on the hand Henry held tightly in his. "Let go! I got to help." She moved quickly away from him when he released her hand.

"If you're going to help Ma, I'll help Kain. Kain," Henry called and went loping toward him. "I'll picket the horses. Mary Ben liked the ribbon."

Mary Ben stood nervously beside Ellie. When the older woman didn't look up at her, her anxiety grew.

"Mrs. Hill? Are ya mad cause Henry give me the ribbon?" Her voice was a bare whisper.

Startled, Ellie turned and looked into the young, worried face of the girl. "Mercy, no, child! I think it was very thoughtful of Henry to buy the presents."

Tears spurted into Mary Ben's big brown eyes. Her lips trembled and she clamped the lower one between her teeth. "I . . . can keep it—and the toilet water?" Her voice was shaking so that the question came out on a sob.

"Of course you can." Ellie could see that Mary Ben was doing her best to keep from crying, and did the only thing she knew to help her. "But landsakes, child, we got to get the supper on. We're running late and it'll be dark before you know it. Bring me that pan, Mary Ben, and take this one and put it in the oven. See to the coals under it first, dear," she called as Mary Ben, relieved to be doing something, hurried to obey.

Darkness fell, quiet settled over the camp and everyone gathered for the evening meal. Vanessa filled her plate and went to sit on a stool with her back to the wagon wheel.

Kain sat on the other side of the cookfire and talked to John. She watched him. He ate very little for a man his size, she thought. He nibbled on a biscuit and ate a helping of rice and gravy. John had bought a pail of milk from a woman at the campground, and Kain drank several cups.

His face was thinner. The thought went through her mind as she studied it. He had lost weight since she had first seen him in Dodge City. A stab of fear caused her heart to pound heavily. But he didn't look sick, she told herself. Traveling every day was hard on a person, even a man as big and strong as Kain. She had lost weight and so had Ellie. She regreted having to put more worry on him, but he had to be warned to be on the lookout for Primer Tass.

The trip, Vanessa thought, had taken a toll on Ellie, too. She had always been proud of the soft, white skin on her face and had protected it with a sunbonnet. Now, in spite of the sunbonnet and applications of olive oil, the wind and dust had chapped her cheeks and dried and cracked her lips. When Kain joined their party, Ellie's nerves had been stretched to the breaking point. She was still fearful—Vanessa had even heard her crying in the night. She didn't know if her aunt's tears were caused by her fear of the outlaws who preyed on travelers or fear of what she would face when they reached Junction City. Vanessa was determined, if at all possible, to shield her aunt from the extra worry of Primer Tass' threats.

When it was Mary Ben's turn to take the first watch, Henry would stand it with her as he had done for the past week. He would also stay with Vanessa when she took the second watch. It was Kain's idea that she and Mary Ben take turns and that Henry stay with them. It was a way, he had explained to Ellie, to give Henry some responsibility.

John and Ellie had gone to bed, and Henry and Mary Ben, with the yellow dog beside them, had settled down for the first watch. Vanessa moved quietly to the outer edge of the camp where Kain had opened his bedroll. She wanted to share her anxiety with him; the burden was just too great for her to bear alone. In his calm manner, Kain would know what to do.

She stood hesitantly a few feet away from him, not knowing that he had watched her from the time she left the wagon, and that his heart had begun to pound with a new rhythm. Her hair was untied and hung down to her waist. She looked so small and so lonely, standing there. He lay still, gazing at her. Hungrily his eyes slid over her slim figure, silky hair and light face. God, he thought. Did she know what she as doing to him? She was so sweet, so beautiful, and he was trying so hard to keep distance between them. He had no future beyond Junction City, and he loved her too much to take her for just a few short months or weeks. And the thought of her seeing him at the end was unbearable.

"Kain? Are you awake?"

"I'm awake. What's wrong?"

"I . . . want to talk to you."

"Can't it wait till morning?"

The harshness of his query cut her to the heart. Vanessa felt a knot in her throat and incipient moisture under her eyelids. She was struck speechless for a moment. She hadn't expected him to be angry with her for seeking him out. And then the hurt blossomed to indignation.

"No, it can't wait until morning," she said sharply. "I have something to tell you that I especially want to keep from Aunt Ellie."

"If it's about Henry and Mary Ben—"

"It's *not* about Henry and Mary Ben. It's about one of the men who stole our mules—the dark one, Primer Tass." There was a break in her voice, and then a pause while she swallowed with difficulty. "He told me to tell you that he'd be waiting for you . . . up ahead. I thought you should know so you can be prepared to defend yourself. That's all I have

to say. I'll not take up any more of your time." She turned to
go.

Kain rose from the bedroll as if pulled by invisible strings
as soon as she said the man's name. John had told him what
he knew of Primer Tass, and it was all bad.

"Vanessa!" he hissed. "Come back here." He got to his
feet and grabbed her arm. "Where did you see Tass? Was he
here?"

"He was down by the river, where we set the boiling pot
to wash." Just saying the words made her voice shake.

"Goddamn!" Kain swore in a husky whisper. "Tell me,"
he demanded roughly, "did that bastard . . . force himself on
you?"

Vanessa turned a stricken face toward him, and words
gushed out of her mouth like water out of a fountain. "Oh,
Kain! He was behind me when I turned. I was washing
myself . . . I had my shirt off! He'd watched me bathe! He
looked me over with those snakey eyes. They're awful!" She
shuddered. "I shouldn't have gone down there without my
gun, but it wouldn't have made any difference, he's so . . .
quick. He pounced on me when I turned to run. He pinched
me and rubbed me against him."

"Did he . . . did he molest you?" The question tore out of
his throat in a hoarse, desperate whisper. She could feel
trembling in the hands that gripped her shoulders so tightly it
pained her. "Did he? Tell me, goddamn it! Did he violate
you?"

"What . . . do you mean?"

"Goddamn it to hell! You know what I mean! Did he go
inside you?"

"No! No, not that. He touched me . . . in places and he
kissed me. His mouth was all wet and slobbery. I was so
scared, Kain, and I wanted to throw up." She felt once again
the chill of panic, then her nerves steadied. Kain was with
her. "I bit him, though," she said spiritedly. "I wanted to kill
him!"

"Jesus Christ!" Kain was so relieved he didn't realize that he had pressed her down on the bedroll and flung himself down to sit beside her. His arms slid around her and he held her so tightly against his chest she could scarcely breathe. "I should have killed that bastard when I had the chance." His voice was muffled against her hair.

"Oh, no! I'm glad you didn't try. He might have killed you!"

"John said I'd have to kill him sooner or late. He said you don't give a snake a second chance at you, and by God, he's right. If Tass comes near you again I'll shoot him down like a mad dog, without a second thought!"

"He said to tell you he'd be waiting for you." The pent-up tension of the day came flooding out in the form of tears that ran down her cheeks and seeped into her mouth. She didn't want him to see her cry and tried to move away from him, but his arms held her. For a moment she resisted the pressure of his embrace, then suddenly she hid her face against his chest in a rush of anguished despair.

"What else did he say?" he prompted gently.

"He said that then it would be . . . just him and me." The last word came out on a sob. "And, Kain . . . he cut my hair! He cut a big chunk out of the top to take away with him." She took his hand and carried it to the top of her head where the stubby ends barely covered her scalp.

Anger and jealousy sent waves of rage reverberating through him. His fingers fondled the inch-long hair, then cupped the back of her head and held it to him. The thought of another man—especially a man like Primer Tass—touching her in private places and having a strand of her hair to carry with him brought a predator's gleam to his leonine eyes.

"He wants you." His voice was low and harsh. "The nervy bastard!" He was quiet for a moment, then murmured, "At the same time I can hardly blame him." He moved back, staring at her, and asked in a controlled voice, "Why didn't he take you when he had the chance?"

"He said he wasn't ready, that he had things to do first. He talked of taking me to the mountains." Her words were muffled against him when she hid her face against his shirt. His big arms squeezed her more tightly.

"That's probably his territory, the mountains of New Mexico or even south of the border. He's thinking you have money in that fancy wagon. He'll need someone to help him get it, because he knows he'll have to go through John and me."

"That *fancy* wagon has been nothing but trouble. What are we going to do, Kain? What can we do? He's been watching us and he said he knew that you're . . . not my man."

"How does he know that?"

"He said we didn't sleep together." In this sweet intimacy the words came out unhesitantly.

Kain was silent for the duration of a few heartbeats. "There's been only a few places where he could get close enough to see much without us knowing he was there. From now on we'll camp out in the open."

"He's going to try to kill you. Can't we report him to the soldiers at the forts?" she asked hopefully.

"They're not here to police civilians. Even if they were they wouldn't go after him for just making a threat." His hand absently stroked the length of her hair while he spoke.

An owl spoke mournfully from the cottonwoods down near the river. Was it an owl? Or was Primer Tass calling to a friend of his? Vanessa clutched Kain's arm and snuggled closer to him. Being in his arms was marvelously comforting.

"Do you think we should go on alone?"

"It's the only thing to do. He could lose himself among a crowd of people. Out on the trail he'll have to come at us point-blank."

"I'm afraid for you, Kain. He said several times he was going to kill you. And he said it calmly, as if he had no doubt." She pulled back and looked up into his face. "You were gone a long time today and I was afraid he'd found you. I watched and waited for you to come back. It would break my heart if you—if something happened to you!" Her attempt to speak calmly was weakened by the depth of her emotion. She gave no thought to her words or her actions. Her arms wound around his waist and she clutched him to her fiercely.

His hoarse, ragged breathing accompanied the thunder of his heartbeat as the realization of what she had said came to him. She was saying she cared for him—maybe even loved him! She was distraught, he thought, and frightened. She didn't realize what her words implied.

"You don't need to be afraid, Vanessa. I'll take care of Tass. He'll have to go through me to get to you again. And I'll see you and Ellie safely to Junction City. Then I've got things to do—"

"Thunderation!" Anger stiffened her body. "Do you think that all I care about is staying out of the clutches of Primer Tass and getting to Junction City? I'll blow his worthless head off before I let him take *me*. It's *you* he wants to kill. He'll wait behind a boulder and ambush you! That's his way. He'll not come at you head-on. Don't you understand that? He hates you because you showed him up that morning. And it's my fault for not staying out of sight like you told me to." Her anger dissipated, and tears of rejection and humiliation poured down her cheeks. She lowered her head until all he could see was her bowed head.

"Vanessa, girl, I didn't mean—"

"Oh, yes, you did! You think I'm throwing myself at you! Good women don't do that, do they? They wait for the man to speak first."

"I've never had anyone so sweet, or so beautiful thrown

at me. I just didn't know how to react." He chuckled and a wild, wonderful feeling engulfed him.

"Don't laugh at me."

The sad note in her voice whipped him into speech. "Vanessa, darlin' girl," he murmured, the endearment coming unknowingly from his lips. He lifted her face with a firm hand beneath her chin and pressed his cheek to her wet one. "I wasn't laughing at you. I was laughing because it makes me feel good to know that you're concerned for me."

"It's the . . . same." Her heart fluttered and she drew her face back to look at him.

"No, ma'am, it isn't." He grew tongue-tied looking down into her white face, and the absurdity of it made him half angry. Her eyes glistened in the darkness and her breath came out in little buffs of warmth. His amber eyes drank in every feature as if he wished to imprint them on his soul. They stared at each other for a moment that was so still it seemed time had stopped.

Looking into his eyes, Vanessa felt a wild, heated longing stab her body and race through her veins with the speed of lightning. She raised both arms, letting her hands move up his chest to his shoulders. The buckskin shirt was smooth and soft beneath her fingertips. Her hands reached his throat, moved up beneath his ears, and paused. She could feel soft, silky hair against her fingers, and moved them around to the back of his neck. His hair came to the top of his shirt and was cut off bluntly. The boldness of her action sent a thrill of excitement through her. Her fingertips wandered up to his eyes, traced the straight brows above them, traversed the slope of his nose down to his lips, and traced the scar that slashed across his cheek.

Then slowly, haltingly, she gathered her hair in her hand, lifted it and wrapped it about his neck, binding him to her. Again she slipped her hands into his hair at his nape, let them remain there and leaned her cheek against his shoulder. It was a moment in which they both knew that something had changed forever. For as long as they lived there would be a bond between them.

Kain could feel life pounding in his throat, his temples. He was achingly aware of her small, firm breasts, warm clinging arms and her breath on his neck, and the intimacy of her body resting so trustingly against his sent a wave of desire through him. He forgot there was no future for him, nothing but this moment.

As if compelled by forces stronger than he, Kain lowered his head and pressed gentle kisses to her wet eyes, and sipped at her tears with utter gentleness. Then a sound of urgent longing escaped his throat, and he whispered against her lips, "Vanessa, Vanessa . . . I can't help myself."

Their breaths mingled for an instant before he covered her mouth with his. He kissed her lingeringly, tasting her mouth, learning its shape and texture, but softly, gently, as though she were infinitely fragile and precious. The streak of flame spreading through his groin jolted him, and he drew her closer, holding her tightly against him, drinking in her sweetness until his senses reeled. Her body was pliant against his, his lips soft and clinging, and he took them hungrily, again and again.

"I wish—oh, God, how I wish I'd met you sooner," he murmured against her lips, and there was pain in his voice. His mouth trailed over her cheek, along the curve of her jaw and down the column of her throat. "You're so sweet, so sweet," he muttered feverishly, then caught her mouth again, desperately needing the taste of her, rubbing her lips with his until they parted so his tongue could roam her soft inner lips.

Time was lost in the hot excitement flowing from his body to hers and back again. He was loath to end it and his mouth trailed over her eyelids, her cheeks and her firm little chin before nuzzling in the softness of her hair.

"Sweet, sweet, wonderful Vanessa. I never meant to . . . kiss you like that." He stuttered and tremors shook his tall frame. He kissed her again, reclaiming her full bottom lip in a long, fiercely possessive kiss.

"I never knew kissing was so wonderful," she said weakly while he was placing small kisses along the line of her jaw. "I feel like I have no bones, no muscles."

"It isn't always this wonderful." His voice was thick and husky.

"I didn't think it was. It was special, wasn't it, Kain?"

"For me it was."

Her hand moved to his cheek. "For me, too, my darling Kain. How did you get this scar?"

"By being careless. I took a man's gun, but not his knife."

"You've been to a lot of places I've never heard of. Have you known many . . . women?"

"A few. But none as beautiful as you."

"I like to hear it, even if I don't believe it. Kain? I feel so much better about . . . Primer Tass. You'll be careful?"

"Of course." Just looking at her and holding her gave him pleasure. Feeling the swell of her breast, her firm hips and breathing in the scent of her breath sent a golden warmth spreading through him.

"Kain do you still think Adam Clayhill is Henry's uncle?" The question came softly from beneath his chin where her face was nestled.

"Yes, I do. If there was a rich, powerful rancher in that area by the name of Adam Hill, I think I would have heard about him. Ellie will not receive the welcome she's expecting from Adam Clayhill," he commented in a soft whisper.

"Tell me about him. You said he married your mother. Did she love him?"

"I think he swept her off her feet with his charm. He can be very charming when he wants to be, and he thought my mother was rich. The man is totally without compassion. Henry Clayhill raised Adam's son by an Indian woman. And when Henry died he left his fortune to Adam's son, Logan

Horn. That brings up another question that's been dogging my mind. Why didn't he leave his money to his widow, Ellie? Perhaps he died before he had a chance to change his will. But if that was the case, Adam would have known Henry had a wife and out of pure meanness to keep Logan from having the money he would have seen to it that Henry's marriage was made public."

"I don't think I'll like this Adam Clayhill."

"Hardly anyone does. There is a bright side, however. Logan Horn is a fine man. If Ellie is Henry Clayhill's widow, she and Henry will be welcomed by Logan and his wife."

"I think Aunt Ellie is terribly worried, but she needn't be. We have money to start our bakery. We don't need help from anyone."

Vanessa found herself waiting, hoping and praying that Kain would say they had him now. But the silence went on and on. He sat quietly, his fingers massaging the nape of her neck. Although his arms still held her close, a sixth sense told her he had pulled some part of himself away from her.

"I'd better get some sleep." She hoped he'd ask her to stay a while longer. He didn't, and she pushed herself away from him, then smoothed her hair with trembling hands. He stood and pulled her up beside him.

"From now on I want you to stay in the wagon. Henry can drive John's, and John and I will ride alongside. You're not to leave camp. Understand? If you can stand the pace we'll travel from dawn to dusk. I know a shortcut that will bypass Denver and cut days off the travel time to Junction City. I think we should take it."

"Don't worry about me. It's Aunt Ellie—"

"I'll tell her we have to hurry and get there before the cold weather sets in. Now run along and get some sleep. I'll stand your watch."

"No. I—"

"Yes. If I'm in charge, I'm in charge, Vanessa. Don't

argue . . . please. Run along now." He added the last words tiredly as if he were speaking to a rebellious child, and they put more distance between them.

"All right. Good night."

"Good night."

Vanessa went to the wagon, confused and hurt by the swift change in Kain's attitude. He had dismissed her as if he hadn't held her in his arms, called her darling, or kissed her. It was as though what had happened between them had meant nothing to him at all.

Chapter Nine

The sun was making its first appearance of the day when Kain tied his horse to the rail in front of the store outside Fort Lyon. Even at this time in the morning wagons, both covered and freight, dray horses, mules, riders from the campground and drifters mingled in the street. He stood with his back to the wall of the store while his sharp eyes roamed. There didn't seem to be anyone paying particular attention to him and he saw no one who resembled Primer Tass. He entered the store and greeted the big man behind the counter.

"Morning."

The storekeeper stood in the same place as the day before, wore the same clothes and had the same surly look on his face.

"What're ya back fer?"

"If it was a friendly greeting I came for I got short changed by a mile," Kain answered curtly.

"Friendly ain't what I'm here fer." He shot a healthy spit

of tobacco toward the gaboon, and the sound of the splash that followed indicated he had hit it.

"I want to hire a couple of good men for a few weeks. I thought you'd be the man to point them out."

"Why me?"

"Because anyone as cantankerous as you is bound to have run into the best and worst of the lot that hangs around a place like this."

"You wantin' to kill somebody, steal somethin' or overthrow the gover'ment?"

"I want to get a good woman to some folks up north, and there's a lowdown son of a bitch that wants to carry her off against her will. I want men who will kill if they have to, steal if they have to, or do whatever is necessary to keep her safe."

"Wal, now . . . ain't nobody goin' to sit still if'n a good woman's bothered. Ya ort a know that."

"I do know it, and I'm that somebody who's not sitting still. Do you know a couple of good men who would hire on to ride with us for wages?"

"A train pulled out fer Denver this mornin'. Why didn't ya hook up with 'em?"

"That's none of your damn business, but I'll tell you anyway. We're moving light and fast and I've no wish to nursemaid a bunch of pilgrims."

A grin twitched the storekeeper's stern mouth for an instant. "Don't know as I blame you none. That kid you had the run-in with, he 'n his bunch was in the saloon last night. Is it him yo're lookin' out fer?"

"That kid doesn't amount to a pimple on a jaybird's ass compared to the *hombre* we're up against. Do you know the kind of men I'm looking for? If you don't, say so and I'll look somewhere else."

"Crotchety, ain't ya? Yup, I know 'em. Texans. Pure hickory is what they is. Come up with a herd. They keep to themselves, but they don't take no shit off'n nobody."

"Where can I find them? My party has pulled out and we've got to catch up."

"I'll get 'em." The storekeeper went out the back door, slamming it behind him.

Kain backed against the counter where he could watch both doors. The ribbon table and the spool of blue from which he had purchased the length for Vanessa were directly in his line of vision. The ribbon was still in his pocket. He had intended to give it to her at supper the night before. With everyone present, he had planned to say something like, "Henry thought you should have this," and carelessly toss it in her lap. It would have been less personal that way. But somehow, when the time came, he couldn't bring himself to do it. And later, when she had come to him, he'd forgotten about it. In fact, he'd forgotten everything except that he had been alone in the dark with her.

He knew when she left him she had been hurt and confused. Damn! Why had he kissed her the way he had? Knowing her sweetness was going to make it twice as hard to stay away from her. But, hell, he reasoned, wasn't he entitled to a few pleasures? Logic battered his mind. With death creeping up on him, he had no right to let her think they could make a life together. She had a future, if he could keep her safe from Tass. He had no future to offer her. He had a thing inside him that was slowly eating his life away. It was still hard for him to believe that he was dying, yet it was happening. He was a man who had always lived with his muscles as well as his brain, and at times he felt as strong as he always had.

The storekeeper came back followed by two men in dusty trail clothes. They stood side by side, looking at Kain while he looked at them. The storekeeper went behind the counter without a word. Kain studied each man, one at a time. His experienced eyes told him the first one had been up the trail and over the mountain. Years in the saddle had bowed his legs and bent his back. He was tall, thin, and almost as old as John. He had sharp eyes, a handlebar mustache and wore down-at-the-heel boots. His hands were large and gnarled from hard work. He hooked his thumbs in the gun belt slung around his lean hips and eyed Kain in much the same manner Kain was eyeing him.

The second man was slightly younger, shorter, heavier. All else was the same. Both men had quiet faces and eyes that seemed to see everything. They were sizing him up as they had no doubt sized up a hundred men before him. He knew instinctively that if they didn't like his looks the money wouldn't make any difference.

"Did the man tell you what I needed?" Kain jerked his head toward the storekeeper.

"Yup," the older man said.

"The man we're up against, name of Primer Tass, is meaner than a rutting moose. Ever heard of him?"

"A bit, now 'n then."

"Then I guess you know he doesn't play by the rules. He's not one to meet you straight out unless he's forced to. He'll be ahead of us and will put a hole in your back if he gets the chance. He wants one of the women, and if he gets her he'll not leave anyone to tell the tale."

"I heared it's his way." The younger of the men looked straight at Kain without the slightest change of expression on his weathered face.

"The cards are on the table. That's what we're up against. Are you still willing to sign on?"

"I ain't heared nothin' to change my mind none. Have you, Clay?"

"Nothin'."

"I'll pay each of you fifty dollars in gold, feed you, and help you find work if you want it when we get there."

"It's good enuff fer me."

"Me, too."

"I'm Kain DeBolt." Kain held out his hand. He could tell

a lot about a man by his handshake. The ones he got were firm, and he wasn't disappointed.

"Clay Hooker, Van Zandt County, Texas."

"Jeb Hooker, same place."

"Brothers?"

"Yup."

"By the way, these women make the best pie you ever ate. They're going to start a bakery up north."

Clay grinned and the dry skin on his face seemed to crackle. "I ain't had no good pie since I left Texas."

"Ya shoulda said that first off. Clay's stomach is arubbin' on his backbone pert near all the time."

"They're *good* women." Kain looked first one man and then the other straight in the eye.

"In Texas a woman's a woman. Makes no ne'er mind if'n they be good or bad." Jeb took out a long thin knife, cut off a chaw of tobacco and stuck it inside his cheek.

"I know. I've been to Texas, but I needed to hear you say it."

"Don't blame ya none." Jeb passed the plug of tobacco to his brother.

"Do you have good horseflesh?"

"Yup."

"Then get your belongin's and let's ride. The folks started out behind the train for Denver and we'll catch up. I figured if Tass was ready to make his move he'd have done it last night. I'll meet you out front."

"Much obliged." Jeb nodded at the storekeeper.

"Me, too." Clay, the younger one, followed his brother out the door.

"They don't talk much," Kain said.

"Shee . . . it! I thought ya wanted men what'd shoot, not talk ya to death."

Kain ignored the sarcasm and tossed a ten dollar gold piece on the counter. "We'll need extra grub. Give me some coffee, raisins, soda crackers, and a few sticks of candy. Put in some beans, rice, tobacco and a few plugs of whatever the Hookers are chewing. Whatever is left, keep it for your trouble."

He dipped into the cracker barrel and took out a handful of crackers, then went to the front door and looked out into the street. He had discovered the pains didn't bother him so much after he had eaten. He nibbled on the crackers and waited for the Hooker brothers to appear.

They rounded the corner mounted on strong, long-legged horses that stood at least seventeen hands high. They had bedrolls tied behind their saddles and rifles in the scabbards. When they stopped one of them was looking down the street one way, and the other swung around facing the opposite direction. Trail wise men, Kain thought. They've seen a lot of country and trouble to go with it.

Kain gathered up the cloth bag of supplies and offered his hand to the storekeeper. "I'm obliged to you, mister."

"Good luck to ya. I stuck in a bit more a that laudanum. The poor bastard what's got a cancer'll need it afore he gets to the Pearly Gates."

"Thanks." Kain set the sack back down on the counter, took out the bottle and put it in his pocket. "Thanks," he said again before he left.

When he reached the porch he nodded to the Hooker brothers and mounted Big Red. He kept the big horse at a leisurely pace until they reached the Santa Fe Trail. Up ahead he could see the dust cloud from the wagon trial. Vanessa would be right behind it. He kicked his mount into a fast canter, anixous to be near her. The Hooker brothers kept pace with him.

"Go on, missy. Go on 'n puller 'er out."

"Where's Kain?" Vanessa climbed up on the wagon seat and took the reins from John's hand.

"Rode out. He said fer us to go on; he'd catch up." John

was mounted on Vanessa's horse and Henry was driving his wagon, Mary Ben sitting on the seat beside him.

"I knew that he'd ridden out." There was a deep note of irritation in Vanessa's voice. With a flip of her wrist she snaked the whip over the backs of the team, harnesses creaked, the mules strained, and the wagon rolled up onto the trail.

"He went to the mercantile," Ellie said when they had pulled in behind the twenty-five wagon train headed for Denver.

"Why did he go back? He was there yesterday."

"He asked me if I was sure we didn't need anything more from the store. My, my, Vanessa. Do you know he wouldn't take a cent for what he got yesterday? He said for us to keep our money stashed away and not be flashing it—as if I'd do a thing like that."

"This fancy rig makes folks think we're rich. He's thinking of robbers."

"Oh, dear! I thought we were through with such as that. It seems more civilized now that we're in Colorado with the army and all." The dust billowed up from the trail, stirred by a hundred wheels and an even greater number of livestock. It hung like a cloud over the train. Ellie took a small vial of olive oil from her pocket and smeared a few drops on her face with the tips of her fingers. "I hate this dust!"

"So do I. Kain said he knew a shortcut that would bypass Denver. I hope we'll be turning off soon and get away from the other wagons."

"Flitter! I never heard him say that."

"He said it last night, after you went to bed."

"I wondered where you were. Did you walk out with Kain? That's nice, dear," she added before Vanessa had a chance to deny it. "Here, let me put some oil on your cheeks." Ellie coated Vanessa's cheeks with the oil, then dropped the bottle in her apron pocket. "I wonder why John asked Henry to drive his wagon? Mary Ben can drive every bit as well as you or Henry."

"I get the feeling Mary Ben can do a lot of things better than me and Henry." Vanessa looked back. There was no sign of Kain, but John was riding between them and the growth that lined the river. "John probably wanted to ride horseback today. Are you worried about Henry and Mary Ben?"

"A little. Did you see the ribbon and the toilet water he bought for her?"

"Henry loves to give presents. He's never had anyone but us to give to. I bet he was excited. I hope Mary Ben didn't disappoint him."

"The poor child was afraid I'd not let her keep them. That's downright pitiful, isn't it? She's scared to death of us, Vanessa. What in the world will I do if Henry wants to marry her?"

"Mary Ben might not want to marry him. But if she does, talk to her. She knows Henry isn't like other men."

"What would I tell her? That Henry will never be able to support a family?"

"You don't know that. Henry's a grown man. We've got to stop thinking of him as a boy. He's changed a lot since we left Springfield. If he had a shop where he could make whips and quirts—"

"I couldn't bear to have people make fun of him!"

"I know. I couldn't, either."

"And they would. I know they would. He's good and sweet and he'll work his fingers to the bone if someone tells him what to do. I'll have to tell Mary Ben that he'll always have to have guidance. She's got to know that. If that's enough for her, I'll give them my blessing."

"I've been thinking about it, Aunt Ellie. If Mary Ben loves him and he loves her, it may be the best thing in the world for Henry. He should have a wife and a family like other men. And there will be someone besides you and me to look after him."

"But after a while she might get tired of him. She may meet someone else that's . . . brighter, and it would break his heart. We don't know anything about her background, her breeding."

"Poo-poo on breeding, Ellie dear. You didn't know anything about Henry's father when you married him."

"I loved him!"

"Maybe Mary Ben *loves* Henry. He is handsome and sweet too. We don't know anything about Kain, either, but we let *him* join us. We took *him* on trust, why not Mary Ben?"

"But marrying is different—that's forever. Vanessa! Are you thinking about marrying Kain?"

"Oh, for crying out loud! Whatever gave you that idea? He's an adventurer—you've heard his stories. He'll not settle down. He's not the marrying kind."

"I wish he was." Absently, Ellie watched the rolling wagons ahead. "You two would be perfect for each other."

Vanessa had tried to put all thoughts of the night before out of her mind. Her actions had implied that she wanted to be kissed and he had obliged. That was all there was to it, and it was best forgotten. But her mind kept straying back to it like a tongue seeking a sore tooth. She had thought about him through the night and into the morning. He had seemed so sincere and loving when he had held her. Then he'd told her to run along. At the thought of those words, waves of humiliation rolled over her.

An hour after sunup, Kain came alongside and flung the cloth sack of supplies onto the floor of the wagon.

"I bought a few extra supplies, Mrs. Hill. I ran into a couple of friends from Texas. They're riding north, so I invited them to ride with us to Junction City. I hope you won't mind cooking the extra grub."

"Of course I won't mind. Weren't you lucky to run into your friends way out here in the middle of nowhere?"

"How much longer do we have to eat this dust?" Vanessa spoke crossly to keep her voice from wobbling.

"Until the train stops for nooning. We'll pass them and go ahead. There are raisins and crackers in the sack if you get hungry and I'll bring a canteen of water. When we're well ahead of the train, we'll find a place to water the stock. I want to make thirty-five or forty miles today."

"What in the world for? Is there something wrong, Kain?" Ellie had a sixth sense where trouble was concerned, and it always amazed Vanessa that she could ferret it out.

"Well, yes, ma'am. I heard that the weather up north is turning ugly. Snow comes early to the Rocky Mountains. I sure don't want you to arrive in a snowstorm, so we're picking up the pace."

"I hadn't thought of that. Why, of course. Junction City is quite a bit north of Springfield, and higher too. Oh, my! I'm so glad you're with us, Kain. Whatever would we have done without you?"

"You'd have managed, and I'd have missed out on the best pie in Kansas and Colorado."

Vanessa glanced at him. His smile was charming and wholly for Ellie. She sailed the whip out over the backs of the mules with unnecessary force and gritted her teeth. Damn Kain! her mind screamed. She loved him so damn much it hurt, and he didn't even look at her.

"Are you doing all right, Vanessa?" His voice knifed into her thoughts.

"Uh-huh."

"If you get tired, sing out. Henry can move up here and spell you for awhile. Mary Ben can drive John's wagon."

"Henry wouldn't like that. Mary Ben wouldn't, either." She kept her eyes on the swishing tails of the mules.

"I suspect not. They're chattering away like a couple of magpies." He reined in his horse to turn around.

"Kain, I want to thank you for taking an interest in Henry," Ellie said before he could ride away. "I wish we could have known you or someone like you before. I see such a big change in him."

"Don't give me all the credit, Mrs. Hill. I don't believe Henry had as much incentive before. Don't be offended, but you and Vanessa have done too much for him. You've weakened him by protecting him. He needed to learn to take the hard knocks like the rest of us."

"I'm not offended." There was a sadness in Ellie's tone. "I didn't realize we were doing that until just a few weeks ago. We did it because we didn't want to see him hurt."

"Hurting is part of life. You have nothing to compare being happy with if you don't hurt a little."

"But sometimes there's a lot of hurting and only a little happiness."

"That's true. We have to play the game according to the cards we're dealt."

"Mr. DeBolt? Kain? Has Henry said anything to you about . . . Mary Ben?"

"He likes her, Mrs. Hill," Kain said bluntly. "He may be in love with her. I cautioned him about forcing himself on a woman, if that's what's worrying you. I'm sure he'll not do that."

"Of course he won't!" Vanessa glared at Kain, her blue eyes sparkling with indignation. "Whatever gave you the idea he'd do a thing like that?"

"Vanessa?" Ellie looked at her in surprise.

Kain laughed. "Don't get in a snit, my fiery redhead. Henry asked me about what took place between a man and a woman, and I told him. I gave him a few suggestions about how to handle women."

"Of course! You'd know all about that!" Vanessa felt the flush that covered her cheeks. What in the world was the matter with her? She was making a fool of herself.

"Thank you, Kain." Ellie looked as if she wanted to apol-

ogize for Vanessa's outburst. "I wanted to ask you to explain
. . . a few things to Henry, but I couldn't get up the courage."

"You should have had Vanessa ask me." He saw Vanessa
grip her lower lip between her teeth.

"That would hardly have been proper." There was a cool-
ness in Ellie's voice.

Kain realized he had said the wrong thing, but it was the
first thing that had come to his mind. Damn her, when he
was near Vanessa he was as rattled as a sixteen-year-old
meeting a girl for the first time.

"You're right, Mrs. Hill, and I apologize. Vanessa isn't in
a very good mood today. I'd better leave before she takes the
whip to me." He tipped his hat to Ellie and wheeled his
horse.

Vanessa looked back to see him stop and talk to a man on
a big roan. The stranger and John moved to the other side of
the wagons. They were flanked now by four riders. Kain
was doing everything he could to protect her from Primer
Tass, but what about him? Oh, Lordy! Tass wanted to kill
him! How could Kain protect himself from a shot from behind a clump of trees or a boulder? Her stomach did a slow
turnover. Fear for him was tearing her apart, making her
unreasonable.

The next few days found them traveling along the fringe
of the rolling foothills, and at times they passed over naked
rock or plains barren of any growth. The wind, cool and
constant, blew up dust particles that reddened Vanessa's eyes
and chafed her cheeks. In the light of day it seemed as if she
had never been alone with Kain, that he had never kissed her
or called her darling. Reality was her fear that Tass would
follow up on his threats to kill him. Her eyes constantly
sought the distant trail, searching for a place where Tass
could be waiting.

The Hookers, Clay and Jeb, who Kain had introduced to
Ellie as friends, were quiet, polite men. They ate the hearty

breakfasts and evening meals Ellie and Mary Ben prepared, thanked them, and disappeared. After the clean up, the fire was doused and the women went to the wagons. Vanessa was glad for Henry's sake that he wasn't excluded from guard duty along with Mary Ben. He and the yellow dog, who now accepted him as an extention of his mistress, stood the first shift. All the horses were picketed close to the camp. Bred with a strong survival instinct, they would warn them of any approaching man or animal.

Days turned into a week with no sign of Primer Tass. The weather turned cold and wet. Wrapped in a slicker, Vanessa drove the team, her mood as dark as the weather. She didn't even have Ellie's chatter to keep her company since Ellie rode in the back of the wagon, sheltered from the driving rain. Kain was relentless in his drive to make as much time as possible each day. At times he rode up ahead where Vanessa could see him, at other times he was out of her sight for a half a day at a time. It was times like that when she thought she would lose her mind with worry.

One night Vanessa looked at Kain when he came to the cookfire and was shocked by the haggard look on his face. There were deep, dark circles beneath his eyes and his cheeks, covered with a brown stubble, were sunken. She had wondered and worried for several days if he were ill. He silently filled his plate and moved away. He didn't looked directly at her anymore. Had he come to despise her for getting him into this situation? If so, why did he stay with them? He could ride out and leave them anytime.

An idea began to glimmer in the back of her mind. Perhaps she should start thinking about eliminating Tass herself. She, and only she, would be able to approach him without fear of being killed. If she rode out to meet him, he would think she had changed her mind and decided to go with him. When she was sure she was close enough that she wouldn't miss, she would shoot him. The idea took root in her mind and she began to plan.

After two days and two nights of drizzling rain, morning brought the breaking up of the rain clouds. It was still a dark and dreary day, but a brisk wind was blowing the clouds away. They were able to travel only because the trail at this point was rocky. In the middle of the morning a heavily loaded freight wagon pulled by a span of eight mules overtook them. The driver stopped and waved his hand. John rode over and he handed him a paper, then moved on past them. John brought the paper to Vanessa.

"The man said this here was given to him to pass on to a woman named Vanessa."

Vanessa took the paper with an unpleasant feeling in the pit of her stomach. The brief message was written by a crude hand and she could scarcely make out the words: *Ain't nobody gonna keep me away from my woman.*

She crushed the paper in her fist and shoved it down in her pocket while her mind scrambled for a plausible explanation to give her aunt.

"What's that all about? Who in the world knew you were out here, Vanessa?"

"You know how men are, Aunt Ellie. It's from one of the men on that train. I looked at him a few times and he thought I was flirting. Forget him. Oh, look!" On a small knoll two graceful does stood quietly with a buck at their side, unmindful of the wagons passing down the steep trail. "Aren't they pretty? They're so wild and free. This is beautiful country."

"Kain says we should reach Junction City in two or three days. I can't believe it. I'm scared, Vanessa. Somehow I wish we could put it off a little longer."

"For Pete's sake! I can hardly wait. I'm sick of traveling. I want to get in one place and stay there."

"I'm tired of traveling, too. But I keep thinking that we've come on a wild goose chase, and I've decided that when we get there I don't want to try and find Adam Hill or his family."

"You don't have to decide that now."

They reached a valley and the mules walked easily on the ribbon of trail that ran through the green grass. The mountains filled the western sky and ahead of them the forest loomed thick and green. They crossed a creek that ran clear and cool. Birds sprang up from the grasses and a jackrabbit, its ears erect, took giant leaps down the trail ahead and disappeared into the red and gold sumac.

Vanessa saw none of the beauty of the place. Her mind was filled with dread. Primer Tass would do whatever he was going to do before they reached Junction City, she was sure of that. He wouldn't have followed all this way if he hadn't intended to carry out his threats.

"You're worn out, aren't you, Vanessa?" Ellie's calm voice broke into Vanessa's thoughts. "You haven't been yourself since we left Fort Lyon. It's unfair of Kain to expect you to drive every day."

"I don't mind," Vanessa said absently. Then she amended, "Yes, I do! I'm going to tell John I want my horse this afternoon."

"It would be a nice change for you, dear."

Kain was nowhere in sight when they stopped beside a stream to water the horses. The wind had whisked away the heavy clouds and the sun was shining for the first time in days. Vanessa climbed down off the wagon seat and went to where John had tied the horses before he led the mules to water. When he and Henry returned to hitch them up again, Vanessa was mounted and the shotgun was in her hand.

"I'll ride awhile, John."

"No, ma'am. Ya ain't ort a." He walked toward her, and she danced the mount away from him, a frown tightening her features. "Kain said yo're to stay with the wagon, missy."

"Kain has no right to tell me what to do. Besides, this is *my* horse and I'll ride him if I want to." The stricken look that crossed the old man's face cut her to the quick. But, she reasoned, it was better to hurt John than have Kain killed. "I'll stay close by," she promised to soften her previous words.

When the wagons were strung out again, Vanessa rode alongside the lead mules. She could see one of the Hookers riding on the left, and although she couldn't see him, she suspected his brother was on the right. A half hour passed. the only sounds were the jingle of the harnesses and the dull thud of shod hooves on the hard packed trail. Vanessa heard Mary Ben laugh, and looked back to see her and Henry deep in conversation. They had eyes only for each other, and loneliness, too, settled in Vanessa heart.

Time dragged to the middle of the afternoon. There was still no sign of Kain. The uneasy feeling that had been with her since meeting with Tass turned into dread that perhaps what she most feared had happened. The country ahead was wooded and strewn with boulders. The trail inclined gradually and the wagons slowed as the tired mules strained against the traces.

Vanessa suddenly put her heels to her mount and went ahead. She heard John shout but ignored him. This was her chance, maybe her only chance to get to Primer Tass before he got to Kain. In a matter of minutes she was out of sight of the wagons. She studied the terrain before her with careful eyes. There was nothing on the trail, no movement of any kind. But *he* was out there, she could feel it. The dirty, slinking animal was out there waiting to kill Kain!

A wild turkey gobbled and scurried into the underbrush. Fright made Vanessa pull up sharply on the reins. The gelding wheeled and danced nervously. She spoke to him calmly and the big horse quieted, but he was restless. His ears perked and his nostrils flared. Then Vanessa saw the reason for his distress. There was a piece of paper fluttering on a bush beside the trail. She knew immediately it was another message from Primer Tass. She hurried to it and snatched it from the twig that pierced it.

Nothin's changed, purty woman. Nothin' a'tall. We be meetin' soon.

The hateful image of Primer Tass' face flashed across Vanessa's mind with sickening clarity. She urged her horse into a canter to leave the place where he had been. Days and nights of worrying about Kain had frayed her nerves until she couldn't bear it. Something had to be done. Waiting for Tass to make his move was driving her crazy! Deep breaths of cool mountain air lifted her firm breasts and shuddered through her lips as she fought to calm herself for what she had to do. The right or wrong of her intentions didn't enter her mind—she had stopped thinking of Tass as a man.

Suddenly a distant sound behind her caught her ears. She drew up her mount and turned, listening. The gelding's ears began to twitch, then stood straight. He blew through his lips and stared back down the trail. What she had heard was the sound of a running horse, and seconds later Kain's big red horse rounded a bend in the trail and came toward her at full gallop. Should she run? No. He could catch her easily.

"What the hell are you doing out here?" he shouted while he was at least fifty feet away. "Have you lost your mind? Get back to the wagons! *Now!*"

She felt herself go hot with anger beneath the stinging command in his voice. His tone and his angry expression raised her hackles. This time she would not "run along" as she'd done the night they were camped by Fort Lyon. Kain reached her and his hand grabbed for the bridle. Before she thought she lashed out with the ends of her reins and hit him on the arm.

"Keep your damn hands off my horse!"

"You brainless little fool! Get back to the wagon. He's just up ahead. Go back!"

"I know that!" She waved the paper in his face. "Here's another message from him."

"There have been messages left along the trail for the past

week. He's goading us to do something foolish and you're taking the bait."

"I don't care. I'm going to meet him and kill him!"

"For God's sake! That's the most harebrained idea you've had yet. You're no match for him! He's a killer and he's got two men with him. I spotted them and went back to stop the wagons and get the Hookers. Now, goddamn it, go before you get us both killed!"

At that instant, Kain heard the click of metal and saw the flicker of a darker shadow among the thick pines to his right just as he was struck a wicked blow on the shoulder. Searing pain tore through him and he grabbed wildly for the gun in his holster and clutched it with a desperate grip, but couldn't raise it. Pain stabbed him again and he seemed to tumble forward, over and over, round and round in the velvety darkness. His last thought was of Vanessa. He couldn't die now. He couldn't leave her to him.

Chapter Ten

Three shots had been fired in rapid succession. Two struck Kain, the third tore the hat from his head. Vanessa watched him pitch from the saddle to lie facedown beneath his horse's belly. Through the roaring in her ears she heard another sharp, splitting crack of a rifle coming from slightly behind and to the right of them, then more shots farther away. Her feet hit the ground running. Kain! Nothing mattered but Kain. Desperately she pushed at the big red horse who stood protectively over his master.

"Move! Get away from him!" The animal finally moved and Vanessa threw herself down on top of Kain, shielding his head and shoulders with her body.

"Darling, I'm sorry! Please, please don't be dead!" Her hand burrowed beneath his body and sought to feel his heartbeat. The pounding of her own heart and the sobs that came from her throat made it impossible for her to find it. In a frenzy to know if he lived, her experienced fingers moved to the base of his throat and detected a pulse. "You're alive! Oh, thank God! Oh, darling, darling . . ."

It seemed an eternity before there was silence. Vanessa raised her head and looked around. Her shotgun lay on the ground a few feet away where she had thrown it in her haste to get to Kain. Cautiously, she lifted herself off him and made a dash for the gun. With it clasped tightly in her hand, she ran back and hovered over the still figure that lay on the thick bed of pine needles. Her mind refused to think beyond the fact that Kain was still alive and if the bastard that shot him came to finish the job she would kill him.

She heard the sound of a snorting horse and cocked the gun. Crouched over Kain, her finger on the trigger, she waited. To her relief the Hooker brothers came riding toward her from the stand of pines. They reined their horses to a stop and jumped off.

"Is he still out there?" Vanessa's heart was pounding so hard she could scarcely hear her own voice.

"He's gone."

"Gone? You let him go?"

"He ain't goin' far. Is Kain shot up bad?"

Jeb gently turned Kain over and held open his coat. His shirt was soaked with blood from wounds in his side and his shoulder above his heart. It took all Vanessa's willpower to keep from crying out when she saw that his eyes had sunk back into his head and the week's growth of beard on his face did nothing to hide the hollows in his cheeks.

"Is he alive?" Clay asked.

"Yes, he's alive." Vanessa looked up at the men with tear-filled eyes. For the first time she fully realized she had been the cause of this horror. She knew she couldn't bear it if Kain should die and had to be left behind in a lonely grave. Oh, God! Kain couldn't die. He couldn't die!

She had to stop the blood, but she had nothing to stop it with except her shirt. Without hesitation, and unmindful of the two men, she shrugged out of her blanket coat, turned her back, yanked off her shirt, and slipped the coat back on to cover her naked torso.

"Get our wagon up here." She began to think as her father taught her to think when fighting to save a life. *Think of what has to be done, Van. Don't think of who it is you're working on.* "We've got to get the bullets out." Clay was on his horse by the time she finished speaking. She folded her shirt and held it firmly against the two wounds on Kain's upper body. "Why did you let Tass get away?" She spoke without looking at Jeb, her voice resentful. "Why didn't you follow him and kill the dirty backshooter?"

"He was hit bad, ma'am. We put three bullets in him. He was jist ahangin' in the saddle with the horse runnin' full out. Me 'n Clay thought to get back, cause we knowed Kain was hurt bad."

"You're right, of course. But if Tass lives he'll be back."

"He ain't in no shape to do nothin'. Buzzards'll have him by mornin'. If'n they don't, Injuns will. Thar's a mess of Cheyenne camped down thar, 'n he was headin' straight at 'em. They ain't got no use a'tall fer whites right now, 'n I 'spect no more fer a Mex."

"I hope they kill him. I hope they kill him an inch at a time." She looked down at her hands, sticky with Kain's blood. "I wish they'd hurry. Build a fire, Mr. Hooker. I've got medical supplies in the wagon. As soon as it gets here, we'll heat some water and get these bullets out."

"We'd best figger on campin' here, ma'am. I'll build a fire yonder in that clearin'. It'll be out of sight like."

Guilt was a heavy burden on Vanessa's heart, but she would not allow herself to think beyond what she had to do to save Kain's life. Quietly and efficiently she asked that water be heated in two different containers, one she could wash in, the other brought to boiling so she could rinse the instruments she would used to probe the wounds. She had Kain lifted gently into the caravan and placed on her bunk.

After that was done the Hookers went out to stand guard and John tended the fire. Henry and Ellie undressed Kain while Vanessa scrubbed her hands, a procedure her father had insisted was essential when treating an open wound. She and Ellie had worked together before, but never had they worked on one who was as beloved to them as the still man who lay in Vanessa's bunk.

Without having to be told, Henry got out the wooden case containing his late uncle's surgical instruments. He dipped each one in the boiling water and carefully placed them on a clean cloth. Mary Ben watched him with awe and admiration.

The wound in Kain's side appeared to be the most serious at first. But to Vanessa's relief, the bullet had deviated from it's original direction when it struck his hip bone and went out without passing through any vital organs. The problem was getting all the foreign matter out of the wound. She did that by filling a syringe with clear cold water John brought up from the mountain spring and gently squirting the water into the cavity. She dabbed at the wound with clean lint using the tweezers. When this was done she disinfected the lacerated flesh with Lambert's listerine and left the closing of the wound to Ellie.

The bullet that went into Kain's shoulder above his heart was lodged beneath his shoulder blade. Henry's strong arms were needed to lift and hold him while Vanessa made a cut through the skin and extracted the bullet with pincers. Kain moaned and jerked when she did it, but she went determinedly ahead with what she had to do. She wet a compress with the listerine, pressed it on the cut, and then Ellie applied a strip of sticking plaster before Henry gently laid him down.

The three worked as quickly as possible. Hardly a word was spoken except to ask Henry to fetch something. When they had finished, Ellie and Henry dressed Kain in a pair of Henry's long underwear Mary Ben had been warming by the campfire. Vanessa left the caravan and wrapped hot stones to be applied to his feet, between his thighs, to his sides and beneath his armpits.

That Kain would die from shock was what Vanessa feared the most now. Her father had said that during the war many of his patients had died of shock that followed severe bodily injury rather than the injury itself. He had schooled her in what to look for and what to do. Kain had not regained consciousness; that worried her. His skin was cool and his limbs trembled, which were signs of shock. She silently listed the things she could do. She would keep him warm, rub his hands and arms briskly and hold the open bottle of ammonia four to five inches from his nose. What else? Whiskey and honey in hot water. They had the honey Mr. Wisner had given them and there was whiskey in the medicine chest.

Vanessa went back to the caravan. Mary Ben and Henry brought the hot stones to the door. As she and Ellie packed them around Kain's body, he began to tremble even more.

"Henry! Bring a cup of hot water with some honey in it," Vanessa called. "Get the ammonia, Aunt Ellie, and hold it under his nose while I rub his arms."

They worked untiringly, and half hour later warmth returned to Kain's body. His pulse had been weak and rapid but was strong again. He roused briefly after each whiff of the ammonia and then lay quietly.

"We've done all we can do, dear. Now we wait."

"That's the hardest part. It's my fault for riding off like I did. What's wrong with me, Aunt Ellie? Why am I so headstrong?"

"I think things have been going on that everyone knew about but me. John said it was one of the men who stole our mules that shot Kain. You knew he was following us, didn't you? Kain knew it, too. That's the reason he asked his friends to ride along with us. I'm disappointed in you, Vanessa. I thought we were close enough that we could share the bad things that came along as well as the good."

"I didn't want you to worry."

"I'm not a child. I have the feeling you acted unwisely, and that you feel responsible for what happened to Kain. Am I right?"

"Yes, you're right. Later I'll tell you about Primer Tass, but not now. I think if I say another word I'll cry my head off. Stay with Kain, Aunt Ellie, while I wash my hands. Then I'll come sit with him."

Evening came suddenly. The slow column of the campfire smoke drifted upward and was scattered by the thick branches of the pine trees. There was something so everlastingly normal about a cookfire, about boiling coffee and cooking a meal. Vanessa wondered how many times they had done that since they had left Springfield. Regardless of how tired, frightened or worried they were, a simple fire gave comfort and security.

The Hookers came in one at a time, to eat, talk to John and depart after they went to end of the wagon to inquire about Kain. They were polite, but Vanessa knew the men blamed her for what had happened to Kain. She didn't blame them. She'd heard their comments. Voices carried in the still mountain air.

"That woman ort a be pure 'n shamed fer what she done," John said to one of the Hookers. "Kain rode out ever'day lookin' fer that varmint. He done ever'thin' he could. All she had to do was stay with the wagons. It's just plumb bafflin' why she rode out like she done. He jist had to go chasin' her 'n put hisself right out fer Tass to aim at."

"Ain't no use hashin' o'er the whys a woman does what she does. He has to think a heap a that woman, him bein' sick 'n all 'n a ridin' hisself to death. I saw him pukin' his head off a day or two back."

Tears rolled down Vanessa's cheeks. Her heart contracted

painfully as she gazed down at Kain. The light from the kerosene lamp that hung from the ceiling of the caravan played shadow games on his face. He was so pale, so still. John was right. She *should* be pure and shamed by what she'd done—and she was. Leaning over, she kissed his still lips tenderly.

"Please get well, Kain. Wake up so I can tell you how sorry I am," she whispered. "I love you so much it hurts, but it's a hurt that I like. I was afraid Tass would kill you. I was so afraid I was sick. I'd rather have gone off with him than have him hurt you like this."

Ellie came to the door of the caravan with a plate of food; but Vanessa shook her head and Ellie took it away. The camp settled down after the meal. The fire was allowed to die down, but kept alive to heat the flat stones should Kain need them. He was uppermost in everyone's mind.

Vanessa sat beside him and held his hand between her two palms, or stroked the back with her fingertips. Suddenly his eyes were open and he was looking at her.

"Tass?"

"You're awake! How do you feel?"

"Weak. What about Tass?"

"Gone. Don't worry about him. Oh, Kain! Please don't go back to sleep until I tell you how sorry I am. I *am* mule-headed. You're right about everything you said to me. I'll never forgive myself for being so foolhardy."

He grimaced a dismissal of what she was saying. "How bad am I?"

"You were hit in the shoulder and side, but nothing vital was damaged. Unless there are complications, you'll be all right."

"Tass . . . is dead?"

"Jeb said they put three bullets in him and killed the other two. He said Tass rode off, but he didn't think he'd get far. I'm so sorry, Kain. I'd rather have gone with him than have him hurt you like this." Tears rolled from her eyes and fell on their clasped hands.

"Hush talking foolish," he said tiredly. "Get me a cracker. I've got to have something to eat so my gut won't hurt."

"Can you drink some broth?"

"No. Get me a cracker..."

Vanessa hurried out the door. "He's awake. He wants a cracker. Where are they, Aunt Ellie?"

"Cracker? Landsakes. In the blue tin."

Vanessa grabbed the tin and vaulted up the steps, swinging the lower half of the door shut behind her. She pried open the lid with shaky fingers, took out a cracker and held it to his lips. He took a bite and chewed slowly, his tawny eyes fastened on her face. She fed him several soda crackers before he spoke again.

"Was my horse hit?"

"No. When you fell he stood over you and I had to push him away."

"Where's my coat?"

"It's here. Your clothes and your guns are here, too. The rest of your things are in John's wagon."

"Look in the pocket. I brought a ribbon."

Vanessa set the cracker tin on the floor and reached for the coat. Her fingers delved into the right pocket and she found the tight coil of ribbon.

"Is this it?"

"It's for you. I got it back at the fort."

The blue satin ribbon flowed through her fingers. Vanessa looked at him with tearful eyes and her lips trembled when she spoke. "It's lovely. Thank you."

"A red-headed woman should have a blue ribbon. Put it in your hair."

"Oh, Kain! How can you even be nice to me?"

"I want to see it." He lifted his arm and a small grunt of pain came from his lips.

"Don't move this arm," Vanessa said quickly, and placed

his hand gently on his chest. "The bullet that went into your shoulder lodged beneath your shoulder blade. I had to make a hole in your back and take it out."

"You?"

"Of course. I told you my father was a doctor. I helped him take out bullets, and later I took out a few by myself with the help of Henry and Aunt Ellie. I'm sorry we don't have something for the pain. Papa didn't believe in giving laudanum. He said it was too habit-forming."

"Put the ribbon in your hair."

"I've had to be careful about letting my hair down," she confessed nervously. "Aunt Ellie has eyes like a hawk. She would have spotted that bare spot on top of my head right away." Vanessa tried to smile while her fingers worked at the hairpins. He lay there watching, his great tawny eyes wide open and staring. She unraveled the thick braid, then bent over and raked her hair with her fingers until it hung from the top of her head. She tied it at the crown with the ribbon and when she lifted her head it hung down her back like a flowing mane. "This is the only way I can hide my bald spot," she said lightly and waited, hoping Kain would smile.

He didn't—not even slightly. There was a strange quietness about him and he lay staring at her. She didn't know what to say. He lifted his good arm from the bed and she clasped his hand in both of hers. His fingers squeezed hers then reached upward. She flung her hair over her shoulder and he grasped the strands between his fingers.

"I . . . hated for Tass to have this. I was going to get it back."

"It's just hair. It will grow back."

They looked at each other for a long time. Her eyes were brilliant with unshed tears. Her eyes were what he'd noticed about her the first day he met her in Dodge City. Now they anxiously searched his for a glimmer of forgiveness.

"I don't know if I can get up. You'll have to get Henry or the Hookers to help me."

"You can't get up. You'll break the stitches and start bleeding again. If you lose any more blood you'll go into shock."

"I can't stay in your wagon."

"You certainly will! You don't realize how close you came to being killed."

"It doesn't matter. Call Mrs. Hill. I want to talk to her . . . alone."

She met his gaze evenly. "You're not going to forgive me, are you?" she whispered.

"There's nothing to forgive."

"I almost got you killed! John said I should be ashamed for what I did. I am ashamed, terribly ashamed. Why am I so headstrong, Kain? Why is it so hard for me to let someone else take charge?"

"Vanessa . . . Vanessa, you can't help the way you are. You're a woman who needs a strong hand."

"A chore you're unwilling to take on?" She almost choked as the enormity of her words hit her. When he didn't answer her taut nerves made her rush into speech. "I was going to meet him and kill him before he killed you. I couldn't stand to just sit and wait for that . . . animal to make the first move," she told him, unable to keep the quaver out of her voice. His rejection was the hardest thing she had ever had to endure.

"It isn't easy to shoot a man, and while you hesitated, which you would have, he would have had you. You didn't stand a chance. Now, say no more about it," he added impatiently.

Vanessa looked down at him. Even his voice was closing her out. When he said nothing more she placed his hand gently on the bed beside him and stood.

"I'll get Aunt Ellie. Are you going to tell her about Adam Hill?"

"No."

Kain watched her leave and closed his eyes wearily. She

was hurt. But what the hell could he say? He had nothing to offer her. It would have been better if Tass had killed him, he thought. But then Vanessa would have had to live with the guilt that she had caused his death. He opened his eyes, afraid he would fall asleep. He had something to do, something he should have done before this.

Ellie came in and took the stool beside his bunk. Her cool hand smoothed the hair from his brow and then rested on his forehead for an instant.

"No fever, thank goodness. We were so worried about you. Are you hungry?"

"No, ma'am. I want you to write something for me. Will you get a pencil and paper?"

"Of course . . . but Vanessa writes a beautiful hand."

"I don't want her to know about this yet. Please, Mrs. Hill."

"All right, Kain."

Ellie took a box of writing supplies from the compartment at the front on the wagon and returned to sit on the stool beside him. She opened a tablet of lined paper and took a pencil in her hand.

"I want to make a will." Kain's quiet words dropped into the stillness and Ellie almost dropped the pencil.

"Oh, no! You're not . . . Didn't Vanessa tell you that we have every hope you'll—"

"There's a chance I won't die from the bullet wounds, but nevertheless, I'm going to die soon," he said calmly. "I want Vanessa to have a house and some land I have near Junction City. If I die without a will, my estate will go to . . . a relative I'm not fond of and I don't approve of."

"Oh, Kain! Oh, dear boy! What are you talking about?"

"I have a cancer that will surely kill me."

"Oh, dear God!"

"I want your promise to say nothing about it."

"Of course, I promise. But . . . are you sure?"

"I'm sure. Now write, please. I, Kain DeBolt being of

sound mind. . . ." He dictated slowly, then asked her to read back what she had written. He nodded his approval, and she handed him the pencil and held the tablet so he could sign his name. "Date it at the top, and sign your name as a witness," he instructed wearily. "You'll find the address of my solicitor in New York in my saddlebags. If . . . when something happens, write to him and tell him about the will. He'll know what to do."

"I can't believe you're saying these things to me." Ellie clasped his hand tightly. "Don't you have anyone? Family or—" She sniffed back the tears. "Oh, shoot! I'm trying hard to not . . . break down."

"Don't cry for me, Mrs. Hill. I asked you to do this because I know you're a strong woman. You've got to be to endure what you have and still hold your head high."

"Thank you, Kain. You'll not be alone. Vanessa and I will take care of you."

"No! Vanessa is not to know. When the time is near I'll know and I'll go away."

Ellie brought his hand to her tear wet cheek. "I'll do whatever you want me to do. But until . . . I'll be with you."

"Thank you. It means a lot to know someone cares."

"You've become very dear to me, Kain. I care, and Vanessa cares. She may be in love with you. I've never seen her in such a state as she was today while we were working on you."

"She feels guilty is all."

"Oh, no. It's more than—"

"Aunt Ellie?" Vanessa's voice reached them from the end of the wagon.

"Put that away," Kain whispered.

"Don't worry." Ellie lifted the lid of her trunk and slipped the tablet inside.

"Are the Hookers out there?" Kain asked in a louder voice.

Vanessa climbed into the wagon and glanced curiously at her aunt as she moved aside.

"You're awfully pert for a man with three holes in him."

"Three? You said I was hit twice."

"Don't forget I had to cut a hole in your back to get the bullet out."

"I bet you enjoyed that," he said dryly.

"He's going to live, Aunt Ellie. He's back to being mouthy." She gave a nervous little laugh.

Kain tried to smile, but it was a meaningless flexing of his facial muscles.

"Could you eat a cup of potato soup?" Ellie asked.

"Don't go to any bother, ma'am."

"I saved it from supper. I'll get it."

"Did I hear you ask for the Hookers?" Vanessa inquired after Ellie left. "They're not out there, but John and Henry want to see you if you feel up to it. They—we were all so worried about you. We're glad you're going to be all right."

"Is this your bed?"

"Yes. I'll sleep in Aunt Ellie's so I can hear you if you need anything. She'll sleep in with Mary Ben. It's all been decided."

"I'll get up tomorrow."

"Tomorrow? You'll do no such thing. You'll stay flat on your back for a week if I have to tie you to the bunk."

"We should get to Junction City the day after tomorrow."

"We're not traveling tomorrow. We're staying here so those wounds can start healing."

"Damn it, Vanessa! John and the Hookers know this is dangerous country. We have to leave here at daylight."

"I was thinking of you. Tomorrow you may feel a lot worse than you do now."

"I know. I've been shot before. I could be out of my head with a fever by this time tomorrow. That's why I'll tell you this now. Do what John and the Hookers think best and don't give them any sass."

"All right, Kain. If that's what you want, I'll—" she had to stop when sobs threatened to close her throat. She found herself looking directly into his eyes and watched his gaze fall away and become fixed on her blue sunbonnet hanging at the end of the wagon.

"When we get to Junction City, ask directions to a place called The House. All you have to say is The House. It's about five miles out of town. I own it and the land around it. The woman that rented it wrote that she left it boarded up. I want you to stay there—all of you. Don't argue, Vanessa," he said tiredly. "Do this one thing for me without arguing."

"We'll take you there and stay until you're on your feet." She said the words as though they were being dragged out of her against her will. "Do you want to see John and Henry?"

His gaze returned to her white face and he felt his mind grind to a halt. The silence that enveloped them was so complete that he could hear Ellie's voice in the Wisner wagon telling Mary Ben how glad she was they were nearing the end of their journey. Every word was as distinct as though she were speaking a few feet away. Into that continuing stillness, he turned his face away and murmured, "I guess so."

At the end of two days of hard travel they came down out of the foothills and entered a wide valley that stretched for miles. On each side lay rolling hills topped with glossy evergreen, and beyond were snow-capped mountains. It was a breathtaking sight, one Vanessa was unable to appreciate because she was so worried about Kain. He was hurting and as cross as a bear. His stomach had been troublesome, and he would allow only Ellie to attend him.

Junction City was a town of unpainted buildings and rutted streets. Small boxlike houses set in rows fanned out from the main street which was lined with false-fronted stores. Vanessa drove into town with Jeb and Clay Hooker leading the way. She looked with dismay at the crude buildings, the curs that ran out from between the buildings to nip at the heels of the mules, the big-wheeled freight wagons, the loafers sitting along the boardwalks and the drunken Indians who staggered along the street. The double swinging doors of the saloon opened and a man was tossed headfirst into the street.

Ellie sat stiffly erect, her face white and drawn, her hands clenched tightly together. She turned her head and stared dully at Vanessa.

"We've traveled hundreds of miles for this?" she asked in a low, strickened voice.

Chapter Eleven

Jeb reined in his horse and waited for the wagon to catch up.

"Stop here, ma'am, and I'll do some askin'. Ain't no use us goin' on if'n the place we're lookin' fer is back yonder."

Vanessa pulled up on the reins and the wagon stopped in front of the harness and blacksmith shop. It was no longer difficult for her to remain quiet and let someone else take over. Humiliation had drained her of energy and she hurt as she had never hurt before.

"Hey, thar, mister." The man Jeb spoke to had come out of the harness shop with several horse halters hanging from the crook of his arm. The cowboy put his foot in the stirrup, swung into the saddle and turned his mount toward them.

"Were ya talkin' to me?"

"Howdy. We'd be obliged if you'd give us some help in findin' a place. We're looking fer The House. That's what the feller said the place is called: The House. Would ya be knowin' where it'd be?"

"The House? Why shore. Ever'body knows where The House is at." A huge grin split the cowboy's weathered face. He leaned on the saddle horn and grinned with open admiration at Vanessa and Ellie, then craned his neck to see who was in the wagon behind. "Yo're a-goin' to open The House?"

"Figgerin' on it." The Texan's voice was less friendly and he edged his horse between the cowboy and the caravan.

"The House is openin'?" The cowboy threw back his head and let out a wild yell. "Yahoo . . . ee!"

Vanessa looked at him in astonishment, then looked quickly around. His bellow hadn't attracted the slightest bit of attention from the people in the street or on the boardwalks.

"Yo're a-goin' to open The House!" he repeated excitedly. "Doggy! I'm pure proud to hear it. If thar's anythin' I can do to help ya get settled in, ma'am, jist send out a call fer Stan Taylor. Now, don't ya be fergittin' that name. Yes siree, Stan Taylor'll shore be proud to help ya ladies out. Jist wait till the fellers hear."

"Give us a pointer, mister, so we can be on our way." Jeb's voice was hard with impatience.

"Jist go right on through town and foller the river road. Hit's a plank house painted white. Hit's a right purty place, but it's been boarded up fer 'bout a year now." The cowboy leaned over and spoke to Ellie. "Don't ya be frettin' none, ma'am. Stan Taylor'll spread the word. The boys'll be plumb tickled to hear The House is openin'."

Jeb nodded to Vanessa and she slapped the reins against the backs of the mules and the wagon moved ahead.

"We're obliged to ya." Jeb dismissed the man with a nod of his head.

The cowboy grinned. He tipped his hat to Mary Ben when she passed, then headed for the saloon to tell the news.

"What in the world was that about?" Ellie drew her shawl closer about her shoulders. "He was sure friendly."

"Too friendly, if you ask me. He acted as if he hadn't seen a woman for years. What's the matter with these men out here?"

"I doubt he's seen one as pretty as you. You *are* a pretty girl, dear. You don't know what a beauty you are, do you?"

"Pshaw! Beauty doesn't get you anywhere, Aunt Ellie. I might as well have been as ugly as a mud fence."

"Speaking of Kain—"

"Who is?" Vanessa countered sharply.

"Anyway, dear," Ellie said patiently, "when we get out of town, stop and let me get in back with him. The last time I looked in on him he was sleeping. He may want a drink of water by now."

"I get the feeling he'd just as soon never set eyes on me again. If I hadn't promised him we'd stay at his house we'd leave him there with the Hookers and camp while we look around for a place of our own."

"He didn't mean anything last night, Vanessa. He'd suffered something terrible jostling around back there all day."

"It was his own fault. He wouldn't let us stop."

"I'm sure he had his reasons, dear."

"Why are you always defending him? You heard him tell me to get out and leave him alone. That was awfully hard to take, Aunt Ellie."

"I'm sure he didn't intend to speak so sharply."

"I told him I was sorry. What more can I say?"

"He was throwing up, dear. I don't think any man would want a young woman to see him vomit. Especially if he was fond of her."

"Oh, fiddle faddle! Don't give me that nonsense about him being *fond* of me. We've been at swords' point since the day we met and he can't stand the sight of me."

They reached the edge of town and Vanessa stopped the wagon. Henry rode up to lift his mother down. When they started up again he rode alongside.

"What did you think of the town, Henry?"

"It's nothing like Springfield. I don't think I want to live in town, Van."

"Maybe we won't have to. We'll stay at Kain's until he's better, then we'll decide what to do."

After only a few minutes of conversation, Henry drifted back to ride beside John's wagon so he could be near Mary Ben, and Vanessa allowed herself a moment of self-pity. Henry was so in love with Mary Ben that he wanted to be with her all the time, Vanessa thought painfully. They shared what they had seen or done during the day, how the country looked, how tired they were or how scared. Loneliness crept into her bones like an ache. There was a clammy, sick feeling in the pit of her stomach. It had been there for the previous two days, sapping her strength, eating away at her self-esteem and so controlling her thoughts that she had not been able to eat or sleep.

The night before she had just stepped into the wagon to see how Kain was feeling when he asked her to go and leave him alone. His tone had hurt her even more than the words he had spoken. Thank God she had been able to hold back the tears until she could grab up a bucket and go to the stream for water. There she had cried as she had not done in years. After supper she had crawled into the wagon with Mary Ben, leaving Ellie to tend to Kain during the night. Even now, thinking about it, she blinked her eyes rapidly to keep them from filling.

Vanessa brought her attention back to the mules and slapped their backs with the reins. The road ran alongside a rushing stream. It was level and meandering and quiet after the noise of the town. Several riders were on the trail ahead. As the distance between them and the wagons grew smaller they shifted into a single line and curiously eyed the fancy caravan and the girl driving it. They tipped their hats and Vanessa nodded coolly.

When Vanessa first saw the white house in the distance, it didn't occur to her it was Kain's house until they drew closer and she could see the planks nailed across the doors and lower windows. It was larger than she had expected and had a shiny tin roof. Surrounded by large oaks, it loomed tall and square with a barn and several sheds and outbuildings behind it. Dry, brown weeds were knee-high in front, and porch and window boxes were empty of flowers. The place looked sadly neglected, Vanessa thought, but with some work it could be beautiful again.

Jeb rode ahead and opened the wire gate so the wagons could enter. Vanessa drove through and pulled the team to a halt between the house and the barn. She sat on the high seat looking around, uncertain as to what to do. Evening was approaching and a chill wind was blowing down from the mountains. She shivered, but more from nervousness than the cold. The back door of the caravan opened and Ellie called to Henry.

"Kain said to get some tools and pry the boards off the door, son. We'll cook supper on a cookstove tonight."

Vanessa climbed down and began to unhitch the tired team. She and Mary Ben helped John turn the mules and horses into the pole corral where they rolled in the dust, then began cropping the sparse grass. Henry called to Mary Ben to come look at the house.

"Go on. I can finish." Vanessa slung the heavy harness over her shoulder and went to the barn. John followed carrying the horse collars. It was the first time she had been alone with him since Kain had been shot.

"John, I want you to know I'm sorry for what I said that day you tried to stop me from riding away from the wagon. You see . . . I thought I was so right, that by riding out to meet Tass I could keep him from killing Kain.""

"It's all right, missy. I knowed why ya done it."

"I heard you say I should be ashamed. I am, and for the way I talked to you. If not for you and Mary Ben and Kain——" She stopped, turned her head and sniffed back tears, hating herself for being weepy. "We were dumb to think we could make it out here alone, weren't we, John?"

"Ya might be lackin' in knowin' the trail, but ya know how to crack heads," he said with a grin that showed his tobacco-stained teeth. "Don't ya be worryin' none, missy. Ya got grit. Ain't no city woman I ever heard of could a stood up to drivin' that span of mules clear to Colorady."

"Oh, John, if you don't be careful I'm going to start liking you a lot."

"Wal, now, wouldn't that be plumb grand? I ain't had no purty redheaded woman after me fer quite a spell."

They left the barn just as Mary Ben and Ellie came out of the caravan with armloads of sheets and bedding. The young girl was talking excitedly to Ellie.

"Now don't that jist beat all?" John took off his hat and scratched his head. "Women's jist like a cluck a hens when it comes to buildin' a nest. They jist can't wait ta get at it without givin' a thought to a man's empty belly."

"Aunt Ellie's in her glory. I guess I better go help. Thank you, John, for not being mad at me."

"As long as we're apassin' out thanky, I thanky, lass, fer bein' friendly like to my . . . Mary Ben."

"I think Henry wants to marry her. How do you feel about it?"

"If'n it's what she wants 'n if'n Mrs. Hill ain't carin', I'm plumb tickled. Mary Ben ain't goin' to be no drag on nobody. She'll hold up her end 'n be a heap a help to Mrs. Hill."

"Henry will be good to her, you know that."

"I know it. I done took his measure. He'll do jist fine with Mary Ben helpin' him."

Vanessa looked at the old man. He dipped his head sideways and studied her. She had the feeling he was trying to reassure her about something. The smile on his face was hard and bright and strangely pleased.

Her legs were unsteady, but her shoulders were square

and her back straight as she walked up the path to the house. She stopped at the end of the caravan, glanced in, and saw Kain sitting on the bunk trying to put on his boots. She didn't even consider offering her help; she didn't think she could bear another rebuff from him. He looked up and held her with his gaze. They continued to face each other, neither speaking, neither moving, while the silence built up between them. Vanessa watched him carefully for some slight break, for a softening in his expression, but there was none. She turned and walked slowly to the house.

She stepped up onto the lean-to porch feeling somewhat like an unwelcome guest, paused uncertainly, then entered the kitchen. It was large and square, with cupboards along one side and a black iron cookstove on the other. An oblong table large enough to seat a dozen people took up the far end. She could see into a pantry through one open door and into a hall through the other. The sounds of a hammer and male voices came from somewhere inside the house.

Ellie came in from the hall followed by Mary Ben.

"Isn't this a lovely house, Vanessa? Mary Ben and I have been preparing a bed for Kain. There's a bedroom down here and five more upstairs, plus rooms in the attic. Did you ever see the like? There's twice the room we had back home. Oh, it's grand to be in a house again! I didn't realize I was so tired of that wagon."

"What do ya want me to do now, Mrs. Hill?"

"You can start a fire in the cookstove, Mary Ben. The house has been shut up for so long it has a damp feel about it."

"I ain't never seen such a fancy stove. I don't know as I know how."

"Vanessa, will you show Mary Ben how the stove works? Kain is worn out. I want to get him in here and in that bed as soon as I can."

"I'm in."

Vanessa turned to see Kain leaning against the doorframe.

The part of his face not covered by whiskers was pale, and there were deep dark circles under his eyes. He was holding his hand to his side.

"My goodness, Kain." Ellie rushed to him. "You shouldn't have gotten out of that wagon by yourself. Mary Ben, help me get him to bed."

"No," he said. "Not yet."

Vanessa made a quick turn and stepped into the hall, but not before she had gazed up and been caught by the look in Kain's eyes. Surprise held her immobile for seconds, unable to tear her eyes away from his brooding amber eyes, which held something other than physical pain. What was it? she wondered.

Kain took a quivering breath and sank down onto the chair. Damn! He was weaker than he thought. The look on Vanessa's face had cut him to the quick. She was hurting. An old saying came to mind, "you always hurt the one you love the most." After he had shouted at her to get out the night before he would have given anything to recall the words. Later, trying to justify his outburst, he told himself he was desperate to keep her from seeing the blood in his vomit. Damn! Why did he have to have the attack just when she entered the caravan? It had been almost a week since he'd had the terrible pain in his stomach.

Kain watched Ellie move swiftly and confidently about the kitchen, preparing to scrub away a years accumulation of dust and mouse droppings from the counter and tables before she started the evening meal. She reminded him of Cooper Parnell's mother; slim, blue-eyed, blond hair. However, she was younger than Mrs. Parnell. It had been a comfort to him having her know what he faced. It surprised him to realize he had become fond of her. He only hoped that he would be around to help her when she had to face Adam Clayhill.

While he was flat on his back the last two days with the worry that Tass would steal Vanessa lifted, he'd had plenty of time to think. There was enough land here to support a good-sized herd of cattle. If the Hookers, with the help of John and Henry, would stay on and work the place, he was sure it would pay off. His friend, Griffin, would make him a loan, or go partners, but—he put a halt to his thoughts. He wouldn't be around to see a loan paid off.

"The first thing we need to do is get a cow. I miss having fresh milk and butter. Kain? Kain, are you awake?"

Kain lifted his arms so Ellie could wash the table. "I'm awake. Mr. McCloud at the mercantile can tell you where you can buy one."

"I think I'll ask John if he'll go in tomorrow and find us two good milch cows. I want some hens and a rooster or two. Next spring we'll set some hens and get some chicks. Mary Ben, find Henry and tell him when he finishes what he's doing to bring in some wood for the cookstove."

"Winter comes early here and it takes a lot of firewood to keep a place this size warm in the winter," Kain said as he watched Mary Ben skip happily out of the room. "There's plenty of timber in the hills behind the barn."

"My goodness! There's so much to do. This is a grand place, Kain. I feel so much better with a solid roof over my head."

"Don't get too used to it, Aunt Ellie. It shouldn't take more than a few days for Mr. DeBolt to get on his feet, then we'll go back to town." Vanessa stood in the doorway, her hands deep in the pockets of her britches.

"But dear, it will take a good while for him to be strong enough to take care of himself. The least we can do is get this place clean and livable for him. My land, it's beyond me how a place can get so dirty closed up, but it can. The floors are filthy, and the windows—"

"Are you hiring on as his housekeeper?" Vanessa cut in quietly.

"Well . . . I—"

"Cows? Chickens? It sounds as though you plan to stay here permanently."

"We . . . can take a cow."

Vanessa saw the look exchanged between her aunt and Kain and willed herself not to just walk away.

"Have you forgotten that we came out here to find Henry's relatives and open a bakery, not work in someone's home for our keep?" She forced herself to look directly at the man sitting at the table. He was watching her and she refused to be moved by the shadow of hurt in his amber eyes.

"No, dear, I haven't. I also haven't forgotten that it's possible we wouldn't have gotten here at all except for Mr. DeBolt."

Ellie stood at the end of the table with the wet cloth in her hand. Was that guilt on her face? Vanessa wondered. Ellie had not only been like a mother to her, but also her best friend and confidante. Ellie had always been there when she needed her. She had changed; Henry had changed. Ellie had switched her loyalty to Kain DeBolt. Henry had fallen in love with Mary Ben; and although she was happy for him, it seemed strange to not have him depending so much on her. In Springfield they had been a close family. Here, they each had a different priority. Was that what this country did to people?

"I suppose there comes a time when families break up." Vanessa spoke slowly because she felt as if she'd swallowed a cup of sand. "I hadn't expected ours to do so quite so soon. I understand why this place appeals to you, Aunt Ellie. It's something like the farm back home. It's ready-made for you—a house to tend, meals to cook for hungry men, and you have Mary Ben to fuss over. Perhaps it's best that you and Henry stay here. My only advice would be that you find out how long your employment will last, because I don't think Mr. DeBolt is the kind of man who will be content to stay very long in this dull place after seeing the wonders of the world."

Vanessa's brilliant blue eyes went from her aunt's stricken

face to the man sitting quietly in the chair. She was proud that she could keep her eyes steady as they looked into his.

"How do you know I wouldn't be content to stay here?"

Vanessa didn't answer.

"I don't understand what you're talking about." Ellie twisted the wet cloth around and around in her hands. "Are you saying that . . . that you'd rather we not stay here for awhile?"

"I said that I'm not staying, Aunt Ellie. That doesn't mean that you can't stay. You feel obligated to take care of Mr. DeBolt for what he did for us. You can do that without me. I'm sorry I was responsible for his being shot, but I don't intend to spend the rest of my life on my knees because of it." She walked around the table and headed for the door.

"Obligated? You're not obligated to do anything for me you stubborn little redheaded mule!" Kain snapped.

"Vanessa! You're not going now?" Ellie's voice stopped her at he door, and she turned.

"Of course not. The mules are too tired. I'll go in the morning." She went out without a backward glance.

Ellie stood looking at the closed door. "Oh, Kain! She means it. It isn't a threat."

"No. It isn't a threat. She's just that bullheaded."

"Oh, my. I knew she was hurt, but—"

"But she's stubborn, feisty, sharp-tongued, and irritating!" Kain's voice reflected his annoyance, Ellie's eyes mirrored her distress.

"If she's so *irritating*, then why are you so desperately in love with her?" Ellie demanded, facing Kain. She was shocked and hurt at Vanessa's attitude, but she rose to her defense.

"Because . . . I can't help myself!"

"Oh, Kain!"

"Do you think I want to love her now that it's too late? It only complicates things."

"Tell her," Ellie urged. "Tell her and be happy for the time you have left. She loves you. Give her something to remember."

"No! She'll meet someone else."

"I didn't. I had one love in my life. It may be the same with Vanessa."

"I'll not leave her to raise my child alone."

"I've never regretted having Henry, not for one minute!"

"I'll not saddle her with that responsibility."

"But you may not—"

"I won't take the chance."

"Then Henry and I will leave with Vanessa in the morning. I'm sorry, Kain. She's my daughter in every sense of the word except for the fact I'm not her natural mother. I raised her and I love her, stubbornness and all. If she's uncomfortable here we'll go."

"Don't say anything until I can talk to her. Right now I've got to lie down." He pushed himself to his feet with a grimace of pain. "After supper tell her I want to talk to her. She should be cooled off by then."

"She may not go."

"Then tell her I need some more stitches, or that I'm bleeding all over the floor—tell her anything, but get her in there and see that we're not disturbed."

The door opened and they both looked quickly to see if it was Vanessa. Henry came in with an armload of wood for the cookstove.

"I found some already cut, Ma. Mary Ben is coming with the kindling."

"Put it in the woodbox, son, then help Kain into the bedroom. He's worn out."

Henry dropped the wood into the nearly empty box, then held out his arm to Kain. "I sure do like it here, Kain. Mary Ben likes it, too. She's never lived in a house before."

"There's a lot to be done before winter." Kain panted from the effort it took to walk out of the room. "You'll have to haul in some hay for feed and drag some logs down from the hills for firewood."

"I can do that. You just tell me what to do." In the bedroom at the back of the house he eased Kain down onto the bed. "You want that I pull off your boots?"

"I'd appreciate it, Henry. Bending over is the hardest thing to do right now."

"You're bleeding. Van should put on another bandage."

"I'll have her do it after supper. Right now I'm so tired all I want to do is get into bed." Kain unfastened his belt and Henry pulled his pants off and covered him. "Thanks. When you get around to it, will you get my gear out of the wagon and bring it in here?"

"Sure. If there's anything you want, call out." Henry walked out of the room and closed the door.

Kain lay listening to the sounds coming from the other rooms. He heard Henry's voice and Mary Ben's giggle and their footsteps going up the stairs. He knew that as soon as they were out of sight Henry would grab Mary Ben and kiss her. Being in love with Henry had put a bloom in the cheeks of John's young waif and a sparkle in her eyes.

Kain closed his eyes and saw Vanessa's white face, fiery hair and brilliant blue eyes. His breath became heavier and a hunger to have her to love and care for centered in his loins and pulsed there. It seemed to him he had searched through a lifetime of emptiness to find her. Now forces beyond his control were closing in on him, forcing him out of the warmth of this family circle. He would be left alone with the Hookers if he couldn't persuade Vanessa to stay. He sighed deeply.

Ellie filled a plate with food, set it on a wooden tray she found in the cupboard and took it to Kain. When she returned she took her place at the table. Henry and Mary Ben were still excited about being in the house and chatted about the things they had found in the different rooms.

"There's a tin bathtub in the closet room, Van. It's big at one end and little at the other, just like the one you had back home." Henry's smile faded when he couldn't get a response from his cousin. "You like a bath. I'll carry the water for you, Van."

"Thank you, Henry. Yes, I'd like very much to have a bath."

The Hookers and John finished their meal and took their hats from the pegs on the wall beside the door.

"You're not leaving?" Ellie's worried face expressed her concern.

"No, ma'am. We'll turn in if there ain't nothin' we can do till mornin'." Jeb always turned his hat around and around in his hand while talking to Ellie.

"You're not going to sleep outside when there's all this room." She waved her hand toward the front of the house.

"No, ma'am. There's a bunkhouse. We'll bed down there."

"But . . . sheets and things—"

"Don't worry none 'bout that, ma'am. It'll be a plumb treat to sleep on a bunk."

"Mr. Wisner, can I sleep in here if it's all right with Mrs. Hill?" Mary Ben got up from the table and stood behind her chair. Ellie turned and looked at her in surprise.

"Of course you'll stay in here. A bunkhouse is no place for a young girl. Isn't that right, Mr. Wisner?"

"Right as rain. Stay with Mrs. Hill, Mary Ben." He slammed his hat down on his head and followed the Hookers out the door.

"Well, now." Ellie took a big tin pan from the hook on the wall and set it on the cookstove. "Mary Ben and I will clean up while you take a bath, Vanessa." She poured water from the teakettle into the pan. "There's hot water in the reservoir, Henry, and plenty in the teakettle for the dishes."

"I'll help with the dishes first," Vanessa said.

"No. Go take a bath. Mary Ben would you like to have a tub bath?"

"Oh! Could I, Mrs. Hill?"

"Of course. By the time we're finished here the water will be hot again."

"I'll carry the water for you, too." Henry placed his hand on Mary Ben's shoulder and smiled down at her lovingly.

Vanessa saw her aunt watching him. Aunt Ellie, too, was losing something, she thought. Aloud she said, "I'll get some clean clothes out of the wagon." She threw her shawl around her shoulders and went out into the darkness.

Inside the caravan she felt around on the shelf for the matches and lit the lamp. She could smell the listerine she had used to wash Kain's wounds and her eyes sought the pillow on her bunk that showed the indentation where his head had lain. She had tended to him, loved him in secret, offered herself and been refused. What more was there? she asked herself. Nothing at all, the practical side of her nature replied, and she had to face that discouraging fact.

She took a dress and undergarments out of her trunk. She would have to wear a dress tomorrow when she went into town, she reasoned. Anyway, she was tired of wearing the britches.

It was sheer luxury to sink down into the tub of warm water. Vanessa sighed deeply, leaned back and closed her eyes. This was what she had missed the most during the long trip from Missouri; the moist heat, scented soap, the joy of being clean. After she scrubbed every inch of her body she worked a thick lather into her hair, rinsed it once in the bath water and again in the bucket of water Henry had left beside the tub.

When she had dried herself and dressed she wrapped a towel around her head and went back to the kitchen.

"Feel better, dear?" Ellie hung the dish cloth on a rack beside the stove.

"Oh, yes. That's a wonderful tub. Whoever lived here before must have liked a bath as much as I do. There's even a hole in the bottom of the tub with a stopper in it. It looks like the water runs out through the pipe in the wall. You won't even have to empty it, Henry."

"Sit here and dry your hair, Vanessa." Ellie pulled a chair up close to the stove and lowered the oven door. "I was telling Mary Ben about those two dresses of mine that are so short I can't wear them any longer. The water I washed them in must have been too hot, they shrank so. I'll go out to the wagon and get them and my sewing box. I'm sure they'll be too big around."

After Ellie left Vanessa sat for a moment rubbing her hair with the towel. Suddenly she realized it was quiet and looked over her shoulder. Mary Ben and Henry stood close together. Her arms were about his neck and he was kissing her. It hadn't taken Henry long to learn about women, Vanessa thought dryly. Kain must have been a good teacher. She opened her mouth to make a teasing remark, then closed it, not wanting to intrude on their time alone. She turned back to smooth the ends of her hair with a wide-toothed comb so she could twist it and pin it to the top of her head before her aunt returned. Only Kain knew that Primer Tass had cut the swath of hair from the top of her head. Thank God she no longer had to worry about him.

"Stop, Henry. Yore mama'll come in—"

"I like kissing you."

"I like it, too, but not now."

The whispered words reached Vanessa's ears as she was pinning up her hair, and she turned to see Mary Ben pushing herself away from Henry. He had a grin on his face and hers was beet red. Mary Ben walked over to stand beside the stove and Henry went to empty the tub.

Mary Ben stood on first one foot and then the other, her hands clenched together in front of her. Vanessa looked up to see her staring at her with her bottom lip caught firmly between her teeth. She was worried, Vanessa thought, that she didn't like what was happening between her and Henry.

"You like Henry a lot, don't you, Mary Ben?"

"Yes'm."

"He's a handsome man. The girls back home eyed him, some even came to the farm on the pretext of visiting me so they could see more of him. When they realized that he's still very much like a small boy they either ignored him or said hateful things to him. It hurt his feelings. He didn't understand it."

"That wasn't nice of them. Henry ain't got a mean bone in him." Mary Ben's voice rose defensively.

"He's in love with you. Did you know that?"

"Yes'm. He told me he was."

"How do you feel about him? A few kisses are one thing, but how do you feel about spending the rest of your life with him? He'll never be any different. He'll always be happy and he'll never worry about where the next meal will come from."

"I know it. I guess I love him. I don't know, I ain't never loved nobody before. I jist know I want to be with him, take care of him and be a help to him. I ain't never goin' to let nobody do no hurt to Henry," she added fiercely.

"That's the way I feel about him. I've been looking after him all my life." Vanessa stood. "I'm glad there'll be someone to help me."

"Does that mean you don't care if . . . Henry likes me?"

"It means I'm happy for both of you. Henry is like a brother to me. Now I'll have a sister, too."

Ellie came through the door and the wind sucked it closed behind her. The loud bang resounded throughout the house. Her arms were full.

"It's cold out there and the wind has come up. I'm glad we're not camping out tonight." She put the things she was carrying on the table and smoothed her hair back from her face. "I brought in the medical chest, Vanessa. Kain's side has broken open again and we've got to put a new bandage on it. Will you do it, dear, while I take up this dress for Mary Ben?"

"No."

"No?" Ellie spun around in shocked surprise.

"No, I won't do it."

"Vanessa Cavanaugh! In all these years you've never said that word to me when I've asked a favor of you. Have you lost all compassion and turned uncaring and hard? We have never turned away a man, woman or animal who needed our help. No man has ever taken greater risks for us than Kain DeBolt! He knew that man was waiting up ahead to kill him. He could have ridden away from us anytime, but he chose to stay and help." Ellie's cheeks had turned red and she stood tall with indignation, glaring at her niece. "When we left Missouri you were a sweet, happy girl, always ready to help the sick and the weak. What has this godforsaken country done to you?" she asked slowly.

Vanessa was dumbfounded by Ellie's outburst. She hadn't seen her aunt that angry since she walked out of a store in Wichita and saw a teamster hitting a mule on the head with a plank. She had grabbed one of the whips they were selling and struck the man a blow between the shoulders—much to the delight of the crowd that gathered. Vanessa knew her aunt had the family temper, but she usually kept it well under control.

"Well, my land! If it means that much to you, I'll do it." Vanessa grabbed the wooden case containing their medical supplies. "I'm not the only one this country has changed, Aunt Ellie!" She flung the parting remark over her shoulder and flounced out of the room, her head held at a defiant angle, the skirt of her blue dress swirling around her legs as she walked rapidly down the hall.

Had Vanessa turned to look back at her aunt she would have seen her stiff features relax and a pleased smile curve her lips. But she was too angry to look back. She stalked to the door of Kain's room, grasped the doorknob and shoved open the door.

Chapter Twelve

"Well how do you expect me to put on a fresh bandage without a light?" Vanessa demanded, staring into the darkness.

"There's a lamp on the table to your right." Kain's voice came from the far side of the room. A match flared briefly, then went out. "Shut the door, there's too much of a draft."

She stepped inside the room and pushed on the door. It closed with a bang. Seconds later another match flared. She set the medical case on a chair, removed the glass chimney from the lamp and lit it. The room was large and square, with windows on two sides. Vanessa observed this as she crossed the rag-rug to place the lamp on the table beside the bed. Without looking at Kain, she went back for the case.

"This is only the second time I've seen you in a dress. It's the one you wore in Dodge City the first time I saw you."

Here it comes, she thought. He was going to practice his

charm on her. If it worked, he'd have something else to tell Henry about how to handle women.

She didn't comment or look at him. In a businesslike manner she placed the case on the table beside the lamp, opened it, pulled a chair up close to the bed and sat down.

"Aunt Ellie says you're bleeding again." She yanked on the sheet, pulling it down to expose his naked chest. The bandage on his shoulder was held in place with plaster strips. She pulled at the end of one. It left his firm skin reluctantly and she heard him take a quick breath. Adjusting her body so her shadow didn't obstruct her view she peered beneath the pad. Her head was inches from his face and tendrils of copper hair tickled his nose.

"Your hair is damp. You should have dried it completely before you put it up."

Vanessa shifted her position and replaced the plaster strip. "This one is all right. The bandage won't need changing until tomorrow. Ellie put petroleum jelly on it, so it won't stick."

When she moved the sheet lower to look at the wound in his side she suddenly realized he was completely naked beneath the covers. Her hands faltered for a second, then angled the cover so that only his wounded side was exposed. She noted that his stomach had sunk even more since he had been shot, and that little tremors rippled his skin as if he were chilled. His torso was smooth except for a small patch of golden brown hair that grew on his chest and a narrow strip that started beneath his navel and disappeared beneath the white strip wrapped around his waist to hold the bandage in place.

The pad over the wound was red with blood. Vanessa took scissors from her kit, and with fingers not quite as steady as she wished, cut the band and removed the bandage. She dabbed at the wound with a pad soaked with listerine. When she had washed away the blood she could see that although the wound had opened at one end, the flesh around it looked pink and healthy.

"Are you going to put in more stitches?"

"No."

"What are you going to do?"

"Put on another bandage."

"When are you going to look at me?"

"I am looking at you," she answered calmly.

"Look at my face, damn it!" His hands clenched into fists.

"I'm not interested in your face, Mr. DeBolt. Only in the wounds I was responsible for."

"It galls you to think that you *owe* me, isn't that it, Vanessa? Are you afraid I'm going to try to *collect* something from you? Is that what bothers you so much that you can't even look at me?"

"You're right about one thing, at least. I don't want to owe *you* anything."

"Do you think I joined up with you so that you'd owe me? You attracted me, Vanessa. I'll admit that. You're beautiful and I admired your spunk. I couldn't ride away knowing what would happen to you, your aunt, and Mary Ben if those men got their hands on you."

"And we've thanked you—repeatedly." She made a thick pad out of the clean lint and put some salve on it.

Kain grabbed her wrist. "Leave the goddamn wound alone and *look* at me!"

Vanessa's angry blue eyes flashed up to meet his. "Turn loose of me!"

"So you can turn tail and run? You're a coward, Vanessa. For all this spitfire image you carry around like a cloak you're a coward."

His unexpected words threw her completely off balance.

"You think I'm afraid of *you*?" Hard blue eyes stabbed down at him.

"Yes. You're afraid of what you feel for me, and you're

hurt and embarrassed because you think I don't return those feelings."

She closed her eyes tightly and moved her head from side to side. When she opened them they blazed into his.

"You're the most egotistical man I've ever met. Just because I'm grateful and let you kiss me doesn't mean I'm . . . in love with you!"

"Vanessa!" he said with angered insistence. "You didn't *let* me kiss you. We kissed each other because we both wanted to. But I will say no man ever kissed a sweeter mouth." His voice dropped to a whisper and his eyes moved to her mouth, as if he were remembering. His hand on her wrist slid down and his fingers entwined with hers. There was no warmth in her eyes, and he suddenly wanted that warmth, needed it. "Don't look at me like that, little red bird. I can't bear for you to look at me as if you hated me."

The very softness of his voice melted some of the cold chill from hers. She watched his lips move, saw the pleading look in his tawny eyes, felt the nervous tremor in the hand that held hers. "I don't hate you, Kain. I could never hate you. I'm too grateful—"

He crushed her hand in his and jerked so hard she almost fell onto the bed.

"Damn you! Listen to me! I've had about all of your independence I can stand. Don't ever use that word to me again! It has no meaning—no meaning at all between us! Do you understand, Vanessa?"

"Why are you so angry? Turn me loose."

"If you promise to stay. I want to talk to you. I need to talk to you about your aunt."

Vanessa's blue eyes moved down to where the bullet had torn a jagged hole in his side, traveled slowed up over his bare chest that rose with every angry breath, and locked with his. There she saw deep tension, but also something else that she'd seen there before. Could it possibly be a yearning for something he could not attain? What could this wordly wise man want that he couldn't have? She pulled on her hand gently and he released it.

"All right. Let me finish with this first."

Kain watched her face as she worked. She was so incredibly beautiful that he didn't even notice the dull ache in his shoulder, the sting where she'd ripped off the plaster, or the sharp pain in his side as she pressed on the salve-smeared bandage. He watched her as a starving man watches a feast. His eyes moved from her small pointed chin up to her mouth that had fit so achingly sweet against his. Her eyes were the most expressive he'd ever seen, he thought. At times they blazed with anger, were flat and cold as ice when she put on her haughty face, shone brightly when she laughed, and when filled with tears, they were like two sparkling pools of clear mountain water. Her head was bent over him and he could smell her cool, clean scent. The lamplight turned her hair to a glimmering flame. He wanted desperately to touch it, but kept his hands at his sides and caressed it with his eyes. Her tongue came out to moisten her lower lip and stayed there as she concentrated on what she was doing. Desire flowed through him, and he feared that his flesh beneath the thin covering would rise and embarrass her. He prayed to God that she would hurry and finish so he could turn over and hide it from her.

Vanessa secured the bandage with plaster strips, repacked the kit and closed the lid. She moved the chair back from the bed and started to sit down. Kain's voice stopped her.

"Don't sit way over there. My voice may carry out into the hall. Here, sit beside me." He moved over on the bed and turned on his side to face her.

Seconds piled on top of each other to make a minute while she stood uncertainly beside the bed. When he lifted his hand, his long, slender fingers reaching for hers, she sank down on the edge of the bed.

"What's this about Aunt Ellie?"

"First I want to tell you that I'm sorry I barked at you the other night. My only excuse is that I was hurting like hell and I didn't want you to see me like that."

"That's silly. I helped my father take care of patients. What few he had," she added dryly. "We took splinters out of behinds, set broken bones, treated boils and all kinds of gunshot wounds. Hill people are always feuding and shooting at each other. Seeing you throw up wouldn't have bothered me at all."

"It would have bothered me."

Vanessa looked into his face. She was calmer now, and her wildly palpitating heart had slowed to a rhythm that left her not quite so breathless. At times like this she was so comfortable with him that she felt as if he might be the other part of her. Something intangible had bound them together since the day they met. She had always known that, even though at times she had pushed that knowledge to the back of her mind.

She took a deep breath that quivered her lips, and her eyes softened and caressed his face. He needed a shave, she thought, and had to contain herself to resist the urge to run her fingers over his rough cheeks. Her eyes were lost in his intent gaze and she held her hands locked tightly together so he couldn't see them trembling and know how badly she wanted to touch him.

Kain watched the expressions flit across her face. She was proud and beautiful but vulnerable, too. He wanted to hold her, to stand between her and anything that would hurt her, as he had tried to shield her against Primer Tass. His hand lifted to push a strand of hair behind her ear; there his fingers lingered, their tips against her earlobe. He watched in fascination as her eyes changed from frosty stones to bright sunshine that penetrated his very soul, grabbed him, and shook him.

"I'm in love with you, pretty little red bird. I wish I could ask you to marry me, but I can't. I'll have to go away soon, but while I'm here, can't we enjoy each other's company and stop hurting each other?"

Vanessa was stunned by his words. She half suspected he was teasing, then saw the look of longing in his eyes. The intense silence that followed seemed to press the breath out of her, drain all coherent thought from her mind until a tremulous joy came over her, so great it was like a pain, and her heart began to race. Then the rest of his words seeped into her mind and dread swept over her like a chill.

"You're going away . . . from here?"

"Yes. I don't know just when, but soon."

"Why? Where are you going?"

"Away . . . on business. But I want to know that you're here, safe."

"How long will you be gone?"

"I'll not be coming back."

His words hung in the air between them. He watched her with dark and anxious eyes, and through them she sensed the mental agony he was suffering.

"Kain! Oh, Kain! You don't mean that!" Dear God! She loved him so, and that gave him this awesome power to hurt her.

"I don't want to go, love, but I must." His hand moved up and down her arm as if he couldn't bear not to touch her.

"But if you love me—"

"I do. You must believe that."

"Then don't go. Please don't go!" Vanessa's words echoed back to her like a lost wail.

"I must, my sweet love. Don't think about it. We've got now. Lie down beside me and let me hold you—for just a little while." There was a deep huskiness in his voice and he closed his eyes tightly, unable to bear the pain in hers and let her see the moisture in his.

Vanessa didn't know that she was crying until she felt the tears running down her cheeks. She sank down on the bed, her back to his chest, and he pillowed her head on his arm.

Wrapped in his arms, even with the bed sheet and her clothes between them, she could feel the pounding of his heart against her back. He had said he loved her, said he was going away and was not coming back . . . and he had not asked her to go with him. Her face crumbled. This was both heaven and hell.

Kain pressed his lips to the white flesh beneath her ear, and tears ran from his eyes into her hair. He hadn't meant to tell her of his love. It had just come out. What had he done to this sweet woman? She cared for him; he had been sure of it since the night she had told him about Tass. This would make his leaving all the harder to bear. Was Ellie right? Should they take what happiness they could get in the short time left?

"I know you don't understand, my love." His whispered words caressed her neck. "I shouldn't have told you and put this burden on you. It would have been easier for you if you were angry at me, hated me. But I'm a selfish bastard. I wanted your love, your warmth. More than anything I wanted to hold you in my arms and see love shining in your eyes for me . . . only for me. Pull me into your heart, my love, and hold me there."

"Oh, Kain," she whispered and brushed his bare arm with her lips. "All I can say is . . . I love you, and I don't want you to go."

"They're the most beautiful words I've ever heard." His voice vibrated with emotion. "You came into my life so unexpectedly and made me feel things I never thought I would feel. Let me be with you for this little while."

"I love you so, I don't know if I can bear it if you go away and leave me."

"You will, dear heart."

"Are you already . . . married to someone?"

"No. I've never met anyone I wanted to marry until now."

"Then why?"

"It's something I have no control over. Don't ask me, love. Let's not think about it, not now. Let's pretend we're going to be together forever. Push it out of your mind. Push everything out of your mind, sweetheart, but me. We've had some hard times, but, darling, there may be some good in knowing we must part because it makes us aware of how precious this time together is and how priceless this thing we feel for each other."

For a long time they lay without talking. Kain's hand gripped hers tightly and he buried his face in the softness of her gleaming tresses.

"Why did you tell me, now? Why didn't you just go?"

"Because I was afraid you'd leave in the morning and I'm not up to following you to town."

"I didn't want to leave here, but—"

"I couldn't let you go. I want you here, with me." His fingers left her arm and curled about her breast in sweet intimacy. He spoke against the back of her ear after a short silence. "And it's best that Ellie and Henry stay away from town, too, until I can find out more about Henry Hill. I want to ride out and talk to Logan Horn. He was Henry Clayhill's adopted son. He may know something about Henry Hill and Adam Hill. Sweetheart, I'm convinced that the man your aunt is looking for is Adam Clayhill."

"If he's as mean and ornery as you say, Aunt Ellie will be disappointed, then just stay away from him."

"He isn't like anyone Ellie's come up against. He can be as nice as pie one minute and like a viper the next."

"Then the sooner she finds out that he'll not claim Henry as a relative the better. She's about ready to admit this was a fool's errand."

"But think about this: If Adam Clayhill is Adam Hill, that would mean that his brother was Henry Clayhill, not Henry Hill, and he married Ellie under an assumed name."

"I hadn't thought about that."

"I want to find out more about this before Ellie meets Adam Clayhill."

Time assumed a dreamlike quality. Their desire to lie quietly together was wholly without passion. Neither intruded on the other's thoughts as they enjoyed the simple pleasure of being close. Kain felt a peace he hadn't known since that unforgettable day beside the river when he realized that soon he would die. He didn't feel so lonely now.

Vanessa thought of the love that had sustained her aunt through twenty years. Would it be the same with her? But Ellie had had a child to lavish her love on. Henry was a part of the lover who had swept into her life and out again in one short month. What would she have when Kain was gone? Nothing? She'd not know the joy of mating with the man she loved, the thrill of having his child grow in her body, or looking into tawny eyes knowing they were his eyes unless. . . .

"I must get up," she whispered. "The house is quiet. Aunt Ellie will wonder—"

"Turn over so I can look at you."

Vanessa swung her legs off the bed and sat up. Her fingers raked her hair back from her face before she looked at him. Her eyes took in the questioning look in his and the small damp puddle that lay on the bridge of his nose.

"I must look a sight. I always get red eyes and a runny nose when I cry," she said with a trembly smile.

"You could never look anything but beautiful to me." God how could this woman make him feel like a king just by looking at him? He felt a surging warmth flow through him like a river. The chilling darkness which had wrapped itself around him loosened and fell way under the spell of her brilliant eyes. His smile answered her, then grew into a low, throaty laugh. "Ah, love, I've never been this happy in all my life!"

She leaned over him, and her soft lips touched the dampness in the corner of his eyes. "We'll be happy while we can," she whispered. "If you say you have to go I must believe that you don't want to leave me and I'll try not to think about it. I've never loved before, Kain, and it hurts." Her voice broke, but she cleared her throat and went on. "Because I love you, I want to make our time together something we'll always remember. I'll not question you, but I want you to know that, if you want me, I'll go with you . . . if it's to jail, or South America or the Yukon." Her tears fell on his face and mingled with his.

"Darling, don't cry."

"This is the last time. I promise. Kain? Are you . . . going to die? Is someone going to kill you?"

"The only one I know who wanted to see me dead was Tass. We don't have to worry about him."

Their lips met and clung. His hand behind her head held her to him. They whispered to each other, mouth to mouth, sharing breath and soft, sweet kisses.

"I must go. Aunt Ellie—"

"She knows I love you."

"You told her?"

"She guessed. I think everyone knew but you."

"You said I was stubborn, mule-headed."

"You are, my sweet." He laughed against her lips. "Even Henry wanted me to court you."

"Then you bought the ribbon to please Henry?"

"To please me. Then I was afraid to give it to you, afraid you'd throw it at me."

"I wouldn't have."

"Kiss me some more before you go and come back early in the morning."

"If we were married I could stay," she whispered.

"Oh, sweet love, don't tempt me!" A groan of anguish escaped his throat and he pulled her to him, disregarding the pain in his shoulder. "Little red bird!" His voice was husky, tender. He held her fast and kissed her wet cheeks.

"I don't want to cry again . . ."

"It's all right." He pressed his mouth close against her temple in gentle reverence and spoke soothingly. "We'll get rid of all the tears tonight, and tomorrow we'll start to live one day at a time."

"I've been miserable the last few days." She couldn't keep the pain from her quivering voice.

"No more than I." His hand began stroking her forehead, pushing her tousled hair back and smoothing it caressingly. "And not from the holes in me, either," he added lightly.

She sighed and their seeking lips found each other and lingered. Held close against him, feeling his heart pounding heavily against her breast, she pushed away the waves of despair that had threatened to drown her when she realized their time together would be brief.

"I can't bear for us to quarrel," she whispered.

"But we will, my little redhead. We'll quarrel, we'll fight and we'll make up. All in the same day. I'll never sleep again with a misunderstanding between us."

"I love you, Kain DeBolt." Her voice was the softest of whispers and she drew back so she could look into his face.

He searched her eyes for confirmation of her words, and when she smiled at him he could see her love in them. She kissed him with fiery sweetness, then stood and looked down at him for a long moment before gently untangling her fingers from his. Without speaking, she swiftly left the room and closed the door behind her.

A light from the kitchen shone out into the hall and she followed it. Ellie sat beside the table sewing one of the dresses for Mary Ben. She looked up when Vanessa came into the room. Her hands stilled, and her knowing eyes searched Vanessa's teary face.

"He loves me, Aunt Ellie, but he's going away. Did you know?"

"Yes."

"He didn't tell me where he's going. Did he tell you?"

"I didn't ask, dear."

"I think someone is going to kill him. He won't tell me about it because he doesn't want me to worry. I don't think I can bear not knowing." Her sight was blurred by her tears. She sniffed and wiped her face on her sleeve.

"He must love you very much."

"But not enough to tell me what's taking him away from me. I don't know, Aunt Ellie. I don't know if I'm strong enough—"

"We're all stronger than we think we are. Take one day at a time and be happy—make him happy. Make this the happiest time of his life. He's a fine man."

"But it's not fair!" A desperate weariness enveloped Vanessa and she began to tremble.

"Who said life is fair? Go on to bed now, dear, and stop worrying over what you can't help. I've fixed a room for you at the top of the stairs, on your right."

"I'm not going to let him go! I mean it, Aunt Ellie. If someone is going to kill him they'll have to kill me, too."

"I don't know what to say, dear. Get a good night's rest. You're worn out. In the morning you'll see things in a different light."

"I won't! Oh, Aunt Ellie, I wish he hadn't told me!"

"It wouldn't have been fair to you. He did what he had to do to keep you from leaving. Take what happiness you can get, Vanessa. Take it and savor it. It comes to such a few of us during our lifetimes."

"I'll not give up, you know."

"I know. Good night, dear."

Footsteps going down the stairs awakened Vanessa and her first conscious thoughts were of Kain. *He loved her!* Then dark misgivings entered her mind. Determinedly she shoved them aside with the hope that something would happen to prevent him from leaving. She clung to that hope. He had told her that they should live each day as if they would be together forever and that was what she was going to do. It was what she was going to *try* to do.

The light of dawn lit the room with a faint glow. It was a small room with one window, a washstand, the bed and a massive wardrobe that stood against one wall. The bed was a white iron bedstead elaborately decorated with scrolls and gold knobs; the mattress was made of feather ticking. The night before Vanessa had paid little attention to the room. She had pulled off her clothes, drawn a nightdress over her head and gone to sleep, too weary to appreciate the luxury of lying in a real bed after weeks of discomfort in the narrow bunk in the wagon. Now she felt a hairpin poking into her neck and realized she hadn't even bothered to take down her hair.

She got out of bed, went to the washstand and splashed water on her face. There was an urgency in her movements as she dressed again in the blue dress and laced her black shoes. She brushed her hair up and tied it at the crown with the blue ribbon Kain had given her. Out of curiosity she opened the door of the wardrobe. Her dresses hung there, and several of her boxes were on the floor.

What surprised her was her image in the mirror on the back of the door. In the long, narrow glass inset she could see herself clearly. Her face was thinner and her eyes larger. She had lost weight! The blue dress had a sash that went around her waist and tied in the back, and since it had always been a little too big for her she hadn't noticed how much looser it had become when she put it on the night before. She looked closely at her face and discovered a generous sprinkling of freckles on her nose. She shrugged. Somehow freckles were not as important to her as they would have been in Missouri. Back there she would have carefully applied a mask of buttermilk morning and night if lemons were out of season until the small brown spots dulled or faded completely.

The door at the foot of the stairs was open and she could

hear voices in the kitchen—Ellie and Kain were there. Vanessa went quickly down the stairs, but her steps slowed and stopped as she reached the kitchen door. Kain sat at the table, his dark head bent over the sheet of paper he was writing on. She had only an instant to observe him without him being aware she was there. He had shaved, and his hair had been combed back with a damp comb. His cloth shirt was a faded blue and he wore the sleeveless, dark leather vest.

"Morning, dear." Ellie opened the door to the warming oven and took out a pan of biscuits. "Everyone has eaten but you."

"Why didn't you call me?" She spoke to Ellie, but her eyes were on Kain, and his on her. He was smiling, his gaze full of adoration.

"Kain said you were tired. Sit down. The biscuits are hot, and I'll heat the gravy."

Vanessa scarcely heard what Ellie said. Kain had held out his hand and she went to him.

"Morning," he said just to her.

"Morning."

He pulled her down on the bench beside him and touched his lips to hers in a gentle, lingering kiss. He lifted his head and smiled into her eyes. Vanessa shot a look at her aunt. He drew her closer and whispered in her ear, "You might as well get used to it, sweetheart. I'm going to kiss you every chance I get."

The back door opened and Mary Ben came in carrying a small glass Daisy churn. Henry followed, his arms loaded with things from the caravan.

"Be careful with that, Henry," she cautioned. "That washbowl was yore grandma's. If you break it yore ma'll have yore hide."

"I'm being careful. Where shall I put it, Ma?"

"Put it in the room Mary Ben's using. I don't think there's a washbowl in that room."

"Oh, no, Mrs. Hill. I . . . I might break it."

"Fiddlesticks! You're no more likely to break it than I am. Is the wagon about emptied, Henry?"

"Another load or two and it will be." He looked at his cousin. "What're you sitting close to Kain for, Van? Is he finally courtin' you? Is he your beau? I told him a long time ago that—"

"Henry Hill! Get along with you." Ellie took the churn from Mary Ben. "Get him out of here, Mary Ben, before he puts his foot in his mouth."

"Yes'm. Come on, Henry."

Henry backed toward the door. "You know what Kain said, Van? He said what this place needed was two good hounds. Two of them! He said after they got used to the place they'd set up a ruckus if anyone came around. He's going to get some. Ain't that right, Kain?"

"That's right, but first we've got to get your mother a couple of milch cows. Is John ready to go to town? I've got a couple of letters for him to take to Mr. McCloud at the mercantile."

"He's going to move the wagons back by the barn first."

"He ain't never goin' to do it if ya don't come on, Henry." Mary Ben tugged on his arm.

"Oh, all right. Ain't she pretty in that dress and her hair all shiny, Van? She's just pretty and *bossy*, ain't she?" They went out the door, their voices trailing behind them. "Did I say something wrong, Mary Ben?"

"I reckon not, but why did ya have to go 'n say that other fer?"

"What other? About you being pretty? Cause you *are* pretty, honey girl. You're just as pretty as a speckled pup."

"Ah, Henry."

"My, my." Ellie shook her head as she set a jar of grape jam in front of Vanessa. "Those two are the limit! Henry's underfoot all the time, but that girl can get more work out of him than you and I ever could."

"A pretty woman can just twist a man around her little finger." Kain looked at Vanessa and she could see the amusement in his amber eyes.

"The same can be said for a certain man I known." Vanessa tilted her chin pertly. "He can be oh so charming—when he wants to be."

"Love brings out the worst and the best in us." Kain smiled into Vanessa's eyes as he spoke.

"I know," Ellie said, "and I'm so grateful."

Chapter Thirteen

Several days passed in rapid succession. Breakfast was at first light, and the women spent the rest of the day cooking and cleaning. They scoured the cupboards, aired bedding, washed windows, scrubbed floors and beat carpets. Gradually the musty odor left the house, and it took on the pleasant smell of wet wood and strong lye soap.

The Hookers decided to postpone their trip back to Texas until spring. They cleaned up the quarters in the bunkhouse after Ellie's inspection had pronounced the place unfit to live in.

With a shy grin on his face, Jeb told Kain, "That woman do be bossy, but she sets a mighty fine table."

Henry worked alongside the Hookers. They snaked deadfalls down from the hillside behind the house and with a two-man saw cut them in stove-size lengths. Clay explained to Henry that the wood would split more easily when the weather turned cold. John took over the chores in the barn.

He liked working with the cows, and to Ellie's surprise he did all the milking, which she had fully expected to do herself. Clay liked to hunt and brought in a pronghorn antelope buck which he hung from a branch of a tree and dressed.

Ellie insisted that Kain drink cup after cup of the fresh milk in order to get his strength back. His shoulder and side no longer pained him unless he stretched or moved suddenly. He lived in constant dread of having one of his attacks and planned on what he would do when it happened: he'd go into his room, bolt the door, and depend on Ellie to keep Vanessa away.

If Vanessa wondered at the family settling so permanently into Kain's house she said nothing about it. She spent every available moment with him. He watched her while she worked; she scolded when she thought he was over exerting himself; their hands caught as they passed; their eyes met and held in silent conversation. Always in the back of Vanessa's mind was the dread that when Kain was out of her sight she'd not see him again.

At mealtime the "family" gathered around the big table in the kitchen. The Texans had lost much of their shyness and now lingered as John did to visit before returning to work. Mary Ben and Henry sat side by side and Ellie sat at the end of the table. Kain enjoyed these times. Not only because Vanessa sat close beside him, but because it gave him the feeling of belonging, something he'd not had for a long while.

"There's something I need to tell you," Kain said after they had finished a meal of venison, buttermilk biscuits, and custard pie. Vanessa looked up at him with a quick intake of breath. He saw her fear, his hand sought hers beneath the table, and he squeezed it reassuringly. "John already knows about this. He discovered it when he went into town. The truth is, we'll be having visitors any time now."

"Company?" Ellie passed the pitcher of milk to Vanessa so she could refill Kain's glass. "I love company."

"Not this kind, Ellie." Kain's smile broadened when he glanced at John and saw the old man trying hard to keep the grin on his face from breaking out into a full laugh.

"What do you two know that's so funny?" Vanessa's eyes traveled over the expectant faces around the table and she pinched Kain's thumb with her fingernails.

"First I'd better tell you about this place, The House. It was built by a woman named Mary Gregg about ten years ago. She and her husband came up from Texas and filed on land west and south of here. After a year or so they were pushed off the land, and shortly after that her husband died. Mary was left with a little money, but not enough to live on. She was a lovely, compassionate lady, and one day she saw the owner of the saloon throw one of his . . . ladies of the night out into the street. The girl had nowhere to go. It gave Mary an idea. She bought this land, built this house and opened a brothel."

"A what?" Vanessa gasped. "You mean . . . a wh—"

"That's exactly what I mean, sweetheart." His amber eyes glinted with amusement as they traveled from Ellie's shocked face to Vanessa's. It was deathly quiet for the space of several seconds, then both women erupted in laughter.

"That's why . . . that man in town was . . . so friendly!" Vanessa gasped between bursts of laughter, her eyes shining like sapphires.

"My land! I wondered why he was so pleased The House was going to be opened." Color had stained Ellie's cheeks and she kept her eyes turned away from the men.

"'Don't ya worry none, ma'am,'" Vanessa mocked, laughter making her so radiant Kain couldn't tear his gaze away from her, "'Stan Taylor'll spread the word.'"

"Vanessa!" Ellie chided, but smiled despite her embarrassment.

"According to what John heard in town, Stan did a good job."

"For goodness sake, Kain. You mean men are coming here thinking that . . ."

"Yes ma'am. They'll be coming here thinking that! The House is well known among cowboys and drifters, traveling men and, no doubt, some respectable husbands."

"Well, I never!"

"Mary just ran the place," Kain hastened to add. "She wasn't one of the girls. The House is known all over the territory as a place where a man can come if he's sick or hurt or needs . . . ah, whatever."

"Sounds like a mighty fine place to know 'bout," John said, then his weathery face turned beet red and he looked fixedly down at his plate.

"What're you talking about, Kain? I don't know why Van's laughing." Henry had a puzzled frown on his face. "It ain't funny if a man's sick. We had sick people come to the farm back home and Ma and Van didn't laugh."

"How did you come to buy the place, Kain?" Vanessa asked quickly, teasingly, to fill the void after Henry's question.

"Whew . . . thank you, sweetheart," he said softly. "Mary's childhood sweetheart, a man named Case Malone, came up from Texas. He worked for awhile with Logan Horn out at the Morning Sun Ranch, then he and Mary went back to Texas when his brother died and someone was needed to run things there. Mary rented the place to Bessie Wilhite and she carried on in Mary's tradition. When Bessie married a man from Wyoming and moved there, I bought the place from Mary just because I didn't want someone else to have it, I guess. Now I'm glad I did." He smiled down at Vanessa and his fingertips caressed the palm of her hand.

"That's why there are all those rooms up there—for sick people," Henry announced.

"Does anyone want more pie?" Ellie asked so quickly that even the faces of the somber Texans were creased with wide grins.

Later in the afternoon a visitor arrived, but it wasn't a male visitor. Vanessa was washing the upstairs windows in the middle hallway when she saw a shiny black landau driven by a Negro servant in livery stop at the front gate. Two escort riders reined in a distance away and sat their mounts. The servant jumped out of the buggy and handed down a woman covered from neck to toe in a dust coat. She had a large scarf over her head. She removed the coat and scarf and handed them to the driver. She was dressed all in white from the small brimmed hat perched on her high-piled blond hair to the tips of her buttoned shoes, except for something pink that fluttered from the neck of a hip-length, form-fitting jacket. She daintily lifted the sides of her white wool, tiered skirt to keep it from brushing the dry weeds that edged the walk and came toward the door, a floating vision of white and pink beauty.

Vanessa dropped the wet cloth in the bucket of water and hurried down the stairs, knowing Ellie and Mary Ben had gone to the barn and Kain was resting in his room. At an insistent rap she opened the door and stared. The face she looked into had the perfection of an exquisite cameo.

The woman lifted artfully plucked eyebrows and looked at her coolly. Blue eyes traveled over Vanessa with appraising frankness and pink lips opened to reveal small, extremely white teeth.

"I understand Kain is here."

"Yes," Vanessa managed to say.

"I want to see him." The woman stepped across the threshold, stopped, turned, and once again studied Vanessa with a certain cool and rather amused patience. "Well, get him."

The words were ordinary, but the tone was not. It was marked by a commanding rasp designed to place the beautiful but untidy redhead firmly in the pigeon-hole marked "inferior." Vanessa's eyes flashed with anger and her proud chin lifted. Unconsciously her hand lifted to the straggling curls on her forehead, but she lowered it quickly when the woman's pink lips twitched knowingly.

"You can wait in here." Vanessa swung open the double doors to the parlor and the woman swept past her.

In spite of her soiled, damp dress, dirt-smudged face and unruly hair that had sprang loose from the ribbon, Vanessa marched with dignity down the hall to Kain's room. She opened the room without knocking and found him sleeping soundly, his boots on the floor beside the bed.

"Kain, wake up." She shook him gently. "Kain?"

"I'm awake, sweetheart. Hmm . . . what a nice way to wake up." His hands reached for her face and pulled it to his. As her mouth came to his, she felt the soft mating of their breath before his lips opened gently beneath hers. He kissed her, lingeringly, lovingly. When the kiss was over, she gazed down at him, seeing the tenderness in his eyes as his fingers touched the fair skin of her neck where her pulse beat so rapidly.

"Come lie down with me." His voice had a sensual rasp. When his arms moved to pull her down beside him, she pulled back.

"You have a visitor."

"A visitor? Let him wait, I want to hold you, love you, kiss you." He grasped her hand and slipped it inside his shirt so her palm lay flat against his chest. "It was worth getting shot to feel your hands on me."

"It's a woman. She's waiting in the parlor."

"What does she want?" Kain's hands reluctantly fell from her when she stepped back. He sat up on the side of the bed, reached for his boots, slipped them on and ran his fingers through his hair. Vanessa was at the door when he looked up. "Wait a minute, honey."

The woman was standing in the parlor doorway when Vanessa walked down the hall and turned to go up the stairs. She heard Kain's boots on the floor behind her, then the woman's soft laugh and lilting voice.

"Kain, darling. It's so good to see you."

Kain heard the door to the stairway close as he went down the hall. "Hello, Della."

"Well, aren't you glad to see me?"

"Overjoyed," he said dryly, and shouldered past her into the parlor.

"I heard in town that you were back. Are you opening this place?" She closed the parlor doors and turned to look at him. "Have you been sick? You've lost weight."

"Get to it, Della. You don't give a damn if I've been sick. You want to know if I lost all my money in the crash. I lost some but not all." Kain looked at his sister's beautiful face and felt not a trace of affection for this woman who was born of the same parents as he. He would be damned if he'd let her know that this place and a few dollars were all he had salvaged from the crash.

"You don't have to be so defensive, brother dear. I thought if you needed money I'd take The House off your hands. I've had it in the back of my mind for a long time to reopen it. I've got places in Denver and one in Greeley. Papa wouldn't care if I had one here as long as I didn't run it myself. I've done very well, Kain."

"I know. You're a very rich whore."

"My, my! What a nasty word. Don't tell me you've never used the services of a whore, brother."

"Perhaps, but that doesn't make it any easier knowing my sister's one."

Della laughed, the musical sound reaching the upper floor where Vanessa stood clutching the wet cloth.

"I'm good, Kain. I've fucked royalty and they said they'd never had better."

"Say what you came to say and get out, Della."

"Do you want to sell this place?"

"It's not for sale."

Della shrugged. "How long are you staying, Kain? And who is the grubby-looking redhead?"

"How long I'm staying is no concern of yours, or your *dear* papa's. And the redhead, grubby or not, is far more a lady than you'll ever be."

"Come now! What's a *lady* but a female with a slit between her legs? We've all got a twat under our clothes. Without it you men wouldn't give us a second look. Is she better on her back, Kain, or her knees?" Another tinkling laugh followed the question. "If she's good I may be able to use her. Her hair is different, but I can't say much for the rest of her."

Kain gazed at his sister. She looked like a porcelain doll. He thought about the night he'd walked into a saloon in Denver and saw a beautiful naked woman dancing on a table. He hadn't realized it was his sister until she took off her mask just before she slipped behind a curtain. He thought of how she had tried to have Logan Horn hanged for rape after he had refused her advances, and the rumors that she had been old Clayhill's mistress for years. He wondered how anyone so beautiful could be so rotten. He went to the door and opened it.

"Good-bye, Della."

"So *you're* opening The House. Well! If you plan to use the redhead, my advice is to clean her up a bit. She smelled like a wet goat! And although she'd only be servicing drovers and drifters, even they like—"

Kain slammed the door. "Shut up! You don't have a decent bone in your body."

"Decent? What's *decent*? Does it make you feel good? Does it put money in your pocket?"

"Why don't you get the hell out of here?"

"Does Papa know you're back?"

"I suppose he does. The old son of a bitch knows everything that goes on in the territory."

"Are you going out to see him?"

"Why in hell would I do that? You know I despise his guts."

"Papa isn't well. Joseph said he had a sinking spell one day. I'm staying to take care of him."

"Don't give me that line of bullshit, Della. You're staying to be sure you get his money when he dies."

"Of course. I didn't screw that old bastard for nothing!" Della opened the door and stepped out into the hall. "This place is ideally suited for what it was built for. It's drab, but that could be fixed in a hurry. If you need any help in training your girls, Kain, let me know. Or would you rather do that yourself?" She made sure her lilting voice carried, glanced over her shoulder to the stairway and laughed.

Kain could hear Ellie's voice in the kitchen. He opened the door, took Della firmly by the elbow, and pushed her out of the house.

"Get out of here, Della, and don't come back."

"You'd better not lay a hand on me, even if you are my brother. Papa's men might shoot you. He pays them well to protect his little girl."

"His own private whore, you mean. I'm glad Ma never knew what you turned out to be."

"Oh, she knows. She's probably up there clucking her tongue and saying, 'Don't be a naughty girl, Della. It's naughty to fuck your steppapa.'" Della went down the walk laughing, turned and called, "Bye, darling. If you want to see me you know where to find me."

Kain watched the servant help her on with the dust coat, then place a small stool on the ground so she could step up into the landau. She waved a white handkerchief as the buggy, followed by the outriders, pulled away from the gate. Kain stood on the steps for several minutes trying to rid himself of the feeling that he'd been surrounded by something dirty.

At the window of the ranch house, Adam Clayhill watched his stepdaughter alight from the landau with all the grace of a queen. A smile hovered on his lips beneath the neatly trimmed white mustache. She was something to see. She could fit herself into any society. On the outside she was every inch a lady, but the truth was she was every inch a whore. She had been a lanky ten-year-old when he had married her mother. Even then she had liked to sit on his lap and wiggle until she had him worked up. She was a born courtesan, and even then had known instinctively what to do. Four or five years ago they had become lovers; she was the best he'd ever had. Then, after the business with the Indian, Logan Horn, she had gone to Denver and become quite a businesswoman. Over the past several years she had come back to the ranch often; this time she'd been here several weeks. He chuckled. Della intended to be here when the money was counted. By God! She was more of an offshoot of his then either of the two known bastards he had sired.

Yes, he thought gleefully, Della was thinking he was about to cash in his chips. He looked at his reflection in the shiny glass window pane. He was still a handsome, robust man. His hair was thick and white, his carriage erect. It would take more than one sinking spell to do him in, but if Della thought so, let her if it would keep her here. He was vigorous despite his years. Cecilia, his little Mexican whore, could still get a rise out of him. So far Della hadn't come to his bed, but he knew her strategy was to let him wait. He chuckled again and went to the door to let her in.

"Hello, Papa Adam. How are you feeling?" Della took the pins from her hat and handed it to the silent Mexican girl who stood waiting. She took off her coat and hung it carefully on the halltree.

"Fine. I've been waiting for you. Dinner is ready."

"You're sweet." She kissed his cheek.

"Who did you see in town?" he asked when they were seated at one end of the long table and the Negro servant had gone back to the kitchen.

"There's nothing in town half as handsome as what's here

on this ranch." She smiled, reached across to caress his arm with her fingertips, her eyes lingering on his mouth.

"I could've told you that."

"You *are* a conceited old bastard, aren't you?" She laughed. "Mr. McCloud said he's holding a letter for an Adam Hill. He wondered if it could be for you."

"Where was it from?"

"Springfield, Missouri."

"It couldn't be for me. I don't know anyone in Missouri."

"Kain is back."

"I heard that this morning."

"You do have your network of spies, don't you, Adam? Did they tell you he's at The House? I stopped there to see him. He's been sick, or hurt. More than likely some jealous husband shot him. He was walking slow and carefully."

"Did you hear any news about Cooper or the . . . Indian?" It was still hard for Adam to speak of Logan Horn.

"I heard Mr. McCloud at the store telling someone that Cooper's little boy had been sick and that his mother, Mrs. Henderson, had been out at the ranch. I guess he's all right now. You're former . . . ah, mistress has gone back to Morning Sun to be with her husband. Is it true that you had some men break his legs a few years ago thinking it would make Sylvia pressure Cooper to come work for you?"

"Humph!"

Della ignored the scowl on his face and continued talking.

"Your grandson looks like his mother, Adam. Lorna Parnell is a wild, dark-haired, mountain-bred bitch! She goes into town in britches with a bullwhip over her shoulder. I'll swear, it amazes me that Cooper lets her do it. Everyone knows he's a Clayhill. It reflects badly on all of us."

"Everyone knows you're a whore, too, sweeting, but that doesn't seem to hurt my standing in Denver one bit."

"No. Because if one bad word about you reaches my ears, I could more than likely ruin whoever said it. And I would, too, Papa. I have a little book tucked away with a lot of valuable information in it."

Adam basked in her affectionate smiles. "What a team we would have made if we'd met when I was young."

"You're not *old* darling! I refuse to let you say you're old."

"Did you hear anything about that Griffin fellow down on the Blue?"

"No. He's Kain's friend, isn't he? He and Kain killed those two bullies you had working for you a year or so ago. What was the name of that redheaded man? Dunbar? If they hadn't killed them, folks would have strung them up when they found out they had horsewhipped a woman. You don't get away with that in this country. I never did find out what they had against Lorna Parnell."

"That son of a bitchin' Dunbar. He bungled the job, or I'd be owning that place on the Blue. Cooper's got a hand in it, too. The stiff-necked son of a bitch. He'll not get an inch of this land, by Gaw!"

That was just fine with her, Della thought, then said aloud, "Oh, yes. I saw the *Indian*'s squaw in town with the teacher they've hired to run the school at the ranch. She was dressed fit to kill, but everyone that's anyone refused to have anything to do with her. She's pregnant again. Does this make three? Good God, Papa! You're going to have descendants all over the territory." Della couldn't resist bringing up a subject that was sure to rile him.

"Hush that stupid twaddle! That red ass and his mites are no kin of mine."

"That red ass is your son—there's no way you can deny it, Adam darling. He's got your crooked finger, so has his boy." Della kissed her fingertips and laid them against Adam's mouth. "But, don't get all worked up about it now. Save all that delicious anger for later."

Adam asked about Kain as they walked arm in arm to his office after the meal.

"He's got some women there cleaning up the place as if he were going to open it. If he does I'm sure he'll have someone run it for him. He won't stay around long. Junction City is too dull for my world-traveled brother."

"Hmm . . . hmm . . ."

"What do you mean by hmm . . . hmm? It sounds as if you had something on your mind." Della drew back the velvet drapes that hung over the door and they entered the office.

"Kain turned out to be a good man—"

"There's no such thing as a *good* man!"

"You said I was," Adam replied with a grin.

"As a lover you're . . . wonderful. As a man you're rotten! That's why I love you so much." Della had studied men all her life. She knew just how to stroke their egos. She watched the pleased expression settle on Adam's face.

"I could use a man like Kain."

"You'd not be able to manage him, Papa," she cautioned. "He's stubborn, and so very self-righteous. He's like Mama —all wrapped up in right and wrong. I'm like my Papa. He knew what he wanted and went to any length to get it. That's how he amassed a fortune."

"And left it to your brother."

"Yes, left it to my brother, and he lost a lot of it when the New York Stock Market crashed this year."

"Then he might be reasonable about an offer from me." Adam had sat down in the big leather chair, and now he pulled Della down on his lap. He opened her dress immediately and pressed his face between her bare breasts. "There's a smell to you, girl, that's different from that of any woman I've ever known."

Della fumed inwardly. He hadn't paid a bit of attention to what she had said about Kain.

"It's the expensive perfume from France."

"It's more than that. It's hellfire and brimstone. You're hot for a man and you smell like it." Laughing huskily, he slipped his hand up under her skirt and felt his way up her bare thighs to the dampness that he knew he'd find. He chuckled again with pure pleasure. "I'm glad you're not one of them women who wears drawers. Open your legs, girl."

Della let her arms circle his neck. He had been a good lover in his day. But now the skin on his chest was beginning to sag and his middle thicken. He was still an attractive man and would stand out in any crowd with that magnificent head of white hair and the way he carried himself. Adam Clayhill was born to give orders, not take them. But he was still only a man, Della mused, with the majority of his brains in that piece of flesh that hung between his legs.

"You're my horny stud, Papa Adam," she whispered, and her tongue poked moistly into his ear. What he was doing was pleasant, she admitted moments later. Sex of any kind was a necessary part of her life. But as badly as she wanted it now, she'd make him wait a little longer before she would let him have it all. Before she was through she would make him desperate for her, make sure *she* was like life's blood to him. The strong cantharides she had brought from the Middle East would help. Once she took him she would have to work on him everyday. She would drive him crazy with what she'd do to him. Kain wasn't going to come waltzing in here and share in *her* inheritance. Clayhill Ranch was the largest holding in the northern territory and she meant to have it all.

Adam was still a lusty man, she reasoned, even if some of the lust was in his head and not in his pants. She had something Kain didn't have and she'd use it, by God; she'd use it to get what she wanted. She opened her legs to his seeking fingers, wound her arms about his neck, and pressed his face between the soft mounds of her breasts.

"Cecilia might poison me for stealing this from her," she murmured in his ear as her hand slid slowly down his chest and her fingers delved between them to find firm flesh that took longer now to harden than it had just months before.

"I . . . got enough for both of you," he panted and bit her

nipple roughly. His lovemaking had become almost painful of late because he was so desperate to reach fulfillment.

Della smiled down on his bent head. She didn't mind the pain at all. She squeezed his hand between her thighs. The old man, she thought, had *nothing*! But if he wanted to think he did. . . .

"Ahh . . . Papa Adam, you know just what to do. I love that. You know I love it, but I want more, much more. I want this big thing . . ." She gripped him hard. "I want it, but we can't now. I'll ruin my dress."

"To hell with your dress," he growled. "Take it off!"

"It'll take too long to undo all these buttons, and then I'll be out of the mood. Come to me tonight. We'll do everything we've done before and more. I'll show you something a Turkish sultan taught me to do."

"Now! You hot little bitch! You want it as much as I do. Don't you put me off again, hear?" he shouted. "You do and I'll beat your ass!" He pulled his hand from between her legs and grasped her arm to hold her.

"Don't yell so loud," she cautioned. She slid from his lap, jerked free from his hands and stood back. Her dress was open and her naked breasts exposed, but she made no attempt to cover them. "The servants will hear—"

"Screw the black sons of bitches! You don't give a gaw-damn about the servants you fuckin' little tease!" He sat up in the chair, yanked off his belt, and worked at the buttons on his britches. "Get over here you little slut, and finish what you started." His face was florid, and beads of sweat stood out on his forehead.

Go ahead, old fool, Della thought. Have a heart attack. If she thought it would help she'd screw him to death, but it would just be her luck that he'd thrive on it.

"You're not so bad off, darling." She reached down and stroked the hardness he was trying to release, letting her breast brush his face. "You can hold it for awhile . . . it'll make it better."

"Better, hell! Gawddamn you!" he snarled. "I want it now! Are you playing the whore, Della? Are you wantin' me to *pay* first?"

"Well! If that's how you're going to talk." She sniffed daintily. "I thought there was something . . . special between us."

"Special my ass!" he shouted.

"I love you. You know that—"

"All you love is money and a thick prick!"

"Hush talking like that."

"You love dirty talk! The dirtier the better. Well? Are you going to stand there or are you going to bring that tight little ass over here?"

Della slowly shook her head and saw his face swell with rage.

"Then get that hot twat of yours out of here!" His bellow could be heard in every corner of the house. "Cecilia! Cecilia, get your fat little ass in here!"

Della went out the door as the Mexican girl slipped in. The bitch, Della thought. She had been waiting.

"I've done all the hard work. He's primed and ready for you," Della said sweetly, pulling her dress over to cover one bare breast.

"But he wants me."

"He needs something to poke it into. A cow would do!"

If it hadn't been so funny, Della would have slapped the satisfied smirk from the Mexican girl's face.

Cecilia could have his wobbly old pecker. *She'd* have his money.

Chapter Fourteen

Kain waited a full ten minutes after the buggy was out of sight before he went into the house. What stood out in his mind was that Della was in town and she wanted the place he had planned to give to Vanessa and the Hills. Would they be strong enough to hold out against her without his being there? Would Della be able to go to court and take it regardless of the will?

An idea began to take root in his mind. As his wife, Vanessa would have the place and whatever of his assets the solicitor could salvage from the stock market crash. He would have to make sure his death was recorded in order for her to inherit.

He took the makings for a cigarette from his pocket and began to roll a smoke. Although he had tried to blot from his mind the fact that he was dying, he thought about it now. Thank God he'd had only one attack since he was shot. How much time did he have left? He knew as the end drew near the time between attacks would shorten, then come daily. When that happened he'd simply disappear in the middle of the night.

His mind kept going back to the idea of making Vanessa his wife. Was he being foolish to want her, knowing he might leave her with a child? At the mere thought of a son, his own red-haired son, growing in her body his somber features softened and a smile curled his lips. A part of him would pass on to the next generation, marking his time on earth. Perhaps he would live to see his child, although it seemed unlikely. The sheriff in Arizona had lived only a month or two after he started vomiting blood.

The door behind him opened and Ellie walked out. He dropped his smoke and stepped on it, grinding it to fragments before sweeping them away with his foot.

"Are you all right, Kain?" Ellie asked quietly.

"Sure. That was my sister, Ellie."

"Your sister? My, my. Why didn't she stay?"

"I told her to leave."

"Oh. Oh, I'm sorry—"

"Don't be, Ellie. I've seen very little of her during the past twenty years. She's not the type of person to be around you and Vanessa. She's a completely self-centered, greedy woman who caters only to her own peculiar needs. I don't talk about her or think about her."

"All right, Kain. Has your stomach been bothering you?"

"Not except for a constant little nagging pain."

"I wish you'd see a doctor."

"And have an old quack tell me I've got worms?" He smiled down into her concerned face. "Don't worry, Ellie. I may go along like this for weeks with only an occasional attack."

"I think what you eat has a lot to do with your attacks. I remember Vanessa's father telling a man back home to drink milk for a bad stomach. Of course he wasn't as sick as you are."

"So that's why you insisted on getting the cows right away. Ellie, I may hug you."

"Feel free to do so anytime." Her soft eyes smiled up at him and her expression was gentle.

"Ellie . . . do you think I'd be a selfish bastard if I asked Vanessa to marry me?"

"No, Kain. I think it would give her something to hold on to . . . later on."

Kain's hand went to her shoulder and squeezed it thankfully before they went back into the house.

Vanessa heard Kain walking up the stairs and slipped into her room and closed the door. She needed just a few more minutes to compose herself before she faced him. While he talked to the woman in the parlor she had had time to think about the shards of jealousy that had knifed through her, and about the life Kain had lived before he met her. No doubt he had known many beautiful women well enough to call him darling. She could accept that. The fact that *this* beautiful woman had neatly regulated her to the position of a servant was what had so angered her. Even that, she told herself, wasn't as bad as the insolent way she had looked at her, and the inferior feeling that had followed that look. This new, strange feeling was one Vanessa had not had before.

She looked at a sliver of sunlight on the floor without seeing it. A calmness came over her. She knew herself, knew what she was. She'd not let the woman's insensitivity touch her. She heard Kain's voice calling her name and opened the door to look into tawny gold eyes that smiled at her.

"You're not up to climbing those stairs," she scolded gently. "I was coming down."

"I'd climb clear up to the heavens if you were up there waiting for me." He came inside and closed the door. "Did anyone ever tell you that it isn't proper for a young lady to entertain a man in her bedroom?"

"It seems to me that I've heard something about that not being nice. But as you know, I don't pay too much attention to what's proper."

"I'm glad."

Vanessa wanted to bury her face in his chest and cry with relief. He was the same Kain. His feelings for her hadn't changed with the coming of the beautiful woman. The light, quick intake of his breath and the subtle narrowing of his eyes told her that he knew her thoughts and that her light words were to cover deeper feelings.

"I love your eyes, sweetheart," he said and drew her to him. "They're so honest. They don't know how to deceive." His lips found her, touching her nose as they moved over her cheeks with small kisses until he found her mouth. He covered her lips with a deep, hungry kiss. The kiss ended abruptly as he dragged his mouth away. He picked up her hand and slipped it, palm down, into his shirt, laying her fingers over his heart. She felt the warmth of his skin, and, as he held her hand there, the increasing thud of his strong heartbeat. "You do that to me, pretty little red bird. You and no one else."

"Now it's my turn to be glad," she answered softly, smiling into his eyes.

"Do you suppose we can sit down on the bed? I'll try not to attack you, though I'll be sorely tempted."

"If you promise to not try to hard," Vanessa said as Kain sat down on the edge of the bed. She wiped the beads of sweat from his forehead with a handkerchief. "You're still weak," she murmured when his arm reached out and pulled her down beside him, pressing her close.

"That woman was my sister." He entangled her fingers in his and lifted their locked hands to his mouth so he could kiss the back of her hand. "The beautiful Della Clayhill," he announced dryly with an expression of distaste.

"Your sister?" She repeated the words blankly.

"You knew I had one?"

"Yes, but I thought she lived in Denver."

"She does, part of the time. She's now out at Clayhill's ranch."

"She's very beautiful. I've never seen a more beautiful woman."

"Yes, she's beautiful . . . on the outside. On the inside, she's filth."

"Oh, Kain! No . . ."

"Yes." He tilted her chin and looked into her eyes. "My sister is a whore. She's a whore because she wants to be one. She enjoys her work. She has a place in Denver where a man can have a woman, any color, any age, any size, and any way he wants her. She specializes in the exotic. She's opened a place in Greeley, and she wants this place, The House, so she can open another. I'm telling you this because I want you to know the facts about my family when I ask you to marry me."

"You want to . . . marry me?"

"Is that so strange? You're beautiful, lovable, exciting, and the most desirable woman in the world. I want you more than I could tell you if I talked all day."

His words sent a shower of joy whispering through her. She closed her eyes for an instant and shivered with pleasure. She opened them to look into the amber depths of his eyes, and what she saw there was more love for her than she had ever thought she'd ever have. His fingers smoothed the hair back from her ears.

"I want it too." Her voice was low and full.

"I'll love you forever." His mouth found hers and covered it with fierce, hungry kisses, random and violent, different from the gentle kisses he had given her before. Clasped tightly to his chest she could feel the hammering of her own heart. "I want you so much," he whispered against her lips.

"You have me . . . for as long as you want me."

He pulled back to look at her. His eyes were bright, raw with feeling. He brushed her lips with another kiss. "I was just thinking—this feeling is a miracle. Do you suppose anyone else has ever felt like this?" His voice was gently curious.

"Not like this. I think I could fly!" She felt free, glowing and a little crazy. Her hands cupped his face. "When?"

"Now. The next five minutes." He turned his face and kissed her palm. "Whenever you say. I want you to be mine, wholly mine . . . soon. I want to be yours. I want what I have to be yours."

"I want you, too." She placed her lips on his and kissed him gently and sweetly, and with deep dedication. "I won't ask you how long we'll be together like this. I know you'll be in my heart forever."

"Sweetheart! Don't stop loving me." His voice was no more than a ragged whisper, a strand of breath. "It's so good to know you love me."

It had been so long since anyone had loved him, almost a lifetime. He wondered if she realized that or guessed how her sweet, caring presence filled that vacant place in his heart. He drew her close so he could feel the lovely fullness of her small breasts pressing into his chest. He moved his hands to her hips. She was perfect and perfectly desirable, the source and fulfillment of all his dreams.

They sat quietly for a long while just holding each other. The wonder of the love they felt for each other kept them in an awed silence. Vanessa no longer felt drab or inferior. She felt beautiful and loved. She loved this man with the golden eyes. She loved the sound of his voice, the line of his jaw, the curve of his mouth and even the scar across his cheek that had given him pain.

She made a silent vow to do everything in her power to keep him with her forever, but if fate tore them apart, she would have a thousand sweet memories to cherish. She would store them away inside so that when she was alone she'd be able to take them out of her heart like little treasures. She didn't want it to be that way, but if that was all she could have. . . .

Kain announced their plans to be married while they were at the supper table. Vanessa had already whispered the news to Ellie. The men stood to lean across the table and shake his hand. His smile was beautiful and his eyes flashed continually to the woman beside him. Her slightly flushed cheeks made her sparkling eyes seem all the brighter, clearer. Her hair was piled on top of her head and the blue ribbon Kain had given her was wrapped around the bun. Ellie looked at her with misty eyes. Vanessa had never been lovelier.

"You're going to *marry* Van? Well, dog my cats, Kain. You just started courting her." Henry, excited by the news, forgot what he was doing and piled more and more rice on his plate, until Mary Ben reached over and gently took the bowl from his hand.

"Have you decided when and where?" Ellie asked. "Oh, my! Will we have time to make a dress?"

"If you can do it in a week," Kain said, squeezing Vanessa's hand tightly under the table. "I'll see if we can get the preacher out here next Sunday."

"That's six days from now!" Ellie's voice squeaked.

"I don't need a new dress, Aunt Ellie. I can wear the blue silk with mutton sleeves. I've only worn it once. There'll be enough to do without you staying up nights to sew. Isn't that right, Kain?"

"You can wear just what you have on, honey. It'll be all right with me. Anything," he said with a chuckle. "Even those britches you wore on the trail."

"They were comfortable. It isn't fair that women have to wear yards and yards of skirts flapping around their legs."

"It's a shame, sweetheart, that they hide all that prettiness from the world!" Kain had to force his teasing eyes from her glowing face to look at Ellie. "Vanessa and I want to be married here. I want to invite my friends. One of them is

part Indian and he and his wife wouldn't feel welcome at the
church. It'll mean extra work for you, preparing food and
finding places for them all to sleep."

"I don't mind that. Oh, dear, what *will* we have in the
way of food? Thank goodness for you, Clay. Do you suppose you could get another antelope?"

"I 'spect I could, ma'am. But I got a idea. Me 'n Jeb's
cooked many a steer fer a whoop-de-la. If 'n ya want, we'll
get ya one 'n cook it fer ya, Texas style."

"You mean dig a pit, fill it with coals, put in the steer and
cover it for a few days?" Kain saw the pleased look that
covered the Texan's face.

"Ya've et pit-cooked steer meat?"

"You bet! Down in Fort Worth. It'll be a treat to have it
again. They've got stock pens in town. Let me know when
you want to go pick one out."

"It's settled?" Ellie asked, then sighed with relief when
both men nodded. "Now all I have to worry about is the rest
of the food and the sleeping arrangements. How many will
be here, Kain?"

"There'll be the Cooper Parnells, the Logan Horns, and
my friends, Fort Griffin and Bonnie. They live down on the
Blue, and I don't know if there's enough time to get word to
him, but if he can't get here in time for the wedding it'll be
shortly after. And, oh yes, Cooper's mother and her husband. They live on the Morning Sun and can come over with
Logan and his family."

"We can use four of the bedrooms on the second floor.
I'll sleep in with Mary Ben, and Henry can go to the bunkhouse with John, Jeb and Clay."

"Ma, I want to say something." Henry spoke up firmly.

"Yes, son?"

"Remember that I told you that Mary Ben and I want to
get married?" Ellie's quick intake of breath could be heard in
the quiet following Henry's statement.

"Henry!" Mary Ben hissed and nudged him with her elbow.

"Don't be Henryin' me, Mary Ben. I'm going to say it. I'm going to marry Mary Ben sometime, Ma. Why can't we get married when Van and Kain get married?"

All eyes turned from Henry to Ellie. "Well, son—"

"I already asked John. Kain said I ought to ask him because John's like Mary Ben's pa."

Vanessa looked at her cousin with pride. Henry *had* changed. He was speaking out for what he wanted.

Ellie's troubled eyes turned to Kain.

"If they have your consent and John's, Ellie, Vanessa and I would be proud to share our wedding day with Henry and Mary Ben," he said.

"What do you think, John?" Ellie asked. "Mary Ben has been with my son enough to realize what it will mean to be married to him. I'm very fond of her. If they marry, she'll be like a daughter to me."

"She ain't no rattle-head, ma'am. If she wants him fer her man, it'll be her that says it."

"Mary Ben?" Ellie realized that being the center of attention was agony for the girl. Her head was bowed and the lamplight cast a rosy glow on her flushed face. Slowly she looked up and met Ellie's eyes squarely.

"Henry ain't no rattle-head either, ma'am. He said right out he wanted me. And I'm sayin' right out I want him 'n I'll stand by him." It was the most positive statement any of them had ever heard her make.

When Vanessa looked at her aunt she saw tears rolling down her cheeks. She and the young girl who sat within the circle of her son's arm were looking at each other as if they were the only two people in the room. An understanding was being forged between the two women. Ellie's lips quivered when she spoke.

"I'm proud to welcome you to the family, Mary Ben."

"Thanky, ma'am. I aim ta be a help to ya."

"Well." Ellie took a deep breath. "We'll have two weddings. Things are happening so fast my head is dosey. Oh, my! Mary Ben must have a new dress!"

"Remember that pink and white striped dress you made for me, Aunt Ellie? It's so tight I can scarcely breathe. We'll have time to fix it for Mary Ben if she wants it."

"That's right, Vanessa. It'll be perfect. She looks so pretty in pink, and she should have some pretty white slippers. You have your white ones, Vanessa, to go with the blue dress. We must go in to town and get some ribbons and things, and streamers to decorate the parlor. Oh, dear, I'll have to get a tablet and make a list of things to do."

The Hookers and John rose from the table. Each of them slapped Henry on the back and congratulated him.

"It's plumb disgustin'," Jeb said. "This young scutter come 'n took this little purty when I ain't had me no luck a'tall gettin' me a woman."

"If'n ya took a bath like I tole ya, ya might stand a chance." Clay hit his brother on the back with his hat before he slammed it down on his head. "Ain't that right, Henry?"

"I never thought Jeb smelled bad—"

"He's joshin' ya, Henry. I had me one this past summer. It pert near killed me 'n didn't help none a'tall to get me a woman. Get on outta here, Clay, afore we have us a real chicken-flutter set-to."

While the women cleaned up after supper, Kain sat at the table and wrote letters for Clay to take to town the next morning. McCloud, at the store, would send them out with riders going toward the Parnells and to Morning Sun Ranch. In his letter to Logan, he asked him to invite Cooper's mother and Arnie, and to get word to Griffin.

He hoped that Della wouldn't hear about the weddings, although it was hard to keep such an event secret. She just might decide to come, especially if she thought Logan Horn would be there. It would matter little to her if she were invited or not. Should that happen, Kain would meet her at the gate and turn her away. He'd not allow her to disrupt this most important day of his life.

Henry was sitting patiently beside the door waiting for Mary Ben. Kain wondered what the years ahead would be like for him. Immature as he was he was luckier than most. He had his health, and with the love of a woman like Mary Ben and support from Cooper and Logan, he'd make out all right.

This would be a good opportunity for Ellie to meet Logan and Cooper and Sylvia Henderson, Kain thought, because if what he suspected were true, Ellie was due the surprise of her life.

The sound of hooves on the hard-packed road made Kain lift his head and listen. There could be as many as half a dozen horses approaching the house. He got to his feet.

"Henry, slip out the back door and go tell Clay and Jeb we have visitors. You women stay in the kitchen out of sight," he said tensely, then went quickly to his room. He took his gun belt from the peg on the wall and was strapping it on as he strode down the hall. He picked up a lamp and set it on the table beside the door just as a loud bang on the door rattled the oval glass.

"Open up!" The voice was loud and raspy; the owner drunk or near to it. "We come to have us a real sockdolager whoopla!"

Kain opened the door. A drover with dusty clothes and a weeks growth of whiskers stood on the porch. Four more of the same stood behind him.

"Where's the women?" he demanded and pushed on the door. Kain held it partly closed with his foot.

"You've been given the wrong information, men. I know what this place was in the past. It's a private home now."

"Ya mean it ain't no whorehouse no more?"

"That's exactly what I mean."

"I don't believe ya. This's always been a whorehouse.

Yo're jist ahoggin' the women is what yo're adoin'." A short man with a walrus mustache elbowed his way to the front. "Stan Taylor told us The House is openin', by Gawd, 'n we come to get our rocks knocked off. Stan said there was two wagons a women."

"Stan Taylor was wrong. The women here are not that kind of women. Now leave before there's trouble."

"Who's goin' ta give it?" The cocky little man hitched up his gun belt.

"I am, if you don't leave."

"Looky here, fellers. We got us a rooster what's goin' to run us outta his chicken yard all by hisself. I think we ort a pull his tail feathers."

"If you want to get your rocks knocked off with a bullet, go ahead and try it. But I think you should know that if I miss, there's a buffalo gun pointed at your belly that won't miss and a couple of Texan six-guns pointing at the rest of you. You better think about it before you start trying to pull tail feathers."

"C'mon, Lyster. Stan could a been wrong."

The man named Lyster shook off the hand that tried to pull him back from the door. "We're Clayhill men. Clayhill runs thin's round here, and he don't stand fer havin' his men pushed round. It was a long ride out here. We ort a have us a drink fer it."

Kain's temper flared. "Listen you stupid shithead. Clayhill doesn't run this place. You'd better get the hell off it before I forget I didn't want any trouble."

"C'mon, Lyster. Quit yore jawin'. Yore makin' a ass a yoreself. Sorry, mister. We ain't aimin' fer no trouble."

"Yo're the ass fer backin' down, Matson. Shee . . . it! This piss 'n vinegar blowhard's don't 'mount to no more 'n a fart in a whirlwind. He thinks to run us off so's he'll have the women all to hisself."

"Do ya want that I let loose on that thar blabbermouth, Kain? I got this here ole buffalo gun loaded to the brim 'n she's jist itchin' to go off." John's voice came out of the darkness.

"That 'n what's got the floppy mouth is mine." The drawl came from one of the Texans. "I got my sight right on them rocks a his he's wantin' to get knocked off."

"Ya got the last floppy-mouthed bastard we run on to, Jeb. I got my sight on jist the place to give 'em a new asshole."

The men turned and left the porch in a body, and headed for the horses. Lyster stood alone on wobbly legs, then turned and followed, threatening what he was going to do to Stan Taylor when he caught up with him.

"Dadgummit! Why'd they have to go 'n be so confound reasonable fer?"

"Hit's the night air, John. Hit's plumb calmin'."

"Twas what I said 'bout the asshole what done it. Ya can't get along without one, but I ain't never seen no feller what wants two of 'em."

"If'n ya wants to think ya run 'em off, Clay, go ahead. Me 'n John knows it ain't so."

Kain waited until he could no longer hear hoofbeats, then called out, "Much obliged."

"Don't mention it." The trio headed back to the bunk-house.

Kain closed the door, shot the bolt, and went back to the kitchen.

"They were a bit rowdy, and mad because they made the long ride for nothing. Stan Taylor spread the news all right. They'll probably take a piece of his hide for sending them on a wild goose chase, but they'll spread the right word, and I doubt if we'll be bothered again."

"I hope not." Ellie hung the dishpan behind the stove. "Imagine them coming out here thinking . . . that!"

"I think it's exciting, Aunt Ellie."

"Vanessa!" Ellie scolded, but here eyes were bright with excitement, too.

"What did they want, Kain?" Henry asked with a puzzled frown. "One of them said something about rocks. They didn't ride out here to get *rocks*, did they?"

Kain looked at Vanessa's sparkling eyes and twitching lips. She raised her brows and the expression on her face was expectant.

"I think they came out here to drink and watch a show. They'd heard there was a redheaded woman out here who danced the cancan."

"Van can't dance like that!"

"Henry Hill! I can too dance the cancan!"

"I ain't never seen you. I only saw you at a barn dance, and then you got mad and kicked Martin McCann on the shin so hard he had to be helped in his buggy. You said he pinched your bottom."

"I'm glad to know she doesn't like her bottom pinched, Henry. I don't want my shins kicked until my side is healed."

Mary Ben hung the wet towel on the rack beside the cookstove and glanced at Henry. She hesitated for a moment, then said, "Is there anythin' else fer me to do, ma'am?"

"Not tonight, dear. In the morning we'll have to put our heads together and make plans. There will be a hundred things to do between now and Sunday. We'll have to figure out what day we'll go to town. What do you think, Kain?"

"Give me another day and I'll ride in with you. I need to call on the preacher and see if he can come out next Sunday. Come to think of it, I should see him before I send out the letters asking folks to come."

Henry lifted Mary Ben's coat off the peg, put it around her, and they slipped quietly out the door. As soon as it closed behind them he wrapped her in his arms, kissed her, then held her away from him and looked down into her face.

"What's a whorehouse, Mary Ben? I heard talk about it, but nobody would tell me what it is."

"It's a house where women'll do *it* with men for pay."

"Do what?"

"Get in bed with 'em, couple with 'em. Ya know, like what we'll do when we marry."

"They want to do it with women they don't even *know*?"

"If'n they don't have a woman they do. There's a lot a women who do it. It be the way they make their livin'."

"I'll have my own woman, won't I? We're going to get married! After next Sunday you'll be mine forever."

"I'm already yores, Henry Hill!"

"I know it, but then everybody will know it, too. I'm just so proud of you, Mary Ben. Kiss me again, my sweet and pretty girl. I thought you'd never get through with those old dishes."

"I'll be a help to yore ma. I promised her I would."

"Ma likes you."

"I like her, too."

"Let's go to the wagon."

"We'd better not. Yore ma trusts me, 'n I ain't wantin' to let her down. It's gettin' harder 'n harder to hold out against ya. We ain't got much longer to wait now. After we get married we'll be together ever' night."

"I was looking at you while you were drying dishes, Mary Ben. You're just so pretty and you're *my* girl. I wanted to pinch myself to see if I was dreaming."

"If'n I am, I don't want to wake up."

"Let's sit down here on the end of the porch. You can sit on my lap and I'll keep you warm."

"I was surprised at ya speakin' up like ya did in front of ever'body," she said after he had sat down and pulled her onto his lap. The old yellow dog came out from under the porch and lay down beside them.

"Why? You knew we'd get married sometime. I just didn't like hearing about Van and Kain when we wanted to get married, too." He leaned back against the wall and covered them with her coat. "I like holding you like this.

You're . . . just a little girl, and sweet." His hands roamed over her small body, and his lips nuzzled her ear. "Do you think we'll know what to do when it comes time?"

"We'll know *what*, but maybe not *how*, at first," she whispered and slipped her hand inside his collar at the back of his neck. She moved her face so their lips could meet. He kissed her gently, as always. "We'll learn how. Most folks have younguns 'n they have to do it to get 'em."

"Kain said it'd hurt you at first. I don't want to hurt you." He hugged her fiercely. "I don't think I could stand to hurt you, my sweet girl. Kain said I'd have to be careful, and I will. Sometimes I get so big and so hard, and I think I can't put this in Mary Ben, she's too little."

"Yes, ya can, silly. Babies come outta there, so it stretches. You ain't to worry about it, Henry. Ya ain't to worry a'tall, hear?"

"Kain said men want to do it more than women. He said men could do it every day and not get tired of it. He said if you didn't want to I wasn't ever to force you, and I won't, I promise I won't. He said when we both wanted to do it it would really feel good."

"Kain must a told ya a lot of thin's."

"He did. He said if I wanted to know something to ask him and he'd tell me the best he knew how. He knows about women and a lot of other things. He said if I touch myself when I'm big and hard it'd not make me go crazy. I always thought it did."

"What else did he say?"

"I told him I got like that when I was with you, and that I wanted to kiss you awful bad. He said it was all right for a man to get that way when he was with a pretty girl he liked. I guess he does when he's with Van. You know what, Mary Ben? I've got you now, and I won't have to be asking Kain."

"Do you want us to have a baby, Henry?"

"Won't we get one if we do it?"

"Some people don't have but one youngun, some none.

My ma jist had me. That mean old bastard that took us to Oklahoma put it to her lots of times, but she never had no more. He'd make her bend over, throw up her skirt 'n poke it in her. He tried to do it to me when I was just a little girl, and Ma cold-cocked him with a spoke from a wheel."

"Did she kill him?"

"No. I did. Later I shot him dead. He was nothin' but a mean dirty old skunk. He was hurtin' Ma. I told him to stop 'n he wouldn't." She shuddered and cuddled closer in his arms. "I didn't even stop 'n think 'bout it, I jist shot. I'd shoot somebody hurtin' you, Henry."

"You would? Ah... honey girl," he whispered between kisses. "I'm suppose to take care of you."

"We'll take care of each other... 'n yore ma, too. I jist love ya so much, Henry." She felt his breath heat and quicken as his kiss deepened. He pressed her against the elongated hardness that sprang up between them and moved his hips in jerky little motions. She pulled away and framed his face with her hands. "We'd better stop, sweet man, afore you get to hurtin' bad," she cautioned. "Soon I'll not have to tell ya to stop. I'll be with ya all night long 'n we'll do all the lovin' ya want."

"Ah... Mary Ben, I just hurt to have you."

"I know ya do," she crooned, and stroked his cheek with a feather touch. "Jist be still. It'll go away, like it done afore."

Chapter Fifteen

"Thank you, God," Ellie prayed, "for bringing Mary Ben into our lives. She's a sweet, dear girl, and I promise to love her as if she were my own, for this great joy she has brought to my son."

Ellie sat in the kitchen sewing on the pink and white striped dress she had made for Vanessa several years before. It was hard for her to believe she was remaking it for her son's future wife. She had been proud of Henry earlier that night. He had spoken up like a man. A few weeks before he would have pulled her away from the others and whispered in her ear if he had wanted to tell her something. He was going to be married. *Her Henry was taking a wife.* One day there could be children, her grandchildren. One of her greatest sorrows had been her belief that her son would never know the fulfillment of loving, as she had loved his father. That was over now. Mary Ben was mature beyond her years and seemed to understand Henry far better than she and Vanessa.

There was no doubt in Ellie's mind that the girl loved him. He was such a handsome man, the image of his father. If only Henry could have lived to see their son on his wedding day.

The country had changed Henry, changed all of them. Here she sat in the kitchen thinking it was perfectly respectable for Vanessa to be in Kain's bedroom with the door closed, and Henry and Mary Ben alone in the dark outside. My, my, she thought. What a difference a few weeks could make in a person's life.

She had completely given up the idea of trying to locate Adam Hill. She realized now he was indifferent about the relationship. Otherwise, he would have answered her letters. Should their paths cross, so be it. If not, she and Henry wouldn't miss having a relative they'd never had. Of more importance was Kain. He was an extraordinary man. He had brought them through that rough country to this place. She had the feeling he would have done it even if he hadn't fallen in love with Vanessa. She prayed to God he was mistaken about his illness. But he seemed so sure.

Her thoughts were interrupted by the happy laughter coming from Kain's room.

"I need to have my bandages changed." Kain stretched out on the bed and grinned up at Vanessa.

"No you don't. I changed them this morning."

"They itch."

"You're lucky. That means they're healing."

"I hurt . . . something terrible—"

"Big baby! You're after sympathy. Eeow!" she screeched, falling heavily beside him when he jerked on her hand. "You idiot! I could have fallen on you and hurt you."

"I made sure you didn't. I want nothing to interfere with my wedding night." He laughed, dragged her close, turned her over on her back and, leaning over her, kissed her hungrily. "I can't keep my hands off you. I want to touch you, look at you, kiss you . . . here and here." His lips moved from her mouth to her eyes, her nose, and down her cheek to her chin.

"Hmmm."

"What does that mean?"

"It means don't stop what you're doing."

His fingers scarcely touched her skin as they played along the line of her chin and then began to caress her throat. He smiled down at her, and it warmed her like sunshine. She arched up in mute appeal for his hand to cup the aching fullness of her breast. She watched his eyes move down as his hand slid from her throat and his fingers slowly stroked back and forth across her aroused nipple, visible through the cloth of her dress.

"Ah, sweet woman," he whispered. "I'm desperate to make love to you. I want to see you, touch you, feel you. I want to come into you and worship you with my body, give you my soul."

She reached for his hand and brought it to her lips. She turned it over and kissed his palm with a tender, lingering caress while still looking into his eyes. His eyes were deep and warm and golden. An instant hotness like a flash of heat skittered along her nerves and a burning ache stabbed her lower body with awful, stunning suddenness.

"Then why don't you, my darling?" She wasn't sure she had even said the words. Her fingers guided his to the buttons on her dress. In utter silence they continued to stare at each other with openhearted longing. She moved her hands up over his shoulders to the back of his neck, giving him unrestricted access. His trembling fingers worked at the buttons, but not until he released the last one did he fold back the top of her dress and pull on the ribbon that held her chemise.

She felt the throbbing beat of her pulses high in her throat, and the pounding of his heart when first his eyes and then his fingertips touched her breasts. The gentle, seeking touch of his hands sent delicious quivers through her as he held her warm and naked breast in his palm.

He made a low groaning sound. "My love, my love."

Unable for a moment to do anything but look at her, his warm, loving gaze caressed the coral tips of her breasts, the smooth white skin of her ribs and upper belly.

She watched his eyes follow his fingers as they stroked from one side of her firm globes to the other, across taut and aching nipples. Her breath came in long, deep waves, enjoying the moment, waiting heedlessly for the next. He bent his head and his mouth traced a path from her collarbone to the tip of her breast. He kissed it reverently and took it into his mouth. She felt the roughness of his tongue and her breathing came deeper and faster.

"Kain..." She palmed his face with her hands and brought his mouth to hers. Their lips met and parted, then met once again in a deep, clinging kiss, his tongue gently circling the soft, pink flesh of her inner lips.

"I've never known such pleasure or seen such beauty," he whispered, and pressed his mouth to her moist parted lips again. "This means I love you." His mouth trailed to her eyes and his kiss closed them. "This means I love you. And this," his voice faded to no more than a breath of a sound as he pressed his face into the valley between her breasts, "means I love you."

"My sweet and gentle man," she crooned, and caressed his head with her two hands. "I'm yours, now and for always. Show me what to do. I want to give you all of me, and I want all of you."

He raised his eyes to hers, not daring to believe she could want him as much as he wanted her.

"I can wait—"

"I don't want to wait, Kain darling. I don't want to waste a minute of my time with you."

With great suddenness he was holding her fiercely. She heard his gasping, almost sobbing breath; felt his quivering, eager mouth against hers. His tenderness thrilled her to the marrow. The rough drag of his cheeks against hers, his masculine odor, the sweet, tender way his fingers held the back of her head as his lips played with hers all sent delicious quivers throughout her melting flesh.

"Do you want me to blow out the lamp?" His voice in her ear seemed only a breath.

"No."

"Thank God!" he said fervently. "Oh, thank God you are what you are, my love."

He slipped off the bed and knelt down. He untied her shoes and slipped them off her feet. Slowly he pulled off her black stockings, his hands caressing her knees and calves. He lifted a bare foot and tenderly kissed the red mark on her instep made by the tight shoelaces.

He said her name and reached for her hand. She stood before him and he untied the sash of her dress, smoothing it from her shoulders until it fell around her feet. She stood proudly, her eyes on his face, the chemise that hugged her narrow waist and slim hips her only covering. His fingers were so shaky that he fumbled with the pins in her hair, but as each one slid away he placed it carefully on the table. He could only stare at her when her fiery hair fell in curling wisps over her gleaming white shoulders and pink-tipped breasts.

As his eyes roved over her, Vanessa's body burned with a joyful and alien longing, new and unknown sensations that had lapped at her senses since she had met him. He pulled her into his arms, buried his face in her drifting hair, and stood quietly holding her as if he were holding something far more precious than life. After what seemed like an enchanted eternity, he released her and stepped away.

His whole body flamed and hardened, his arms and legs began to quake. He quickly pulled his shirt off over his head. Watching her, he worked at the buckle of his belt, unfastened it but then waited, willing himself to contain his almost insupportable eagerness before he released the throbbing, elongated hardness to her innocent gaze. He had to go slow, he cautioned himself. He reached for her again and she came willingly. Her soft breasts against his flesh set him to trembling and constricted his chest until he thought he would suffocate.

"Tell me what you want. I don't want to frighten you," he muttered thickly.

She gazed up at him, seeing through her desire-misted vision the anxious, tender concern in his eyes. "Nothing about you could ever frighten me."

"I could blow out the light."

"No. I want to look at you."

He released her and stepped back. His heart was drumming so hard he could barely breathe. He was too stunned with his happiness and joy of her to utter a word. He shrugged out of his tight buckskin britches and stood before her. His body was dark against the white bandage on his shoulder and side. His wide shoulders narrowed to a sinewy waist without an ounce of superfluous flesh. He stood on muscular legs, and where they joined she saw the thatch of dark brown curls that enclosed the root of his maleness. The mystery she had expected to fear and shrink from was beautiful. It stood firm and hard against his belly, a monument of his love.

She stared at him with the dull, fixed expression of the hypnotized before her lips parted and the air from her lungs escaped with a pleasurable sound. "Ahh . . ."

With a freedom that surprised even her, she slid the chemise over her hips, and when it fell to the floor she stepped out of it. She stood still, only her glorious hair covering her while his eyes roamed from the top of her head, down over rose-tipped breasts to her flat belly, on to the soft, red-gold hair that nestled between her thighs, and down long slender legs to the tips of her toes.

She smiled a quivering smile and went to him. Her hands

fluttered up and over his smooth, muscled shoulders, and moved down along his ribcage to his narrow flanks. A half choked cry came from him as she stroked the quivering flesh of his belly with her fingertips.

"Once I saw a picture of a statue called *David*. You're beautiful, like the statue." She looked up into his eyes and her hands slipped from his shoulders down his arms so her fingers could interlace with his. Slowly, she pulled him toward the bed. "I must have done something good sometime, or God wouldn't have let me be with you like this."

He moaned and murmured, "I've never truly thanked God for anything before. I do now. I thank Him for bringing you into my life."

They sank down on the bed, arms holding each other, lips touching, releasing and touching again. If he had hoped for or expected anything, it had not been this swift honesty with which she had offered herself to him. He had had no experience at all with a good woman, only a succession of the other kind. He had not expected this sweet willingness, the astounding passion that lay slumbering beneath her patient innocence.

Her mouth was trembling and eager against his as his hand traveled down her back to the fullness of her hips and pressed her to him. The silky down between her thighs teased his hardened flesh. In a frenzy his heated blood raced to it, swelled it even more, and pulsed there. An inarticulate sound escaped him. He gently turned her onto her back and raised himself on quivering arms to hover over her. His thumb caressed her lips before he kissed her, gently, wonderingly, the touch filled with praise and promise.

"I love you, Vanessa Cavanaugh." The words were wrung from him, accompanied by a soft moan.

Her murmured reply was lost in his kiss.

Borne beyond constraint, he lifted himself above her and positioned himself between her thighs with firm but gentle insistence.

Almost believing this was a dream and she would awaken alone in her bed, she opened her legs to welcome him when she felt the first firm touch of his hardened flesh probing the moist opening in her body. In the sweet freedom of letting go, she was wholly caught up in the sensations trembling from that secret place. She instinctively lifted her hips to the indriving shaft of pleasure that stole into the enchanted grotto, and her body perceived a gradual, gentle filling where before there had been emptiness.

In a haze of ethereal delight she was conscious of only a slight, swift tinge of pain. Then she was rocking, rocking, borne on a floating rhythm of a mighty wave. Seeking more of the delicious feeling, she thrust upward to envelop his entire length, and her hands slid around his waist, down to his taut buttocks, gripped hard, and pulled him to her, helpless to suppress the unending moan of pleasure that rose in her throat with every surge of his magnificent prodding flesh. She writhed in her search for gratification, and when it came she found she was no longer herself and whole, but a body of many fragments, alive with vibrant sensations. The explosion sent her rising, gasping, upward and onward until all that held her together was the glorious spear that pierced her to her very soul.

Knowing the time had at long last come when there was no need for hesitation, he drowned his burning, bursting body in the writhing sweetness he had entered. Kain felt himself enveloped in a sheet of flame that ignited his every nerve and tissue. He was enclosed in sweet softness, pillowed in a warm and silken place. There was no more thinking, only feeling and a quick, ecstatic, irreversible tempo building toward the consuming release. Then, with only the warm sheath to hold him, he was floating free above the earth, flying and drowning all at once. He felt the heated flow of his life giving fluid spurt from his body in a great flood, filling her. And then he was beyond himself.

His body and mind came gradually back together with his

gasping breath. He roused and lifted himself on his elbows, looking down into her magnificent blue eyes. Beholding her perfection and feeling her physical warmth that still enclosed him convinced him that it had not been just a dream. With gratitude he saw that she was smiling at him with worship in her eyes. For a long moment he had courage for no more than silence.

"I think I died and was born again," he said when he was finally able to speak. The words were whispered against her lips before he kissed them as if he had never kissed them before. "You've given me the greatest treasure I've ever had." She could feel his deep voice vibrate against her breasts. "Thank you."

She pressed her hands against his back when he would have moved from her.

"Not yet," she whispered. "Please stay."

He looked into her eyes for a long moment, and when he chuckled a low, loving sound, she felt the tip of him touch her womb. She gave a gasp of pleasure and flexed her hips upward, trying to bury him more deeply.

"Did you like it, my love?" He was amazed and pleased to discover he was fully distended inside her, despite the violent completeness of the act they had just finished.

"It was heaven. I'd heard it was something a woman had to endure." She laughed softly at the absurdity and wiggled her hand down between them. "You are all the way inside me," she said with wonderment.

"You'll be sore tomorrow. I should leave you."

"Do you want to?"

"God no!" He advanced his pelvis, deliberately letting her feel the hardness of his erection.

"I hope to have callouses . . . there," she whispered, moving her hands down to his buttocks and kneading gently.

Her brilliantly alive eyes laughed up at him. Her face was damp and flushed and covered with a happy smile. He began to caress her mouth gently but firmly. A little noise came from his throat, and he moved his hips in small circles as gentility gave way to greed. His need was a tumultuous pressure in his groin. His mouth nuzzled her rigid nipples, and she held him, clutching fiercely and stroking the back of his head, loving his weight, his warmth, the throbbing pressure that nudged at her womb.

His movements became frenzied. The pull of his lips on her nipples was both pain and pleasure. He left them to cover her mouth with his. She opened to him in wild abandon, giving her love with a wild recklessness, wanting to make him need her as much as she needed him. She drew him deeper and deeper into her as if she could hold him to her forever, chaining him to her with bonds of warm flesh.

Suddenly and violently her own body began to splinter and fall apart. During her shuddering convulsions he lay rigidly still inside her, giving her maximum pleasure, letting her feel the full impact as each trembling wave washed over her. She keened a quiet, soft cry of rapture as he brought her to an ecstasy far beyond the one of moments before. Finally he could no longer hold himself back, and poured his stream of life into her, his heart pulsing violently. In that final moment he experienced fulfillment, contentment and blazing passion beyond anything he'd ever imagined.

She held him to her with all her strength while violent shudders rocked his powerful body. For an undetermined time she was aware of nothing but his fullness inside her and his weight on her body. Then she floated back to consciousness and found her hands moving across his back, feeling the smooth shifting pattern of his muscles as he moved, feeling his breath on her cheeks. Then she heard the hoarsely whispered, shakily spoken words in her ear.

"You are more, far more than I ever dreamed a woman could be. I feel as if I had come home after a long lonely voyage." Slowly he pulled himself out of her and slid down her body to lay his dark head on her breast.

He lay quietly and she stroked his hair. Love for him

filled her heart. Now that she knew of this pleasure she could give him, and he her, she would banish the hungry look from his golden eyes.

"Am I too heavy for you?"

"I want to keep you here forever."

"I'm so sleepy."

"Rest, darling, I'll hold you."

She reached for a bedcover, pulled it over them, and brought it up to cover his back. She delighted in the sensation of his warm body on top of hers. The cover closed them in their own private world. Never, never had she felt so safe and so complete. And never had she been more determined that nothing or no one would take him away from her.

When Vanessa woke Kain was sitting propped against the headboard, studying her with an ineffably tender expression, his fingers entwined in her flaming tresses spread out on the pillow. He reached over and smoothed the tight curls from her forehead, and trailed his fingertips down her cheeks, rosy from the roughness of his face.

"Morning, sweetheart." He put out his arm, inviting her to move up beside him. She did so, leaning her head on his shoulder. "I'll have to be more careful. My whiskers have scraped your soft skin." He kissed the top of her head and his hand moved beneath the cover and spread over her soft belly. "Are you sore?"

"I don't know. I haven't moved enough to find out." Aware that she was naked, she pulled the cover up and over her breasts.

"There's no need to close the barn door after the horse is gone, sweetheart." He laughed and his arms tightened.

"You're right, of course." She let the cover fall to her waist and grinned at him.

"Brazen hussy!" he chided with rough tenderness. "We can ride in to the preacher today, sweetheart. We don't need to wait until Sunday."

"There's no need. Standing in front of a stranger so he can say the words won't make me your wife any more than I am now. We'll be married on Sunday. Aunt Ellie is looking forward to it."

"And you?"

She turned her head and pressed kisses along the smooth warm skin of his chest. "I'm looking forward to every night between now and then."

"I was hoping you'd say that." He lifted her face and kissed her parted mouth. "Thank you for making me happier than any man has a right to be." His smile fired her with new tenderness. She slid upward in his hold and kissed the corner of his mouth.

"Thank you . . . for showing me that mating with the one you love can be the most precious gift God gave to us humans."

"I brought warm water from the kitchen for you to wash in. I'll fix us some breakfast while you get dressed. It will be a while before everyone comes in."

"Kiss me first. It will have to last for at least ten minutes."

The hours of the day disappeared as if by magic. An air of gaiety permeated the house and all its occupants. Clay went to town to get a steer to barbecue. Jeb and John began clearing the weeds around the house and repairing the gates. Ellie made list after list of things to do, things to buy, things not to do, and things not to forget to do at the last moment. She set Henry and Mary Ben to unpacking the good dishes they had brought from Springfield, and when that was done they took down the heavy, velvet draperies in the parlor and hung them on the line so the wind could whip the dust away.

Before John left the kitchen after breakfast he motioned Ellie to follow him outside. He pressed several gold pieces into her hand.

"When ya go to town, buy shoes 'n ribbons 'n all them folderols fer Mary Ben. Is that enuff?"

"It's more than enough, much more. One coin will do, with enough left over for dress goods." She took his hand and returned all the coins but one ten-dollar gold piece. "John, I don't know how you feel about Henry, but I want to assure you that he'll always be kind to Mary Ben. He has his limitations, but there isn't a mean bone in his body."

"I ain't got no doubt of it, ma'am. That little gal's had it mighty hard. She ain't ne'er had nobody. From what I hear her ma was pert nigh mindless at the end. It jist might be she'll be the makin' a Henry 'n him a her."

"You'll always be welcome. I want you to know that, and I hope you're with us for a long, long time."

He took off his hat and scratched his head. "That's mighty good a ya, ma'am. I'd kinda figgered to stay round." He slapped his hat on his head. "I figgered somethin' else out. I'd better get ta workin' on that ol' wagon a mine. Clean it out 'n fix up somethin' decent to carry you women to town in. I'm thinkin' of goin' along 'n buyin' myself a new shirt fer the weddin'."

Kain came out of the house with his hat and vest on. "It's not safe in there, John. We men better stay outside or we'll get swept up in all the doings. My woman tried to set me at the table to run the flat iron over ribbons for her hat. That's when I remembered I had things to do, like stretching my legs." His smile was spread all over his face.

"Don't stretch them too long or too far," Ellie cautioned and went back in the house as Henry came out. "Don't run off, son. I need you to bring down that mattress from the attic."

"I won't. I want to talk to Kain."

"Come walk with me. I'm going out to the gate and back. I can stand just so much sitting around."

"Ain't it something, Kain? We're going to get married on

the same day." They were walking side by side down the two-wheel track, the yellow dog at Henry's heels.

"Sure is. Things have happened in a hurry."

"I don't have to ask you so much now that I've got Mary Ben. She tells me most everything I want to know. She told me what a whorehouse is and why the man said he come to knock off his rocks. Mary Ben knows about a lot of things."

"I'm happy for you, Henry. She's a fine girl. She'll make you a good wife."

"There's something worryin' me, even if Mary Ben told me not to worry about it. She's such a little girl, Kain. She only comes to my shoulder. I just worry that when I'm all worked up, you know, that I'm too big for her."

"You've talked to her about it?"

"Oh, sure. We talk about everything."

"If she told you not to worry, don't worry."

"But I can't help it. I'm afraid I'll hurt her."

"I see your mother has a large jar of plain salve. Dip some out and put it in a small can and keep it in your room. If you're afraid you'll hurt Mary Ben, use some of it, and you'll be able to enter her more easily." Good God! Kain thought. He was actually giving a lecture on sex. Was that what he would have told his son someday?

"Put it where?"

"On yourself . . . or Mary Ben. There's one thing I'd better tell you. It's something Mary Ben might not know about. You be sure that when you're with her you give her as much pleasure as she gives you."

"How can I do that?"

"By going slow, holding back. It will take longer for her to feel pleasure than it will for you. Once you've let yourself go, that's it for awhile. So hold off as long as you can."

"I will, Kain. I want Mary Ben to be happy. More than anything I want her to be happy."

They reached the gate and started back toward the house. Henry was silent for awhile.

"Mary Ben told me she'd killed a man for hurting her ma. She said she'd shoot somebody for hurting me. I've got to take care of her, Kain. I've just got to. I've got to work and make a home for her and Ma."

Kain looked into Henry's tormented eyes, realizing Henry knew his inadequacies. Kain stopped and put his hand on his shoulder.

"You can do that right here. There's not a doubt in my mind that you'll be able to do it, Henry. You're a good man. You're not lazy, you take direction, and with Mary Ben beside you you're going to make it a hell of a lot better than most folks."

"Do you think so?" Henry began to smile. "I wish I'd known you a long time ago, Kain."

"I do too, but wishing doesn't change things. I'm proud to know you now."

Kain was seated at the table when the sharp pain made itself known to him and he felt the familiar sickness rise up in his throat. He had been forced to lounge about the house because Ellie and Vanessa watched him like hawks to see that he didn't over-exert himself. He had drunk cup after cup of strong black coffee, idling away the time while everyone else was busy. Now the coffee was like bitter gall in his mouth. He set the mug on the table, put on his hat, and murmured something about seeing to his horse.

"Kain?" Vanessa called as he headed for the door.

Ellie saw the drawn look on his face. "He's going to the barn, dear. Will you help me put the draperies back up in the parlor?"

Kain went quickly down the path to the barn, swung open the door and went to Big Red's stall. He stood there, arms folded on the heavy timbers, breathing heavily. Damn! Damn! He had thought his stomach was better lately. The pains had not bothered him so much. Perhaps this was the onset of that feeling of well-being he remembered had struck the sheriff several times before the end. It was something about the cancer eating through one place, and pausing before going on to another.

It was only at times like this that he really believed he was dying. At other times, there was the faint hope he would cheat death. But it was inevitable, or so the experts said. There was no cure. Still he had read of miraculous recoveries despite all the medical prophecies. He considered that for a moment. Were the miraculous cures proof of mind-over-matter? Could faith in God win over cancer? Or was there some strong force within the body that could be summoned forth and set to working against the disease?

Men critically wounded had survived against all odds during the war. Was it the will to live that saved them? Did they have something as precious as he had to live for? He had the will, but would it be strong enough to defeat his illness?

While he was thinking the pain subsided to a dull ache, but the sickness remained. He swallowed repeatedly so that he'd not retch. Beads of sweat formed on his brow and his face felt clammy. He rested his forehead on his crossed arms and stared down at his feet, willing the sickness to leave.

If he died today, he thought, he had already had more than most men. Vanessa . . . Vanessa, his sweet, sweet woman. He had slept little last night after the first hour of deep slumber. The rest of the night he had lain awake, holding her in his arms, vainly wishing he could see her with her belly swollen with his children and when silver streaked her fiery hair. He wanted to grow old with her, sit in a porch swing holding her hand and reminisce about the time she hit the young bully over the head with the shovel and later worked him over with the end of her shotgun. He wanted to tell their grandchildren about her wearing britches on the trail when as few as a dozen women had dared to be seen in men's attire. Most of all he wanted to sleep every night with her in his arms, even long after the urge to procreate had left him.

The barn door creaked open. He raised his head to see Vanessa standing there, the late afternoon sun behind her. She came quickly to him. He held out his arm to pull her close.

"Are you all right?"

"Of course I'm all right. I came out to see Big Red."

"I was afraid you'd hurt your side or your shoulder. You had a lot of exercise last night."

"Ah, sweet woman! That was the most wonderful night of my life. I'm thinking about a repeat tonight." The last words were whispered in her ear before his lips traveled around to place a lingering kiss on her lips.

She wrapped her arms about his waist, being careful of his side, and buried her face in his shirt. "Kain? I can't bear to let you out of my sight. I'm so afraid! Please tell me why we can't plan a future together. Everyday I'm dying a little inside not knowing. Is someone coming to kill you? Why are you so fatalistic about it? You weren't that way about Tass. I'm hoping, praying something will happen, that . . . you are mistaken, that we can get help from your friends if you think we can't handle it here. Please don't put me through this hell of not knowing."

"Sweetheart . . . you promised to not think about it." He almost choked on the words. "Please, please don't ask me. If I thought it would make you feel better I'd tell you." He held her tightly against him and stroked her hair.

Vanessa squeezed her eyes shut as tears welled. Her heart constricted and she struggled to keep the sobs from breaking loose. When she raised her head to look at him there was a smile on her face, but her lashes were wet. She took a deep breath.

"I can't promise I won't think about it."

The look she saw in his eyes, the look of love, adoration, and utter helplessness brought a great swell of emotion within her. She clasped her arms about his waist and her lips gently brushed his chin.

"I love you. It will make no difference if we are a million miles and a million years apart. Always remember that I love you."

Chapter Sixteen

On a cool, still autumn day John drove the team with Henry beside him on the wagon seat, and Kain rode alongside the wagon on Big Red when the trail widened to permit it. Jeb and Clay stayed behind to slaughter one of the two steers Clay had brought out from town.

"It's best," Clay had said that morning at breakfast, "to let the meat hang fer a day or two. 'Sides, it'll take Jeb that long to dig the hole to cook it in."

The sense of humor the Texans concealed behind their quiet faces came out more often now that they felt more at ease around the women.

"If'n I got to dig it by myself, I jist might dig it out by the outhouse," Jeb retorted, then turned brick-red when he realized what he had said. When Ellie paused on her way from the stove to the table to look at him, he said, "I'm jist joshin', ma'am."

"Course you are, Jeb. I never thought for a minute you'd do such a thing."

"Hogwash!" Clay snorted. "I remember the time we was at a shebang down on the Red River. The ramrod we was workin' fer was half sloshed 'n meaner 'n all get out. He was sittin' there shootin' off his bazzoo 'n Jeb put a frog in his whiskey jug. He took a swig a that whiskey 'n that frog dang near choked 'em to death."

"Oh, my goodness! You men must have ironclad stomachs!" Ellie exclaimed and shuddered with revulsion.

Jeb sent a quelling glance at his brother, gulped his coffee, and got to his feet. "You've run off at the mouth enuff, Clay. Get outta here afore Miss Ellie throws ya out on yore ear 'n I got to skin that steer all by my ownself."

Thinking about it now as she sat behind John and Henry with Vanessa and Mary Ben, Ellie recognized how fortunate they were to have such good friends. John had worked most of the day taking the top off his wagon and building a seat in the back for them to sit in. And Kain . . . when she thought of what awaited him and the pain Vanessa would have to endure, her heart felt like a rock in her breast.

Vanessa pulled the gray wool shawl tighter around her shoulders when they left the shelter of the timber. A cold wind coming down from the mountains made her aware that winter was but a month away. Her dark print bonnet allowed wisps of copper colored curls to show around her face, making the skin of her face appear all the whiter, her eyes bluer.

As they approached town, Kain reined in and waited for the wagon to catch up. "I'm going to turn off here and go on to the preacher's house. I'll meet you at the mercantile in about half an hour."

"Oh, please! Don't go off by yourself!" There was a kind of desperation in Vanessa's voice.

"There's nothing to worry about. Believe me, honey. I'll

see you in a little while." Feeling the warmth of her concern, Kain's eyes were reluctant to leave her face. Here was the consummation of all the yearning dreams he had had through the years of empty waiting. Her smile told him she had received the message of love and assurance that he had sent with his eyes, and her lips formed a kiss that he carried with him as he turned his horse and rode away.

A freight wagon took up most of the space in front of the store, so John turned the corner and went a good way beyond the saloon before he pulled up. Henry jumped down and helped the women from the wagon while John tied the team to an iron ring in a post.

"It isn't a very big town, but it's busy," Vanessa remarked, and moved back as another wagon rounded the corner.

"It's cause towns is scarce out here. Go on, Mary Ben, go on with Henry," John said when she stood uncertainly beside the wagon. "I aim to be here awatchin' the sights 'n keepin' my eye on the wagon."

Mary Ben reached down and patted the head of the old yellow dog who had trotted behind the wagon all the way to town.

"Yo're plumb wore out. Ya stay here with Mr. Wisner, now. Me 'n Henry'll be back in no time a'tall." She tucked her hand in the crook of Henry's arm and they headed toward the main street.

John reached into the wagon for Ellie's basket. "She's mighty purty all duded up in that dress 'n bonnet with ribbon on it, ma'am."

"Yes, she is. Our children make a handsome couple, don't they, John?"

A smile made the wrinkles in John's weathered face even deeper, and his blue eyes shone with pride. "Yes'm, they sure do."

Ellie walked beside Vanessa down the boardwalk. "There seems to be an awful lot of men here and a very few women.

A bakery would do well, Vanessa. I didn't see one as we came through town, did you?"

"No, but I saw an eating place. And it's a good one, if the woman I saw standing on the porch is an indication. She was so fat she'd have to go through the door sideways."

"I'd still like to try my hand at a bakery sometime. Oh, my, look at that fancy buggy coming into town. Oh, shoot! It turned. I was hoping it would come on by so I could see who was in it."

"It looked like the buggy Kain's sister was in. I hope we don't run into *her*."

Mary Ben and Henry were waiting beside the open door of the mercantile and followed them inside. At first glance Vanessa wasn't sure they would find what they wanted. It was as different from a ladies' emporium in Springfield as day from night. Here farming tools were set beside dress goods, and tins of crackers, barrels of rice, beans and jugs of sorghum were set alongside ribbons and scented soaps.

"Howdy, folks." The storekeeper walked from behind a screen of hanging harnesses. "Cooper! I didn't know—" His voice stopped as he came face to face with Henry. "Young man, I thought for a minute you were a friend of mine. By jinks damn if you ain't the spittin' image of Cooper Parnell."

"Do you know Cooper Parnell?" Henry smiled broadly. "He's gettin' an invite to our wedding. He's a friend of Kain's." He glanced at his mother, then stuck out his hand. "I'm Henry Hill, and this is my intended, Mary Ben."

"Glad to meet you. And you too, young lady."

Henry looked proudly down at Mary Ben, but she was gazing at the floor.

"I'm Henry's mother, Mrs. Hill. And this is my niece, Vanessa Cavanaugh."

"Name's McCloud. Are you folks moving in or passing through?"

"We're at Mr. DeBolt's place about five miles north of

town," Ellie said. "I believe the place was *formerly* called The House."

"Ah . . . so you're the ones. I heard you had visitors the other night."

"A few," Vanessa said dryly.

McCloud chuckled. "I hope you ladies wasn't too put out. It'll take awhile, but folks'll come to know it ain't . . . what it was. I've not seen Kain since he come back."

"He's to meet us here later on."

"Good. Good. What can I show you?"

"Shoes, for one thing," Ellie said, digging for her list in the purse that hung from her wrist. "And ribbon, sewing thread, and a piece of white goods. We need something to make streamers to decorate the parlor and eggs for the cake."

"Sounds like you're having a real shindig."

"It will be as nice as we can make it on this short notice. A woman cherishes the memory of her wedding all her life, Mr. McCloud. My niece is marrying Mr. DeBolt, and my son is marrying this young lady."

"A double wedding! That's something. You'd better not noise it around or you'll have half the town out there. Let's see, now. The shoes are right back here." The storekeeper went toward the back of the store.

Ellie urged Mary Ben along with a gentle hand on her back. "Something nice and soft. Oh, yes, do you have white stockings?"

After Mary Ben had been fitted with shoes, she sidled over to stand close to Henry. He was examining the collection of whips that hung from the ceiling on a wire.

"Looky here, Mary Ben, at this six-plait whip. The feller who made it didn't pull his strips tight and he should of run them through the splitting gauge one more time to get all the hair off. Did you know I can make a eight-plait whip? Someday I'm going to try my hand at a twelve plait."

"Why, that'd be grand! I couldn't even cut the strips straight. Mine'd be all katty wampus."

"Sometime I'll show you how to plait. I got a whole sack full of strips already cut."

"I'm just so proud of ya fer knowin' how to do that." She slipped her hand through his arm and hugged it to her.

"Are you, Mary Ben? My land! It's nothing."

"It is too somethin'," she protested. "Not ever'body can take a ole cowhide 'n make a whip."

"We sold some at stores on the way out here," he said proudly. "Van said I was helping to pay the way."

"'N ya was. Lordee, ya was jist doin' ever'thin' when I saw ya. They'd never got to Dodge without ya."

"You're just saying that." He covered her hand with his and squeezed it. "If Ma and Van don't need you, why don't we go out and see the sights?"

"I'll tell 'em we're goin'."

They walked past the land office and stepped off the boardwalk into the rutted street, crossing it to walk in front of the tall and gaunt feed store. Between the livery and the feed store a barbed wire was stretched and a cow with a bell around her neck grazed contentedly.

"Is that there a telegram wire, Henry?"

"Yup. That building is the telegraph office. It's not nothing like the one in Springfield, though."

"Can we cross over 'n go up the other side? This be the first time I ever did jist walk up 'n down the street of a town."

"Didn't you in Dodge?"

"No. I was scared. I'm not scared with you, Henry."

They walked the length of the other side of the street, crossed and started back down the boardwalk. They strolled past the barber shop, and the barber sitting in his chair waiting for a customer nodded a greeting. They looked down a side street and saw a Negro man wiping the dust from a fancy buggy.

"Look at that, Henry. Oh, my! He must be richer 'n Mr. DeBolt."

"He don't own it. He's the driver. There's a lot of nigger drivers in Springfield."

A group of riders came down the street and stopped at an empty hitching post. They tied their horses to the rail and stepped up onto the walk. The jingle of spurs could be heard over the loud thumping sounds of their boot heels on the boards.

"There's one of 'em that tole me The House was openin'." The cowboy that pointed the accusing finger toward Henry had a split lip, a cut on his cheekbone and a black circle around an eye that was almost swollen shut. He stood on bowed legs in the middle of the walk and confronted Henry and Mary Ben. "Ain't you one of them fellers that came through here with the fancy outfit sayin' ya was openin' The House?" he demanded.

"Ah . . . Are you talking to me?" Henry saw the anger and the hostility in the man's eyes and was utterly confused.

"I don't see nobody else. Ya 'n that other feller said The House was openin'. Ain't that what ya told me? Looky at what I got fer tellin' it." He gestured toward his face. "I got me a notion to do to you what was done to me."

"I never told you anything, mister."

Mary Ben tugged on his arm. "C'mon, Henry."

"Jist stay where ya are!" The belligerent cowboy grabbed Henry's arm and spun him around. "Ya ain't gettin' off that easy, ya lyin' son of a bitch!"

"Let go of me. I don't—I didn't—"

"He didn't do nothin'!" Mary Ben pulled on Henry's arm.

"I'm sayin' he lied!"

"He never—"

"He ain't even wearin' a gun! What we got us here is a plowboy." He shoved Henry up against the side of the building and held him there with his hands against his chest. "Ya tell 'em what ya told me. Nobody's brandin' Stan Taylor a liar."

"I . . . never told you nothing—"

"Tell 'em!" Stan slapped Henry across the face.

"Stop that! I never—"

Stan cut Henry's words off with another slap.

"Ya ort a be careful, Stan. Ya'll hurt him." After one of the watchers spoke the others began to laugh.

Mary Ben stood on the edge of the porch and looked frantically up and down the street for help. There was no sign of John or Kain. She heard Henry trying to explain, but the cowboy kept hitting him and she knew she had to do something.

Wild with fear, she jumped off the porch and ran to the horses tied to the rail. She slipped between them and snatched a rifle out of a saddle scabbard. It was cocked and ready by the time she reached the front of the eatery. She pointed the barrel upward and pulled the trigger. The sound of the shot vibrated up and down the street. The men on the porch turned in a body to see a small girl in a bonnet holding the rifle as if she knew how to use it, the barrel pointed at them.

"Get away from him!" Her voice was high and shrill.

"What the hell?"

"That's my rifle!" A lanky drover moved to the edge of the porch.

"If'n you hit him agin, I'll shoot ya!"

"My God! Do ya reckon she means it?"

"Wal, I'll be hornswoggled! Ain't this somethin'? Ya shore stirred up a hornet's nest, Stan. This little gal's a fighter even if her man ain't."

"Yo're shore enuff gettin' bested by a petticoat, Stan. The fellers'll roast ya alive!"

Henry moved around and hurried to the street to stand beside Mary Ben. "Where did you get that gun? What are we going to do?"

"Ya got to do what Kain taught ya," she hissed. "Ya got to fight that cocky little bastard or ya can't show yore face in this town no more."

"I can't fight," he whispered hoarsely. "I know, I can't—"

"Ya can too. When he comes over here jist spin 'round an' kick his balls like Kain showed ya. Ya got to do it fast 'n hard. Don't pay no mind to none a the rest of 'em. Jist spin 'n kick like Kain showed ya."

"It'll hurt him something awful!"

"If 'n ya don't, they'll hurt us. There ain't nobody to help. We got to stand 'em off, jist you 'n me."

"I'll . . . try, if you want me to—"

"Stan Taylor, are you 'fraid to fight by yoreself?" Mary Bent threw out the challenge. "Henry'll fight ya man to man. Step out if 'n ya ain't scared."

"Scared of a bush-bottom plow-pusher?" Surprised by the challenge, Stan glanced at his friends and grinned. "This'll take 'bout as long as it'll take to spit." He unbuckled his gun belt, hung it on a nail and stepped off the porch. "I'll clean yore plow, boy, 'n I'll get yore gal to boot. She's a mite too feisty fer the likes a you, nohow." He strolled cockily toward Mary Ben. "I reckon I'll get me a kiss first."

"I reckon you won't!" The words burst from Henry when Stan moved toward Mary Ben.

"What'll you do 'bout it?" Stan taunted.

Henry whirled, his arms flung wide so his opponent would be watching them, just as Kain had taught him. His right foot swung around and the toe of his boot landed in Stan's crotch. The air went out of Stan's lungs with a loud grunt, and as he doubled over, Henry struck him on the back of the head. His other looping fist caught Stan on the chin with all the weight of his body behind it, knocking him to the ground. He lay there moaning and writhing with pain.

"I didn't want to hurt you, mister." Henry stood over him, his fists still clenched. "But I will again if you bother Mary Ben."

"I knew ya could! Oh, I knew ya could!" Mary Ben rushed to him and hugged his arm.

The surprised drovers stepped off the porch. The tall lanky cowboy came to Mary Ben and held out his hand for his gun.

"Thanky," she said shyly and handed it to him.

"Anytime, ma'am. Jist anytime, a'tall. Yo're a woman to ride the trail with, ma'am. My hat's off to ya fer takin' up fer yore man."

"Ya shore cleaned old Stan's clock." One of the men held out his hand to Henry. "Name's Bill Cooney, late of Iowa. My pa farmed. It warn't fer me, though."

"Henry Hill, and I'm glad to know you."

"What the gawdamn hell is going on here!" A white-haired man in a black serge suit stood on the boardwalk in front of the eatery and glared at them from beneath the brim of his black hat. "You're Clayhill men, goddammit! I'll not have Clayhill riders brawling in the street, by Gawd! Do your brawling in the back alley, hear?"

"Yes, sir." Bill Cooney and the lanky drover helped Stan to his feet. "We was just goin'."

"Get back to the stockpens. If you're finished there get back to the ranch. I'm not paying you to hang around town."

"Yes, sir."

Stan Taylor was helped into the saddle and they left hurriedly.

Adam Clayhill's angry gaze passed over the girl and the tall blond man beside her, then returned to the man. His head was tilted down toward the girl in such a way that Adam didn't have a full view of his face, but he looked somehow familiar.

"Do you work for me?" he demanded, his brows beetled questioningly.

"No, sir. I'm sorry for—

"Henry! Mary Ben! What in the world?"

Vanessa was almost running in her haste to get to her

cousin, and Ellie was not far behind. They had been in the store when they heard the shot fired, and Mr. McCloud had said it was not unusual for a rowdy to discharge a weapon. When they left the store, they had seen Henry and Mary Ben standing in the street surrounded by men.

"Van! Wait'll you hear what I did." Henry and Mary Ben stepped onto the walk. "I did what Kain told me. He was going to kiss Mary Ben and . . . Kain said kick 'em where it hurts most, and I did." Ellie reached them and he put his arm about her shoulders and hugged her. "I did it, Ma," he exclaimed happily.

"I'm jist so proud of him," Mary Ben held tightly to Henry's arm.

"Oh, son! Taking up for yourself is one thing, but—"

"I didn't start it, Ma. Honest I didn't."

Adam Clayhill felt as if the wind had suddenly been knocked out of him. The boy was a simpleton, a dummy, but his face was Cooper's face, his voice Cooper's voice. Was he losing his mind? The woman and the boy turned to look at him. The woman's face went white. A wordless cry broke from her as if her senses were shocked by what she was seeing.

"Who the hell are you?" Adam spoke clearly, urgently, and he raked her with sharp, unkind eyes.

Hearing the sound of a voice that had echoed in her dreams, Ellie's vision blurred and her heart leaped to pound in her throat. She blinked her eyes rapidly so she could see, and her hands reached blindly for Vanessa's arm. In a near state of devastation her mind sped back through the years. She looked into the face of the man before her. It was an older face, but yet the same as the one she saw in her dreams and in the tintype she cherished.

"Henry," she gasped in a barely audible voice. "Henry," she said again. His face floated in and out of her vision as she sagged on Vanessa's arm.

"Aunt Ellie! What's the matter?" Vanessa looked up to

see Kain swinging from his horse. "Kain, come quick. Aunt Ellie is going to faint."

Kain realized what had happened the instant he saw Adam Clayhill standing on the boardwalk, and he cursed himself for taking the chance Clayhill would not be in town today. Poor Ellie!

"Henry, get your mother's arm. We'll take her down to the barber-shop where she can sit down."

"No!" The gray mist floated from Ellie's mind and she pushed the hands away from her. "I've got to know!" She stiffened her legs, lifted her head and looked pleadingly at Kain. "Who is he?" Her raw voice thinned to a wail.

"Adam Clayhill. Ellie, I wanted to tell you before you saw him—"

"It's Henry. I know he's Henry!" Her eyes moved from Kain's to Adam's face. "It's not Henry's brother. It's Henry!"

"His name is Adam Clayhill. But I think he's also Henry Hill, your *late* husband," Kain said bluntly. He put his hand beneath her elbow to steady her.

"Yes," she whispered, and staring unblinkingly at the man who returned her look with fixed intensity. "Oh, dear God! It is you!"

Adam shifted his gaze to Kain. "What are you up to now, DeBolt?"

"I think another of your sins has caught up with you. We can discuss it out here on the street or in privacy over there at the barbershop. The choice is yours. But this woman is going to know before she leaves here if you're the bastard that married her in Missouri under the name of Henry Hill, sired a son, then deserted her."

Adam started to answer, choked, and swallowed. Finally his voice came, and he stridently shouted, "I don't know what the hell you're talking about!"

"I think you do."

Kain watched the red flush that started at the neck of

Adam's white shirt and rose to cover his whole face. He realized the man was suddenly possessed by an almost overpowering fear.

"What's the matter, Ma?" Henry's anxious voice brought Ellie's attention to him. "What does Kain mean? Henry Hill was my pa."

"We're about to find out, son," she said, her voice unnaturally quiet.

"Move, Clayhill."

Adam's face was gray when he turned and led the way to the barbershop. His incredible self-possession had never failed him, and he was determined it would not fail him now. Thank God he had sent the ranch hands scurrying out of the street. His mind searched frantically for a way out of this dilemma without the entire town knowing about it.

"Get out," he said to the barber, who stood when he walked through the door.

"But Mr. Clayhill—"

"He'll pay for the use of your shop for a private conversation," Kain said, entering behind Vanessa and Ellie.

The man took off his apron and hung it on the chair. Something was going on here, he thought. Something big! He left the shop hurriedly.

"Close the door, Henry. Do you want to sit down, Ellie?" Kain asked.

Ellie seemed not to have heard him. Her eyes were glued to Adam Clayhill. He had the same thick hair, gray now where once it had been blond like her son's. Even his mustache was the same as in the picture made on their wedding day. He had the erect carriage of Henry Hill, and held his head at the same angle. He was dressed as fashionably as Henry had been dressed twenty years before.

"You are Henry Hill." Her flat, unequivocal statement brought an even deeper frown to Adam's face.

"I'm Adam Clayhill. I've never seen you before in my

life. What game is this? Are you trying to get money out of me?" There was a fleeting trace of desperation in his voice.

Ellie rejected this with a slow shake of her head. "You lie. Let me see your hands. The forefinger on my husband's right hand was crooked. My son has that same crooked finger."

"Husband? I'd know a woman if I'd married her, for Gawd's sake!"

"You married me in Springfield, Missouri and left me a month later to go to Chicago."

"He was on his way to Boston to marry my mother, Ellie," Kain said.

"Gawddamn you, Kain. You dug this woman up to embarrass me. What are you getting out of it?"

"I want to see his hands, Kain. That way I'll know without a shadow of a doubt that he's Henry Hill."

"Show her, Clayhill."

"I don't have to show her a damn thing!" Adam almost strangled on the words. His hands were deep in his pockets and he left them there. The emotion rioting through him was plainly written on his face.

"Show her or I'll break your goddamn arm!"

"There!" Adam jerked his hand out of his pocket and held it palm out in front of Ellie's face. The forefinger curved outward at the second joint. She drew in a sharp breath when she saw it. "It doesn't prove a damn thing!" he bellowed.

It was a moment before Ellie could speak. She watched Adam shove his hand back in his pocket. "Show him your hand, Henry."

"I wish you'd tell me what's going on, Ma."

"I will, son. But first show him your crooked finger."

Henry obediently held out his hand. The finger on his hand was identical to that of Adam Clayhill.

"Why did you do it?" Ellie asked quietly. "You sent me the letter saying Henry was dead. I grieved for you all these years."

"Jesus Christ, woman!" He loomed over her, his gaze locked with hers. "Are you trying to shove your bastard off on me?"

Ellie's hand flashed up and struck him across the face. "My son is not a bastard!"

"He sure as hell isn't out of me. I'd not sire a gutless, whining weakling—"

Ellie struck him again, and he caught her wrist in a cruel grip. Both Kain and Henry sprang toward them. Henry struck out blindly. The blow landed on the side of Adam's face. Caught by surprise, he dropped Ellie's wrist and staggered back.

"Don't you hurt my mother!"

"Jesus Christ! I'm getting out of here." Adam started toward the door and Kain barred the way.

"Not yet."

"What the hell does she want from me? She's got no proof I married her. She married a Henry Hill. She said she did."

"I have my marriage papers, Kain. And the photograph taken on our wedding day. I married him, and our son was born of that marriage."

"Papers? I signed no papers."

"You signed the marriage papers at the preacher's house and he sent them to the hotel. The clerk gave them to me. I had them recorded at the courthouse, just as I had the birth of our son recorded."

"So that's your game! You're wanting me to claim him for my legal son so he'll inherit. I got news for you, madam! That will never happen. I'll get my lawyer on you and sue you for slander if you spread that story around."

"Don't worry about that, Ellie," Kain said dryly. "He married you under an assumed name, and then married my mother. I think they call it bigamy. It's against the law in Missouri and in Boston. What would the Republicans down in Denver think of that, Clayhill?"

An agony of fear shot like a fiery bolt through Adam. He gritted his teeth and clawed at the collar of his shirt, then struck back in the only way he knew.

"Gawddamn you, DeBolt! You buck me on this, and you'll wish to Gawd you'd never come back here! I'll ruin you—both of you! And you, woman. Take that imbecile and get the hell out of this territory or I'll drag your name through such filth and slime you'll be spit on when you show your face on the street. Hear? I made this town, by Gawd! I was the first white man to snatch this land from the savages, and no split-tail woman is going to ruin my name. I never had to wed a woman to fuck her! And I'd certainly not have wed *you*, madam!"

Ellie looked closely at the man, noted the sickly pallor of his skin and the sheen of desperation that shone in his eyes. His ruinous brutality, crudeness and ungiving hardness had been there all the time, smoldering behind a charming facade. She recognized it through the layers of pain that dulled her senses.

"What a fool I've been to waste my life on such as you," she said slowly in a flat voice. "You bedazzled a young girl; and in order to get her to bed, you went through a ceremony using another man's name. You left me to raise our son alone. You're the lowest, most vile creature I have ever known."

"Your opinion means less than nothing to me. *You* mean less than nothing to me," Adam sneered.

The door opened and Della stood poised in the doorway. Her white felt hat was adorned with a white feather that brushed the top of the doorframe. She had a white fringed shawl folded over her arm and a pale blue scarf at the neck of her princess styled coat.

"Hello," she said cheerfully. Silence followed her greeting. "I didn't have any trouble finding you. Everyone up and down the street is waiting to hear what's gong on. What *is* going on, Papa, darling?" She moved inside and closed the door. She stood with her back to it, and her glance fell on Henry. "Oh, flitter! I can guess. Another one of your bastards has showed up."

"Shut up, Della," Kain roared. "Get out of here, and take this old son of a bitch with you before I kill him."

"You're going to get violent? Naughty, naughty." Her smile stretched to show pearly white teeth and a pink tongue she stuck out teasingly at Kain. "He's my brother, you know," she announced proudly.

"They know the miserable fact. And they also know I'm not proud of it."

His blunt statement had no apparent effect on Della. Her smile was brilliant, but her eyes were insulting as they toured up and down Vanessa's body.

"The redhead cleans up pretty good, Kain. You might be able to use her at The House when you open it, if you do something with that awful hair. But good God! Where in the world did she come from, and where did she dig up that horrible, backwoods sunbonnet?"

Vanessa's head jerked up and anger flared in her blue eyes. "Where I came from people have some manners. What back alley did you crawl out of?"

"Oh, dear. She's got an Irish temper, too. Her breeding is showing, brother. That's what happens when you take up with the lower classes."

Kain's fury burst forth in a strangled shout. "Damn you, Della. You and that old bastard make a pair!" He flung open the door and shoved Della out onto the boardwalk. People were gathered in small groups, all looking toward the barbershop. "You're a bitch, Della!" His raised voice echoed up and down the street. "You're nothing but a bitch!"

"Sure I am," she said sweetly, and touched his cheek with her fingertips. "A very well paid one at that. You're making a fool of yourself, brother," she added softly. "But then you always were a fool."

Adam shoved his way past Kain and grabbed Della's arm.

"You keep that two-bit whore away from me, hear?" he snarled, and propelled Della down the boardwalk, looking neither left or right. They turned the corner and Kain went back into the barbershop. Ellie stood with her hands gripping the arms of the barber chair.

"Are you ready to go, Ellie?"

"Why don't ya let me run 'n get Mr. Wisner?" Mary Ben moved protectively close to Ellie. "He can brin' the wagon 'n she won't have ta walk out there with all them folks starin'.'"

"That's a good idea. Tell him to bring it up the side street." Kain had never felt as sorry for anyone as he felt for the white-faced woman holding onto the chair.

"We left our packages at the store," Vanessa said.

"I'll get them, honey. I've got to post my letters with McCloud."

"There are eggs . . . for the cake," Ellie murmured.

"Me 'n Mr. Wisner'll swing by there 'n get 'em." Mary Ben put her hand on Henry's arm. "Stay right here by yore ma, Henry."

After Mary Ben left, Ellie looked up at Henry's troubled face. "She's a dear girl, son. You must always cherish her."

"I will. What happened, Ma? Is he—"

"I know this is confusing to you, but can you wait awhile longer? Later I'll tell you everything you want to know. Right now I feel like something inside me has died."

Chapter Seventeen

"Stop pushing me, Adam!" Della said testily.

"Hush up your damn mouth and get in the buggy. We're going home."

"Back to the ranch? We just got here for God's sake! We can go to the little house here in town until you get cooled off."

"Joseph!" he shouted. "Flag your black ass in here and get this thing moving. We're going home."

"Ta the house on A Street, suh?" The man hurried to untie the horse and climb into the driving seat.

"I said *home*, you fool!"

"Yassuh." Joseph sailed the whip out over the backs of the team and the buggy lurched.

"I'm not ready to go home," Della protested. "You said we'd stay the night in town. I'm tired of being stuck out at the ranch. Now, damn it, Adam—"

"Pull up, Joseph. Get your gawddamn ass out and stay or stop your damn whining!"

"Well, for God's sake! What's put you in such a state? Go on, Joseph."

"Yas'm." Joseph flicked the reins on the back of the horse and the buggy rolled smoothly out of town. The master was in a state, all right. Joseph was grateful he didn't get the toe of his boot in his back.

There were two bright spots of color high on Adam's cheeks, his eyes were as bright as glass, and the cords in his neck stood out and throbbed. He didn't seem to notice the sweat that rolled from his forehead down his nose.

"Gawddamn that son of a bitchin' brother of yours. I could kill the fuckin' meddling bastard! He's bucked me from the first time I laid eyes on the arrogant, know-it-all pissant!"

"I told you all along Kain wasn't our kind," Della said gleefully, knowing now there wasn't a chance she'd have to share her inheritance with her brother. "Has my dear brother flushed out another one of your bastards, Papa Adam?" She loved it when Adam was so angry he used filthy words.

Adam ignored the question. He placed his foot on the back of the driver's seat and looked off toward the mountains. Joseph put the horse into a brisk trot and turned down the winding river road they had traveled not more than an hour before.

Adam smoldered with rage at Kain. Even as a boy Kain had hated him. He'd shown his dislike the instant his mother had promised to marry him. The sulky little bastard had dragged his feet coming West, making his dislike for Adam known every chance he got. He had stayed only a short time before going back East to school. Now he was back and had set out to ruin him. Christ! How the hell had he managed to find that woman? The one time in his life when Adam had done something stupid was catching up with him.

Adam had been on his way to Boston to marry Etta De-Bolt and bring her back as his wife. He had stopped in Springfield to do some business with a banker who owned stock in a mining company he wanted to buy. He had met Ellie and, as he admitted to himself now, she had been a pretty little thing. She had made him horny as hell but refused to bed with him until after they married. He had gone through the ceremony, thinking it invalid unless the papers were recorded. He had enjoyed her day and night for several weeks.

Before he left town he had pressed the preacher for the marriage document. He had been told it was given to the clerk at the hotel, who a day later had run off with the hotel owner's wife. Ellie hadn't mentioned them, and deciding the papers were lost, Adam had dismissed the legality of the marriage from his mind. Later, after a number of letters from Ellie, he had sent the letter saying Henry was dead and promptly forgot the whole affair.

Now what in hell was he going to do? The woman didn't have the brains to press the suit; but Kain did, and he'd not let it rest. And the boy—he was a weakling, a throwback! He had the look of a Clayhill, had the Clayhill crooked finger, but he didn't have the brains to go with them. In fact, he acted like a gawddamn kid still shitting yellow! He wondered how he could face having folks know that dolt was his son?

"Adam?" Della slipped her hand through his arm. "Are you all right?"

"Yes, I'm all right! Hush your mouth and let me think!" He threw her hand away from him and turned in the seat, giving her a view of his back.

"I'll not take much more of this," she said in a shrill, tight voice, and dug her elbow in his back. "You'll not talk to me like I'm one of your servants. I don't know what Kain has done and I don't give a damn. But you'll not take your anger out on me. Do you hear me, Adam?"

There was no sound from him to indicate he had heard her. She leaned forward to see his face. It was rigid and he was staring straight ahead.

"Shit!" she muttered, and sank back on the seat.

As the miles dropped behind the speeding buggy, Adam asked himself why this had to happen to him now. He had overcome the stigma of having sired a half-breed son and the fact that his other bastard hadn't wanted anything to do with him. The Republicans in Denver had slapped him on the back and said, "There's a skeleton in the closet of every great man. Look at Thomas Jefferson. It was said he had bastards, both black and white, strung all over the South." Adam was sure that they would not be so tolerant of bigamy.

Adam had no doubt that Kain would use the woman and her simpleminded son to ruin him, getting his own back for Adam's bringing his mother and sister West. All his plans for becoming the governor of the territory would be washed away in the face of a scandal. A murderous hatred for Kain began to fester in Adam's mind. It was boundless and unchangeable, too complete to allow any vestige of reason to disturb its fathomless depths. It clamped its hot fingers around his throat, pinching off his voice so that when the curses rolled from his lips they came out thin and unintelligable. He brought the curses up out of the burning pit of hatred and they spewed out, laced with every filthy word he had ever heard. For endless minutes his cursing went on, and when it finally ceased he turned and stared fixedly at Della.

She stared back, vainly waiting for some break in his expressionless face. But there was no change at all in the steady look he gave her; and in the end, it was she who turned away. Not since the time he had slapped her in front of a crowd in Junction City for lying about Logan Horn's alleged rape of her had she been so frightened by his rage.

* * *

Kain watched the wagon roll down the dusty street and out of town before he went back to the boardwalk fronting the stores. As he passed the open door of the barbershop he tossed a coin to the barber and walked on, ignoring the curious stares of the bystanders. When he reached his horse he stepped into the saddle and rode the block to the mercantile.

McCloud met him at the door. "Howdy. I heard a few days ago you were back." The men shook hands. "Guess you know the town's buzzin' with news of the set-to you folks just had with Clayhill."

"Yeah, I guess I do." Kain pulled the letters from his pocket. "I need to get these out to Logan Horn and Cooper Parnell. It's an invite to my wedding. I'm being married on Sunday."

"I've already met your bride. Mighty pretty woman, and the little gal isn't bad looking, either." He held his hand out again. "Congratulations, Kain."

"Thanks. Ride out Sunday for the doings. We'd be glad to have you."

"I'll see if I can make it. I remember the day Logan married Rosalee Spurlock," he said looking at the envelope with Logan's name on it. "They had to sneak out the back door of the store because Clayhill had his gunmen hunting him."

"I think Clayhill has finally come up against something he's not going to crawfish out of. The woman who was in here is his legal wife, and the boy who looks like Cooper his legal son and heir. I'll telling you this because I'd not put it past the old son of a bitch to send someone out to kill us all. I want somebody to know the straight story. I aim to make sure Logan and Cooper know it, too."

"You don't say? Well, I swan." McCloud shook his head. "If it don't beat all what that man gets away with. The woman seemed a real nice lady, just as Mrs. Parnell is."

"She is. He deserted her and the boy, just as he deserted

Cooper's ma. Pass the word around town if you want to. It'll not do Ellie any harm, because I imagine he'll be doing all he can to smear her name."

"I'll do that. Folks aren't as keen on him as they were. There's not many in town he's not had a run-in with." The storekeeper placed the envelopes on the cash register. "Now, don't worry about the letters. I know just the man who'll take Logan's. He'll be back in before he leaves town, and Cooper'll get his if I have to send my stable boy out with it."

"Much obliged, McCloud. I appreciate it."

"There was a fellow in here asking for you yesterday. He said he'd heard you were headed this way and wanted to know if you'd got here yet."

Kain had turned to go, but turned back. "Did he say who he was?"

"I don't reckon he did say a name, now that you mention it. He knew you were traveling with some women in a fancy wagon and that you had an old man and a couple of other fellers with you."

"What did he look like?"

McCloud lifted his shoulders in a noncommittal gesture. "A Mex, or part Mex. Thin, dressed in black with silver studs in his gunbelt. There was one thing kind of queer about him, though. He had a braided rope of red hair hanging around his neck with a button on the end of it."

For a long moment, Kain stood gravely studying the wall behind McCloud's head, then finally he nodded. "Thanks, McCloud. I'll see you Sunday, if you can make it."

He mounted Big Red, and as soon as he left town he put the animal into a reaching trot, the easiest of all gaits. His anxiety to get to Vanessa far overshadowed the pain that throbbed in his side and the one in his stomach that was gnawing at his vitals.

So the Hookers hadn't killed Primer Tass after all. If he'd followed them to Junction City it was certain he knew they were at The House. Holy damn! Kain had thought Vanessa

was safe from that bastard. He wasn't going to give up trying to get her as long as there was a breath left in his body.
The thought of his wearing Vanessa's hair around his neck
caused a kind of frustrated rage to boil up inside Kain. He
was determined to see to it that that scum would not bother
Vanessa after he was gone. He'd kill him on sight whether
he was armed or not. What did it matter if they hanged him
for it? He was dying anyway.

The fresh tracks of the buggy wheels and the prints of the
trotting horse told Kain that Adam had wasted no time getting out of town and that he was probably only a few miles
ahead of the wagon. He kept Big Red at a steady trot until he
overtook the Wisner wagon. Then he moved to the side of
the track and pulled up on the reins and rode alongside. Ellie
sat between Vanessa and Mary Ben, her hands clasped in her
lap and her eyes straight ahead.

"You look tired, Kain." Vanessa had taken off her bonnet
and hooked her shawl up over her head because a cold wind
was now coming down from the mountain.

"I am, a little. My stomach is growling for food."

"Did Mr. McCloud think he could get your letters out to
your friends?"

"He said there was a man in town today from out Logan's
way, and he'd see to it that Cooper got his letter, too."

"I forgot to ask you about the preacher. What did he
say?"

"He said he'd be out Sunday, just as soon as church service was over. He's a pleasant fellow. Came here last winter
from Ohio."

Kain caught himself before he pressed his hand to his
side. He didn't want Vanessa to worry. But damn, he would
be glad to get home. The pain in his stomach was worse,
and his side hurt like hell. He was hungry for one thing. He
had noticed that as long as he had a little something in his
stomach it didn't bother him quite so much. If not for Ellie

meeting Clayhill they could have eaten at Mable's Restaurant.

When Ellie first told him about Adam Hill, the brother of her dead husband, he had suspected that Adam Clayhill was actually both men. It was something Adam would do—seduce a young girl and then desert her. The resemblance between Henry and Cooper was uncanny, and of course Kain had noticed Henry's crooked finger. Ellie had unknowingly outwitted Adam when she had the marriage and her son's birth recorded. She was Adam's legal wife, and Henry was his legal son. Old Adam must be about out of his mind wondering what would happen next. All his life he had done exactly as he pleased without consideration for anyone. It could be that this kind lady and her son would be his downfall. Despite his aching side, Kain had to chuckle.

It was high noon when they arrived back at the house and John pulled up to let the women out before he drove on to the barn.

"Aunt Ellie, Mary Ben and I will set out a meal if you want to lie down for awhile," Vanessa had removed her own wrap and took her aunt's shawl from her shoulders and folded it.

"Thank you, dear. I think I will. Be sure Kain drinks his milk." Her voice grew weaker and ceased altogether as she went up the stairs.

Kain came in and sat at the table. Henry had offered to take his horse to the barn and tell Jeb and Clay to come to the house. The thing foremost in Kain's mind was the danger to Vanessa from Primer Tass. Tonight he would have to tell her so she'd stay close to the house. She walked over to him carrying a cup of milk.

"Before Aunt Ellie went to her room she said to be sure you drank your milk."

She set the cup on the table and Kain pulled her down on his knee. "Thank you, sweetheart." He drank the full cup before he lowered it. "That was better than whiskey." He grinned at her frown and placed a gentle kiss on her lips.

"Poor Aunt Ellie. Did you see her face when that man said those awful things to her?"

"Yes, honey, I did. But she's a strong woman and she'll weather this. Now, get some food on the table. Your man's hungry."

After the meal, Kain motioned for John and the Hookers to go outside. They followed him to the woodpile where he sat down on a stump, and they squatted down on their heels.

"Primer Tass isn't dead. Somehow the bastard lived and followed us to Junction City."

Jeb and Clay looked at each other and Clay mumbled, "Shee . . . it!"

Jeb leaned over to spit out a played-out chaw before he spoke. "If'n ya say he made it, he did. But I'll be horn-swoggled if I know how he done it. The bird was jist a barely hangin' on when I seen him last."

"He had three holes in 'em, Kain. Two of 'em high up," Clay said disgustedly.

"He hung in the saddle and got to someone who patched him up."

"Warn't nobody 'round but a parcel a Cheyenne. I was thinkin' they'd get a easy scalp. Ya don't reckon *they'd* patch him up?"

"Someone did. I guess it's not important who. He was in the store asking about me. By now he knows where we are. I'm surprised he hasn't made a move."

"We ort a follered 'em, Jeb."

"Ain't no use thinkin' that now. When yo're in a tight, ya do what ya think ya ort a. We coulda follered 'em, got tangled up with a mess a Cheyenne 'n Kain could a bled to death."

"He's a mongrel cur, is what he is." John spoke for the first time. "Raised on wolf milk 'n thinks like one. Hit's my idey, he'll try 'n pick us off one at a time. It ain't his way to sneak in till he evens the odds some."

"I think you're right, John." Kain's sharp eyes surveyed the area like an army general planning to defend a position. "There's a couple of places where he could get a shot at us without our seeing him. I guess you know where, the same as I do. We'll have to watch ourselves and watch out for Henry, too."

"Hit 'pears like y're goin' to have to dig another hole, Jeb. I ain't doin' no cookin' less'n the barn's atween me 'n that clump a pine yonder." The grin Clay showed was one of pleased innocence.

Jeb was not amused. He cut off a chaw with his pocket knife, stuck it inside his jaw and gave his brother a disgusted look.

"Shitfire! Ya can't cook nohow."

Kain was seated at the table watching Vanessa prepare the evening meal when Ellie and Henry came downstairs. They had spent several hours in Ellie's room. Ellie was pale, but otherwise she was like her old self; calm and smiling. She had combed her hair and put on a fresh apron. She poured coffee for herself and Henry and they sat down at the table.

"Henry and I have had a long talk. I've explained everything to him." She smiled at her son and her eyes mirrored her love. "We have decided that we are the same people who left here this morning to go to town. Nothing has changed. I'll continue to carry in my heart the sweet memory of the time my son was conceived, even if the man was not what I thought he was. I must believe that for a few weeks of his life Adam Clayhill loved me in his own warped fashion. He's my husband; he's Henry's father. There is nothing we can do about it. My only regret is that I didn't find out a long time ago that he wasn't worth a single moment of those wasted years that I grieved for him. Other than that, I'd not change one moment of my life if it would mean I'd not have had Henry."

"Ellie, I'm glad you're taking it like this." Kain reached across the table and clasped her hand. "It's strange, but the mothers of Clayhill's sons were all good women. My own mother was attracted to him. The man has charm; there's no doubt of it."

"He's also evil. I told Henry that his father was not a nice man and how lucky we were that he inherited the crooked finger and not the other traits."

"I didn't like him, Ma. I wish he wasn't my pa," Henry said staunchly. "He's not ever going to hurt you, or I'll hit him again."

"Believe it or not, Henry, there is something good to come out of this," Kain told him. "You have two half brothers who feel exactly the same as you do about Adam Clayhill. Cooper Parnell and Logan Horn are two fine men, and you'll be proud they're your brothers."

"Golly! I'll have brothers? But maybe they won't like me. Maybe they'll think I'm—"

"Don't worry about that," Kain broke in.

"Oh, my. They'll be here Sunday." Ellie turned the cup around in her two hands.

"Cooper's mother will be here, too. Adam seduced her when she was sixteen. Her parents put her out and she washed clothes at an army post in order to feed herself and her son. She held up her head, and eventually married a man named Oscar Parnell who gave her son his name. When he died she and Cooper worked to build a horse ranch. Now she's married to Arnie Henderson, who works for Logan on Morning Sun."

"Poor woman. She had it harder than I did."

"Have you decided what you're going to do, Ellie?"

"I'll not ask anything of Adam Clayhill," she said quickly. "If I had the money to pursue it I'd have my marriage papers and Henry's birth recorded with the correct name of husband and father. Not that I want to use the name, but for the sake of any children Henry might have."

"Do I have your permission to talk the matter over with Logan and Cooper? One of them might have an idea of how it can be done."

"They'll not want to be bothered with us."

"I think you're wrong about that. You'll know after you meet them. They've had to fight Adam Clayhill every step of the way for what they have."

Henry's thoughts never remained long on any one subject; the mere mention of a fight was enough to divert them into a new channel.

"You know I beat that Stan Taylor today, Kain, but I've not had a chance to tell you about it. I did just what you told me. At first I was afraid, then I was afraid I'd hurt him. Mary Ben said I could do it, and if I didn't I'd not be able to face folks in town. Then he was going to kiss Mary Ben and that made me mad. He was watching my hands, Kain, and I kicked him right in the balls, ah—in the rocks. Mary Ben said kick him hard, and I did. Boom! He doubled up and I hit him on the chin." Henry's arms waved as he demonstrated how he had hit Stan. Kain listened intently, nodding his head in approval.

Ellie got up from the table with her red face averted. She didn't have the heart to put a damper on her son's victory by telling him to watch his language.

Vanessa sat on the edge of the bed and unbraided her hair. Each time she unpinned the coronet from the top of her head she felt with her fingertips the short, inch-long curls at the crown where Primer Tass had cut the swath of hair. It was growing out, but slowly. She pulled the heavy mass over her shoulder so the ends lay in her lap. She stroked it with a wide-toothed comb, starting at the end and working upward until she had removed the snarls and could run the comb through the full length of the copper colored tresses.

Kain, lying on the bed behind her, marveled. She was so beautiful. His eyes feasted on her shapely head with its fiery aureole of hair, the curve of her perfect back and her slender body through her transparent thin nightdress. He shut his eyes, giving himself up to the wonder and the glory that she loved *him*. He took the comb from her hand and placed it on the table beside the bed.

"It's going to get all messed up anyway, sweetheart. Comb it in the morning." He tugged gently on the sheeve of her nightgown. "Why do you bother to put this thing on? You'll only have to take it off."

"Because it's what decent young ladies wear to bed." She raised her brows haughtily. "It's not easy to just suddenly throw all trace of modesty out the window."

"Modesty? With me?"

"I'm not used to parading around without my clothes on while my naked *lovers* lie in bed watching me." She smiled down at him with false sweetness, showing white teeth, while she tied her hair at the nape of her neck with a ribbon.

"How many naked *lovers* have you had, lady?" He made an angry growling sound and tugged on her arm. "Blow out the lamp. This naked lover wants to hold you, kiss you, love you, and he might wear himself out, go to sleep, and leave it on."

"Why did you cover the windows tonight? They're so high no one can see in."

"They could if they stood on something."

"Yes, but who would do that?"

"Come to bed and love me." His voice was soft and beautiful and his amber eyes were achingly anxious.

Vanessa blew out the lamp. She slid her nightdress from her shoulders and let it fall to the floor before she surrendered to the arms waiting to hold her. She pressed her body's full length to his and he felt her satiny breasts crush against his chest, felt the down of her brush his hardening body and the warm writhing skin of her slender thighs interlace with his. He gathered her close to his long, muscular body with a tired little sigh.

"Sometimes the day is a week long while I wait for this." His hand slid down her smooth back and pulled at her body so that it fit snugly into every curve of his.

"I'm not hurting your shoulder or your side?"

"No, my pretty, little sweet-smelling, angel of a woman," he muttered thickly between kisses. "The only part of me that hurts is something I dare not name for fear it would shock my lady's modesty."

Her arms went up to hold him closer, her body straining against his. He covered her face with kisses, releasing his pent-up desire with each touch of his lips. He stroked her firm breasts and was struck with that irreversible progression, that steady, beating drum of blood that demanded the eternal forward beating to the final flourish. His hand moved between her thighs, stroking her soft inner skin, moving upward. She gave a muffled, instinctive cry as his fingers found her wetness and probed gently inside.

Minutes later they were interlocked and breathlessly surrendering to a voracious hunger that found her as impatiently eager to receive him as he was to insert himself into her yielding warmth. And then they were one fierce flesh, seeking the peaks that could not be found alone. He was deep inside her and she gloried in the delicious invasion. All conscious thought left them as the maelstrom overcame them and they were swept beyond the limits of return, into a primordial wilderness that outdistanced the mind.

"I love you. Oh, I love you, Kain, darling." She held his head pillowed against her breasts until his breathing audibly calmed. Caught in the grip of sudden yearning, she wondered how she could possibly go on without him.

"Mmm, I could stay here forever." He placed a kiss on her breast and laid his cheek on it with a long, gusty sigh. "I've got something to tell you," he murmured. "Something unpleasant." He felt her stiffen and realized immediately she was thinking that their time together had come to an end, that he was leaving. He raised his head. "Not that! I'm sorry, sweet girl. It was stupid of me to put it that way." He moved up until his head lay on the pillow beside hers. His mouth was warm and gentle on her eyelids and came away with the taste of tears on his lips. "Don't cry, darling, please don't cry."

"I'm not."

"Sweetheart . . ." He smoothed her hair back from her damp face and spread it out on the pillow. "I never dreamed that love would be like this."

"Nor I." She moved her lips to his and they shared a deep, tender kiss. "What do you have to tell me?"

"I wish I didn't have to tell you, sweetheart, but I do. Primer Tass survived the three bullets the Hookers put in him. He was in McCloud's store asking about me."

"Oh, no! Will he come here? Is he the one who is—"

"Sweetheart, I don't think he'll give up trying to get you until he's dead. I've seen his kind before. In his warped mind he thinks you belong to him. Damn his blasted hide!"

Vanessa's arms closed tightly around Kain's shoulders. "He's trying to kill you! You knew it all along!"

"No. I didn't know he was alive until today. We'll be on the lookout for him, and I'll tell Griff, Cooper and Logan when they get here."

"You'll be careful? He's so sneaky!" She shuddered, remembering the beady black eyes and the way he turned his head, like a snake, to look at her. "Don't go out looking for him. Please, Kain."

"You can bet your life I'll be careful. I aim to get to him before he gets to me. You've got to stay close to the house, honey. Don't even go to the barn without me or John or one of the Hookers." Kain's arm tightened and she could feel the heavy thud of his heartbeat.

"I'm not worried for myself. He won't *kill* me. It's you, my love. He wants to kill you!"

"Don't worry. I'm not going to make it easy for him. Wait until you meet Fort Griffin, honey. He would chew Primer Tass up and spit him out."

"I've never heard of anyone named Fort."

"He's usually called Griff. He was embarrassed when he told me how he got the name. His mother was a whore at the fort, and she thought it a joke on the men to name him that."

"Poor little boy!"

"I met him down in New Mexico and we spent more than a year together. He was the toughest kid I'd ever met. When he was thirteen he killed the man who had killed his mother and was sent to Yuma Prison for five years. I met him about a year after he was out. He's as square and honest as the day is long, but he's also deadly with a gun. I want you to know him and Bonnie. If you're ever in trouble or need help, you're to go to them, Cooper, or Logan."

"You have such good friends here. Why didn't you stay?"

"They were all family men, building for future generations. I just never seemed to fit, so I drifted on."

"You'd fit now."

"Yes," he said wearily. "Now I know what I was searching for." And found it too late, he added silently to himself.

"I promised I'd not ask what's taking you away from me. But sometimes, my love, I get so angry!" Her voice choked on the sobs in her throat. "Sometimes, I think I'll die, not knowing when, or how."

"I'm a selfish bastard for putting this burden on you. But I love you too much to deceive you. Put it out of your mind, darling, and hold me. Hold me, love me . . . make me forget."

She turned her face to his, angled her nose alongside his and caressed his lips with her own, nibbling, stroking with her tongue, deepening the kiss and withdrawing.

"I'll try, love. Oh, it's been such an eventful day. Henry finally found the courage to take up for himself, thanks to your teaching, Kain. Ellie met a husband she thought had been dead for twenty years, and Primer Tass wasn't killed after all. But even if the moon fell from the sky it wouldn't mean more to me than this."

All the adoration in her heart was given to him now. She murmured his name as her lips glided over his straight brows, short, thick eyelashes, cheeks rough with stubble, and over to his waiting mouth.

"Ah, love! Don't stop!" His voice came huskily, tickling her ear. His hands kneaded her rounded bottom and pressed her tightly to the aroused length of him captured between their bellies. "I can't get enough of you." His leg glided off hers and his hand moved to spread her thighs. He lifted her with strong hands on her waist. When he settled her on him, she made a purring sound like that of a pleased kitten. "Just be still, sweetheart. Just be still." His hands glided up over her hips to the sides of her breasts, which were flattened against his chest. He grasped her head and turned it so his lips could reach her mouth. "We fit perfectly, my love. We're perfect together," he said, breathing deeply. His voice was a shivering whisper that touched her very soul.

Much later, as she lay quietly beside him, he turned and buried his face in the curve of her neck like a child seeking comfort. She held him, stroked his thick brown hair back from his forehead, loving him, wanting him to feel loved. She tried to dismiss the feeling of impending heartache. In torment she tightened her arms around him and pressed her mouth to his forehead. She wondered if she would be able to bear the loneliness without him. It was lonely now, knowing he was going, she told herself, but how would it be when she knew he'd never . . . She rolled her head, not wanting to think about it. Finally she fell asleep, wishing the night would go on and on.

Chapter Eighteen

Saturday morning came, and everyone was up early and in a state of excitement. Kain was sure some of the guests would arrive by early afternoon. Ellie had set her jaw, called on her reserves, and gone through each day with bulldog tenacity. Now she was afraid she'd not have enough food and, after stirring up the cake, made a rice pudding. Vanessa and Mary Ben did last-minute cleaning.

The Hookers came to breakfast while John sat in the loft of the barn where he could see anything that moved within a half a mile of the house. They ate hurriedly so they could escape the kitchen where the floor had been scrubbed, the iron cookstove polished with stove black, the curtains washed, and the women were fussing with the cooking.

"Your clean shirts are on the hook by the door, Jeb," Ellie called from the pantry. "Don't slam the door when you go out. The cake will fall."

"I warn't goin' to slam it nohow," Jeb mumbled to his brother on the way to the barn.

The steer was ready to cook. Between the barn and the clump of pines that had worried Clay, another pit had been dug and lined with adobe bricks. A tin cover was fashioned to hold in the smoke, and hickory wood was stacked nearby. The brothers were pleased with their part in the gala event, and when not taking a turn in the loft to watch for Primer Tass, they were fussing around the pit.

Vanessa took Mary Ben upstairs to try on her wedding dress one more time to be sure the hem was right.

"I'm jist scared pea-green, Van. What with all them folks comin' 'n all."

Vanessa, on the floor with pins in her mouth, looked up at her worried young face.

"It is scary meeting a lot of folks for the first time. I'm a little scared, too. I keep wondering if Kain's friends will like me. We'll just be scared together, Mary Ben. Goodness, you'll be as pretty as a picture, and Henry is so proud he's about to burst his buttons."

"I'm scared I ain't got enough manners, 'n what if somebody asks me to write somethin'?"

"Oh, shoot! I forgot you'll have to sign your marriage paper." Vanessa stood. "I'll tell you what we'll do. I'll write your name on a paper, and you stay here in your room and copy it until you can write it. It doesn't have to be good. No one will see it but you and Henry and the preacher. Later, I'll teach you how to write all your letters. Now, off with the dress so we can get started."

Vanessa went to the kitchen to report to Ellie.

"Poor child. Of course she would be embarrassed." Ellie finished crimping the crust around a pie, moved it aside and began filling another pie shell. "I can't think of anything else that has to be done except shake that rug you're standing on. We all had baths last night, so our guests can use the tub tonight if they want. Don't shake it, Vanessa, unless you put something over your hair. Goodness, we don't want to have to wash it again."

"Where's Kain?"

"He and Henry are polishing boots. Good heavens! That man is beside himself. He's so happy, he keeps grinning all the time. I think he feels better, too." Ellie rolled out another crust and fitted it into a granite pie plate.

"I took the stitches out a couple of days ago—"

"That's what I mean, dear," Ellie said hastily. "He feels better now that the bandages are off."

In the middle of the afternoon the first of the guests arrived. Kain stood on the porch, his face wreathed with smiles, as Cooper and Lorna Parnell rode in. He was in the yard before they could dismount and hurrying to lift Lorna from the saddle. Time hadn't changed her. She wore britches and a pullover shirt belted at the waist, a blanket coat, and a flat-brimmed hat. Her black hair hung like a curtain about her shoulders and her violet eyes laughed down at him.

"Lorna! You're as beautiful as ever."

He set her on her feet and she reached up to hug him. "You're just saying that because you're getting married! I told Cooper I was half in love with you myself."

"Don't tell him that! He'll shoot me." He stuck out his hand to Cooper, who was still sitting his horse. "Glad to see you, Cooper. What've you got here?" A small dark-haired child with large blue eyes bashfully turned his face to his father's coat. "Come here to me, young man, and let your pa get down off that tired old horse." Kain lifted the child from where he sat in front of Cooper and Cooper got down. The child reached for his father and Cooper took him.

"He's his papa's boy, Kain," Lorna said with a short happy laugh. "He doesn't let his pa out of his sight if he can help it."

"I'm glad you came early, Cooper. I've got a surprise for you that you'll not believe."

In the quiet of the barn, Kain told them about Ellie and Henry and their connection with Adam Clayhill. "She's a nice woman, Cooper. She reminds me a lot of your ma. I wanted to warn you before you saw Henry. Even McCloud mistook him for you."

"There seems to be no end to the lives that old man has messed up. He keeps a distance from me and Logan; and after his men had a run-in or two with Griff, he steers clear of him, too. He'll try to run the woman off, you can bet on it. You say the old man married her under the name Henry Hill? The rotten old bastard used his brother's name."

"Young Henry isn't as bright as you'd expect a man of twenty to be, but he'll work like a demon if someone tells him what to do. He'll make it with a little guidance."

"I bet that was a blow to the old man."

"He was terribly cruel to both of them. It was a sad thing to witness, Cooper. Ellie was stunned. For twenty years she'd thought he was dead. Henry favors you, and he's got the Clayhill crooked finger, so there's no doubt about his being the old man's. I'll bet old Clayhill is trying to figure a way to get out of this one."

"If young Henry is about twenty, that means the old man was already married when he married your mother, Kain."

"I figure he stopped off in Springfield and married Ellie on his way East to marry my mother." Kain picked up the bag Lorna had tied to the back of her saddle. "Ellie and Henry know who you are. Come on in. I'm eager for you to meet Vanessa."

"Yes, Cooper. I want to see this beauty who won Kain away from me." Lorna said with a small smile.

"You just keep on lipping off, woman, and you'll get a hiding when you get home," Cooper said gruffly, and plucked their son from her arms. "Come to papa, Douglas. Your mama's being feisty again."

* * *

"Oh, my," Ellie said when Cooper walked through the kitchen door. Her eyes clung to his face and without her knowing it, they filled with tears. "Oh, my," she said again and blinked rapidly. "I'm sorry. It's just such a shock."

Cooper's eyes had gone beyond Ellie to the tall man who stood behind her. "I know how you feel, ma'am." He took a step toward her and held out his hand. "Cooper Parnell. This is my wife, Lorna, and our son, Douglas."

"How do you do? This is *my* son, Henry." Ellie turned so she could see both men. They were staring at each other. Henry spoke first.

"Is he the one, Kain?"

"Yes, Henry. He knows that he's your brother."

Henry looked at the hand Cooper extended. "Are you . . . mad about it?"

"Of course not. I'm glad to know my son has another uncle."

The smile that could come so quickly to Henry's face appeared now. He looked at the small boy in Cooper's arms, and then at Cooper and grasped his hand.

"Ma! Did you hear that? I'm an uncle!"

"Yes, son, I heard." Ellie's shoulders slumped with relief.

"Mary Ben, you'll be an aunt." Henry pulled the girl from behind him. "Mary Ben, this is my brother, Cooper Parnell."

Kain had moved over beside Vanessa and put his arm around her. Together they watched the meeting between the brothers. Vanessa saw the relief on her aunt's face and was sure she was going to cry. Henry was so excited the words poured from his mouth. And Cooper's face never changed expression when it became apparent that Henry's mind hadn't kept pace with his body.

Cooper's wife watched, too. She was the prettiest woman Vanessa had ever seen. The skin of her face was white, a startling contrast to the blue-black hair that framed it, her mouth was red, and large, magnificent violet eyes adoringly watched every move her husband made.

"I don't think Douglas will want to come to you yet, Henry," Cooper was saying. "He's a mite shy. After we're here awhile he'll crawl all over you. I think I'd better meet Kain's bride. She's got to be something to bring Kain back here and keep him in one place."

"She is, Cooper. Believe me, she is!" Kain was gazing at Vanessa's blushing face, his eyes filled with tenderness, and smiled with loving mirth when she pinched his arm.

The introductions were made amid laughter, teasing, and congratulations. Finally Ellie began to shoo them from the kitchen.

"You men can go in the parlor where you can visit. Mary Ben, take Lorna's things up to the room we set aside for them. That baby must be hungry and want a nap after that long ride. And my, oh, my. I've still got two more pies to make."

"I'll help you, Aunt Ellie."

"No, dear. You and Lorna go get acquainted. Enjoy yourself. Tomorrow is your wedding day."

"I'd offer to help, Mrs.—" Lorna paused and lifted her straight black brows.

"Call me Ellie, Lorna." Ellie smiled and then a trembling laugh burst from her lips. "You know, I don't know what to call myself, now." With that admission, a weight she had carried since the trip to town lifted from Ellie's heart.

"I'd offer to help, Ellie, but I'm no hand at making a pie. Ask Cooper." Lorna giggled and looked around the corner into the hall to see if the men were out of hearing. "He swore he was going to starve to death after Sylvia married and moved to the Morning Sun. She had to come back and teach me how to cook something beside beans and Hopping Jack. She and Arnie will be here later on. She'd not miss a wedding for anything, especially Kain's."

"I'm worried about meeting her."

"You don't need to worry about meeting Sylvia. You'll like her. Everyone does. Come on upstairs with me, Vanessa. I'll have to tell you about my first visit to this house. I'd lived on Light's Mountain all my life and I didn't know about such things as whorehouses. I thought this was a school for young ladies! When I found out what it really was I got Cooper out of here in a hurry." Her happy laughter rang throughout the house.

Vanessa was fascinated by Lorna's openness. Kain had told her that Lorna had been raised wild and free on Light's Mountain. He had said she could sing like a bird, throw a knife, shoot a gun, and was the best with a bullwhip he'd ever seen. Vanessa knew she was also a happy woman, terribly in love with her husband.

The lamps were all lit and the table set for supper when Logan's party arrived. The buggy accompanied by two riders pulled in at the gate and Kain and Cooper went out to meet them. Henry would have gone, too, but Lorna asked him to hold Douglas. Ellie smiled at her gratefully, knowing that Kain needed some time with Logan, just as he had with Cooper and Lorna.

When Cooper came in sometime later, he was leading a small dark-haired boy by the hand. The child looked around the room, spied Lorna and grinned a gap-toothed grin.

"Hello, Henry. Do you have a kiss for Aunt Lorna?"

"Naw. Boys don't kiss girls."

"Your Uncle Cooper does."

The boy tilted his head back so he could see his uncle's face. "Why do you do that?"

"You'll know soon enough. I want you to meet another uncle. His name is Henry, too." Young Douglas spied his papa and set up a howl until Cooper took him.

It seemed to Ellie a long time passed before she heard boot heels on the porch and the door opened again. Her heart was fluttering like a trapped bird in her breast, and she had unknowingly wrapped her hands in her apron. People filed in and suddenly the kitchen was filled.

The pleasant-faced woman who came in first greeted Lorna with a kiss on the cheek, nuzzled her grandchild, then looked directly at Ellie and smiled.

"I'm Cooper's mother, Sylvia Henderson. Kain said your name is Ellie." She glanced at the stove and the shelves where the rows of pans were covered with a white cloth. "Goodness gracious! You've been cooking all day. I told that Arnie we should get a wiggle on or we'd come in on you right at supper time."

"But we have plenty," Ellie almost choked on the words.

Kain went to Vanessa, put his arm around her, and held her close to his side while he made the introductions. There was a continuous proud smile on his face.

Rosalee Horn was a pretty woman with light brown hair and blue eyes set wide apart in a calm face. She was pregnant. Her husband stood behind her with his hands on her shoulders. He was a big, handsome dark-haired man with the high cheekbones and dark skin of ancestors who had roamed the land long before the white man came. He had a full mustache shaped in a wide downward curve around his mouth, reaching almost to his jaw, giving him a stern, forbidding look until he smiled, which he did when he looked down at his wife.

"Tired, honey?" He took the wrap from her shoulders.

"A little."

Lorna jumped up from the chair she had moved out from the table. "Sit here, Rosalee. I remember how my back hurt when I was carrying Douglas."

Henry hadn't said a word. Ellie's heart ached for the uncertainty he was feeling, and she wished there was something she could do to make this easier for him. Sylvia's eyes went from him to Cooper and back again. Logan Horn's dark gaze settled on Henry's face, too. Henry fidgeted.

Logan crossed the room and offered his hand to Henry.

"Kain was telling me that there are three of us now. You and I and Cooper."

Henry seemed overwhelmed. He didn't say anything, and Ellie wanted to cry. It was Cooper who eased the tension. He clapped Logan on the shoulder.

"Henry, I know just how you feel when you look at this big galoot. When I first laid eyes on him I didn't know he was my brother, and I thought he was as ugly as a mud fence. After I found out he was my brother, he got better looking. He grows on you. After awhile you might even forget he's got a face that would stop a clock."

"I don't think he's ugly," Henry stammered. "He's just . . . big."

"Yeah. Big and ugly and mean."

The two big were smiling at each other and Logan didn't look quite so fierce. Henry began to grin. "I think you're joshing me, Cooper."

"I think you're right, Henry," Logan said. "Our brother has quite a sense of humor."

Sylvia pulled an apron out of the travel bag that sat by the door, tied it around her waist, and went to the stove to help Ellie.

"I can't get over how much Henry looks like Cooper did at that age. Now, what can I do?"

"We'll have to set two tables. We'll feed the men first and get them out of the way, and then we women can sit down and eat. Did your husband come?"

"Oh my, yes. He thinks the sun rises and sets with Kain. He's putting away the buggy. Here he is."

"Hang your hat there beside the door, Arnie, and come meet the folks," Kain called to the man who stood beside the door shaking his head at all the confusion.

"I was fixin' to eat in the yard, Kain. Them fellers has a steer cookin' in a pit, 'n it smells larrapin'. 'Sides, I'd not have to listen to the hens acluckin'."

"Arnie! Behave yourself until these folks get to know

you. They'll think I married an Illinois hillbilly," Sylvia scolded.

"Ah . . . there ya are, sweet thin'. I done told ya there ain't no hills in Illinois to speak of. I might a knowed you'd be right in the middle a the cookin'." He crossed to where Vanessa stood beside Kain and held out his hand. His friendly eyes smiled into hers and he held her hand between his two hard, calloused palms. "Hit's a good thin' ya got me afore I saw this little pretty, honeybunch," he said over his shoulder to Sylvia. "Or ya might not a got me a'tall."

"Oh, Arnie!" Sylvia threw up her hands. "He's just a talker, Vanessa. I couldn't get rid of him if I tied him to a span of mules and shot them in the rumps with a slingshot."

Rich laughter filled the room. Vanessa looked up to meet Kain's tawny gaze. She had seen those eyes in so many moods; they had laughed, teased, smiled, grown fierce with anger. Now they were filled with warmth and love and happiness. The smile she adored claimed his face.

He leaned down to whisper in her ear, "Look at Henry with Logan and Cooper. Look at Ellie and Sylvia. They're chattering away like a couple of magpies. It's working out for both of them."

"It's all your doing. Thank you, darling."

"I know how you can thank me . . . properly."

"I can't imagine how."

"I'll show you tonight," he promised.

Her mouth curved in a contented little smile. He was safe! With his friends here, he was safe!

By sunrise everyone had had breakfast except the children, who were still sleeping. The night before, long after the women had gone to bed, the men had sat around the kitchen table, drank coffee and talked. Now they were outside, gathered around the pit where Clay was cooking the steer. John called down from his perch beside the loft door that two riders were coming.

Fort and Bonnie Griffin rode into the yard amid shouts of welcome. At Ellie's urging, Vanessa threw a shawl around her shoulders and went out onto the porch. She saw a slim, wiry, young man jump from the saddle and pump Kain's hand vigorously. Cooper lifted the woman down. Lorna came from the house, vaulted off the porch, ran to the woman and threw her arms around her.

"Oh, Bonnie! It's been so long since I've seen you. Wait till you see how Douglas has grown."

Kain called to Vanessa and she went to meet his out-stretched hand.

"Honey, this is Griff and Bonnie."

Bonnie smiled and nodded a greeting. She was as tall as her husband and looked even younger. She wasn't pretty. Standing beside the petite, curvaceous Lorna she looked thin and gawky. But she was sweet looking, with her wide mouth and large, soft brown eyes that made her appear vulnerable.

"I'm shore proud to meet ya, ma'am." Griff shook Vanessa's hand. "Kain saved my bacon a time or two." When he laughed he looked more boyish. "Cooper and Logan have, too. Cooper even cut me down from a hangin' tree once."

"There are times when I think I should have left him, huh Bonnie?" Cooper clapped him on the back.

"We didn't get to town till after dark," Bonnie said to Lorna on the way to the house. "Griff was bound to come on out, but I talked him into stayin' at the hotel. We shoulda come on. We didn't sleep a wink cause of all the racket in town."

Kain held onto Vanessa when she would have followed Lorna and Bonnie. He pulled her close and placed a quick kiss on her lips.

"Kain! Stop that! What'll they think?"

He let loose a rich, satisfied laugh. "They'll think that I'm madly wildly in love with you, which I am." He let her slip from his arms and she hurried to catch up with Lorna and Bonnie.

* * *

The morning slid away in a flurry of activity. The men were banished from the house.

"We're working on two weddings and we've got to get the kitchen cleaned," Sylvia said. "You men are not necessary."

"Not necessary?" Kain protested. "I'm one of the grooms."

"Very minor part. Now scoot to the barn. You and Henry can come in later and get yourselves cleaned up."

"See what yo're in fer, Kain." Arnie stood obediently and slammed his hat on his head. "But I don't reckon yore woman'll be bossy as mine. She takes the cake when it comes to bossin'."

"Oh, Arnie! You'd complain if it was rainin' soup."

"I do love ta tease that woman," Arnie said with a chuckle as he followed the men out the door.

Mary Ben and Bonnie took to each other right away. Mary Ben was fascinated by what Bonnie could do with one hand. Lorna had told them the night before how hard Bonnie's life had been until the time she met Griff. She told them that because Bonnie had been born with one hand, her folks were ashamed of her and sold her to a man who abused her, and that Griff had killed the man. Amid giggles, Lorna told about meeting Kain in town and that he had thought she was one of the girls who worked at The House. On a more serious note, she told them how Cooper, Kain and Griff had rescued her from the men who had burned her home and killed her father.

Bonnie and Lorna decorated the parlor with streamers Rosalee cut from folded paper. When they finished they stood back, admired their work, then scurried upstairs to dress.

When all was ready and they were waiting for the preacher to arrive, Ellie slipped into the room where Henry was waiting.

He was wearing a black serge suit and white shirt. "My, you look handsome. I'm just so proud of you." She went to him and placed a kiss on his cheek. "Mary Ben is ready, and she looks real pretty."

"Ma, I think I'm glad that old man's my pa. I don't want you to feel bad about it anymore. I sure do like Cooper and Logan. I never thought I'd have brothers. I think they like me, too."

"Of course they do. And I don't feel bad, son. We came out here to find you some kinfolk, and we never dreamed what we'd find, did we? We can talk about that later. This is your wedding day. You don't have to stay in here, you know. You can wait in the parlor. Mary Ben won't come down until the preacher gets here."

Ellie met Kain in the lower hallway. His wardrobe being limited, he had chosen to wear a white silk shirt and black tie. He had brushed his dark hair back, but the waves were even now rebelling against the brush. She held out her hand to him and he took it in his.

"How do you feel?" she asked softly. "You didn't drink coffee last night, did you?"

He smiled. "I feel fine, and, no, I didn't drink coffee last night. I drank a gallon of milk. You're going to have to get another cow," he teased.

"Things have turned out so well, Kain. I don't know how I'm ever going to thank you."

"Then don't, Ellie. You and Henry will be all right now, no matter what Adam Clayhill does. Cooper and Logan will keep an eye out for you. Both of them think we should send your papers, the tintype, and other pertinent information down to Denver to a fellow named Randolph. He handles Logan's affairs, knows his connection to Clayhill, and he'll see to it that the records are put in order."

"If you think that's what I should do, I will. I wish... Oh, Kain, you're as dear to me as Henry and Vanessa." Tears filled her eyes. "I don't know if I can bear—"

"You can. I know you can, Ellie dear. It's been such a comfort having you know." His eyes caressed her face fondly. "Now don't pull a long face. This is the happiest day of my life. All of my friends are here and I'm marrying the most beautiful, wonderful, loving woman in all the world." His eyes shone like amber agates, and his happy smile made Ellie want to cry all the more. "I've asked Lorna to sing. Did you know she sings like an angel?"

"Sylvia told me. She's so fond of her."

"Just as I'm very fond of you."

"What's going on back here?" Cooper came down the hallway. "Is he trying to sneak out the back door? Hold onto him, ma'am, the preacher is pulling into the yard."

The parlor was a large square room with windows on two sides. Everyone filed in. The women sat in the chairs, and the men stood. The Hookers and John came in last. John's hair was slicked down on the sides and his bald pate shone. He had scraped the whiskers from the upper part of his face, leaving only those on his chin, and was wearing a new shirt. His hands clutched each other and twisted nervously. This was clearly the most uncomfortable moment of his life.

Mary Ben and Vanessa came down the stairs and were met at the bottom by Henry and Kain. Vanessa's low-necked dress was almost exactly the color of her eyes. Her shoulders and arms gleamed like white marble. Her hair was piled high and secured with a bright comb, and tied around her neck was the blue ribbon Kain had given her.

Kain took her hand and slipped it into the curve of his arm. He stood for a long silent moment, gazing at her as if mesmerized, then he said softly, "Hello, pretty little red bird."

Henry gaped at Mary Ben. The pink dress set off her clear skin and brown eyes. Her hair had been curled and piled on the top of her head and a pink satin bow was tucked saucily in the front.

"You just look so pretty. Don't she look pretty, Van?"

Henry was fairly bursting with pride and his voice boomed, bringing smiles and laughter.

"She sure does. You look pretty good, too."

"How about me?" Kain whispered.

Vanessa stood on tiptoe so she could whisper in his ear, "You look better . . . bare naked."

Kain whooped with laughter, caught her close, and twirled her around, bringing more smiles and laughter. His friends had never seen him in such an open, happy mood.

When they were all in the parlor, Lorna began to sing. She lifted her face, and her voice, true and clear as a bell, filled the room. It had an unearthly quality, like the wind. It was full of love and pain, joy and sorrow, yet sweet and strong.

"Beautiful dreamer, waken to me,
    Starlight and dewdrops are waiting for thee.
Sounds of the rude world, heard in the day,
    lulled by the moonlight have all passed away."

The music coming from the small woman was so hauntingly beautiful it was frightening. Not a soul stirred in the room. Vanessa felt a tingling start low at the base of her spine and travel upward. She glanced at Cooper. He was watching his wife with rapt adoration on his face. Lorna *was* beautiful in a rose satin gown that hugged her full breasts and tiny waist. Beneath the hem Vanessa could see the toes of beaded, white moccasins. Sylvia, holding Douglas on her lap, saw them too, and smiled.

Logan stood beside his wife's chair with his hand on her shoulder. Their son leaned against her knee.

Bonnie sat in one of the parlor chairs in a green silk gown with full sleeves and Griff stood beside her.

It had been decided that Henry and Mary Ben would be married first. When the song ended, with a little prodding from Kain, they moved up in front of the preacher who stood with his back to the fireplace beneath pink and white streamers.

The service uniting Mary Ben and Henry was short.

"Who gives this woman to be married to this man?" The preacher asked.

There was a long silence, then John stepped forward, cleared his throat and said, "I do."

After Henry and Mary Ben were pronounced man and wife, they stepped back, and Vanessa and Kain moved forward to say their vows. Vanessa had asked Henry, as the male member of their family, if he would be the one to give her to Kain. When the preacher asked, Henry spoke the words loud and proudly.

The ceremony was over and Kain was kissing her, holding her close, whispering just to her that this was the happiest day of his life. Everyone began talking at once, the men insisted on kissing the brides, and Ellie wiped away her tears. Douglas, frightened by all the noise, began to cry.

The wedding feast lasted all afternoon. The Hookers carried in huge platters of deliciously cooked meat, and stayed, one at a time, to join the celebration. Arnie had fashioned an extension to the table with a door he found in the barn, and everyone was seated. First Ellie and then Sylvia hopped up every so often to refill the bowls, to serve pie, or fill coffee cups. Even Mary Ben lost some of her shyness and laughed when Cooper wanted to kiss his new sister.

Lorna was persuaded to sing again. She sang several gay tunes and then sang the one she said was hers and Cooper's special song.

"Down the stream of life together,
We are sailing side by side,
Hoping some bright day to anchor,
Safe beyond the surging tide.
Today our sky is cloudless,
But the night may clouds unfold;

Though the clouds may gather round us,
Will you love me when I'm old?"

Vanessa looked into Kain's face and her eyes filled with tears that overflowed and streamed down her cheeks. She would never know the happiness of growing old with him. She would never see him when his dark hair was streaked with gray or when age lines deepened the creases around his mouth. She would grow old alone, with only the memory of this day to sustain her. Was she strong enough to live her life without him? Right now, at this moment, she knew she was not. Without him, life wouldn't be worth living.

His amber eyes, so full of love, told her that he knew what she was thinking. He took her hand, gently drew her to her feet and they left the room. As soon as they reached the hall, out of sight of the others, she turned into his arms, pressed her face to his shoulder and clung to him.

"I'm . . . sorry. Oh, Kain, I've ruined your day. I can't keep from thinking about it . . . hoping and praying . . ."

"Don't be sorry, love. Nothing could ruin this day for me. We'll pray for a miracle, darling, but they seldom happen." The raw pain in his voice made her raise her eyes and look deeply into his. They stood for a long, silent moment gazing at each other.

"If only my love could keep you safe," she whispered.

His eyes devoured her face. This woman, his bride, was so sweetly, sublimely beautiful. Her pink lips were slightly parted and the breath that came from them warm and moist. Her long, tear-spiked lashes framed eyes shining with love. She stood looking up at him, a tight little core of misery. Kain felt a deep sadness for what she was suffering, and searched for words to comfort her.

"We have now, my honey, my love. We'll put a lifetime of loving in the time we have left." His voice was shaky and his breathing ragged in her ear. "You've made me happier than I ever imagined. You're the bright star in my heaven, the shining light of my life. I want to live each day with you as if it were my last. Come, darling, let me dry your eyes."

Evening came, the children were put to bed, and quietness settled over the house. The women changed once again to their everyday clothes to help with the cleanup, and the men gathered in a tight knot around the pit in the yard where Clay was lifting out the rest of the meat to send home with the guests. They had discussed how best to handle the situation if a group of fellows from town should decide to come out and shivaree the newlyweds. The night before, Kain had told them about Primer Tass and his obsession with Vanessa, how he had trailed them to Junction City, and how he had tried to kill him.

"The bird's crazy as a coot 'n sly as a fox," Jeb said. "Me 'n Clay's run into him a time or two. Loner is what he is. Ain't got no feelin' 'bout killin' a'tall. Twas said he'd kill a man fer a chaw of tobaccy if he wanted it."

"Sounds like a lobo." Griff was squatting on his heels, whittling on a twig with his pocketknife.

"Coldest looking bastard you'll ever see."

Kain told them about the hair Tass had cut from the top of Vanessa's head and how he wore it around his neck with a button from her shirt on the end of it. While talking about it Kain could feel his stomach stir restlessly.

"I didn't know about that," Henry said.

"Vanessa didn't want to worry you and your mother."

Logan stood, and the others followed suit. "We'll take care of the shivareers and Tass if they come without any help from you two. This is your wedding night. Unless you want to be dunked in the horsetank, you'd best get back to your brides."

A big grin slashed Kain's dark cheeks. "I sure don't want a dunking, do you, Henry?"

"Why would you do that, Logan?" There was apprehension in Henry's voice.

"It's a custom out here in the West to cool the bridegroom off on his wedding night by dunking him in the tank."

"I'm not hot. It's so cold now I can see my breath—"

"Come on, Henry. I know a couple of ladies who will appreciate our company more than these galoots."

Chapter Nineteen

"Mary Ben? Are you in here?" Henry opened the door to a darkened room. "Mary Ben?"

"I'm here."

"Why don't you have a light on? What are you sitting in the dark for?"

"I . . . jist wanted to."

"Are you sick or something?"

"No, silly. I'm in the bed . . . waitin' fer ya."

He stumbled against a chair as he groped in the dark for the foot of the iron bedstead. "Do you want me to light the lamp?"

"Can't ya undress in the dark?"

"I do it all the time."

"What ya been doin'?"

"Talking. Did you know that out here they put bridegrooms in the horse tank to cool them off?"

"Who tole ya that?"

"Logan."

"Ya liked 'em, didn't ya?"

"Yes. They're nice, like Kain is nice. They never laughed when I asked them something." He dropped a boot on the floor. "I can't believe the time has finally come, can you, Mary Ben?" Another boot dropped into the silence. "How long have you been up here?"

"Not long. Yore ma kissed me, 'n told me not to be scared, that you'd never, never, be mean to me. I told her I already knew *that*."

There was a long silence.

"Don't go to sleep now." Plunk! Something dropped and rolled across the wood floor. "Oh, shoot!"

"What was that? What dropped, Henry?"

"It was . . . something out of my pocket. Something Kain told me about." The words were muffled through the shirt he pulled off over his head.

"What?"

"Well, I told him that you were so little, and that sometimes I got awful big with wanting you. I said I was afraid that—"

"That what?"

"That I'd not . . . that I'd hurt you."

"Why'd ya have to tell him *that* for?"

"'Cause I wanted to know what to do."

"Ya could've asked me."

"You've not done *it* before. How would you know?"

"I told ya not to worry 'bout it."

"I know that, but I did anyhow. Then Kain told me about the salve."

"Salve? You mean that . . . gooey stuff your ma put on his bandage to keep it from stickin'?"

"Kain said to use it on my—"

"I don't want to hear any more of what Kain said," she said quickly. "We'll figger out what to do all by our ownselves."

"But, honey girl." Henry edged his way down the side of the bed until he felt the pillow. He got carefully into the bed, and reached out to Mary Ben lying on the far side. He pulled her to him gently, as if she would break. He didn't speak until she lay fully against him, but she could feel the wild excitement begin to build in him. "You feel so warm and soft." His lips snuggled in her hair. "What've you got on?"

"A nightdress. Your ma give it to me. It's . . . white, 'n I put the pink ribbon ya give me on it." She groped for his hand and brought it to the neck of her nightdress. "Here. Can you feel it?"

"I feel it. You're so . . . little without your clothes on, and soft, like a kitten. You smell good, too. You put on the toilet water, didn't you?"

"Uh . . . huh . . ."

His lips moved down her cheek until they found her lips and kissed her until he began to tremble. "I don't have to stop, now, do I?"

"Not if ya don't want to."

"I sure don't want to."

"Why didn't ya take off yore underpants?"

"I didn't know if I was suppose to."

"Silly."

When he turned back to her she had pulled up the nightdress and the long, throbbing hardness that lay against his bare belly was pressed tightly between them. His breath came in quick gasps and his heart thundered against her breast. The naked hunger that caught him was both sweet and violent. Every part of him that touched her carried a fiery message to the depth of his masculinity.

"My sweet . . . my own honey girl . . ."

His hands on her hips pulled her tightly to him. Her arms were around him, her lips nibbling at his. He quivered violently and unknowingly moved his hips so that the aroused part of him rubbed up and down against her soft belly. When the pressure became unbearable, he grabbed frantically at her hips, gave a little strangled cry and exploded with a pain-pleasure so intense that he spun off into a mindless void. The first fantastic sensation was closely followed by another and then another. When he emerged from the long, unbelievable release he realized what had happened and groaned.

"Oh, sweetheart! Oh, damnit! Look what I've done. I've made you all . . . messy. I was supposed to wait, but I just couldn't—"

"It's all right. Ya ain't to worry 'bout it, hear?"

"But I ruined it—"

"No, ya didn't," she crooned and kissed every part of his face her lips could reach. "Ya didn't ruin nothin'. We can do it lots more times. It ain't like ya was goin' to wear *it* out."

"Then it's all right?"

She laughed softly at the breathless, rather ridiculous question. "Course it is, my sweet man."

"I love you, Mary Ben. There's not a girl in the whole world like you. I'm so glad I got you!" There was raw emotion in his voice. He held her to him fiercely. "I'm so glad."

"I'm glad I got ya, too. Sometimes I'm jist so proud I can't hardly stand it." She whispered words of comfort and kissed away the moistness on his face.

In the bedroom downstairs, Vanessa lay close to Kain's side, her head on his shoulder. His hand moved down to her bottom and then to her thigh and pulled it up so it rested across his. His hand returned to caress the soft, rounded flesh of her hips.

"Are you sorry you didn't save yourself for your wedding night?"

"No! It gets better every time." Relaxed and dreamy, she listened to the steady beat of his heart beneath her cheek and marveled that his hard muscles and angled frame could provide such a comfortable resting place.

She tilted her head to look at him, and he caught her lips.

They shared a deep hungry kiss. She felt his heartbeat soar. The kiss ended and they lay quietly, her hand stroking his chest.

"I'm glad everyone could come. I think Aunt Ellie feels better about things now."

"Cooper's mother hadn't been here any time at all before she and Ellie were acting as if they'd known each other forever."

Vanessa turned her face to kiss his bare chest. "I don't think Lorna ever meets a stranger. Rosalee is harder to get to know."

"She had a hard time before she married Logan and a hard time since. Folks have this idea that because Logan is a breed she somehow sinned against God when she married him. They have a few friends but not many. If Logan were all white folks would think he was grand."

"I knew a woman back home who was part Indian. She married a haberdasher and no one thought anything of it."

"There are two sets of standards out here in the West, sweetheart—one for men and one for women. A lot of men have taken Indian women, but if a white woman takes an Indian for a husband she's ostracized."

"It doesn't seem fair."

"Many things in life are not fair," he said with a deep sigh. "I imagine that a few generations from now there will be men with Indian blood in high government positions. It will take time. You know, honey, we white people have been terribly cruel to the Indians. We've treated them as if they were less than human. Rosalee is one of the few women I know who had the courage to flout the taboos."

"She must love him very much."

"They love each other. There's no doubt about that. He's gone through obstacles that would have stopped an ordinary man in his tracks. Sometime I'll tell you how they met."

"When we met in Dodge, I never dreamed that someday we'd be married."

"You were beautiful today, sweetheart. And now you're all mine."

"I was yours before. Now I'm Vanessa DeBolt. I've not said it aloud before. Vanessa DeBolt, Mrs. Kain DeBolt. If we have a baby I'm going to name it Kain, no matter if it's a boy or a girl." Her voice broke on the last word. He felt a tear drop on his shoulder.

A low growl of protest came from his throat. "Sweetheart! Please . . . no tears! Oh, precious love," he muttered thickly. He turned her on her back, leaned over her and kissed teary eyes.

"I'm sorry. I know I promised, but sometimes it's so hard."

"I know, darling." His lips traced the rivulets to her temples.

"I keep hoping, praying something will happen and you'll not have to . . . leave me. Can't we tell Cooper and Logan and Griff? Maybe they can help."

"I've told them about Tass."

"But about the . . . other?" she pleaded.

"It wouldn't do any good. Darling, I keep hoping that you're never sorry you gave yourself to me. I hope the happiness is worth the pain."

"I'll never be sorry! These past few weeks have been the happiest and the most painful time of my life."

"Mine, too. Go to sleep now, sweetheart. If you keep kissing me, I'll have to make love to you again."

"I'd not mind it at all if you did." Her caressing hands moved down his back to his buttocks. Her fingers dipped and squeezed.

"I'd not mind it either! Absolutely, positively . . . not mind it," he whispered just before his mouth covered hers.

Much to the relief of everyone, no one showed up to shivaree the newlyweds.

The wedding guests stayed over another day, which delighted Henry. His admiration for his new brothers grew daily. He spent as much time with them as he could. Whenever the men gathered in the yard to visit, he squatted beside them, listening intently to every word they said. They treated him with the fondness and patience they would give a younger brother. They teased him, gave advice when he asked it, and listened when he talked. He showed them the tools he used when working on leather, and gave each of them a quirt and a whip. He gave Lorna a fourteen-foot bullwhip, and she showed him how she could snap a leaf from a tree and slice in half a potato that Cooper held in his hand.

Henry said repeatedly that this was the happiest time of his life. He had Mary Ben and now he had brothers. Both Cooper and Logan made him promise to come visit and bring his bride and his mother.

Both men offered to stay until the matter with Tass was settled, but Kain knew they each had work waiting at home and declined the offer, saying it could be weeks or months before Tass made his move.

Griff and Bonnie stayed two extra days. Kain and Griff spent one afternoon looking for a sign that Tass might have been lurking around the homestead, and the next afternoon they went into town and inquired about him there. He had not been seen since the day he was in McCloud's store. Kain left word in town that Tass was dangerous and that if the man were sighted he'd appreciate it if someone rode out to tell him.

That evening Kain had a long visit with his friend, and told him that life was uncertain when he was being stalked by a man like Tass, and if something did happen to him, he would appreciate it if Griff would see that no harm came to Vanessa.

"Ya didn't have to ask. Ya know I'd do it. If'n I get my sights on Tass he'll not get a chance at ya. Ya know, Kain, ya don't stand round 'n wait fer a snake to strike. Ya kill it afore it lets its poison go."

They all stood on the porch and waved when Bonnie and Griff rode out. Mary Ben and Bonnie had become good friends, and Mary Ben had promised that she and Henry would go see the Griffins. Griff felt the need to get home. His men were breaking a herd of horses for the army, but he promised to return as soon as they were delivered.

After they left, the house settled into a routine. Always on the lookout for Primer Tass, Jeb and Clay snaked logs down from the hills, John spent his odd hours working on an old buggy that had been left in the barn, and Henry and Kain reset posts for a pole corral.

One afternoon Kain had vicious pains and headed for the barn where he vomited violently. When he saw blood mingled with the vomit panic surged through him. It had been over a week since he'd felt the hot agony in his stomach. It took several minutes before the pounding of his heart slowed down and he realized he'd released only a small amount of blood, not the great gush the Arizona sheriff had thrown up at the last. He walked out of the barn and sat down on a stump to wait for the weakness to pass.

Living with death, he had come to a new appreciation of all that was about him—the warmth of the sun, the eagle soaring in the sky, a cold drink of water after a long thirst. He remembered things, felt things more deeply, now that they soon would be taken from him. Vanessa, his wife, his love—Everything about her was precious to him. She was soft and yielding in bed, lovely and proud across the table, beautiful and tempting in a faded dress with her arms buried deep in soapsuds. She would never know what being with her had meant to him. Should he tell her that he was dying? She was already carrying the burden of knowing he would be leaving her one day soon. No. He couldn't bear to see the misery that would fill her magnificent eyes. He would write her a letter and leave it with Ellie. In it he would tell her how much he loved her and that he wanted her to live her life to the fullest. And if she should meet a man she could be happy with, she was to remarry and not feel guilty. Kain's heart swelled and he struggled to keep a sob from breaking loose at the thought of his wife in the arms of another man.

He had already begun to make his arrangements. Logan had taken with him, along with Ellie's papers, a newly written will to send down to Randolph in Denver. There was no way Della could get her hands on this place now unless Vanessa sold it to her. Vanessa and the Hills would be able to make a living here with the help of John and the Hookers. Logan and Cooper would keep an eye on them.

The other thing he had to do was kill Primer Tass. He did not doubt that Tass was stalking him. But he would not attempt a shot until reasonably sure of a kill. It could be a duel of wits that could last for weeks, and he didn't have time for that. If Tass didn't make a move soon he would go looking for him. There was the chance Tass would kill him. If so, he would have John and the Hookers to contend with. Kain knew with a certainty that if Tass got him Griffin wouldn't rest until he tracked him down. He also knew that if Griff got to Tass first he would kill him. Griff played by no rules of fair play; he didn't believe in letting a man who needed killing have the first shot. Life in Yuma prison had made the young rancher hard, and he had become even harder since his struggle to get his horse ranch going. Adam Clayhill had not made it easy for him to keep his range.

Vanessa came out of the house. She had a shawl wrapped about her shoulders and a worried look on her face. He watched her come across the yard toward him.

"My sweet, adorable little red bird," he sighed, and held out his hand to her.

"Henry said you were sick."

"It was nothing. I must have eaten something that didn't sit well in my stomach." He drew her to him and pulled her down on his knee.

"How could beef stew not sit right in your stomach? Have you been eating that spiced meat the Hookers cooked?"

"As a matter of fact, I did," he lied. "Stop worrying, sweetheart. I've even gained weight lately. It's all that milk Ellie makes me drink."

"If you throw up anymore, you'll see a doctor. Rosalee said one set up practice in Junction City about a month ago. She said he's young; but his father was a doctor, and she thinks he's good."

"I'm glad of that. Civilization has come to Junction City. I don't think there's been a doctor here before. The first thing we know there will be a town sheriff, a chamber of commerce and prayer meeting night—"

"Stop trying to change the subject. If you're sick again you're going to see that doctor." She wrapped her arms about his neck. "I love you."

"You shouldn't have said that. Those are dangerous words to say out here in broad daylight. I might have to take you to the barn or to our room." He laughed softly at the shocked, exasperated expression on her face.

"You're a glutton, is what you are, Kain DeBolt. We've been married for five days, and every night of those five days we've—"

"If you're counting days, love. Let's be correct and go back to before we were married."

"You're no gentleman either! It's mean of you to bring *that* up." Her brilliant blue eyes regarded him with insolent appraisal. She cocked an eyebrow and pressed her lips together in order to keep a stern face.

He laughed and his arms tightened about her waist. "Lovely Vanessa—my own." His teasing had shifted to a low, husky murmur.

"That's better." She sighed. "Darling, do you think it's decent for us to be kissing out here in broad daylight?"

Chapter Twenty

Adam Clayhill sat in the big chair in his office. His legs were stretched out in front of him, his hands clenched together over his stomach, his eyes on his stockinged feet. He was in one of his quiet moods. Since the chance meeting with Ellie Hill he had alternated between these quiet spells and fits of rage. When the rage was on him he paced the floor, cursed, threw things, bellowed unreasonable orders, and cuffed the servants until the only ones left were Joseph and Cecilia. The laundress left after he slapped her, and the cook and the kitchen girl slipped away quietly at night after he had thrown a bowl of hot soup at them saying it wasn't fit to use for slop.

Della walked the floor in her room and fumed. For the first time in her life she had been unable to get Adam to tell her what was bothering him. She knew it had to be more than the fact that another bastard had showed up and he was not as bright as Adam would expect a Clayhill to be. She had done everything she knew to try and pull him out of his depression. She had offered sex, and he wasn't interested. That led her to believe he was both mentally and physically ill.

Della stood gazing out the window thinking that she'd never seen Adam so unkempt. His hair was uncombed and he hadn't bathed. Until today he hadn't even shaved. She had taken the soap and razor to the den and shaved him herself. He had sat there, indifferent to her coaxing, refusing to talk to her, staring straight ahead, lighting one cigar after the other, letting the ashes fall on the floor.

The dammed old fool! She wished she knew for sure if he had made out a new will. At one time he was going to leave everything to her and Kain. Later, when Kain sided with Cooper Parnell and the rancher, Griffin, he told her Kain wouldn't get a dime of his money or a foot of his land.

She spun away from the window. There was only one way to find out—*ask him*! She checked her hair in the mirror, dabbed some perfume on the white globes of her breasts that swelled above the neckline of her dress, and went downstairs.

The house was quiet except for the rattle of pans in the kitchen where Joseph and Cecilia were preparing a meal. Della swept aside the velvet draperies that covered the doorway to Adam's office and went inside. He sat in the same position as he had when she left him hours earlier, legs stretched out, head resting against the back of the chair.

"Papa, darling, are you hungry? You didn't eat anything this morning, and I had Joseph fix scrambled eggs with peppers, just like you like them." Della leaned down, so that her face was close to his, and pouted prettily.

Adam looked at her without moving his head, then back down at his feet. Exasperated, Della moved a small stool in front of him and sat down. She leaned over so the front of her dress gaped invitingly, and covered his hands with hers.

"Talk to me, Adam. I'm so lonesome."

He looked at her again. His eyes stayed on her face, and she smiled. Then he pulled his hands from beneath hers and looked away.

"What's the matter, darling? Tell Della. You know I love you. You can tell me anything, Papa Adam. I'll understand. We're family." He didn't acknowledge her words by as much as a bat of an eyelash. Anger flared and blazed brightly, fed by a wounded ego. Who the hell did he think he was to sit there like a great lump and ignore her? Men had paid as much as a hundred dollars an hour for her company, and here she was wasting her time on him, sitting at his feet, begging the bastard to look at her!

She got to her feet and began to pace the room. It wouldn't do to speak to him when she was angry. She had to choose her words carefully, ease into the question she was determined to ask. She calmed herself by planning her strategy, then went back to the stool and sat down.

"Darling, I need advice and you're the only one I know who can tell me straight out what to do. Are you listening?" His eyes flicked to her and away. She was encouraged to go on. "As you know I've been quite successful with my business and I've accumulated a sizeable amount of property. I've made out a will, darling, leaving it all to you. I'm wondering if there is any way Kain, as next of kin, can step in and take it from you after I'm gone. I don't want him to have anything that's mine. Not after what he's done."

He looked at her and his eyes began to brighten with interest. They honed in on her face, narrowed, and glinted. It was as if a light had suddenly gone on in his head.

"Is that all that's worrying you?" His voice was rough, but she didn't care as long as he talked to her.

"No, darling. I also want you to tell me if there's any way Kain can take my inheritance away from me."

"What inheritance?" he asked quietly.

"Well, this place." With a wave of her hand, she gestured to the area around them. "That is, if you leave it to me."

His move was so quick and unexpected it brought a startled cry from her. He jumped to his feet with such violence that she almost fell off the stool. His arms swung around and his hand just missed her face. She didn't know if he meant to hit her or if she was just in the way. As soon as she could get to her feet she backed away from him. He stormed across the room, pounded the opposite wall with a balled fist, turned, and came back.

"I thought that was what you were getting at, you bitch! All of you gawddamn women are alike. All you want to do is get your greedy hands on my land. You want to know if *I* have a will, isn't that it, Della? And you want to know if I'm leaving everything to you. You're thinking the old man is going to cash in his chips, and you'll have your own private little stud farm—a whole bunkhouse full of cowhands to screw." He threw his arms wide and his head jutted forward. "Ain't that right, Della? Ain't that right? You've never cared a gawddamn for anything but money and a stud in bed—"

"Don't be vulgar, Adam. I merely asked you a civil question."

"Hush up!" he bellowed. "Hush your fuckin' mouth! I know what you are! Everybody knows what you are, Della. You're a whore! A slut!"

"Yes, I'm a whore, and a damn good one. And I won't hush! You've moped around here like a love-sick calf since you saw that woman in town and I'm sick of it. I'm sick and tired of taking your abuse. Don't throw that word slut at me again, Adam. There's a world of difference between a whore and a slut," she shouted.

"Get your hot little twat off my ranch! Go! I sure as hell don't need you," he roared. His face had turned crimson and the cords stood out on his neck. He kicked over a halltree, strode to the desk and swept the ink bottles to the floor.

A long ribbon of fear that she had spoken too hastily unfurled in Della. "Now, Papa. Don't talk like that—"

"Don't *now papa* me, by Gawd! I'm not your papa. I'm

not your anything. I wasn't even married to that straight-laced, prissy bitch."

His appalling words rocked her. "What do you mean?" she asked with biting urgency.

He ignored the question, turned and stomped to the end of the room, flung back the drapery and looked out the window. Then, as if jolted to action, he spun around and strode back across the room.

"I'm leaving this ranch to the United States government to be made into a park. They'll put a statue of me right out there in the yard, sittin' on my white horse—a monument to a great man who wrestled this land from the gawddamn red asses." He threw his arms wide and brought his fists back to pound on his chest. "That's *me*, Adam Clayhill, the first white man to take a chunk of this wilderness, tame it, and hold it. *Adam Clayhill* ran off the savages, *Adam Clayhill* held this land to keep the scum that follow the trailblazers from coming in and cutting it up. *Adam Clayhill* did it all. By Gawd, when they hear what I'm going to do they'll *beg* me to be the governor of Colorado, or they'll not get an inch of my land!"

"I doubt if your lawyer would make out a will like that," Della said with feigned indifference, although she was desperate to know if the will had been made.

"What the hell do you know about it?"

"He made out your other will, didn't he?"

"I've never made out a gawddamn will in my life! But I'm going to. You can bet your little hot twat I'm going to. I'll go down in history, along with John Fremont, Zebulon Pike, and that great know-it-all Custer, who thinks he's going to fence in the redskins. I say kill 'em and be done with it. Chivington's way is the only way, by Gawd." He paced the floor in long strides, and the words poured from his mouth, laced with curses.

Della was so angry she was almost sick with it. Her fury burst forth in a strangled shout. "You couldn't even kill *one* red ass. Logan Horn has beat you at every turn. His ranch is even bigger than yours. Face it, Adam, you're nothing but an old has-been, and the sooner you die the better I'll like it!"

Adam continued pacing and muttering as if he hadn't heard a word she said. Suddenly, he stopped in front of her, his face frozen in a mask of hate. Spittle ran from the corner of his mouth.

"You whore! You've teamed up with Kain to ruin me. I'd never have married you, but there wasn't a whore in town, and I was bored. That gawddamn clerk said he'd give me the marriage papers, but he run off. Damn you and your half-wit brat! Damn you to hell and back!" As quick as a flash he slapped Della across the face with the palm of his hand, then on the other side with the back of it.

Della was dumbfounded. He was out of his head. She saw that he was completely confused as to who she was. He looked so frenzied, so ugly and maddened that she was paralyzed with shock and fear. She turned to leave, but he grabbed her shoulder and spun her around.

"Hear me, Ellie! You're nothing but hair and bone and skin with a hole in it." His voice rose to a deafening yell, a fierce, wild look contorting his face. "Oh, I know what you thought! Yes, I know, I know. You bitch!" he shrieked. "Gawd, how I hate you. I'll kill you . . . I'll kill—"

He reached out for her and she shrank from his hands, backing away. The corner of his mouth jerked down, his eyes stared, and he hung there as if suspended while his face became expressionless. Then, as if his legs were melting into the carpet, he sagged to the floor.

Della stared down at him, appalled and astounded, not knowing what to do. Then she screamed for Joseph.

Vanessa had gone to the porch to call the men to dinner when the sorrel horse pulling a small, light buggy turned into the lane leading to the house. The horse was halted beyond the porch, and the man stepped down.

"Howdy." He was a tall, thin young man in a wrinkled duster over a black suit. He was clean-shaven except for the beard that outlined his jaws and came together at his chin.

"Good afternoon." Vanessa could see John and Kain coming from the barn on the run.

"I'm Dr. Warren. This poor beast pulling my buggy is going lame. Oh, how do you do, sir?" he said as Kain rounded the end of the buggy. "Dr. Warren. I was just telling the young lady my horse is going lame."

Kain stuck out his hand. "Kain DeBolt. My wife, Mrs. DeBolt, and Mr. Wisner."

The doctor shook hands with Kain, removed his hat and nodded to Vanessa, then held out his hand to John. His face was young and friendly. He had not a single hair on the top of his head, but a thick growth around the edges connected with the hair on his face. His accent had the flavor of the deep South.

John moved over to the sorrel and cautiously lifted the leg the horse was favoring. The doctor patted the animal on the side and peered down at the leg.

"The animal was suffering, and I didn't know if he could make it to town. I wondered, sir, if you could spare a horse. I'll return it later and pick up this one."

"We'll certainly work out something," Kain said. "Meanwhile, my wife was calling us to dinner. Won't you come in and join us?"

"Thank you. I would be pleased."

"The horse has a bad cut on his fetlock, Kain. The doctor can use one of my horses, 'n we'll get this feller in the barn 'n put some pine tar on it." John began to unhitch the horse, who stood quietly as if he knew his ordeal was over.

"Can you doctor it after you eat, John?" Vanessa called. "You know how it irritates Aunt Ellie when her corn bread gets cold."

"I'll be right in, missy."

Kain led the young doctor into the kitchen and introduced him to Ellie and Mary Ben, and then to the others as they filed in. They sat down at the table and Ellie asked Henry to say grace. Ever the polite hostess, she engaged the doctor in conversation while the dishes were being passed.

"Did I hear a bit of the South in your voice, doctor?"

"Yes, ma'am, you did. I was born and raised in Mississipi, not too far from the Shiloh battleground."

"I thought that battle took place in Tennessee."

"It did, ma'am. I'm from Cornith, right across the border."

"That was a terrible battle. Vanessa's father was a doctor, and he told us stories of terrible suffering."

"My daddy was a doctor, too. He spent most of his time in a northern prison." He accepted the meat platter and helped himself.

"I didn't know we had a doctor here until a few days ago," Kain said.

"I've only been here a couple of months. I guess you'd call it the lure of the mountains that brought me here."

"Usually it's the lure of gold that brings people here."

"Yes." The doctor laughed. "I heard before I came here that a man need only to find a stream coming down from the mountains, wade in, and pick up the nuggets. Thank you," he said to Henry, who passed the plate of corn bread. "It isn't what you have that makes a happy life, it's good health. The patient I just attended, a man who seems to have everything, a big ranch, a beautiful home, servants, would probably trade places with the poorest man alive if he could be healthy again."

"Is he someone who lives near us, doctor?" Kain asked the question in the silence that followed.

"As far as I'm concerned, there isn't anything *near* anything else in this country, Mr. DeBolt. It's all sky, plains and mountains. My patient was a Mr. Clayhill. His ranch is about ten miles from here. Do you know him?"

"Yes, we know him." Kain looked at Ellie. She was watching the doctor, letting nothing at all show on her face.

"One of his cowhands came in yesterday to fetch me. I spent the night out there. Mr. Clayhill has suffered a spell of apoplexy." The doctor helped himself to another serving of corn bread, over which he spooned a generous amount of gravy. He was obviously hungry.

"Is Mr. Clayhill paralyzed?" Ellie asked when it seemed the doctor would drop the subject.

"Are you familiar with the disease, ma'am?"

"Yes, a little. I know there are several types of apoplexy."

Vanessa watched her aunt, as did everyone else at the table.

"He did not suffer a temporary fit. It's much more serious. Mr. Clayhill has no voluntary movements except breathing, turning his head slightly and moving the fingers of one hand." The doctor filled his mouth and after he swallowed, he added, "Sad. Very Sad."

"Why do you say that? Is Mr. Clayhill dying?"

The doctor looked down the table at the pleasant looking woman who had asked the question. He glanced at Kain and saw that he also waited impatiently for an answer, as did his wife and the other young couple. Only the old man who had unhitched his horse and the other two continued to eat.

"Doctor," Ellie said, breaking the silence. "I am Mrs. Clayhill. I have the right to know if my husband is dying."

The soberness of Ellie's words brought every eye to her face and drew even a deeper silence. John and the Hookers couldn't conceal their dismay. The doctor was dumbfounded, but rallied quickly.

"I'm sorry, I didn't know. Mr. DeBolt called you—"

"Hill. My son and I go by the name of Hill. Mr. Clayhill and I have been estranged for a long time. Nevertheless, he is my husband. Is he dying?"

"Mr. Clayhill is conscious but cannot speak. He may live a few days, or a year, or he may be gone by the time I return. A stroke patient usually dies within a few days of the attack. If he lives longer than that he has a chance of living for months or even years with good care. Sometimes the paralysis remains, at other times disappearing in the course of some months, partially or completely. It is impossible to predict what the results will be."

"Who is taking care of him?"

"Ah . . . his daughter is there."

"His stepdaughter," Ellie said quickly.

"Cases are known in which the patient's bodily functions have been entirely recovered while various impairments of the mind have persisted. The loss of speech in connection with apoplexy happens frequently if the right side of the body is paralyzed during the stroke, which is what happened in this case. It is interesting to note that Mr. Clayhill understands everything perfectly, but is unable to communicate."

"Is his stepdaughter taking care of him?"

"He's being cared for by a Mexican woman and a Negro servant. Miss Clayhill doesn't seem to have the, ah . . . patience to care for the sick." The doctor looked quickly from Ellie to Kain and back, and a dull redness covered his cheeks. "Ma'am, you may wish to consider—" He cut off what he was going to say when he saw the frosty look that came over Ellie's face.

John moved his chair back from the table and the legs rasped loudly on the plank floor. The Hookers got quickly to their feet, moving fast for them. The tension in the room was being felt by all.

"If'n ya want, I'll hitch up fer ya, Doc. 'N don't ya worry none 'bout yore horse. He'll rest in the barn 'n be fit in a day or two."

"I'm obliged to you."

In the silence after the back door was firmly shut, Ellie got up and brought the coffeepot to the table. She refilled the cups and when she came to Henry, she placed her hand on his shoulder, as if just wanting to touch him. He and Mary Ben sat close together on the bench and she could see her tightly holding Henry's hand. She was a dear girl, Ellie thought, thanking God once more that she loved her son.

"Oh, dear. I forgot the custard pie. It's John's favorite. I'll be sure and save some for his supper."

Nothing more was said about Adam Clayhill until the doctor was ready to leave.

"Mrs. Clayhill—"

"Call me Mrs. Hill, doctor."

"Do you want me to stop by again tomorrow?"

"It would be nice if you could make it at mealtime."

"Thank you. I must say that's the best meal I've had since I came to Colorado."

"It's my turn to thank you."

After the doctor left, Kain and Henry went back to the job of shaping fence posts, and the women began cleaning the kitchen. Vanessa arranged the castor set in the center of the table, set the other necessaries around it and covered it with a cloth. Mary Ben silently took the large granite pan from where it hung on a nail behind the stove.

"Girls, would you mind if I went upstairs for awhile?" Ellie stood in the middle of the kitchen, her eyes focused on the window across the room.

"Of course not, Aunt Ellie. It'll not take me and Mary Ben any time at all to wash up."

"I need to be alone . . . to think." She turned and looked levelly at Vanessa.

Vanessa went to her, encircled Ellie's waist, gave her a quick, firm hug and gently nudged her toward the door. She listened to her footsteps as she went up the stairs to her room.

"What does it mean, Van? Do ya think she could still love that mean ole man?" Mary Ben poured steaming water into the dishpan from the teakettle.

"I don't know. She loved the man she thought he was for so many years."

"I hope she don't love 'em. I hope she hates 'em. Then she won't hurt when he dies. 'N I hope he does fer what he done to her 'n Henry."

Vanessa pondered Mary Ben's logic while she dried the dishes. Ellie had told her one time that love and hate were the two most powerful emotions. They rested side by side in a heart fighting each other. That was the reason people were able to hurt loved ones the most. Like Mary Ben, she hoped that Ellie's love for the man she thought was Henry Hill had turned to hate. For if ever there was a man on earth who deserved Ellie's hate it was Adam Clayhill.

That evening after the supper dishes were washed and John and the Hookers had gone back to the bunkhouse, Ellie made an announcement that astounded them all.

"I have decided that Henry, Mary Ben and I are going to the Clayhill ranch, and that I am going to take my place there as Mrs. Clayhill." Her sincerity was unmistakable.

"Aunt Ellie!" Vanessa sat up straight on the sofa and looked disbelievingly at her aunt as she fiddled with the fringe on the table scarf beside her chair.

"Before anyone says anything, I want to tell you why I have decided to do this. This afternoon, I thought back over the twenty years since Henry Hill left me. I thought of how desperate I was when I knew that I was going to have Henry. I had no money. My parents had died and I had no home to go back to. I had only my sister and her husband to turn to. Thank God they welcomed me. Henry was born there, and my brother-in-law attended me." Ellie's soft words dropped into the silent room. "I stayed on, raised my son and Vanessa after my sister died. My husband, Henry's father, dismissed us as if we were less than nothing. He read my letters begging for a word about the man I thought was my husband

and ignored them. All these years he had been here while I wasted my life grieving for him."

Ellie looked at each of the faces before she spoke again. Her fine eyes misted when she looked at her handsome son, sitting quietly, his young wife on a stool beside his chair.

"That man owes Henry and me twenty years of support. I mean to see that he pays it."

Henry leaned forward anxiously. "You want us to go live with him, Ma?"

"That's exactly what I mean. I am Mrs. Clayhill. Regardless of how I feel about him, I am entitled to be the mistress of his house; you are entitled to live there. He *owes* it to us. I will see to it that he is taken care of. I am sure that I can do it as well as a Mexican woman and a servant."

"But, Ma. He don't want us—"

"I don't care a fig about what *he* wants. He is flat on his back, and according to law, I am his legal wife. *I* will run his home and take care of him as I see fit. I plan to go in the morning."

"Aunt Ellie—" Vanessa looked at Kain for help and was puzzled by the strange little half smile on his face. He picked up her hand and gave it a little squeeze. She turned back to her aunt. "What about Della Clayhill?"

"Della DeBolt," Kain said. "She calls herself Clayhill at times."

"How will Ellie deal with your sister, Kain?"

"She'll not have a thing to say about it." Ellie's confidence seemed unshakable.

"That's right, she won't." Kain's words brought Vanessa's head around again.

"Kain?"

"It seems like Ellie has made up her mind, sweetheart."

"But she's no match for Della."

"I think she is. Besides, we'll go with her."

"Thank you, Kain. I was hoping you'd say that."

"Do we pack up everything?" Henry asked.

"Absolutely. There's no point in doing things halfway, son."

"But I don't like him. I don't want to see him. He's mean. I want to stay here with Kain."

Mary Ben saw the distress on Ellie's face and pulled Henry's head down so she could whisper in his ear.

"I don't like him, either, but yore ma knows what she's doin'. We got to stay by her 'n help her 'n not give her no sass. If'n she can stand that old bastard, we can too."

Henry looked down into Mary Ben's face and his creased with one of the dazzling, beautiful smiles that slid over it when he suddenly understood something that had puzzled him.

"Mary Ben, you're just so smart. I never even thought of that. Ma, Mary Ben says we got to stay by you and help. She says if you can stand that old bastard we can too."

"Henry!" Mary Ben hissed and threw a hasty glance at Ellie.

"What are you all up in the air for, honey girl? That's what you said."

"But ya didn't have to say that word!"

"It's all right, Mary Ben," Ellie said calmly. "I think your description of Mr. Clayhill was perfect."

Kain blew out the light, slipped into bed, and gathered Vanessa into his arms.

"I'm worried for her." Vanessa continued the conversation they had started while getting undressed.

"I think you're going to be surprised, sweetheart. That woman's got backbone and dignity to go with it."

"But Kain, they'll say terrible things to her."

"You mean Della will say terrible things to her. Ellie can take it. Della doesn't have a leg to stand on."

"But if Mr. Clayhill dies and leaves everything to her, she will."

"If that happens Ellie will have to go to court and get a

fair share for herself and Henry. Don't worry, sweetheart. Logan and Cooper would see to it. Now stop thinking about it and think about me." He lifted her arm and pulled it up and around his neck.

Lying in his embrace, drugged with the sweetness, she marveled at how the whole world changed to a dazzling, beautiful place when they were fully entwined, cocooned in warmth, when he was closer than her very heart. She lifted her mouth for his kiss. With closed eyes she perceived his strong, delicate fingers stroking the quivering small of her back. Every stroke, every gesture was marked with grave reverence. He moved his other hand and clasped her head to his chest, murmuring, "My love, my love."

His gentle fingers continued to stroke her hair. She turned her lips to his shoulder to kiss the blessed flesh. She lifted her fingers and touched his face. She could feel him smiling.

And with what surely was a greater passion than ever before, they came together in sweet, familiar, excruciating contact of heated skin, drumming pulses, and shuddering limbs.

Chapter Twenty-one

"Clay, you and John keep an eye out for Tass." Kain was in the barn saddling Big Red. "I don't understand why he hasn't made his move."

"Killin's one thin', Kain. Stealin' a woman's somethin' else. If'n he's smart, 'n I think he is, he's doin' some careful plannin'. Ya've spread the word on 'em 'n folk'll be lookin' fer him. If'n Miss Vanessa come up missin', folks'll be on his trail like flies on cowshit."

"It was Griff's idea to spread the word he was after Vanessa. If he stays around town with that hair around his neck he'll find himself being looked over."

"Hit's the same in Texas. Ya can get yoreself hung quicker botherin' a woman 'n ya can killin' a marshal."

Kain swung into the saddle. "We'll see which way the wind blows out at Clayhills. It could be that Jeb can come on back, and it could be we'll all come on back."

"Ain't nothin' to worry 'bout here. Me 'n John'll hold down the fort."

Henry and Jeb tied the traveling bags on the back of the buggy John had overhauled. He stood proudly by while the women praised his work.

"Well, who'd have thought that rickety old thing could be made into such a handsome buggy," Ellie exclaimed. "You've even put new spokes in the wheels and mended the seat and the top. Isn't this nice, Vanessa? It surely beats riding in a wagon. You're a jim-dandy, John, when it comes to fixing things."

"I tole ya Mr. Wisner could do jist anythin', anythin' a'tall." Mary Ben smiled at him proudly and moved over close so she could speak just to him. "Ya be careful while I'm gone. Don't ya let that sneaky litle ole bastard get up close to ya, hear? Ya carry that old buffalo gun with ya, even when ya go to the outhouse."

"Ya ain't to be worryin', gal," he said gruffly. "Ya mind what Mrs. Hill tells ya."

"I wish ya was comin', Mr. Wisner. I ain't been away from ya since ya come to the Cimarron."

"I ain't goin' nowhere, Mary Ben. Nowhere a'tall. Ya go on with yore man." There was a tender gruffness to his voice now. "Me 'n this ole yeller dog'll be right here. It might be me 'n Clay'll take us a ride over to see that fancy place, if'n yo're thar awhile."

"All right, but ya be careful. Ya stay here with Mr. Wisner, Mister, 'n don't ya let nobody sneak up on him, hear?"

"Come on, Mary Ben." Henry was waiting to help her into the buggy. "Van will drive you and Ma."

"Bye, Mr. Wisner."

"Bye, gal."

"Henry, put this rifle in the saddle scabbard and stay by the buggy so you'll be with the women." Kain, mounted on

Big Red, rode close and handed him the gun. "Jeb and I will scout a little and be back. Keep to the trail, sweetheart."

"Y'haw!" Vanessa slapped the reins against the back of the horse and they moved out of the yard. As they turned down the lane leading to the road, Mary Ben and Ellie waved to Clay and John.

The silence that followed the leave-taking was broken only by the jingle of the harnesses and the clip-clop of the horse's hooves. The terrain that opened before them was a succession of valleys divided by ridges crested with pines, their slopes sometimes dotted with clumps of aspen. Large yellow leaves floated across the trail, pushed by a cool autumn wind. As they traveled in a westerly direction the trail narrowed in places. The scattered boulders grew fewer, the trees thicker.

Ellie was quiet. Vanessa knew that her aunt was terribly nervous. It was evident in her stiffness as she sat in the seat and in the way she kept her hands folded in her shawl. Vanessa wondered what was going on in Ellie's mind as she sat there between her and Mary Ben. She was on her way to a husband who had deserted her, to his home where she would not be welcomed, to take care of a man who despised her. Poor Ellie.

As sorry as she was for Ellie, the danger this trip represented to Kain was foremost in her mind. The old dread she had felt on the trip to Junction City returned tenfold. In a near stupor of fear, she scanned the trail ahead. There were a hundred places where a man could hide and shoot an unsuspecting traveler. She had to believe that Kain knew how best to deal with this situation, that he was doing all he could do to protect himself. Danger to herself from Primer Tass didn't enter her mind. Kain. She prayed to God that nothing would happen to him. A numbness swathed her; she heard nothing of what Ellie and Mary Ben were saying. She saw her hands on the reins and from long training automatically did what a driver would do while she strove to keep panic at bay.

* * *

Kain rode to the crest of the hill, trusting more to his horse than himself, and sat there searching every foot of the landscape with his glasses, as Jeb was doing on the other side of the wagon track that wove among the rocks and trees. He was glad he had Big Red. The horse was spooky, and Kain had deliberately chosen him for just that reason. The animal could hear every sound, and could both see and hear better than a man. If there was a living thing nearby, Big Red would know it.

His horse's ears began to twitch and Kain reached for his gun. A deer darted from the brush and raced toward the cover of thick trees. He nudged the horse and moved down from the hill and up another. He came out onto a bench and saw Clayhill Ranch backed up to the rugged mountain at the far end of a meadow. From where he sat he could see over a far stretch of country.

He took his field glasses out once again and watched the buggy approach. He focused them on Vanessa. Vanessa, his love, his life. Just looking at her made his pulse quicken! She reminded him of a bright new penny. But there was nothing hard and rigid about her. He had never seen a woman who was so beautiful—feminine and soft, sensual and exciting. She was all warm tones from the top of her flaming red hair and brilliant blue eyes to the white skin of her face and hands. And when they were wrapped in each other's arms, when they were one, she was the most giving, most loving—He lowered the glasses and his hand automatically went to his stomach. Every day was precious to him.

When Ellie had announced her plans to take her place in Adam's home, he couldn't have been more surprised but realized it was a damn good idea. Old Adam was flat on his back and couldn't do a thing about it, and possession was nine points of the law. Kain had no doubt that Ellie was in for a bad time with Della, but she had the law on her side or would have as soon as Randolph in Denver set the records right. In the meantime Ellie would run her bluff. Kain chuckled with admiration for the spunky little woman. Adam had finally met his match—if he was still alive. The doctor had said he was in bad shape and was unlikely to recover fully. But if the old bastard just lived long enough for Ellie to be in full possession when he died, even if he left everything to Della, the court would give something to Ellie and Henry.

Kain wondered who was running the business end of the ranch. The roundup would be over by now, but the business end was something he could help Ellie with if she got past the front door.

As the buggy approached the ranch Ellie was thinking the same thing. Would she get past the front door? She wasn't prepared for the elegance of the white frame two-story house. The many gabled house was a splendid example of nineteenth-century architecture. Wide, railed verandas were supported by graceful columns decorated with elaborately carved cornices. Long windows opened up onto the verandas on both the lower and upper floors. Stained glass panes adorned the upper part of the windows as well as the doors. Shrubs and a carefully attended lawn surrounded the house as well as a white picket fence. The elegant house looked as if it belonged on a shaded street of any large city rather than this isolated area. Behind the house was a large barn, various outbuildings and a vast number of pole corrals.

In a glance Ellie knew beyond all doubt Adam Clayhill was a very wealthy man. Resentment burned like a flame in her and solidified her determination that she and her son would no longer be cast aside. They would stay and take what was due them.

Kain and Jeb came down out of the hills and rode with Henry alongside the buggy as it approached the ranch. Vanessa breathed more easily and smiled her relief at her husband. Her ordeal was over for the time being and Ellie's had just begun. As she pulled the horse to a stop beside the front gate, the ranch hands at the outbuildings watched; but none approached. Kain, Henry and Jeb rode to the hitching rail and dismounted. Jeb attached a lead rope to the halter of the horse pulling the buggy and tied it to a iron ring in one of the fence posts, then climbed up into the buggy to wait.

Ellie stood for a long moment before she opened the gate and led the party up the cobblestone walk to the wide veranda. Vanessa had never seen her aunt carry herself with more dignity and determination.

A few minutes after she rang the bell, the heavy oak door was opened by a Negro man wearing a black, long-tailed coat and stiff white shirt.

"Yas'm?"

"I'm here to see Mr. Clayhill." Ellie's voice at first held a slight tremor, but strengthened at the end.

"Mastah done took to de bed. He sick, he doan see nobody."

"I know that. How is Mr. Clayhill?"

"He jist lay dare. Doctor man says he 'spect he gwine ta die." He rolled his eyes upward. "I ain't ta let nobody in."

Kain stepped forward and pushed on the door. "Step aside. We're coming in."

"But, suh, Mis Della say nobody—"

"To hell with Miss Della." Kain pushed him back with a firm hand on his chest and stepped inside. "Come on in, Ellie."

Ellie walked into the wide hallway and immediately took off her wrap and her hat and hung them on the halltree as if she had been doing it for years. The servant stood against the wall. His eyes went from Kain to the top of the stairs and back, and there was a frightened look on his face.

"What is your name?" Ellie asked.

"Joseph."

"Joseph, ask Miss Della to come down. Who else is in the house beside Mr. Clayhill?"

"Miss Cecilia. De rest of 'em gone."

"Who is Miss Cecilia?"

"She be . . . She be . . ."

"Is she one of the servants?"

"Yas'm."

"Tell her to come, too."

"Yas'm." He scurried away and disappeared through a door at the end of the hall.

Ellie turned to the others still lingering beside the door. "Take off your coats. We're here to stay. Henry, in a few minutes you and Jeb can bring our things in."

"What the hell are you up to, Kain? Why have you brought *her* here?" Della stood at the top of the wide staircase that rose from the center of the hall to the second floor balcony. She wore a flowing, white peignoir. Her hair was down around her shoulders and she had a hairbrush in her hand.

"As to what I'm doing, I brought the lady here. As to why, she'll tell you herself."

Della started down the steps. "You've no doubt heard about Adam's fit of apoplexy from that spineless, backwoods doctor. What do you hope to gain by bringing another one of Adam's bastards here? Heaven only knows how many more will turn up. He's screwed enough women to populate the Colorado Territory."

Joseph and a Mexican girl emerged from a room at the back of the hall. They stood with their backs to the wall, watching Della.

Ellie had moved down the hall by the time Della reached the last step. She confronted her there.

"I'm Mrs. Adam Clayhill. I'm here to run my husband's house and to take care of him. If you wish to stay until sundown, I advise you to keep a civil tongue in your head."

Della's body stiffened and her face was as still as a beautiful stone statue. Then she began to laugh; it was high, and shrill and ugly and meant to intimidate. Kain, watching,

knew it wasn't going to work. Ellie had turned her back on
Della and was speaking to Joseph.

"You heard what I said, Joseph. I am Mr. Clayhill's wife.
I am here to stay. I want to see the rest of the house. I'll
need a room for myself and one each for Mr. and Mrs. De-
Bolt and for my son and his wife."

"Yes'm."

"Joseph! You black bastard! Don't you dare obey her.
They're not staying!" Della moved around to face Ellie.
Ellie ignored her and spoke to Cecilia.

"You're Cecilia. What do you do here? Are you the cook?
The maid?"

"Oh, my God! This is rich. She's Adam's whore!"
Della's voice rose to a screech and the look Cecilia shot her
was pure hatred.

"If that's the case, I doubt Mr. Clayhill will be needing
your services." Ellie spoke in a calm, unruffled voice.
"Does your family live here, Cecilia?" The woman shook
her head. "If I told you to leave, would you have somewhere
to go?" She shook her head again. "Very well, you may stay
and work in another capacity. Is that agreeable?" Cecilia
nodded and cast a gloating look at Della. "You can show me
where things are."

"This has gone far enough! Far enough, goddamn it!"
Della threw the hairbrush against the wall. "I don't care if
you married Adam a hundred times, you're not coming in
here and taking over."

"Oh, but I am." Ellie's calm blue eyes looked directly
into Della's blazingly angry ones. "And I believe that as
long as you have this resentful attitude toward me, you'll be
happier somewhere else. I'll have someone drive you to
town. Be ready to leave by noon."

"*You* are telling *me* to leave? This has been my home for
twenty years! I'll not leave because one of Adam's . . . little
diversions tells me to. Jesus Christ! He's amused himself
with dozens of women like you!"

"No, the other women were not like me. Mr. Clayhill and I are married. The marriage is recorded. Our son's birth is recorded. We were already married when he went through the ceremony with your mother. The poor woman was taken in by his charm, as I was. You have no claim here, and you are no longer welcome, even if you are Kain's sister. Joseph, I'll need your help to get settled in. But first you can help Miss Della pack and get ready to leave."

"Goddamn it. Kain—" Della looked at her brother. Kain lifted his shoulders and grinned.

"You may as well go, Della. Your reign at the Clayhill Ranch has ended, and you can kiss Adam's money good-bye."

"Adam's lawyer will put a stop to this," she threatened.

"Why don't you go on down to Denver and talk it over with him? I think he'll tell you you haven't a leg to stand on."

"I'll do that. I'll just do that!" Della flounced up the stairs and turned at the top to look down. The people in the hall below were making themselves at home and didn't even seem to notice that she left them.

"Well, that's settled," Ellie said. "Henry, you and Jeb bring in our things. Vanessa, you and Mary Ben go on upstairs and find rooms to sleep in. I'm going to look over the kitchen with Cecilia, then she'll take me to see Mr. Clayhill. Is there someone with him now, Cecilia?"

Vanessa put her hand into Kain's. "Isn't she amazing? I'm so proud of her."

"So am I, honey. I haven't had so much fun in a long time." He chuckled.

"Shame on you." She reached up and kissed his chin.

"I'll go out and talk to the men and find someone to drive Della to town. She'll not go in style this trip."

"Do you think she can stir up trouble with the men?"

"She might try, but it won't do her any good. Della hasn't been very tolerant of the workers here. She'll want to get down to Denver and see what she can find out from Adam's lawyer. Logan said he was going to tell Randolph to get in touch with him and tell him what's what. She'll know when she gets there what she's up against."

"Will we go home as soon as Aunt Ellie is settled?"

"There's a lot to be done to get her settled in, honey," he hedged.

"I want to go home to our house."

"We'll have to wait and see if Clayhill's going to live awhile. He could get well enough to be up and around, and in that case Ellie's life would be hell."

"The doctor didn't seem to think he would."

"What does that little pip-squeak know? Most doctors tell you what they think you want to hear. I don't have too much faith in any of them."

"My father wasn't like that."

"Not if he was like you, he wasn't. Give me a kiss so I can go."

Vanessa and Mary Ben went up the wide stairway to the second floor. They could hear the sounds of banging and slamming coming from the big room at the front of the house. The door to the room opposite Della's was closed, so they went on down to the next room and cautiously opened the door.

"Oh, ain't it grand?" Mary Ben gaped at the beautiful room with the heavy walnut furniture, silk-covered chairs, and satin spread and draperies.

"There doesn't seem to be anyone using it. Do you want it for you and Henry?"

"No! I'd be 'fraid to sit on them chairs. Me 'n Henry don't need nothin' but a bed 'n washstand. The grandest ort a be Mrs. Hill's."

"We might as well look at all of them before we decide."

They went up narrow steps to the attic rooms, moving quietly, as if they expected to be discovered and told to leave. Two of the four rooms there were occupied. Vanessa suspected this was where Joseph and the girl Cecilia slept. They hurried back down to where Henry and Jeb were piling their boxes in the entrance hall.

Ellie and Cecilia emerged from the kitchen.

"We found a room we think you'd like, Aunt Ellie, and we'll use the rooms at the back."

"That's fine, dear. Cecilia and I have been getting acquainted. She's showing me up to Mr. Clayhill's room."

Ellie went to the closed door at the front of the house, and Cecilia went back downstairs after a fearful glance in the direction of Della's room, where sounds of things being thrown and Joseph being thoroughly cursed came through the closed door.

Ellie was strangely calm as she opened the door to Adam Clayhill's room. She entered and closed it behind her before she looked around. The bed was a tall four-poster made of heavy dark wood. The rest of the furniture matched it in both size and color. It was a luxurious room, and definitely masculine. The wine colored draperies were drawn across two sets of windows, one set was on the front of the house, the other on the side. The only light in the room came from the pane of glass in the door that opened out onto the upper veranda. She opened the draperies on the side to let in more light before she went to stand beside the bed and look down at the husband who had deserted her twenty years before.

Adam stared up at her, his face expressionless and immobile. His cheeks were covered with a stubble of beard and his heavy jowls sagged. Food stains dotted his white mustache, his shirt, and his bedclothes. He lay like a marble statue with no movement except for his eyelids. His huge hands lay at his sides, fingers spread. On the finger next to the crooked forefinger was a huge diamond ring, a monument to the wealth that was of no use to him now.

As she looked down at him, she suddenly realized he was not worth despising. Perhaps he had done her a favor by leaving her. She and Henry had been happy; certainly they would not have been happy with him. Nevertheless, an inner voice told her, the Bible said "cleave unto your husband"; and as sorry as he was, he was her husband.

"Good morning, Mr. Clayhill. I suppose you are wondering what the gullible, naive woman from Missouri is doing here. I am here to take my place in this house as your wife and see that you have adequate care." Ellie spoke slowly and firmly. "I know that you understand what I am saying. I have nursed patients with apoplexy, and although you can't move or speak, there is nothing wrong with your mind. The doctor has explained your condition to me. You may get better and you may not. You could have another fit and go at any time. I want you to understand, Mr. Clayhill, that I didn't come here out of any love for you. The love I had for the man I *thought* you were died a terrible death that day in Junction City. I sincerely regret all those years I wasted grieving for you. How foolish I have been!" She shook her head sadly.

"Our marriage papers, along with the certificate of record and the tintype we had made on our wedding day, have been sent to Denver. I also sent the names of witnesses—the preacher who married us is still in Springfield, as is the banker you went to see when we met. It's airtight, Mr. Clayhill. There's no way out for you. You can't simply cast me and my son aside as if we were so much garbage. We are here. We are staying. I mean to see to it that my son has what is rightfully his. You owe us twenty years of support, Mr. Clayhill.

"I also want you to know that I have met your other sons, Logan Horn and Cooper Parnell. They are both fine men. I've met your grandson, little Henry, with the crooked finger like yours and like my son's. I've met Sylvia Henderson, Cooper's mother. You have hurt so many people it's a wonder God didn't strike you down long before now."

She looked down at him for a long time before she spoke again. His lids had narrowed and his eyes glinted angrily. He knew what she had been saying. Good. She was relieved to find out that there was not an ounce of pity in the feeling she had for him.

"As I said, I will see that you are cared for, and that is all. I would do the same for any of God's creatures. Do not expect pity or companionship from me or my son. You will be fed and kept clean, and I will give you whatever medicine the doctor prescribes. From the smell of this bed you haven't had very good care these last few days. That will be remedied simply because I can't abide slovenliness.

"There's one more thing. Della is leaving. She is no longer welcome in my home even if she is Kain's sister. Cecilia is staying on, even though you are unable to avail yourself of her services. She tells me the laundress and the girl who helped her left when you struck her. They will be back because you will pay them to wash your dirty bed-clothes." She opened the drawer of the bedside table. "It brings up another matter. I will need money to pay the doctor and for household expenses." She closed the drawer. "Never mind. I'm sure the safe is in your office. If it is locked, I'll have the men take it outside and blow the door off."

A rap sounded on the door, then it opened. "Ma? Are you in here?"

"Yes, son. Come in. Leave the door open. It's too close in here." Henry stood in the doorway and made no move to enter. "Come on in and say hello to Mr. Clayhill."

"I don't want to. I don't like it here, and I don't like him. Can't we go back to Kain's place?"

"No, son. This is our home now. I don't like him either, but he's your father. Out of respect for the one who gave you life you must at least be decent, even if he doesn't deserve it."

Henry came forward reluctantly. "Hello, Mr. Clayhill," he said without looking at him. "Ma, that woman threw something at that little nigger and cut his head. It's bleeding something awful. Van is putting a cool rag on it. She said it might need a stitch."

"Oh, dear. The sooner we get that woman out of here the better. I'll be back, Mr. Clayhill, with Cecilia and Joseph, if he isn't hurt too badly, and they can clean you up before the doctor comes."

She went to the window and opened it a bit to let in some fresh air. She and Henry left the room, and she closed the door firmly behind her without giving him as much as a glance.

Della left and the doctor arrived all in a matter of minutes. Henry and Jeb carried Della's boxes down and put them in the back of an open wagon pulled by two mules. Kain could hardly contain his mirth when he saw the look on her face when she saw what was taking her to town.

He had talked to the men, told them Della was leaving, and asked for a volunteer to drive her. A middle-aged drover said he was going in to get a load of grain, and she could ride along with him if she'd ride in the grain wagon. Kain assured him she wouldn't mind at all. There were smirks from some of the men and the twitching of his own lips made them hide grins behind their hands.

Della exploded in rage when she came out onto the veranda and saw the dilapidated old wagon with her fancy boxes piled in the back and the two mangy mules. The driver sat on the seat, chewing his tobacco. Jeb offered to help her climb up the wheel and onto the seat, but she struck him on the arm with her parasol and climbed up by herself, tearing her skirt on a jagged board.

"Damn you, Kain. You'll pay for this."

"Did you say good-bye to . . . Papa, Della?" Kain couldn't resist the parting shot.

"To hell with the old bastard!"

"H'yaw! Hee-yaw!" The driver cracked the whip over the backs of the mules, and startled, they jumped, jerking the wagon. Della almost went over backward. A loud gaffaw came from the direction of the bunkhouse.

"Damn it!" She righted herself without any help from the driver, then sat rigidly in the short-backed seat, looking straight ahead as the wagon circled the yard to leave the ranch.

Kain watched his sister leave. She was more like a stranger to him. There had never been any love between them. This was a setback for a woman who was not used to setbacks. But she would survive. He wondered if she would have turned out the same if their mother hadn't moved West with Adam Clayhill. More than likely she would have been just what she is now. Her brothel would be in New York City or Paris. People were *what* they were, he mused, no matter *where* they were.

Kain greeted the doctor, who drove in as Della was leaving. He had stopped by Kain's and John had told them where they were. They entered the house together.

Ellie went upstairs with the doctor and they stayed for a long while in Adam's room. When they came out she led him downstairs to the parlor where the family had gathered.

"I'm glad to see Mr. Clayhill is clean. The most important part of the treatment of apoplexy consists in sanitary regulations and precautions. Once the blood has seeped into the brain little can be done to remedy the disastrous effects. His head may be kept raised and cold cloths should be applied to it. Mustard plasters may be applied to his feet and to the calves of his legs to help drawing the blood from the head. Another thing, Mrs. Clayhill, a drop of croton oil should be placed on his tongue in order to promote early and active discharges from the bowels."

"Do you forsee another attack?"

"It is extremely likely. You should be prepared for it. You may leave him to return minutes later to find that he is gone. All you can do for him is keep him as comfortable as you

can, give him liquid and soft food. I've brought a glass tube
that he can use to suck it into his mouth."

"Thank you, doctor. Would you like to stay for dinner?"

"I would be delighted."

Several days went by. Ellie had taken over the house easily and completely. Joseph and Cecilia hopped to obey her
kindly given orders. The laundress and her helper, who had
moved in with a family that lived on the ranch, were glad to
return when they were told Della was no longer at the ranch
house.

Joseph was now wearing loose, soft trousers and a clean,
soft shirt. Ellie had told him it was ridiculous for him to be
in a tailed coat and stiff collar while he was working around
the house. His dark face beamed when he looked at her and
he went from one chore to the other humming happily. Her
kind but firm manner had also won over Cecilia, and the girl
was gradually getting over her sulks.

Cecilia and Joseph tended to Adam under Ellie's supervi-
sion. Cecilia fed him and she and Joseph bathed him and
changed his bedclothes every morning. Ellie was usually in
the room, but she never touched him, and rarely spoke directly to him. When they finished, they left the room. After
the morning work was done, Ellie would send Cecilia up to
look in on him, but the girl never stayed very long.

Kain reported that the men were well aware of what had
happened to their boss and were wondering about their jobs.
They had not had a foreman since the roundup had been
completed. He had been quite a decent sort, one of the men
told Kain, but he and Adam had had a violent quarrel and
the man left. Kain asked Jeb if he wanted to stay on at
Clayhill Ranch, but he declined. He said the place was too
big and fancy. He would rather be with his brother and John
back at Kain's, and decided to head on back. Kain then
asked Bill Cooney to step in until other arrangements could
be made and to carry on with whatever was necessary.

Surprisingly, most of the men were understanding about Henry. Stan Taylor had been the one Kain had worried about. But he was the one who was the most tolerant after Henry told him how sorry he was for hurting him and that he would show him the moves Kain had taught him.

A lawyer was brought out from town who attested to Adam's condition, and papers were being drawn up to give Ellie access to Adam's bank accounts so the men could be paid.

At the end of the week the doctor seemed to think Adam would linger for awhile, and the house settled into a routine. When Ellie began the task of thoroughly cleaning, Kain knew she had truly settled in.

Adam Clayhill, the egotistical lord and master of the northwest Colorado Territory, was completely at the mercy of a wife who despised him.

Chapter Twenty-Two

Kain was in a dilemma. He wanted Vanessa to stay with her aunt while he went to look for Primer Tass. He had given his description to the Clayhill men, and earlier that day one of them had told of seeing a man in a black vest and hat sitting his horse on the east ridge overlooking the ranch. The cowboy said that when he turned to ride toward him, the rider disappeared into the trees. Kain reasoned that Tass had followed the buggy tracks to the ranch and was waiting for them to leave.

He also knew that Vanessa would rebel when he asked her to stay. She didn't care for the large house. She didn't like having people other than family underfoot all the time. And most of all she didn't like being confined to the house. The last words she'd said before she fell asleep were, "When are we going back to our house? I want to go home."

In the light of the moon that shone through the window he looked down at the woman sleeping in his arms. As if feeling his eyes on her, she made a little sound and snuggled closer to him. He didn't have to look at her to see her. He knew by heart every feature, every line from her flaming hair frothing out around her proud head, down her body that moved with such voluptuous grace to the tip of her toes. She was perfect. He prayed that she never saw him when he was wasted to skin and bones and looked down on him with pity.

She would be alone at The House after he was gone if Ellie and Henry stayed at Clayhill Ranch. There could be others like Primer Tass who became obsessed with possessing her. The thought brought a surge of impotent rage. He tried to not think about it; he had to clear his mind and plan what he was going to do.

Kain awakened at daybreak. He lay still, listening. A stream of honkers were flying over the ranch heading south. He could see them in his mind's eye, stretching their long necks, following their leader to a feeding ground. Outside the window a bird alighted on one of the branches of a tree and loosed a single brief trilling measure of its song, took wing again, and coasted away on a whisper. He heard the lonely, dismal call of the whippoorwill from the other side of the valley where the pines loomed dark and thick.

Sights and sounds of the changing seasons that he had formerly ignored or forgotten were now remembered and appreciated. Waiting to die he had come to realize how very precious life really was. He had a feeling that this might be the day that it would come down to the line: his life or that of Primer Tass.

He shifted his body so that he was leaning over the soft body nestled close to him. This armful of woman was the sun and the moon, the warm wind in the spring, the drink of cool water on a hot summer day. She was everything good and sweet that had ever happened to him. He kissed her lips. She liked him to awaken her with a kiss. Her lips moved beneath his. His lips moved from her mouth to her eyes.

"Open your eyes, my love, so I can see them."

Unruly bronze curls covered satin white shoulders, pink lips parted invitingly, and sleepy blue eyes smiled up at him.

"Mmm." She arched against him, and her flat palms began to move on his firm, muscled body, stroking, caressing.

His lips rained gentle kisses across the bridge of her nose, placed adoring kisses on her mouth, then rested his lips on her chin.

"You taste good in the morning, my love."

"Are you wanting to love me?"

"Ahh . . ." The sound came from deep in his throat. "I'm desperate to love you."

"What's stopping you?" Her arms curved around him tenderly. "Hurry up and do it," she whispered.

Joy surged through him with heavy urgency. He fitted his body over hers. She wiggled deliciously until they were joined. When he clasped her buttocks in his hands to draw them up to receive his full length, she laughed a rich, satisfied laugh that he felt to his very soul.

"Ahh . . ." The sound came again. "There's nothing more wonderful than this."

"I like it, too. . . ."

"Kiss me, sweetheart."

Her mouth found his and kissed it with gentle reassurance, then with rising passion. His hands moved over her body, touching her with sensual, intimate caresses. She opened her eyes and it was all there, his love, his adoration. The wonder of it filled her with joy and she rocked to bring him deeper.

"Oh. Lie still, darling!" He gasped when she began to move urgently. With a little muffled cry he stiffened and thrust deeply. Her beautiful long body responded to his. In minutes they were panting in each other's arms. They merged into a long, long unbelievable release to the accompaniment of small sounds of pleasure, and lay shuddering in each other's arms. "I love you, little red bird."

"And I love you, my wonderful man." Caught in a drowsy state of sweet exhaustion, they lay entwined for several minutes. Then suddenly, as if heavy chains had been lifted from her control, her arms tightened and she strained him to her, frantically holding onto him. "Hold me, darling. I love you!" Little whimpers came from her lips and she gazed at him in sorrowed despair. "Please! Don't do this to me. I can't bear it! Tell me, how much longer? Do you know? Sometimes I think my heart is so heavy it will stop beating." She pounded on his chest with her fist as the words tumbled from her lips. Tears that would not stay back flooded her eyes and rolled down her cheeks.

"Sweetheart. Please believe me. You don't want to know. If I thought it would comfort you, I'd tell you. Shh, don't cry. We may have weeks, months. Don't think about it. Remember, you promised."

"I know I did, but I didn't know how hard it would be."

"We've had this time. If I hadn't told you we wouldn't have had this much. I just couldn't take you and let you think it would go on forever."

"I keep thinking there's someone out there beside Tass who wants to kill you, and you know they will do it. Or that you are going to be caught and sent to prison. I could take that, knowing you're alive. But if you're killed—"

"It's a lot to ask of you, sweetheart. But don't think of the future. Love me now. I need your love."

He embraced her roughtly, but there was nothing rough about the way he kissed her. There was sorrow in her heart, but also singing because as long as he was with her there was hope. She held him as though he were a dream that would fade away if she let go. He kissed her throat, her cheeks wet with tears, her mouth, and when she laid her palm against his face he turned his lips to it.

"Kain—"

"Shh . . . Don't think about it. I just want to love you,

hold you, kiss you." His exploring hands gripped her buttocks.

A powerful, sweeping tide of love flowed over her, making her feel stronger than the hard-muscled body entwined with hers. Her fingers moved down from the small of his back and pushed him more deeply into her. His mouth closed hungrily over hers in a moist, deep, endless kiss. It seemed to Vanessa that they were no longer two separate people, but one blended together by magic.

"I'm going to name our son Kain V. DeBolt," she gasped, tearing her mouth free, "and we're going to make him now!"

"Oh, God!" he said hoarsely, and shuddered violently with release. They lay so close together each could feel the other's heartbeats. "You were made in heaven, just for me."

Her hand tickled down over his heart to the bottom of his rib cage. "I came right from here, close to your heart."

"I believe it."

When they heard the sounds of a household starting a new day they rose and dressed and went downstairs.

Kain was quiet at breakfast. He ate little, holding Vanessa's hand beneath the table, watching every expression that crossed her face. When Ellie called for her to help her find bread pans, he went to their room. When he came down he avoided the kitchen, found Mary Ben in the parlor and told her to tell Vanessa he was going out to the corrals.

Vanessa was watching Ellie make bread. "You're a cook at heart, Aunt Ellie. Now that you're in this big grand house are you going to give up the dream of having a bakery?"

"Why should I? I love to cook. And there's no guarantee we'll stay here. I'm confident now, Vanessa, that if I have to make a living making bread and pies I can." She smiled. "In the meantime there are a lot of men to feed."

"They have a cook, Ellie, dear."

"I know that, but have you seen the bread that cook makes? Ugh! It's hard and flat."

Vanessa hugged her aunt. "You sure set this place on its ear!"

"Ah, go on with you. There just comes a time when a woman must stand up for her rights. I'm standing up for mine."

"Kain said to tell you he went to the corrals." Mary Ben came through the swinging doors. "What'll I do now, Mrs. Hill—ah, Ma?"

"That's better, child. There's a pan of peas to shell or you can start the churning. Whichever one you want."

"I'll do the peas, Mary Ben, if you want to churn," Vanessa said.

Until mid-morning, Vanessa passed the time doing odd jobs around the house. The hours seemed to move so slowly. She wished that Kain would come back in. Once she asked Henry if he had seen him. He said no, that he'd been watching the blacksmith. She debated walking down to the corral, but remembered her promise to stay in the house if Kain wasn't with her. Feeling edgy and caged, she walked out onto the veranda and looked toward the outbuildings. A string of horses were tied to the rails, but Big Red wasn't among them, nor was he at the rail beside the cookshack where the men gathered to drink coffee and discuss the work.

The uncomfortable feeling she'd had all morning began to intensify. A dark dread settled over her like a heavy cloak. *It was going to be an unusual day.* She dared not think that this was the day Kain feared. In a moment of weakness she had told him that if he had to go away he was not to tell her when he was going. Oh, God, why had she told him that? Was this the day he was going out to meet Tass, or some other man, or a group of men who were determined to kill him? Please, God! Oh, please don't let this be the day.

The cold wind of doom blew over Vanessa and chilled her to the bone. Its pressure booming in her ears set her feet in motion. She ran back into the house and snatched a shawl and a bonnet from the rack and headed toward the stables, stumbling and running, praying and crying.

As the sky grew gray with the approaching daylight, Primer Tass got to his feet. He felt surly and mean. It was getting cold, and there was nothing he hated as much as the cold. He had waited almost too long to make his move, but it had taken time to get his strength back after the squaw had dug the bullets out of him. Luckily he had known one of the Cheyenne braves among the group that caught him after he was wounded. Luck came his way again when he found an old mine shaft that was large enough to conceal two horses, and then again when he saw the drunk miner wave his greenbacks in a Greeley saloon and then carelessly walk out into a dark alley. He now had money and horses to get him and the woman to Mexico.

When he returned from Greeley he had watched the house where the fancy caravan was parked for two days. Nothing stirred but the old man, the dog, and another man working on the woodpile. He never got close enough for a clear shot at either of them because of the damn dog. Then he saw the buggy tracks and followed them to Clayhill Ranch. The day before he had seen her on the upper porch. She had been wearing a blue dress and her flaming red hair had glinted in the sunlight. It was the first glimpse he'd had of her since he was shot and a feeling of jubilance had washed over him. Soon he would have her. She'd not stay there forever. Sooner or later she and DeBolt would leave Clayhill Ranch and return to The House.

He ran his fingers over the hair rope around his neck. The woman had left a mark on him. She had come and gone, but he still had a part of her, and soon he'd have the rest of her to do with as he liked, for as long as he liked. He cursed himself for not taking her at Fort Lyon. But then, he reasoned, he would have had the army after him for taking a woman. He was glad he had waited, it would be all the sweeter when he got her. If the weather turned cold he would have the redheaded woman to warm him, and in a few weeks they would be down south where the sun was hot.

Tass rolled up his blankets and tied them behind his saddle. He dug into his saddlebags for some dried meat and mounted his horse. This could be the day the woman would leave that big, fancy house, and he was ready to take her.

The sun was up when he arrived at the crest of the ridge overlooking the road to the ranch. He tied his horse well out of sight in a heavy growth of brush and settled down with his back to a boulder to watch. He congratulated himself on his patience. He was ready with two horses, supplies and money. Now the waiting was over. As soon as he got DeBolt in his sights, he'd shoot him out of the saddle. He'd done it once and would again. And it would be so satisfying. This time he'd make sure he killed the son of a bitch. He still wondered why he hadn't taken his chance the morning beside the river when they came for the mules. If he had shot when the old man cut loose with the buffalo gun he could have had both of them. But he had had his mind on the woman. Thinking about her had made him careless.

Tass glanced back to be sure he hadn't skylined himself on the ridge. If a man wanted to live in this country he stopped where he had a background against which his shape could offer no outline. He never took a risk if he didn't have to. He had come onto men who had skylined themselves as they slept beside a campfire, had taken a step away from their weapons—and they were dead now.

As the morning progressed the wind picked up and clouds began to form in the southwest. Hell, he thought. They'll not leave if it's going to rain. He watched the cloud bank. It wasn't moving very fast. When he looked back down at the ranch house he saw a buggy turning into the road leading to town.

Tass cursed the Cheyenne brave who had taken his field

glasses while his squaw was saving his life. He searched for a better vantage point where he could watch the road and not be spotted by anyone. Below him and to the right was a clump of bushes. He ran, bent low, until he reached them and squatted down.

Elation flooded through him when he saw a blue skirt flapping in the wind. Looking down, the top of the buggy kept him from seeing her, but he could see her blue bonnet, and there was no one with her. She whipped the horse into a trot and the buggy turned the bend and she was out of sight. He wondered vaguely why there wasn't a rider with the buggy. Then his thin lips quirked. She and DeBolt might have had a set-to and she was leaving in a huff.

This was going to be easier than he thought. He dug in his heels and went back up the hill to where he'd tied his horse. Once mounted, he rode along the crest, keeping the buggy in sight. He'd let her get closer to the old mine shaft before he made his move. An idea began to form. He could conceal the buggy in the mine shaft and they would have a day's start before anyone knew she was gone.

After several miles of riding the crest, he topped a rise that gave him a sweeping view of the road and a way down to it. He watched the buggy for a long moment, then scanned the road ahead of it. From far away he saw another buggy coming down the road. He let loose a stream of curses. He figured the two were a good three miles apart. If he acted fast, he could get to the woman before she met the other buggy. He had waited too long to let this opportunity pass.

Reining around on the shelving bank, he started his horse down the steep incline. The animal skidded on bent hind legs, regained his footing, made it to the bottom, and leaped into a full gallop. The buggy was less than a quarter of a mile ahead. The horse stretched in a ground-devouring stride to escape the cruel bits of the spurs Tass dug into his flanks. He held the black gelding to a straining run down the narrow track while his heart raced with anticipation. The girl had seen him coming! The buggy picked up speed, but the old nag pulling it was not a running horse, and Tass overtook it easily. Knowing the woman was spunky and would try to shoot him, Tass had his gun in his hand and a smile on his face as he came alongside.

He had only a second to realize his mistake.

The blast from the shotgun struck him in the midsection. He was knocked from the saddle of the running horse and was dead before he hit the ground.

Kain pulled the horse to a stop and looked back. Tass lay in a heap on the ground and his horse was running toward the thick stand of trees on the hillside. Kain took off the bonnet and pulled Vanessa's blue dress from around his legs. After he placed her old shotgun on the floor of the buggy, he flipped the reins to turn the horse around.

It was over. His plan had worked perfectly. He pulled the horse to a halt, wound the reins around the brake and stepped down. Lying sprawled on the ground, Tass looked small and harmless. Kain nudged him with the toe of his boot, as he would a snake to see if it was still alive.

"You goddamn little son of a bitch!" He toed him again and turned him over. His stomach and chest were riddled, his eyes open and staring. Kain took his knife from his pocket. A savage anger swept up from deep inside him. He grabbed the rope of Vanessa's hair that hung around Tass's neck, lifting his head and shoulders off the ground. He sawed through it with vicious strokes of the knife and the dead man's head dropped with a thud. Kain held the shining copper mass of hair in his fist. "Goddamn you! This is mine!"

The stomach pains that had nagged him all morning were making him sick. He swallowed repeatedly and pressed his palm to his stomach. He wasn't aware of the approaching buggy until it was almost there and the clip-clop of the horse's hooves penetrated his senses. The doctor pulled up and jumped down with his bag in his hand.

"You won't need that," Kain said tonelessly.

"I heard the shot and came as fast as I could. What happened?"

"I shot him."

"I can see that. Why?"

"He was going to shoot me."

"That's reason enough to suit me."

Kain had only a moment of warning before the terrible pain intensified and doubled him over. He went in a crouch to the end of the buggy, clung there and vomited violently. There was the usual mingling of blood in the vomit that spewed from his mouth. He heaved until there was nothing left and still the bile rose in his throat. Sweat broke out on his forehead. He wiped his brow with his handkerchief and sagged against the wheel.

"You got one, too, huh?" The doctor stood on the other side of the buggy looking at him. Kain didn't answer. "It's the reason I came out here. Slower pace, good air. I hung out a shingle, and if I get a patient, fine. If I don't, that's fine, too. I don't have to worry about it."

"What the hell are you talking about?"

"My stomach ulcer—the reason I came out here. Mine was worse than yours. I was too busy, too tense, worried too much and ate the wrong meals at the wrong times. It gave me a jim-dandy ulcer, but I've about got it licked."

"I've got a cancer you stupid fool!" Kain yelled.

"You don't say?" The doctor walked over and looked at the vomit on the ground. "How long have you had this . . . cancer?"

"Two or three months."

"Hmm. What fool told you that? It doesn't look like any stomach cancer I've ever seen. If it was you'd be throwing up chunks of guts by now."

"I know what it looks like. I was with a man in Arizona who had one."

"Maybe he did. But it still looks like a plain old ulcer to me. Hurts like hell, doesn't it?"

"I've already had the opinion of *one* brainless quack! He said I had worms. The stuff he gave me damn near killed me."

"I can guess what it was. It would be enough to give you an ulcer if you didn't already have one. How much weight have you lost?"

"None. I've gained some drinking a lot of damn milk. It kept my gut from hurting."

"If you had a cancer you'd be skin and bone, and yellow as a pumpkin by now. This *quack* is telling you that you've got an ulcer. I can give you a list of foods to eat that'll help it, and in time it will go away."

Kain gazed steadily at the doctor. He sure didn't look too smart, and there he was leaning casually against the end of the buggy, calmly discussing what was life and death to Kain. Hope blossomed, but he was afraid of it.

"You can't be sure. You could have a cancer, too."

"Nothing is *sure*. But from what you told me, and this," he kicked some dirt over the vomit, "I'm more than ninety-nine percent sure. Fact is, I'd say you're strong as a horse and stubborn as a mule."

Kain stared off at the mountains, not daring to believe.

"Are you sure you know what you're talking about?"

"I may not look too smart, but I graduated at the head of my class from the finest school of medicine in the world. I've seen plenty of cancer and I know what I'm talking about. But damn it, if you want to believe you've got a cancer, go ahead, believe it and worry yourself to death."

Relief washed over Kain like a tidal wave. *He was not going to die. He was going to live!* He would live . . . with Vanessa. Grow old . . . with Vanessa. Have children . . . with

Vanessa. He would hear that stream of honkers return in the spring. He wanted to shout, and did. "Wha . . . hooo!"

"I know the feeling." The doctor laughed and clasped his shoulder with a tight squeeze of his hand. "One time I was sure I had consumption and would die. It was only a bad chest cold, and I was so grateful I didn't say a swear word for a week."

"If you're wrong . . . I'll kill you!" Kain said, and they both laughed.

The distant pounding of hooves on the road brought Kain's head around. When he saw the big horse, he knew immediately it was Vanessa on Big Red. Her bonnet hung by the string around her neck and her flaming red hair waved like a banner in the wind, stirred up by her wild ride. The dark skirt of her dress was up around her knees and her feet were firmly in the stirrups. She looked like a small red bird perched on the back of Big Red who was running all out.

"Kain! Kain!" Her voice came to him like the wail of the wind. He moved out into the track and waves his arms so she would see that he was all right. "Kain—" There was a sob now in the cry that reached him.

Big Red slowed and skidded to a halt. Vanessa threw herself from the saddle into Kain's arms and they both tumbled to the ground. She was sobbing wildly and clutching him with fierce desperation.

"I thought . . . I thought . . . this was the day . . . I heard the shot." Her hands moved over him urgently. "Are you all right? Are you all right? Tell me, damn you!"

"Yes, darling! Yes! Yes! Yes! I'm all right. I've never been so all right." He lay on the ground holding her. "Tass is dead. I killed him. You'll never have to worry about him again." He grabbed her face with his hands so she had to look at him. "And I'm not going to leave you. Listen to me, Van! It was all a mistake. I'll not leave you, ever. Did you hear that, darling? Do you understand? Shh . . . don't cry. I'll never leave you . . . we'll grow old together like in Lorna's song. If I'm lucky we'll have sons and daughters and I'll see this gorgeous hair turn gray."

"It's over? You're not leaving? Ever? There's no one else who's trying to kill you? Say it! Say it again, damn it, or I'll hit you!"

"I'll be with you always, you funny, silly, wonderful, precious girl! You could have broken your neck riding Big Red!" he scolded between kisses.

"Tell me—"

"Later, I'll tell you everything, but look, darling." He held up the rope of flaming hair. "I got it back."

"Don't touch me with it! I hate it. Burn it. I never want to see anything he had or touched."

Kain tossed it over his shoulder. "Put a match to it, doctor. Burn it while I kiss my wife."

EPILOGUE

The House was still called The House, although many people had forgotten the reason. A wide veranda now stretched around three sides of it and it was surrounded by a split rail fence and shrubs and fruit trees. It was a beautiful spring morning and this was a beautiful place. The snow was gone, the robins were back and the trees were budding.

Early that morning Kain had heard the honkers go over on their way north. For fifteen years he had heard them in the spring and again in the fall. And each time they passed over The House he thought of the morning he had held his wife in his arms worrying that it might be for the last time, but it really had been the day they had begun to live.

He loved this place and left it only to take trips to Denver; either his wife went with him or his visit was brief. There was talk of him running for governor, but he hadn't made up his mind about that yet. On mornings such as this he was quite sure nothing could entice him away from his home.

A smile played around the corners of his mouth as a slim, flaming-haired girl of twelve ran out onto the porch and confronted him.

"Papa! I hate brothers! Jason is teasing me again about bumps on my chest. Make him stop it!"

"Hmm, you are getting bumps. I hadn't noticed."

"Papa!"

"You've been calling him a redheaded woodpecker, honey. You've got to expect him to strike back."

"But he calls me red bird. I hate this red hair. Why did K.V. get hair like yours and me and Jason got Mama's?"

"Someday you'll be proud of that hair, and beaus will swarm around you like bees after honey."

"Did they swarm around Mama?"

"If they had I'd have run them off with the shotgun. Yes siree, it sure looks to me like Jason is right. You're growing up."

"Janita!" The commanding call came from inside the house. "Get back in here and finish your chores before you take off on that horse."

"Yes, Mama, I'm coming." At the door she turned and glared at the back of her father's head and stuck out her tongue.

Kain had caught the defiant act several times before and grinned. His daughter hadn't discovered that her reflection showed in the shining window of the side door. She was going to be a handful, but he had no doubt Vanessa would be able to handle her.

It was possible they had made their first son the morning they really began to live. Kain V. DeBolt, called K.V. by his mother, had arrived exactly nine months from that wondrous day. She adored him. He was big and strong like his father and had dark brown hair with just a touch of red. The year before, when he was fourteen, they had sent him back East to school so he could have a taste of a different kind of living. In his letters he said he was homesick for the Rocky

Mountains. Kain was sure he had his eye on Cooper and Lorna's daughter Maggie and was afraid someone would attract her interest while he was gone.

Kain stretched his long legs out before him and thought about Adam Clayhill, who had lived almost a year after his stroke. His body wasted away, but his tough old spirit refused to leave it. He never spoke again, but Mary Ben told of how his eyes followed Ellie wherever she was in the room and how a look of disappointment came into them when she ignored him. Ellie seldom spoke to him, but she saw to it that he was as comfortable as possible.

He died alone in the night and was buried on a plot overlooking Clayhill Ranch. Few people other than Vanessa and Kain had attended the funeral. Ellie, dressed in black, stood beside Henry and Mary Ben when his body was placed in the ground, ensuring that his dust would remain forever in the land he had fought so hard to possess.

Kain wondered if the old man had turned over in his grave when the new sign went up on the posts leading to the ranch. Ellie and Henry's names had been legally changed to Hill. She insisted that Cooper and Logan each take a third of the estate after it was discovered Adam hadn't left a will and she and Henry were to inherit everything. She persuaded them it was the only way she could be sure Henry and his family would be taken care of after she was gone. Horn, Parnell, Hill, the HPH Ranch, under the direction of Cooper and Logan, was prosperous and earned a good living for Henry and his family.

Ellie had married the man Cooper and Logan brought in to manage the ranch, and they lived in a new cottage. Mary Ben took over the management of the big house, and John Wisner had lived with them until he died the year before. Henry and Mary Ben had three boys and two girls. Mary Ben still adored her handsome husband, who wanted nothing more out of life than to be with her and to romp and play with his children. It had been years before the Parnells and the Horns would go to the ranch; but now the families met often, and the cousins raced from room to room in the big house until Joseph firmly put a stop to it.

Della had died in France. It was a violent death. She and her lover had been killed by his wife, who quietly disappeared. It was said she left a fortune to a half-breed Indian who was the only man Della had truly loved. He, in turn, turned it over to an administrator to be used for educating Indian children. Her solicitor never revealed the heir's name, and Kain didn't ask; but he was almost sure the Indian was Logan Horn.

"Kain? Why are you sitting out here on the porch this time of the morning?" Still slim and beautiful after three children, Vanessa came to stand beside him.

"I heard the honkers this morning. They're heading north. Get a wrap and come and sit with me."

"I don't need a wrap." She sat down beside him and pulled his arm around her. "Jason is getting out of hand."

"He's just like you, love. Stubborn, mouthy, willful—"

"You've got to do something about him."

"Right now?"

"Not right this minute. You can kiss me first."

"What're ya doin'?" The screen door slammed, and a redheaded bundle of energy stood before them with his freckled face screwed up in disgust. One arm was encased in plaster.

"I'm kissing your mother."

"Mush! I ain't never goin' to kiss girls!"

"That's fine with me. I'll kiss your share of the girls."

"Go wash, Jason. Dr. Warren is stopping by to look at that arm."

"That old *quack!*" he shouted, and ran off the porch.

"Jasons' right. He is a quack!" Kain looked down at his wife with a teasing light in his amber eyes because he knew she was very fond of the doctor.

"He's no such thing! If not for him I'd still be living with that terrible dread. Damn you, Kain, for putting me through that . . . hell. I'm still mad about it. If only you'd told me. Even *I* knew enough to know you had an ulcer."

"It's been fifteen years, sweetheart. Aren't you ever going to forgive me?"

"I might, if you'd stop bringing up that thing about me calling you a puffed-up jackass, running you off with the shotgun and clobbering folks with the shovel. You've got folks thinking I'm a regular terror!"

"Don't forget about wearing britches, taking off to kill that bird, Tass, riding Big Red at breakneck speed—"

"Hush up and kiss me, you . . . puffed-up jackass. I've got work to do."

He pulled her to him lovingly, and she raised her mouth for his kiss.

"Are you too busy to go upstairs?" He breathed the words in her ear.

She drew back and laughed up at him. "Kain DeBolt . . . you're the limit!"

He laughed happily and hugged her. "Maybe. But there's no limit to my love for a pretty little red bird."

Dear Reader,

I thank you for buying my book, and for the cards and letters I received regarding the first two books of the Colorado Trilogy. I hope they have given you a few hours of enjoyment, allowing you to forget the problems of everyday living while becoming involved in the lives of the pioneers who settled the great state of Colorado.

The reception my stories of the West have received from you, the final critic, have been most gratifying. Please write and let me know the locale and time period in our American history you most like to read about. I would be pleased to know which characters in my Colorado Trilogy you find the most interesting.

You can write to me: Dorothy Garlock, % Warner Books, Inc., 666 Fifth Avenue, New York, N.Y. 10103. Your letters will be forwarded to me immediately. I'll answer each letter as quickly as possible and add your name to my mailing list so that you will be notified when my next book will be released.

At the present time, I am working on the Wabash River Trilogy. The first book is set along the Wabash and upper Mississippi Rivers just before the war of 1812, and is scheduled to be released in the fall of 1987.

Dorothy Garlock
Clear Lake, Iowa